Secrets In Disguise

Chimera Chronicles

Book 4

Published by Stonehenge Circle Press

Cover art by Stephanie Tkach

Page Weaving Cover Designs

ISBN: 978-1-68012-276-3

Acknowledgements

I always have to thank my parents — they encouraged my love of reading all my life. It allows me to travel to other places and times, to step from my life into amazing once-upon-a-times, to go on astonishing and unexpected adventures, and to experience weird, wild and wonderful expeditions from the comfort of my home. Thank you, Dad, for showing me the extraordinary worlds of Fantasy and Science Fiction.

In addition, I have to thank my fellow writers at Stonehenge – I have all your voices in my head as I write. (Yes, that's a good thing!)

And I'm very grateful for the remarkable new friends I've made through this journey. Here's to you, Cheryl, Ruth, Jenny and Jackie!

Table of Contents

Secrets in Disguise

Chapter 1/January/Chimera

Once More Through the Darkness

I came back to myself in fits and starts.

My ears were ringing and pain pulsed in my head in time with my pounding heart.

There was warmth on my face, which didn't seem right. Shouldn't it be cold?

Something pressed against my back, arms and legs, but I couldn't feel any pressure against my feet. That would, I realized, mean I was lying sprawled on my back.

My ears began to clear. Was I hearing voices or a flock of birds? I opened my eyes just a sliver, but that tiny bit of light jabbed straight back into my brain. I winced and squeezed them shut. For a moment I thought I was going to throw up.

There was a shushing sound and everything went silent.

I needed that silence. I started to relax as the pounding in my head receded enough for me to think. But the first thing I thought about was that silence. It was *too* quiet.

It was silent. But it certainly smelled good; like sugar cookies straight out of the oven. I nearly gasped at a distinct memory of eating the last of the Christmas cookies.

Where had that been?

Why didn't I know? That question worried me enough to raise my head. Before I could fully open my eyes, a wave of dizziness crashed through me, knocking me back onto the dirt.

Dirt? Heat? Silence? Sweet smells? Maybe this was…was…

There were sounds again. Now I could tell they were voices. Annoying voices. If they hadn't started up right then, I might have remembered where I was.

Who I was.

That thought drove my teeth together to stop them from chattering. Icy beads of sweat sprang up on my forehead and dripped down into my hair. The air hadn't suddenly grown colder, but I had.

I nearly clapped my hands over my ears. Maybe I could remember *something* if all those voices weren't chattering at each other over me.

No…they were chattering *at* me. There must be at least a dozen people to make that much noise.

I reluctantly slitted my eyes open. And this time, though the pounding in my head grew worse, I could see.

I met the worried gaze of only three people. Three very noisy people. One of them said, "Welcome back, Kat," in a voice that shook with relief.

That's all it took. Hearing my name. Like an avalanche, memories began to click into place.

I was Kat. Katherine Alice Taylor. I lived in Santa Ramona on the Southern California coast.

And those three people were my friends.

"You fainted." Brady's red hair was glowing in the sunlight like a brand new copper penny. He peered down at me in fascination, no doubt calculating the various causes of fainting and potential side-effects. From the sudden frown on his face, the way he tucked his pocket protector deeper into his pocket and straightened the cuffs of his shirt, I was pretty sure I didn't want to hear what he was thinking. Assuming I could even understand his explanation. My brain didn't feel up to science-techno-geek speak right now.

Next to him, Olivia was holding onto his arm. She nodded once, jerkily, making her curly brown hair bounce around her shoulders. The mascara under her eyes had smeared, and her expertly applied make-up was now a smudged mess over her cheeks. She must really have been worried about me to wreck her face like that. She'd even blotted her drippy mascara eyes on the shoulder of her favorite pink shirt. If I felt better, I'd point out that she'd just proved my point; wearing make-up and fancy clothes was a hassle. But why waste my time? Olivia seemed to have made it her mission to get me as interested in clothes and make-up as she was.

Which was *never* going to happen.

Faith stood next to her, tall, slender and fit; nearly the opposite of Olivia's curvy hour-glass shape. Her long hair was pulled back in a thick pony-tail. Though people called it red, her dark auburn was as different from Brady's as you could get. At least she didn't consider it her mission to get me as fit as she was. Thank goodness. She was too busy playing competitive soccer to have other missions in life.

I'd known the two of them since pre-school. More than ten years now. I couldn't even remember the time before we were all friends. So how could I have blanked on their voices for even a minute?

Dirt, heat, sweet air, Brady, Olivia and Faith. We definitely had to be in Chimera. So why wasn't Doug here?

I tilted my head back, searching for him. My eyes locked on him a moment before another wave of dizziness forced me to look away. Darn it. Had that been a look of panic on his face?

I risked another, more careful glance. Sun glinted off his dark blond hair, making me squint slightly. It looked like he'd been running his hands through it, which he did when he was really upset. I'd only seen him do it a few times, even though I'd known him since we were toddlers. He was my oldest childhood friend and one of the bossiest people I knew. But right now he wasn't saying anything. He was just staring at me with a strange expression in his intense, deep blue eyes. An expression I'd never seen before.

What on earth, or Chimera, had just happened? I shut my eyes and forced myself to remember.

I'd gotten up and snatched the last two sugar cookies as I left the house that morning. I could remember that much.

Then we'd met up and made our way to the Santa Ramona cemetery. We hadn't seen any sign of our nemesis… *How do you make that plural? Nemesises? Nemesi? Whatever.* We'd made it without running into any of the Rejects —whose mission in life seemed to be making my friends and me completely miserable. If not actually causing us permanent damage.

After that, we'd taken turns entering the huge old fig tree at the far end of the cemetery — the entrance to Chimera. A world created by magic users more than 400 years ago, in a place just outside our normal space and time. They'd made it to keep safe from everyone in the Mundane world.

It was a fluke my friends and I could get in. Only those born the same year as us could activate the magic keeping it locked. Well, not *all* the time, but during the entire week around the full moon. Like today.

I was feeling better — things were starting to come back. I remembered stepping into the cold damp blackness of the tree. Then…nothing.

It took me two tries to work up enough spit to ask, "What happened?" Even so, my voice came out disturbingly shaky.

I watched in amazement as tears leaked from Olivia's eyes. "You went through the tree first," she said. "It took much longer to get through than usual. For all of us." She looked around and everyone nodded solemnly. She sucked in her cheeks and squared her shoulders, but her voice was defensive. "None of us felt well when we dropped out of the tree so it took Brady a minute to realize you weren't breathing."

That, at least, seemed normal; Olivia always blamed things on Brady.

"I was ready to start mouth-to-mouth," Brady said, "but you began breathing on your own."

What? Eeeoow! Note to self – Don't ever stop breathing again. Especially not around Brady!

I sat up quickly, wanting to make sure he didn't keep thinking that way. It might have been a bit too quick; the world swirled around me for a moment. I decided not to try to get to my feet just yet.

Brady fingered the self-winding watch on his wrist, staring at it intently. He looked at me and smiled. "I timed the entire episode. Your pulse was weak but hadn't completely stopped, and you were without breath for less than two minutes. There should be no lasting negative effects."

Oh great, there should *be no lasting negative effects.*

Now brief snatches of that trip through the tree began coming back. The smothering damp blackness had pressed against me, tightening its grip as time went on.

No sight. No sound. No air.

My lungs heaving desperately by the time I counted to 198.

The sensation of falling, spinning out of control. None of that was unusual, but normally it was followed by being pushed into the warmth of Chimera with the ancient fig tree at my back. This time, I had no memory of leaving the tree. The last thing I could remember was panic. Knowing my air was gone. Knowing I wasn't going to get out in time. One of my worst fears, actually happening.

Doug's voice was gruff as he said, "Are you planning to sit there in the dirt all day, Taylor?"

If they weren't all watching, I'd have run my hands over my arms and legs, just to be sure I was still all there. But Doug stretched out his hand, and when I grabbed it he pulled me to my feet in one fluid motion.

I instantly felt better, though still a bit shaky. But having people standing over me while I was in the dirt was creepy, even if they were my friends. I bent over to wipe dirt from my pants, but straightened when I heard a distinctive rustling. Brady had pulled his map of Chimera out of his pocket. Over the past three years, he'd turned a normal piece of paper with a crudely drawn rendering of this place into something incredibly useful. With a single wish, this map would show where we were, where the Rejects were, or if there was anything we needed to find.

That should be a benefit of being in a magic world; wishes could set off existing magic spells. Sometimes. When things went right, like with the map, it was great. But just as often wishes did something different than you'd intended. Sometimes dangerously, alarmingly different. Which is why we tended to be very careful about using the word *wish* in here.

Brady held up the much creased map and said, "I wish to see the Rejects." All of us scanned the map, looking for their red dots, but there was no sign of them.

Then he said, "I wish to see us." Instantly, five green dots appeared next to the drawing of the large tree.

Brady traced his finger over a road we'd never used before. "This appears to be the shortest way into the town, though I can't tell from a two dimensional image if there are any impediments we should be aware of."

"Why are we going into the town?" Olivia asked.

Brady stared at her like she'd said something in a foreign language. Then he shook his head. "Don't you remember what the Sylph said?"

Now it was Olivia's turn to shake her head.

"I don't understand," he muttered and shoved his glasses higher on his nose. "It was only two months ago."

I couldn't remember the exact words either, but I knew Brady had a photographic memory; what he called eidetic. He'd know every word. I grinned as he said, "*I* remember. Let me quote it for you. 'The last item you seek will be found in a building, somewhere in the town or in the mansion in the South. It will be guarded by a Salamander.' "

Olivia tipped her nose in the air and sniffed. "Fine." Then she turned her back on him.

I decided it was time for me to step in and keep the peace. "What did Ronny call the town, do you remember?"

Brady answered, "Of course. She called it Mystic."

Of course.

Faith had been peering at the map. "At least we won't be going near the forest this time. I've had enough of that place." Her relief was probably more obvious than she'd meant it to be.

I could agree with her. The swamp in our second year in Chimera had been bad, but the 'dark side' of the forest had been far worse. The best thing about being in a town — there'd be roads and trails everywhere, and they'd be protected. The monsters still roaming around Chimera were restricted by magic from entering them. They couldn't even tell where the roads were, not even if they were right next to one. Each road, and everything on it, was concealed from anyone, or anything, that wasn't touching it.

Which meant you could never, ever leave the road, or you wouldn't be able to find it again.

Faith looked back at the tree. "We should get going."

With a start, I realized we'd been standing around talking for a long time. And at any minute the Rejects could come through the tree.

We set off quickly, trying to get out of sight, but we hadn't gone far when Brady came to an abrupt halt. He smacked his forehead. "Darn! I've got to go back."

When we started to protest, he insisted. "I need to wipe out our foot prints. We can't announce the alteration in our venue to the Rejects."

Two years ago we'd discovered the Rejects were following our foot prints in Chimera. That had stopped when we started wiping them away. Although I hated the time it would take, Brady was right. We didn't want them to know we'd started visiting the town.

He was still at the tree wiping out our prints when the quiet was broken by a series of loud barks, and the sleek white body of a Jack Russell terrier leapt into Doug's arms. Rusty proceeded to run his tongue all over Doug's face, though Doug kept turning away, laughing. He tossed the little dog high into the air which scared me, but Rusty wore a doggy grin when Doug set him back on the ground.

The rest of our animals were right behind him.

Olivia started talking baby talk to the small brown screech owl that settled on the top of her head. She reached up and scratched the owl's back. Pyg closed her eyes and looked blissed out; there was no other way to describe it.

Faith knelt in the dirt at the edge of the road and ran her fingers through the silky red fur of the small fox. I was surprised to see Foxy so close to us. The red fox usually kept its distance, like we made it nervous.

Watching our animals made me grin. According to Ronny, my half-magic sister-in-law, they shouldn't exist. Only those with strong magic could call one. Instead, they came from the one wish that brought us nothing but good. I'd made it before we realized how badly wishes could backfire. All I'd wanted was for something to help us in Chimera. The next thing we knew, we had animals. Though they couldn't speak, they somehow managed to communicate and provide us with information and protection.

That seriously confused Ronny. According to her there'd never been a familiar in the long history of the magic world that chose to help one of the non-magical Mundane.

Like us.

I looked back to the tree in time to see Fangface fly around Brady where he was making his way slowly toward us, dragging a small leafy branch. When Brady drew near, I heard him making shrill squeaks and clicks that had the small black bat squeaking back and swooping around Brady's head. I could swear they were in the middle of a conversation.

Then Shadow ran up and I was busy petting her, marveling at the intense blue of her eyes and the beautiful Siamese markings on her fur. She purred loudly as I ran my hands over her back. "I've missed you," I told her, and her purring grew even louder. As if she'd understood what I said. Which should have been ridiculous.

Only, this was Chimera. And in here, anything was possible.

Chapter 2/January/Chimera

Mystic

"We should go," Faith insisted. "We need to get out of sight of the tree."

"Yeah, Brady," Olivia said and grinned. "It would be a shame for all your hard work covering our tracks to be wasted."

Brady gestured for her to go ahead. "Since I must ensure all traces of our presence are eliminated, it's imperative for me to go last. Which means, of course, that you should begin walking first."

Olivia sniffed, then flounced past him down the straight, flat road. The rest of us followed and our animals ranged out around us. All except Pyg, who rode on top of Olivia like a hair ornament. Pyg's head bobbed up and down with each step she took. I almost laughed out loud, but Olivia was already upset with Brady. No point getting her upset with me, too.

We rounded a corner, where we couldn't be seen from the tree, and I stopped dead. I felt the others stop around me, but I didn't look at them. This part of the road wasn't like anything we'd seen before. Oh, the left side looked pretty normal, with trees and shrubs growing thickly down to the edge of the road. But on the right…

There were low rolling hills to our right, covered in flowers that looked like a crazed geometric painting. The flowers in this place didn't look anything like back home. Some were as big as dinner plates. Most of them were odd shapes and many were colors that didn't exist in Santa Ramona. Or anywhere in the normal world.

Back near the tree, some fields looked like a crazed painter had dumped the contents of a paint store all over them. Here, the painter hadn't dumped the paint. The flowers appeared to have been painted in stripes, circles, triangles, rectangles and other strange shapes I didn't recognize. Some areas were small or narrow, while others were huge. The stripes were in every possible direction; horizontal, vertical, and diagonal. Together, it formed the most fantastical patchwork quilt of a garden I'd ever seen.

Faith had to tug on my arm twice to get me moving, then I did so reluctantly. I'd have liked to spend the next half hour exploring that garden.

We'd gone much further before the first obvious signs of civilization began. A short stone fence had been built on the left, as if to keep the woods off the road. Then we came to a small wooden sign. The words on it had been carved delicately and with great skill. We all stopped to give Brady a chance to decipher it.

Fortunately, he'd gotten much better at reading the Chimeran language which consisted primarily of rune symbols, like something out of Lord of the Rings. I don't know why I always expected a message full of significance when we saw one of these signs; I was almost always disappointed.

This was no exception. It took Brady only a minute to announce, "You are entering Mystic, population 164." He made a sound of disgust in his throat. "Actually it's been defaced. Someone scratched out the '4' and changed it to '3'."

It was how he kept his face turned away from me that clued me in. "What else does it say?" I asked.

He flushed and poked at his glasses as if trying to push them into place. Only, they were already in place. He kept his face down and his voice was low and fast as he said, "Be gone, half-Mundane traitor."

"I don't think we need to tell Ronny about that," I said quietly. I tried to relax my fingers where they'd curved involuntarily into tight fists, fighting the anger those words shot through me. It wasn't right. Ronny had been banished to our world, not allowed to return home, just because she married my older brother Chris.

Which was why the five of us were here, heading into a strange town, because she couldn't be. We'd sworn to her that we'd find out what happened to her friends and family. Why they'd all simply disappeared, leaving a world devoid of most everything but monsters.

The worst part was, I'd begun to think we might never succeed. Always before we'd had clues from Ghalynn, Ronny's frustrating, short-tempered elf friend. Granted, most of his clues had been pretty obscure, and his poetry was *awful*. Still, they'd been like sign-posts helping us get where we needed to go. He'd led us to three magic objects he seemed sure we would need, and told us we had to find a fourth.

But this time, we'd be going in blind. A couple months ago we'd found the third object, an old compass. The Sylph protecting it told us Ghalynn probably wouldn't be able to help us anymore. So how the heck were we supposed to find the final object with nothing to guide us? We didn't even know what the final object was. The only clue we had was what the Sylph told us; to look for a Salamander in the town of Mystic.

"Do any of you know what kind of Salamander we're supposed to look for?" I asked.

Brady cleared his throat and proceeded to speak geek. "Are you referring to one of the Scientific Classification of Phylum Chordata, Class Amphibia, Order Caudata? Found in the Holarctic and Neotropical regions?"

"No," Faith said, and rolled her eyes. "She's talking about the elemental, like the other guardians Ghalynn used; the Sylph, Gnome and Undine." She smiled at Brady to show she wasn't getting all over his case like Olivia usually did. "Salamanders are creatures associated with fire, often called fire lizards. At least that should be easy to recognize."

This whole thing was getting ridiculous. We had to watch out for Rejects, blood-thirsty monsters, other clues Ghalynn *might* have left, some unknown hidden object, *and* flaming lizards? Maybe we could ask the map to look for it. Hopefully there wasn't a limit on the number of things the map could watch for.

I shivered convulsively. I wanted to believe it would all be easy. That nearly dying from a lack of air would be the worst thing to happen in here. That we were done with murderous trolls, ogres, goblins, giant spiders and fire breathing dragons.

Actually, I hoped to be done with all monsters, both here and at home. Being grabbed by something beneath my bed and nearly dragged under it a few weeks ago had been terrifying. And, as long as I was hoping like this, I should add the faceless angel statues in the cemetery. The ones that moved each time magic leaked out of Chimera. They weren't be up to any good.

"That's all we have to do?" Olivia asked, interrupting my morbid thoughts. "Look for a fiery lizard?"

"Sal-a-man-der." Faith emphasized each syllable as if that would make Olivia start saying it right.

"Well, there's more to it than that," Brady said. "I have been considering all of the possibilities."

Of course he had.

"We don't know if what the Sylph suggested last November was accurate. It is conceivable that Ghalynn will have placed clues in some of the houses in Mystic. Additionally, we don't know if the," he gave Faith a quick smile, "Sal-a-man-der is actually guarding the final object. The object or clues from Ghalynn could be located anywhere. Inside the town. Inside the houses in the town. Inside the drawers or cupboards in those houses. Unfortunately, it is my belief that we will need to search diligently through everything in order to be sure we don't miss something crucial."

"Why not just check your wonder-map?" Olivia asked.

"We don't know if Ghalynn did something to the other notes and objects that caused them to provide a visual representation on the map. That might not have happened this time. It seems unlikely Ghalynn ever found the last object or he would have left us a clue with the Sylph."

We all gaped at him for a moment, and even though the sun was still bright I felt a momentary chill. I rubbed my arms to warm them.

"But that could take forever," Olivia wailed. "We could be 95 before we finish checking all the houses out."

I bit the inside of my lip, trying not to laugh. I'd been thinking it could take a couple years. But 95 years old? There was no way it was going to take 80 years to get through those houses. From everything Ronny had told us, the town wasn't that big.

As we continued toward it, Olivia and Brady debated how long it could take to go through all of them. Then we topped a small hill and we could see the tree far in the distance. Which meant *we* could be seen from the tree.

"The Rejects could come through any time," I said. "Right now, we're sitting ducks. Let's not waste our breath talking about what might happen." Maybe that would stop Olivia and Brady's bickering, at least for a while.

I started walking faster and the others kept up. I kept glancing back over my shoulder, holding my breath, searching for any sign of the Rejects.

After a few strenuous minutes, we made it over the slight rise, where we could no longer be seen. My fingers cramped and I relaxed them; I hadn't even noticed tightening them into fists.

Brady pulled the map out of his pocket as we walked, and peered at it. Even though, with his memory he had to know where this road went. He sighed. "Unfortunately, our options are severely limited regarding access to the town. There are only two roads now available. All others meant to traverse Chimera are obscured by what we've hypothesized is the potentially lethal fog we encountered on our eighth trip here. It is clearly discernable as you can see." He pointed to the center of the map. "It's represented, as you know, by the expanding void at the center of the map."

The fog. The thought of it creeped me out. Ronny had warned us to avoid it. Inhabitants believed the magic power driving this world had pooled there. And none who entered the center ever returned.

We'd gotten near it the first year we came. *I* couldn't remember if it had been our eighth visit, but if Brady said so I believed him. The fog had been dirty yellow and bone chillingly cold. It reeked like rancid meat, sour milk and putrefying fruit, mixed with a bit of squashed dog crap and vomit. I shuddered at the memory of the disgusting greasy smear it had left on my skin.

Even worse, the fog seemed alive somehow. Drifting tendrils had tried to grab Brady as he walked around the edge of it.

Plus the shadows in the swirls of fog had looked like screaming faces. And there had been sounds of something skittering inside.

You couldn't pay me enough to go anywhere near it.

It seemed like the list of places in Chimera that I never wanted to see again just kept growing. Hopefully the town wouldn't get added to that list.

"So what do you think we'll find in this town?" Faith sounded uncomfortable, as if she'd read my mind.

"It makes no sense to speculate about what we might see now." Brady frowned. "We'll see for ourselves soon enough."

"Oh come on," Olivia said, raising one eyebrow. "Anticipation is the best part of an adventure. And the best way to anticipate something is to talk about what we might see. Come on, try it!"

"No, thank you." Brady met Olivia's narrow-eyed glare casually, a half-smile on his lips.

Olivia must have recognized that he was unimpressed with her do-what-I-say glare. So I wasn't surprised when she changed her tactics. She leaned closer to him and dropped her voice. "Please. I'd love to hear the possibilities you'd come up with." I had to turn away to keep from laughing. She was actually batting her eyelashes at him.

Brady shot her a quick look I didn't understand, then sighed dramatically, giving in to her. "I expect the town will be based on the engineering history of the time Chimera was created. That was the 1600's right? House styles then were based on function and the availability of building methods and materials."

"Oh bother!" Olivia tossed her hair back impatiently. "Who cares about available building methods and materials? They use magic here, remember? There could be castles!"

"Castles?" Brady ran his hands through his hair, looking blank. "Why would there be castles? Castles are normally the private fortified residences of a lord or noble. Why would they be in Chimera?"

"Uh!" Olivia briefly dropped her head in her hands and sucked in a deep breath through her nose. Loudly. Then she looked at him, a sweet pitying expression on her face, and said in an all-too-patient voice, "No, I mean like the places where kings lived. With moats and drawbridges and pennants flying over round towers with decorative cut outs on top. You know, castles!"

Brady sounded like he was channeling Mr. Harper, our history teacher, when the class missed a point he was trying to make. "Round towers are called turrets. And those crenellations on the top weren't for decoration. They were used by defenders to lean out and drop things on invaders. Whether they belonged to a king *or* a noble."

"Eeeow." Olivia stopped and stamped her foot. "Must you always take the fun out of everything?"

Brady lowered his head and scuffed his foot in the dirt. "Sorry," he said, quietly.

Faith grabbed Olivia's arm and tugged to get her moving again. "Come on, let's check it out. Since they have magic, maybe they made it look like Fantasyland in Disneyland."

"Or something out of Lord of the Rings, like Gondor," I said cheerfully, knowing that would get Olivia's attention off poor Brady. He always came across so logical, it was easy to think of him like Spock from Star Trek. But I'd begun to suspect there was a sensitive side to him under all that logic.

We hadn't gone much farther when we passed one of the metal pyramids we'd seen in other parts of Chimera. Like the others, it was huge; taller than a two-story house yet only an inch or so wide. This one glowed as though there were dim lights on inside. None of us suggested touching it to see if it was as hot as the others, and for once we managed to get past without kicking a rock into it.

Good thing. The others had rung like a massive bell when struck, reverberating on and on and on. And when one went off, all of them — all over Chimera — went off. Not only was the sound painfully loud, it made the trolls hidden in the trees scream and howl and break things. That was an experience I'd just as soon not repeat. Ever.

A few minutes after the pyramid, our road intersected with another. The new road bordered fields to our right filled with grape vines. To the left were three small wooden houses with thatched roofs. These couldn't be more different than a castle. I stopped and said, "Do you think we should walk all the way through the town and check everything out first? Or should we start exploring each building we come to?"

Brady spoke up immediately. He was all for a very organized approach, that included checking out the town by dividing it into sections that could be searched scientifically.

Olivia disagreed with him, vehemently. "We need to start with the houses we can see. It doesn't make sense to skip them and come back later. That's just stupid."

I still wasn't sure why Brady drove Olivia so crazy. She argued and disagreed with nearly everything he said. Which was weird because in all the time I'd known her, she had never been like that with anyone else. I'd have to ask Faith what she thought. Later.

"I have to agree with Olivia," Faith said, with an apologetic smile at Brady.

Olivia gave a smug smile. "And, after all, we could find the next object we need right away."

I opted for something between them. "We should take it in sections so we don't miss any," I said. "Like Brady suggested."

I smiled at him, then continued quickly before Olivia could express the protest forming in her eyes. "But we should check each section of town as we get to it," I said. "Like Faith and Olivia suggested." That was a bit of an exaggeration since they'd only been talking about the three houses in front of us. But the frown disappeared from Olivia's face.

Unfortunately, it was replaced with a smirk aimed at Brady.

He frowned and muttered something under his breath, and I continued apologetically, "It *would* be foolish to look at the entire town first, if we could find whatever we need right away." I hesitated then brought up the subject we had all been avoiding. "Does anyone have *any* idea what it might be?"

There, I'd said it. How were we supposed to know we'd found what we were looking for?

"I'm still hopeful that the map will provide us with an indication if we come near enough to any items of interest," Brady said, touching the pocket where he kept it.

"So we're agreed. We check everything in an organized fashion, but do these houses first." Doug grinned and thumped Brady on the back. When we'd started this adventure three years ago, that would have made Brady stagger. Now, he didn't even budge. All that Tai Kwan Do must be paying off. I wondered if he liked it now; he'd only started it to be able to deal with the situations we kept getting into in Chimera.

Brady grunted in acknowledgment though I knew he didn't really agree. He pulled out the map and said, "I wish to see the Rejects."

My stomach clenched as I searched the map for the sight of their red dots. Ray, Andrew and Polly had been bad enough; pushing us down, destroying our things, making us the joke of the school. But their newest recruit, Arnold, was scary.

I was fairly certain Arnold was destined to become a famous psychopath. I'd know who to blame if I heard newscasters describing a desperate search for Southern California's newest serial killer.

If we lived that long... Some days, I was sure we'd be his first victims.

Brady muttered, "Darn." I glanced at the map as my stomach spasmed, then relaxed. The Rejects were here. But they were heading up the main road. The one we'd used last year to go to the forest. That should mean we'd be safe enough.

At least for now.

Chapter 3/January/Chimera

A House is Not a Home

"I wonder what they will look like inside." Olivia was bouncing on her toes. "Like a regular house? Like a fairy tale cottage? Like Snape's potion room?"

"Ronny informed us they created Chimera in the 1600's," Brady said. "It wasn't unusual for the homes of the poor to have dirt floors. Sometimes rush mats were spread over the floor in areas where food was consumed to catch grease and debris."

Olivia made a sound of disgust in the back of her throat. Before she could say anything Brady added, "People had far less knowledge about cleanliness and the use of hygienic practices back then. Don't forget indoor plumbing did not yet exist. Bathrooms were often holes in the ground or chamber pots kept under the bed."

Olivia came to a complete stop and glared at him, eyes narrowed, hands fisted on her hips. "This is a magic place, Brady." Her tone was little better than a sneer. "If they could create a whole separate world, I'm sure they could come up with better methods than that!"

Faith muttered, "That may be, but after all this time there's probably dust and spiders everywhere."

"It's bad enough getting all the negative stuff from Brady." Olivia elbowed Faith gently in the ribs. "Don't *you* start."

"Geez. Can we just go?" Doug stalked around them and turned down the narrow road that led toward the houses. Faith and I followed him quickly, and with a moment's hesitation, so did Olivia and Brady.

It would be more accurate to call these…cottages. They were small, built of wood and covered with thatched roofs. None of them had a yard with grass like I was used to seeing, but they each had a vegetable garden, overgrown and neglected. Sunlight glinted off small glass windows in each house, blocking any view inside. I couldn't help wondering if the insides were as neglected as the outsides.

Though I didn't say so out loud, I'd have bet that Faith was right. A thatch roof didn't sound like a good way to keep dust and spiders and other creepy-crawlies out. I could only hope Brady was wrong. Dirty rush floors and no indoor plumbing would probably stink.

Olivia turned toward the first house, and Doug dropped his hand on her shoulder. "I think we should check out the farthest one first and work our way back to the road."

"Okay, sure," Olivia said. I noticed there wasn't even a trace of a sneer when she spoke to Doug.

He smiled at her and I nearly rolled my eyes. What was it about Olivia that made guys go all goofy around her? She got more smiles in a day than I got in a week. Alright, she was prettier than me. And she really knew how to use make-up, and wore killer clothes, which I didn't. And she looked older than our nearly sixteen, which I definitely didn't. I... I looked down at my average shape and my average clothes, and sighed.

Guys could be *so* shallow.

Doug pushed ahead when we reached the door. "I should go first."

I gritted my teeth. Now he was playing hero for her.

I glanced at Olivia to see her reaction, but she looked oblivious. She was too busy peering around Doug, waiting for him to open the door.

He grunted when it resisted and gave it a strong tug. As it finally swung open I saw it was solid wood, at least two inches thick, and obviously heavy. Our familiars hurried into the house ahead of us; Rusty had a silly doggy grin on his face which made me smile. Then as we all crowded inside, the heavy door swung shut behind us with a loud, definitive thunk.

I heard alarmed exclamations from my friends and would have turned back to look, but our familiars grabbed my full attention. Who knew magic animals would freak at being shut up in a house?

Fangface began circling the small living room, squeaking unhappily. Foxy slunk behind a rather uncomfortable looking brown chair and pressed up against the wall as if she was trying to disappear. Unfortunately, her bright orange fur was even more distinctive against the pale cream paint. Pyg settled onto Olivia's head and hunched down as small as possible. None of those things were a problem, but Shadow started jumping onto higher and higher pieces of furniture — ottoman, table, chair, chair back, sideboard — in a series of graceful leaps. Then she jumped on the mantle over the fireplace and knocked over a large glass figurine which shattered on the hearth in a small explosion of deadly fragments.

In typical cat fashion, she gazed down on her mess unblinkingly, then looked away, nose in the air as if she'd meant to do it. Rusty, on the other hand, began leaping around, barking his fool head off. Doug finally scooped him up to keep him from cutting his little doggy feet on the splinters of glass. Only then did he stop barking.

We stood in the comparative silence, shocked by how quickly everything had gone wrong.

We'd been shut up inside this place.

Shadow had broken the figurine on the mantle.

Fangface had his little bat claws digging holes in one of the curtains while the other one hung askew.

Rusty had managed to knock over a small table with all his bouncing around.

And there were bits of glass and who-knew-what strewn all over the room.

That was bad enough. But even worse, something had closed the door behind us. Or maybe it was *someone*. What if someone was still in Chimera? How could we explain trashing the very first house we'd entered?

"We can't let them come in any more houses," Faith said hollowly, looking where Foxy was still pressed up against the wall, eyes so large there was white showing around the edges.

"No joke," I said, glaring at Shadow who'd started the whole thing and was now sitting there calmly, washing her paws as if nothing had happened.

Doug carried Rusty to the door. I held my breath, suddenly afraid it might be locked or stuck shut, but Doug opened it with little trouble. He set the small terrier outside and patted his head. "You wait for us out here, boy. We won't be long."

Rusty tipped his head to the side and whined softly, his ears and tail drooping.

"It's okay. I'm not mad at you," Doug assured him. "But from now on you guys need to wait for us outside."

Rusty gave a soft bark, like he'd agreed with Doug.

"All of you," I said. "Wait for us outside."

Foxy immediately slunk out the door, followed swiftly by Fangface and Pyg. I raised my eyebrows at Shadow and tapped my foot. She finished washing her paw, then stretched and jumped over the glass and debris onto the rough wooden floor and sauntered outside, nose and tail pointing up in the air. Doug quickly shut the door behind her, a bit more firmly than was really necessary.

Inside the room, thin gauzy curtains let in plenty of light. They were a strange color, kind of cream or maybe more like pale banana. Except, the color seemed to change as I looked. Now I could swear there was a hint of peach or pale raspberry to them.

I tore my eyes away from the curtains. The room wasn't large and looked strangely empty. Then I realized what was missing. There was no TV. No DVR. No Blue-ray player. No stereo or speakers. No collection of DVDs or CDs. No lamps. No digital clocks. Nothing electronic whatsoever.

There was a reason Brady wore a self-winding watch that didn't need batteries. Everything electronic or battery operated — like cell phones and flashlights — refused to work in here. Brady was convinced there was something in the magic in Chimera that interfered with electro-magnetic frequencies. So I understood *why* none of those things were there, but it still looked…weird.

The room was sparsely furnished. There were only three large chairs around a small round table at one end, with several large paintings of fantasy art on the walls; diaphanous winged fairies, jewel-toned dragons sitting on hordes of treasure, and landscapes done in purple and teal and fuchsia.

They looked so much like the paintings in Ronny's house I nearly felt nostalgic.

At the other end of the room was a small dining table and an area I assumed was a kitchen. It didn't look right without a refrigerator or dishwasher. And there was something like an old woodstove in the corner. Next to it was a sink, although I couldn't see any way to turn the faucet on or off. Maybe it was controlled by magic.

Under the sink a cabinet held nothing but bars of soap and worn towels. The rest of the kitchen was filled with drawers and cupboards. I pulled open a drawer next to the sink and almost sneezed when a strange musty scent escaped. The drawer was filled with jars of spices in shades of yellow and red and deep orange. The other drawers were also filled with glass jars, though their contents were easier on my nose.

Above and on either side of the sink were narrow cupboards without doors. On one side, the shelves were stacked with cups and glasses made of pewter and thick glass filled with bubbles and imperfections. The other side held dinnerware; thick grey pottery plates and bowls with strange black symbols around the edges.

I began looking through the remaining cupboards, but my excitement about looking through a magical house was quickly being replaced by a feeling of discomfort. It didn't feel right poking through someone else's things. Even if they were missing.

The last cupboard replaced my discomfort with revulsion. A paper sack had fallen over and split open. A few remnants of some powdery substance were still visible, but most was obscured from view by mouse droppings and a crop of ugly, twisted mushrooms that looked disgustingly similar to Jerusalem crickets — what Mom called potato bugs.

I shuddered and slammed the door, cringing as a furtive sound of movement seemed to drift out of that space.

-xXx-

While I'd been busy in the kitchen, Brady and Doug had been in the only other room in the house. Brady came back in and announced, "There's nothing of interest to us in the bedroom, although the lack of dust is quite puzzling. There should be a considerable amount accumulated after three years. I'll have to ask Ronny if this is a side effect of the magical energy used here."

I turned around and looked at the room again. He was right, there was no trace of dust. And that *was* seriously weird.

"Let's check the other houses," Doug said, and crossed to the door. As he opened it, there was a fusillade of excited barks and Doug staggered back as Rusty launched himself against Doug's chest. Doug managed to get his arms up in time to catch him. But he wasn't fast enough to keep his face out of reach of Rusty's tongue.

I ducked around them and went over to Shadow, telling her what a good cat she was. I stooped down and scratched the top of her head just where she liked it best and was rewarded by a rumbling purr.

Once everyone came outside, I stood up, hoping I'd feel better about searching the other two houses. I asked Brady if he would open the cupboards in both kitchens for me. He did, but I needn't have bothered asking. There were no more creepy mushrooms or rodent droppings.

Olivia pointed out that all three houses looked like they'd had the same decorator. Light colored fabrics over the windows that appeared to change color as you watched. Small spaces filled furniture made of wood and light colored fabrics. Even the paintings on the walls were similar.

She was right, but I couldn't help noticing the other similarities.

Nothing electronic.

No dust.

And other than the kitchens, very few drawers or cupboards in which to keep anything we might be looking for.

The last house did offer a surprise. Lights sprang on as we entered the living room. And in the bedroom, several books were stacked on a low table. When Brady opened them, they were written in what Ronny called Standard Chimeran, full of runes and symbols.

Doug insisted on stuffing the books into my backpack — he refused to carry one — so Ronny could check them out. They were heavy and shifted uncomfortably every time I moved. That was it, I decided sourly. Next time Doug had to bring his own backpack!

This bedroom had both a dresser and a closet. As we rummaged through the dresser drawers I realized looking through a kitchen was nothing compared to going through someone's private spaces. There was something terribly uncomfortable about touching their personal things. I might have felt better if there were signs of dust and decay so it was obvious no one had been there in a long time. But other than the mushroom cupboard in the first house, everything looked like the owners had simply stepped out for an instant, and would come back at any moment.

And demand to know what the heck we were doing.

"Does this feel wrong to anyone else?" At Olivia's blank look I realized I'd said it out loud. "This just feels wrong," I explained. "To be looking through other people's stuff, I mean."

Brady shook his head. "The people who owned these houses have been missing for three years. I'd want someone to look through my things if they were trying to find out what happened to me."

Olivia rolled her eyes. "I wouldn't care why. *I* wouldn't like anyone pawing through my stuff. It's personal."

Faith bit her lip, brows pulled tight, then shook her head. "I gotta go with Brady on this one. I'd want people to do whatever it took to find me if I was missing."

"*I'm* with Olivia," I said. "It makes me feel creepy."

Doug shrugged. "There's no one here to mind. And it doesn't really matter how we feel about it. It has to be done." He turned to Brady. "It feels late. We should probably head back."

Brady checked his watch. "Yeah, we should go back now. I want to ask Ronny about the dust."

Then he glanced at me. "I also want to ask her about those books you're carrying, Kat."

I shifted my shoulders, aware of how much heavier my backpack felt. "Yeah, let's get back quick." I shot a frustrated glare toward Doug. "This thing is heavy!"

Doug ignored me and walked out ahead of the rest of us. He called it taking the point, like he was our leader. *I* called it trying to feel important. I opened my mouth to give him a hard time, then closed it slowly. He was limping. A lot.

He'd had a slight limp ever since Arnold cut his leg a few months before. It hadn't been too bad; long and jagged but not deep. Except that Arnold had unknowingly used a wish, hoping Doug would bleed and never stop.

By the time we got Doug back to Ronny, he'd lost a lot of blood. Ronny had been able to stop the bleeding and heal the cut with magic. But magic didn't work well in Santa Ramona, and Doug had been left with an ugly scar. I'd asked to see it a couple weeks ago, but he'd refused. As far as I knew, he hadn't allowed anyone to see his leg.

I walked up next to him, determined to make him talk. If it was causing him to limp like that, it was more serious than I'd thought.

"Just how bad is your leg?" I asked.

I'd obviously startled him. His whole body twitched in surprise. "What?"

"Your leg. How bad is it?" He stiffened and got his I-don't-have-to-tell-you-anything look. He'd used it on me a lot when we were little. I'd let him get away with it then, but we weren't little anymore.

I gritted my teeth in annoyance, making my voice come out more harshly than I'd intended. "You're limping. No, don't shake your head at me." His pace grew slower as he fought to hide the stutter in his step. "And stop trying to walk normal. It's too late; I already saw you."

He hunched his shoulders defensively. "Drop it, Kat."

"But I— "

"Yes, it hurts when I use it a lot," he snapped. "Yes, it makes me limp. No, there's nothing anyone can do."

"Have you— "

"I've already talked to Ronny. She can't make it any better." His voice dropped and I thought I heard an edge of bitterness. "This is the way it'll be the rest of my life."

"Oh no— "

He shook his head at me. "It's just a stupid limp, Taylor. Lighten up. I never planned to be a professional basketball player anyway."

"Basketball? What—"

"I thought you knew." At my violent head shake, he said, "It's really not a big deal. I had to quit the team. I told the coach last week."

I felt a prickle behind my eyes. Doug had loved basketball.

Now he sounded more tired than anything else. "That last game we played, Ray managed to kick my leg. I went down and thought I'd never make it back up. It was only when the coach started talking about getting the doctor that I forced myself to my feet. How could I explain a magical injury that won't completely heal?"

"Will you show me?"

His hands both clenched into fists, then his left loosened and grabbed his pant leg in a convulsive grip. "No," he said hoarsely. He cleared his throat and said, "No. I'm not going to show it to anyone."

It hadn't looked *that* bad after Ronny had fixed it. I wondered if it had gotten worse since then. I opened my mouth, then noticed the tight set of his jaw, his lips white and thin with strain. Maybe I'd wait and ask him some other time. I fell back, then felt a stab of guilt when I realized the others were all staring at Doug's leg.

We came up a small rise and I could see the huge fig tree in the distance. I heard a faint sigh of relief escape from Doug, and his pace slowed noticeably. I stopped, hoping to give him a chance to rest, and asked Brady, "Can you see the Rejects?"

He already had the map out and scanned it quickly. "There's no sign of them. They must have left while we were checking the houses."

"We'll need to be careful when we leave." Faith started to wrap her arms around her waist then deliberately let them fall by her sides. "You know, in case they're waiting for us in the cemetery."

Olivia rolled her eyes. "You always borrow trouble."

"No," Faith said confidently, no trace of last year's fear in her voice. "I'm always careful. There's a difference."

Olivia sniffed and walked up next to Doug. "Let's get out of here, okay? Since Faith wants us to be careful going through the cemetery, and *Brady* wants to talk to Ronny about dust."

How could she make Brady's name sound like an insult?

Brady folded the map and put it in his pocket. "We should hurry. I have to be home in time for dinner and I still want to talk to Ronny first."

I reached down and scooped up Shadow. "I'd still like to take you home with me," I told her, and ran my hand over her soft silky fur. "I know you can't leave here, but I miss you when we're gone." I smiled as she began to purr.

Ahead of me, Olivia called, "Hey Doug, have you considered wishing for your leg to be healed now that we're back in Chimera?"

Brady muttered, "That would be a particularly dangerous thing to do."

At the same time, Doug said, "No, of course not. Who knows what could happen. Maybe the spell would remove my leg at the knee, or reopen the cut." He grinned as he added, "Or maybe I'd grow an additional uninjured leg, or my leg would turn purple, or—"

"Now you're just being ridiculous," Olivia snapped. I couldn't see her face but I was pretty sure she was pouting. She stomped ahead of Doug, but slowed back down when she got several feet in front of us.

I wracked my brain for something to say to smooth over the awkward silence, but we reached the tree before I came up with something that wasn't totally lame. It wasn't until we stopped and Olivia stepped forward to enter the tree that my blood seemed to congeal in my veins.

I had to go back through that tree.

What would happen if I fell unconscious in there? Could I get stuck inside it forever?

Could I die in there?

I began to feel dizzy and realized I was hyperventilating. It took an effort to slow my panicky breathing. Maybe if I went through next, with three people behind me, their presence would force me out of the tree. Just in case I *did* pass out.

I shoved in front of Faith and said, "I'd really like to go next, okay?"

She looked startled, and I wasn't sure what expression she saw on my face, but she relaxed and stepped back. "Sure, go ahead."

Thankfully I only counted to 36 in the cold, black aloneness before falling face first into the dirt under the tree in the cemetery. I didn't even need to open my eyes to know I was back at home. The air was cool and damp, and smelled of the sea. I'd made it. I hadn't nearly suffocated inside the tree.

Everything was going to be okay.

I opened my eyes and saw a blur of dark stained marble inches from my nose. I'd managed to sprawl at the feet of one of the angel statues.

One of the *creepy* angels that had no face — worn featureless by time and the elements. And of course, it was the one that had moved during the last magic lightning storm.

The one no one believed me about.

I looked up into the shadowed blank face that seemed to be staring at me with loathing, and shuddered. Somehow I had to convince the others about seeing it move.

Because...just because.

Chapter 4/January/Santa Ramona

It's Only Magic...

I always felt relieved when my cell worked once we were back in Santa Ramona.

What had people done before cell phones? I called to let Ronny know we were coming and only a few minutes later we crowded into her living room, taking our usual seats. I plopped onto the rocking chair next to Ronny's recliner, while the others sat on the long green couch that took up most of one wall.

After all this time, everyone looked comfortable here. Olivia scooted back in the far corner and hugged one of the colorful pillows to her. Brady sat down next to her and leaned forward, elbows on his knees. Faith tucked up her long legs, and Doug tossed one of the soft crocheted throws out of his way so he could lean back in the other corner. He had to turn slightly so he wasn't directly facing the window; the sun-catcher there was focusing sparkles of light on his face.

I grinned and turned away to look for Chris, pretty sure he was hovering somewhere nearby, but I didn't see him. He'd been worrying more and more about Ronny. I couldn't blame him. The circles under her turquoise blue eyes grew deeper and darker every month. And lately the least thing seemed to make her upset. All of us had agreed to be careful what we said around her.

Ronny set a plate of cookies on the table and took her chair. As usual they smelled like the best cookies ever. Ronny always insisted she didn't do anything special to them, but I thought she might let some magic slip into the dough.

She'd moved some of the fantastical paintings around in her living room; the ones filled with fairies and unicorns and other creatures people thought were myths. The one that resembled her favorite place when she was young — the glade we'd found in Chimera last year — was now behind her chair where she couldn't see it all the time. I wondered if that was because we'd had to tell her the fairy who lived there had disappeared with most of the other inhabitants of Chimera.

That glade had been one of the few parts of the forest we'd liked. It had been filled with vivid patches of spring green and emerald mingled with turquoise and teal and deep pools of purple shadow. Flashes of light, like lightning bugs had flitted between the trees. The painting made me feel a bit nostalgic.

Then Faith rubbed her ear, shuddered, and looked away. *She* didn't enjoy looking at that painting. I might not either, if I'd been bitten on the ear by a poisonous sprite. Ronny had been able to fix it, but if we'd waited another 24 hours, Ronny said Faith's skin would have started to decay.

I sighed and looked away from the painting. The list of creatures we needed to avoid definitely grew longer every time we went to Chimera. At least we hadn't been attacked by anything today.

I glanced at the tall, narrow curio cabinet in the corner of the room, not sure if this was better to look at or not. In it were all the things we'd found this far: Bad poems with obscure clues from Ghalynn; chests locked by magic that Ronny had to open; the long, heavy metal key we'd found in a cave the first year; the ornate lantern we'd dragged up from the bottom of the lake our second year; and the compass we'd found as dawn broke in the forest a couple months ago. So many things.

And not one gave a clue about what we needed to find next.

I sighed in frustration. No, this was *not* better than looking at the painting. This was…frustrating.

Brady sat forward abruptly. "Kat, can you pull those books out of your backpack?" He waited until I placed them on the table. He tapped them and told Ronny, "We found these in one of the rooms. They're written in Chimeran but it is different than I am used to. Is there anything important for us?"

Ronny absently tucked her black hair behind her ear, and picked them up one at a time to skim through them. "I do not believe so," she said. "They are old novels. Romantic novels, I believe, written in an archaic form of Chimeran." She set them back on the table, and her hand stroked a cover and lingered there.

"You should keep them, Ronny," I said. "We don't need them."

Brady nodded and pushed them toward her. "We entered three houses today." He spread the map out on the coffee table so Ronny could see it and pointed to the houses we'd seen. "None of them had any dust particles on any of the interior surfaces. That isn't logical considering the length of time they have been unoccupied. Yet this one," he gestured at the first house we'd entered, "had something spilled in a cupboard. There were signs that rats had been consuming it, and a form of fungi I am unfamiliar with was sprouting in it. Why is that?"

Ronny looked where he pointed at the map and frowned. "That should not have happened. Houses in Chimera are protected from dust as you are now aware. But they are also protected from mold, bugs, mice, rats and other pests."

"It was just because something spilled," I said.

"You do not understand," Ronny insisted. "You could leave honey or maple syrup all over the floor in Chimera and nothing would get into it. The houses are protected!"

Brady narrowed his eyes skeptically, then rubbed the back of his neck. "You're telling me that magic keeps pests out of your houses?"

"Yes," Ronny said in surprise. "I just said so, did I not?"

He stared at her for a moment then shook his head. "Never mind. I want to know why the last house," he pointed at it for her, "had lights that came on when we entered, while the others did not. I understand about motion sensor lights here in our world. But what made those lights work in Chimera? How did they sense our presence?"

Ronny laughed. It was the first time I'd heard her laugh in a while. "They are witch lights," she told him, then laughed again at Brady's sour face. "It is a spell. It is set to create a witch light when it senses the presence of magick. When the magickal being leaves, the witch light is extinguished."

There was a moment of silence as we all took that in. Including Ronny. I watched as shock stripped the laughter from her face. She grabbed the pendant that hung around her neck, the one her mother gave her, and whispered, "Wait, those lights came on for you?"

I nodded, seeing my friends do the same out of the corner of my eye. Ronny muttered, "Perhaps it was a very sensitive spell. It might have noticed the little bit of magick you absorbed the year you were born." Her gaze became more distant and I was sure she'd almost forgotten we were there. "Or perhaps the spell strengthened after sitting dormant so long. Perhaps it was keyed to something other than magick? But why?"

Doug interrupted her musings. "You told us there was a lot of magical fighting in Chimera the year we were born." She nodded and he frowned. "But you told us magic couldn't be used as an offensive weapon. I don't get it."

She sighed. "No one discovered how it began. Someone wanted to eliminate the Council. First there were terrible rumors. They stirred up everyone. By the time the fighting started, most were so angry they forgot the rules. And by the time the fighting stopped, many had serious injuries; many of their spells rebounded. Mother always believed whoever started the war stole the memory of their responsibility from everyone. It took years to get everything back to normal and to heal all the damage. Mother worried about the effect on the Mundane world. That is why I began to visit here." A goofy smile crossed her face. "And that is why I met my Christopher."

I looked around for my brother. He always loved when she called him *my Christopher*. And he'd been hanging around where he could hear her for months now. But there was still no sign of him.

I turned back and looked at Ronny as she continued, "So much magick escaped during the fighting. Which is why you are able to enter Chimera. All children born here that year absorbed small amounts."

I was suddenly sure she was going to talk about THE-STRANGEST-YEAR-EVER, and sighed. I'd heard about it all my life. Birds flying backwards. Flowers dying and blooming over and over during every full moon. Hundreds of toads raining down on Main Street. Cars turned upside down throughout the town, even those inside locked garages. Sprinklers that kept spraying even after the water was turned off. Alarms going off even when the power was out. It all lasted a full year, then stopped as suddenly as it began.

When I was young, it seemed like that was all most people talked about. They always tried to top each other's wild stories. They had *finally* stopped talking about it, then the strange magic storms started last year. The ones that brought the strange blue lightning. Ronny said the storms were caused by magic leaking once again from Chimera. Now people had started all the TYSE talk all over again.

I was getting a headache from gritting my teeth all the time.

I quickly said, "Um, Ronny, did magical storms leak out of Chimera when we were born? Like they do now? With blue lightning and all?"

She smiled and her voice was nostalgic. "I believe a number of other things happened back then. Mother always liked to say it was because everyone was fighting like bats and frogs."

Olivia had just taken the last bite of her cookie. She snorted, trying to keep from laughing out loud at Ronny's fractured saying, but only succeeded in choking and coughing until she turned beet red.

Doug climbed to his feet and thanked Ronny, assuring her we'd come again next month. The rest of us jumped up and followed him from the house, barely making it out before we broke into stifled laughter. At some point I needed to let Ronny know she should study up on actual sayings.

But right now, they were too much fun.

Chapter 5/January/Santa Ramona

That Was Then/This is Now

The next three weeks were mostly uneventful. I'd actually started to believe it might stay that way. At least until we went back to Chimera that next Saturday.

As I poured myself a bowl of cereal Monday morning, I almost laughed out loud. Looking at us now, no one would think we were the least bit unusual. Dad was seated at the kitchen table, reading the paper, humming under his breath. That meant he was happy about something he was reading. Mom was bustling around the kitchen, rinsing her coffee mug and preparing a sandwich to take to work.

It was such an incredibly normal, everyday scene. But my family was far from normal, though neither Mom nor Dad knew it. After all, I went to a magic land every month. And I couldn't exactly call my brother ordinary. He was ten years older than me, and was married to someone from that magic land. For a moment I wondered what Mom and Dad would do if they ever found out, and had to suppress another laugh.

Not that Olivia's family was completely ordinary. She had *four* younger brothers and sisters. And her mom's whole swearing thing was totally weird. She'd threatened to ground Olivia until she left for college if she heard her use bad language. Years ago, Faith and I had Blood Sister promised not to swear around Olivia. She was convinced if she ever heard a curse word she'd start using it at home. And never be allowed out again.

Faith's life wasn't exactly normal either. She had a single mom who earned barely enough money to keep food on the table. I hadn't really noticed it when we were kids, but Faith wore hand-me-downs and cheap clothes her mom bought off the internet. I'd never realized how bad Faith felt about that until last year when she and Olivia got into a huge fight. It was one of the reasons Andrew detested her. He liked to tell her he didn't want poor trash living in his town.

Andrew's family had made it nearly impossible for Faith's Mom to keep living in Santa Ramona. She was so afraid of them, she kept after Faith, telling her every possible thing that might hurt her.

She'd nearly turned Faith into a basket case. A few months ago I'd been afraid Faith would end up just like her mom, afraid of everything. Then Doug's leg got injured and Faith was partly to blame. She'd been so afraid she couldn't move out of Arnold's way, and Doug had to save her.

You'd think Doug getting hurt would convince her that her mom was right. Instead, she'd sworn not to let fear control her ever again.

Doug's family, on the other hand, was perfectly normal. His parents and mine had been close friends for years. Doug and I spent a lot of time on the same family vacations. Plus we got stuck together for hours while our parents played card games. We were lucky we hadn't gotten killed. Doug liked to try crazy things while our parents were otherwise occupied. He'd been grounded for a month when he nearly burnt down his house after demonstrating how a magnifying glass could start a fire.

Brady, now.... I bit the inside of my lip as I thought about him. It was strange. We'd been friends for three years, but I really didn't know much about his family. I'd never realized it before, but he never talked about them. I knew his great-grandfather was an inventor who'd disappeared without a trace years ago. I also knew his parents had divorced and his dad had remarried. And that was it. But they had to be pretty normal or Brady would complain about them, right?

Mom broke into my musings when she dropped a kiss first on Dad's head then on mine and told us to have a good day. I looked at the clock and gulped. How had the time gotten away from me like that? As the door closed behind Mom, the kitchen grew strangely quiet except for the rustling of Dad's newspaper. Because, I realized, Dad's humming had stopped.

Uh oh.

Any second now he'd be done with the paper and would start asking about my day. And once he got started there was a good chance I'd end up late to school. The trick was to get out of the kitchen while he was still buried in the newspaper. I gulped my cereal in a rush and managed to slap my bowl in the sink and get it rinsed off before he set the paper down.

As I left the room, I told him I'd see him tonight. I knew I'd be a couple minutes early meeting the others this morning, but that was better than getting a tardy.

I grabbed my backpack and headed out the door. Lately Mom had probably decided I wasn't so normal either. Not with my sudden interest in history. Over winter break I'd started digging into some of the library's history books about the 1500's and 1600's. I'd been hoping Ronny had exaggerated when she mentioned how badly the Mundane had treated magic users. But she hadn't exaggerated at all. How could all those history books make the wholesale slaughter of possibly millions of people sound so…unimportant? Almost reasonable. Some books only mentioned the supposed witch trials and werewolf killings as a footnote.

It was really disturbing. In France, tens of thousands were killed for being werewolves. All over Europe and some parts of America people had been killed in disgusting and sometimes stupid ways because they'd been accused of using magic. There was even a book, *Malleus Maleficarum*, which encouraged people to hunt down and destroy witches.

Most people at school probably considered it all ancient history. But it was different for me. It became important when I found out Ronny's grandmother was burned at the stake, while Ronny's mother and her three aunts had to watch her writhing and screaming in agony…

It was why they stayed in Chimera — to keep away from the Mundane. I knew Ronny missed her home, but she always said choosing to be with my brother, even though it got her banished from the safety of Chimera, was worth it.

I had a hard time imagining caring about someone enough to leave my home and my family forever. But the way she got all googly-eyed when she talked about choosing Chris made it hard to doubt her. Which was pretty embarrassing. How could anyone get so mushy over my brother?

I knew she missed her home, but it was more than that now. Because she'd been banished, she couldn't go back to discover why her mother and everyone she knew had vanished. So my friends and I had vowed to go to Chimera for her. We went nearly every month, when the moon was full. When the doorway between our world and Chimera was open.

We'd been at it for three years now. We'd found strange clues from Ronny's elf friend, Ghalynn. They hinted at a dark and dangerous spell. The clues had lead to objects that might be needed to counteract that spell. And two months ago we'd been told to explore the town where Ronny grew up to find the last of those objects.

Searching through town was better than searching the swamp, with deadly puff balls that made us sleep for hours. Or the forest, where giant spiders wrapped us in sticky webs and planned to eat us. And where Doug's dragon nearly burnt us to a crisp. So — maybe — feeling uncomfortable poking through other people's stuff was a small price to pay.

I stopped on the corner where we always met for school and felt a moment of panic when I saw I was the only one there. According to my phone I was five minutes early. I hoped, fervently, that none of the Rejects would come by while I was alone. Someone might as well have posted a sign on me that said 'Victim Here'.

The relief I felt when I saw the others coming toward me was almost embarrassing. Unfortunately that relief soured a bit. Olivia kept us waiting far longer than usual, slathering on her make-up. I might have complained but Doug beat me to it.

"Do you plan to take all day?"he asked.

Olivia gave him the evil eye. "You know I can't do it at home. Mom would have a fit."

Although we finally got her moving, we had to make a run for it. The rest of us managed to find enough breath to give Olivia a hard time; I might have given her a harder time than usual. I hated running several blocks to school, backpack slapping against me, getting hot and sweaty and red-faced. By the time we got to school, we were busy arguing and didn't check who was in the hall.

Big mistake.

Ray and the other Rejects were waiting.

I couldn't stand getting near Ray. I detested seeing his nostrils flare and his upper lip curl in disgust. I loathed how his eyes darkened and his hands tightened into fists. I was always sure he was considering what he'd like to do with those fists.

At least being late had one good point. Ray and his nasty friends didn't have enough time to do too much. It was bad enough when he hawked up a glob of spit into Olivia's face. There were no teachers in the hall to see him, naturally. It made me want to scream.

There wasn't much we could do. We'd tried reporting things in the past, but no one wanted to believe that Ray and Andrew would do such things. Why, they asked, would the Mayor's son risk his reputation like that? In the end, all our complaining had done was to get ourselves labeled as troublemakers. Which meant no one believed us now.

I looked over at Olivia as we'd hurried down the hall. She was wiping away some of her fussy makeup while she wiped spit off her cheek. I had some on me as well, but Faith had it worst of all. Her personal nemesis, Andrew, had spit too. He managed to get her in the eye. She was wiping at it furiously while we ducked into class right as the final bell rang, Faith first, followed by me and Olivia. Ray and Andrew crowded into class right behind us.

I'd just taken my seat when Olivia stopped abruptly, causing Ray to walk into her. He was so much bigger, he almost knocked her off her feet. She caught herself, and in a sickeningly sweet voice said, "You should watch where you're going, Ray. You might get hurt, running into people like that." Then she gracefully swung into her seat, leaving him standing there in the aisle, red with anger.

"Maybe you'd better be more careful if you know what's good for you," he growled. He must be *really* angry; he'd let a teacher hear him threaten someone. He usually protected his image around teachers.

Mr. Kline cleared his throat uneasily and asked everyone to take their seat. Apparently he wasn't going to do anything. I turned to watch Ray just in time to see him deliberately set one of his size 13's directly onto Olivia's foot, leaning on it with all of his weight. She sucked in her breath, the sudden paleness of her skin showing clearly where she'd wiped away her makeup along with his spit. Then he moved past her and took his seat. I had just a moment to see her lift her foot and rub it before Mr. Kline demanded all eyes to the front of the classroom.

I tried to pay attention during class, but I was worried; sure that Ray and Andrew were going to try something when we left.

After the bell rang ending class, Ray and Andrew hung back. No way was I going to let them follow us in the hall. Not going to happen! I asked Mr. Kline if he had a minute, letting Faith and Olivia crowd up next to me. Ray and Andrew hung back, trying to wait us out. I asked about the book Mr. Kline had discussed in class and asked if he had any suggestions for similar books.

"Your mother, as the town librarian, could help you with this, but I can give a few suggestions."

As he finished a dismayingly long list, he turned to Ray and Andrew and told them to come on up. They tried to make an excuse to leave, but Mr. Kline, my new hero, said, "Nonsense. You've waited this long to ask me something. Out with it."

Faith, Olivia and I hurried out of the classroom, sure we were home free. Then I saw Arnold waiting near Faith's locker. With his dark sunglasses, you shouldn't be able to tell for sure if he was staring at you. But I could swear I felt his gaze, like a heavy cold weight when it touched my face. I hated the way Ray and Andrew treated us, but Arnold seriously terrified me.

-xXx-

When the bell rang at the end of school, Faith hung back. "I want to be sure the Rejects are gone before we go out there," she insisted.

Olivia rolled her eyes, but followed Faith into the bathroom. It felt kinda creepy, leaning against the walls of the bathroom, trying to look casual while we waited for the noises in the hall to diminish. Finally, after the longest eight minutes I'd ever spent, Faith let out a ragged sigh and said, "I'm sick of this! Let's get out of here."

I was relieved to get out of there. Right up until we left the building and saw the Rejects walking across the lawn, heading for the sidewalk.

Faith froze like a deer caught in the headlights. She scrunched her eyes tightly shut and began muttering, "Don't let them see us. Please don't let them see us!"

"This isn't Chimera," Olivia said. She sighed and I thought she sounded disappointed when she said, "Wishing doesn't work here."

I wondered briefly just what she'd wish would happen to them.

Faith opened her eyes and glared at Olivia. "Who's wishing? Did you hear me use the word 'wish'?"

"Fine," Olivia said, holding up her hands placatingly. "You were hoping and praying and begging the universe to make it so. But not wishing. Of course, not *wishing*."

Note to self — If you ever want to sound really sarcastic, channel Olivia.

The Rejects probably wouldn't have turned back anyway, but maybe Faith's hoping-praying-begging helped. Because they disappeared around the corner without a backward glance.

"Well," Faith said cheerfully, as if Olivia had never spoken, "let's get home."

-xXx-

Before we'd taken more than a couple steps, Doug and Brady joined us. Doug looked so concerned I asked, "What's the matter? You look like you just lost your best friend." I grinned at him and tried to lighten things up a bit. "Of course that would be impossible. Since all your best friends are standing right here."

He didn't even give me a hint of a smile. Instead he rubbed his hands over his face before looking me in the eye. "We're in trouble," he said.

Chapter 6/February/Chimera

Billy Goats Gruff

"What do you mean, we're in trouble?" My voice squeaked and I quietly cleared my throat, hoping I wasn't blushing.

"I overheard the Rejects talking," he said. Just that. I could have kicked him for making me drag everything out of him.

"So, did they have something interesting to say?" I asked, doing my best sarcastic Olivia impression.

Doug must have recognized it. He shot a quick glance at Olivia, then turned back to me. "Ray was insisting they do something that, uh, that Olivia's old boyfriend Rick suggested before he moved. Rick told them to be nice to their animals because ours helped us."

I was surrounded by groans and startled exclamations. I had to clear my throat, again, before I could speak. "I never told Rick about our animals. Did one of you?"

Olivia was suddenly very busy looking everywhere but at us. "Ooooliiiivia?" I asked, dragging her name out in a sing-song voice so she'd know I'd seen the guilty look on her face.

"I didn't tell him, much," she insisted. "I… I might have mentioned that we didn't know what we'd do without them. He never asked what I meant. So I didn't tell him they were helpful. Not exactly…" Her voice trailed off, with a slight pleading edge to it. Like she was trying to get us to agree.

There was no squeaking now; my voice was strong. "We don't want their animals to help them." I remembered the pathetic spectacle of the small donkey, pink pig, huge rat and disgusting snake trailing along behind them. I'd finally decided the magic required them to follow their human counterpart. The person whose initials referred to the type of animal. There was no way they would follow the Rejects if they had a choice. Not after having rocks thrown at them. Not after Arnold had kicked his snake.

That thought brought up an important question. *"Arnold* agreed to treat his snake nicely?"

"Not really," Doug said. "The others agreed, but Arnold refused to have anything to do with his. He said he'd kill it if it came anywhere near him."

"I guess that's something," Faith said, then shook her head. "I really wish they wouldn't try at all."

"They may not succeed," Olivia said and patted Faith's arm. "After the way they've been treated, maybe their animals won't want anything to do with them."

"What can we do?" I asked. "I mean, if they *are* nice and their animals help them?"

"Such conjecture is useless," Brady said, and clapped his hand on my shoulder. I think he was trying to make me feel better, but now I wanted to rub my sore shoulder. "We'll have to wait and see what happens. Then we can observe the behavior of the Rejects and their animals before we come to any conclusions."

"Brady's right. We'll find out next Saturday." Doug was using his I-am-your-leader-we're-done-talking tone of voice. The one that always made Olivia roll her eyes. This time was no exception. It was a really big eye roll.

"I'll make sure Ronny is available next Monday after school," I said, pulling my cell out of my pocket.

Olivia touched my hand. "Um, about that." She was definitely blushing, big time. "I…uh…I can't go to Ronny's next Monday. It will have to be Tuesday."

"Why can't you go Monday?" Faith sounded aggravated. Which wasn't really fair since it was her soccer practice that kept us from going to see Ronny on Sundays.

"I…well…" Olivia straightened her shoulders and glared around, though she was careful not to look any of us in the eye. "George asked me to go to Johnny's Burger Shack after school next Monday."

"Why would he do that?" Faith asked. "And why didn't you just say you couldn't go?"

"Because!" Olivia was suddenly shouting. "Monday is Valentine's Day. George asked me to Johnny's for Valentine's Day. He likes me. I like him. So I said yes." She turned on her heel and stomped down the steps, face flaming.

I called after her, "No problem, I'll ask Ronny if she can meet next Tuesday."

Beside me, Brady let out a breath that reminded me of a deflating balloon. I glanced over, but he was concentrating on the steps as if his life depended on it. Maybe he was worrying about the Rejects and their animals, even though he'd said there was no point to it. He was probably considering various theories and hypotheses about what that could mean and how we could handle it.

Let him worry about the Rejects. *I* was worried about Olivia. What if this ended up a repeat of Rick? She'd tricked us into telling her first boyfriend about Chimera and insisted on bringing him with us. When they broke up, he was so angry he'd joined the Rejects. And, apparently, told them about our animals. Darn it.

That could not happen again.

I hurried after her and tapped her on the shoulder.

"What?" she snapped.

"Promise me," I said, "that you won't tell him about Chimera." She glared at me, and I repeated, "Promise!"

"Don't worry," she said, sticking her nose into the air and adding a flounce to her steps. "I have no intention of telling anyone about Chimera, ever again."

"Great!" I said and smiled. I chose to ignore the fact that she didn't smile back. She must not be that into George. There was no way she'd agree to keep him out of Chimera if she *really* liked him.

-xXx-

I was nauseous when I woke up Saturday morning. I lay sprawled on my back and considered telling the others I couldn't go to Chimera. I'd had nightmares all night and spent hours sitting up, swaddled in my blankets, shaking as if I was sitting in a freezer. It was bad enough remembering how awful the last trip into Chimera had been. But my nightmares kept making that memory much worse. Because instead of passing out, I stayed awake in my dreams, trapped, unable to breath or see, knowing I'd be stuck like that. Forever.

I'd never enjoyed going through the tree. Having your face shoved into something like a bowl of thick, cold jello was bad enough. But when your whole body is slammed through something cold and clammy and airless... I tried to hold my breath while I went through. It always seemed better to choose not to breathe than to keep trying and failing. Only, after the last time, I was afraid I'd panic in there. That I'd keep trying and failing to suck in air the entire time.

It might be easier if I could see something. Anything. But I wouldn't even be able to see my hand when it was touching my nose. So I always kept my eyes tightly shut in there. It just seemed easier. But I wouldn't be able to keep them shut if I got stuck in there. I'd have to open them and face that impenetrable blackness.

That thought, that I could get trapped in there, had fueled my nightmares all night. Mom's favorite saying about nightmares was a total lie. Things didn't seem better in the morning. Because *this* morning, I'd be going through the tree again. Less than an hour from now.

I dragged myself into the bathroom and stared at my reflection in the mirror. My skin was even more pale than usual, which was really saying something. I tried to care about the lank brown hair straggling around my head and the dark circles under my bloodshot green eyes, but was just too tired.

And what was the point when I was friends with someone who looked like Olivia. Even at my best, I looked pretty ordinary in comparison. Not bad…but, well…forgettable. At least I didn't have to worry about that today. Not when I had a turning-into-a-zombie look going on. No one would find me forgettable today.

Oh well.

I chose my favorite comfortable shirt and jeans. By the time I was ready, in addition to looking terrible, I was going to be late. I ground my teeth in frustration as I left the house. I hated being the last one there. *Olivia* was the one who was always late, not me.

-xXx-

I'd been right, I was last. Olivia was already standing at our usual corner with the others.

"Kat, are you all right? We were worried about you," Olivia said. Her words sounded sincere, but she was grinning from ear to ear. She was reveling in beating me there; she actually looked nearly awake for once.

Wide awake, all made up, and cheerful. I felt like throwing something at her, but was too tired.

"Now that Kat has decided to join us," Doug said, shooting me an impatient look, "we should get moving. There are lots of buildings on the map and we don't know how long it'll take to check them all out."

Olivia grabbed my arm as we headed toward the cemetery. She leaned close and whispered, "I know you must be nervous about going through the tree again. I know I would. But you'll be okay, Kat. I'm sure of it." She squeezed my arm once and smiled, then hurried after the others.

No matter how much she argued with Brady, she was always a really good friend to me.

Brady said, "It may take a considerable amount of time since we must search the houses and other buildings vigilantly," He ignored Faith's groan. "I've considered it thoroughly. We can't rely on the map to show us everything. Not this time. We know Ghalynn may not have been able to leave clues so there is a strong possibility we could overlook something significant. Of course, that is compounded by the fact that we are unaware of the type of object we are searching for."

Brady sounded discouraged, and he was hardly ever discouraged. I wanted to ask what was up, but was distracted when Olivia asked, "So, Brady, why haven't you thought of a way to make my cell work the same way your watch does?"

His eyebrows shot up so high I could see them over his glasses. He shook his head and grinned tightly. "Only you would think I could make a kinetic cell phone. The power that your movements would generate would be insufficient to meet the requirements of a cell phone. I'd have to find a way to amplify and concentrate that power, which would be both heavy and bulky. I don't think you'd like your cell phone to be bigger and heavier than your lap top."

Olivia stopped and stared at Brady. "Ummm..." She drew it out like she was thinking about it, but we all knew what her answer was going to be. "That would be *no*." She glanced at the watch on his wrist. Three years ago, it had hung loose, but now it fit perfectly. It was similar to the watch his great-grandfather had created, right before he disappeared.

Brady grinned at Olivia. "Even if I could make a cell phone that would work in here, you're ignoring the fact that there are no cell towers in Chimera. So there would be no signal. I doubt you could even access a satellite, assuming I was able to perform the necessary modifications on a satellite phone. After all Ronny has described Chimera as a separate part of space and time."

Olivia glared at him and made a growling sound in the back of her throat. "Fine! Just forget the whole thing."

"Can we stop wasting time and get moving?" Doug tapped his foot impatiently. "We sure as heck don't want to bump into the Rejects."

Olivia spun around and growled at him, too. "How often must I tell you not to swear around me?"

I was surprised that Olivia would get so upset by Doug saying 'heck'. It wasn't *that* bad.

"We hardly ever swear," Faith told her mildly.

Olivia crossed her arms over her chest. "Well, it's still too often. 'Cause I almost couldn't come today. I slipped up and said damn. My youngest brother, you remember tattle-tale Jeffrey, right? Well he started yelling damn all over the house. I thought Mom was going to go through the roof. She nearly made good on her grounded-until-college threat."

Doug's lips twisted and he opened his mouth, then closed it and took a deep breath. Then he said, in a strangely formal voice, "I'm sorry Olivia. I'll be more careful in the future."

Olivia stared at him as if she didn't know how to respond to that, then said, "Um, okay. Let's just go, alright?"

When we reached the cemetery, fog drifted in thin patches between the gravestones and wrapped around the mausoleums. It looked like something out of a horror movie. The kind where a group of teenagers enter a haunted graveyard and get picked off, one by one.

Faith increased the pace, not eager to spend any more time in there than necessary, though I'd be glad to delay my next meeting with the tree.

When we got near it, I stopped abruptly and sucked in a startled breath. Olivia wasn't paying attention — too busy tip-toeing over graves — and ran into me, nearly taking both of us to the ground. As she started grousing, I merely pointed. And very nearly cursed, even though Olivia was right next to me. My finger was shaking uncontrollably.

One of the statues had shifted again. It had moved closer to the tree, its blank face fixed upon the path we had to take. The idea of walking by that creepy staring thing made my stomach clench. And I knew I had to try, one more time, to make the others recognize our danger. I cleared my throat; even so, my voice came out pinched. "Um, guys? What do I have to do to convince you that these statues have been moving?"

Faith glanced at me, eyebrows drawn together, a look of sympathy in her eyes. "You must be nervous about going through the tree again," she said, in a soothing voice that made me want to kick something. "You're imagining things."

"My nerves," I bit out, "are fine." That wasn't *really* a lie. More like an exaggeration. Okay, a really big exaggeration. But I wasn't worrying about the stupid tree right now. I was worried about freaking angel statues that kept moving! "Look, I know they've moved. What'll it take to make you believe me?"

"Faith is right," Brady said. At least his voice sounded like he was reciting facts rather than oozing sympathy over my supposedly frayed nerves. "It's fairly common to focus on something other than the issue that is causing distress. You'll soon realize this obsession has no validity. As I've said before, statues are inanimate objects. They don't have the ability to move on their own. It's your perception of their relative locations that is faulty."

I glared at him, eyes narrowed, lips compressed in a straight line. He actually looked surprised that I was angry, and added. "You asked what it will take for us to believe you?" At my stiff nod he said, "You'd have to prove scientifically, beyond a reasonable doubt, that they have changed locations." He must have seen the relief in my eyes, because he added, "And if you proved they were in a different place, I'd assure you that someone must have moved them."

I ground my teeth together in frustration and turned blindly away. I'd show them I wasn't *nervous* or having *issues* that were *causing distress* just because we were going back through that stupid tree.

I'd have been hyperventilating inside there, if I could actually breathe. Fortunately, before I could panic I was thrust out into the warmth of Chimera. It had to be one of the shortest trips ever. Maybe I should have been grateful. Instead, I glared at the tree and muttered, "Why can't it always be like that?"

"Like what?" Olivia asked as she stepped into Chimera.

"It was a nice, quick, easy trip this time. I just wi… um, want. I want them all to be like that." How come, after all this time, it was still way so easy to forget and use the dreaded 'wish' word.

"It wasn't short *or* easy for me," Faith said, panting, as she nearly fell from the doorway. She shuddered dramatically. "I hate when it takes that long in there."

Brady stepped out and pulled the map from his pocket. He scanned it carefully, and Doug joined us just as Brady announced, "No Rejects here yet."

"Great," Doug said. "Let's hope it stays that way." He made a few dramatic shooing motions and we obediently started walking toward the town. We'd made it nearly to the strange metal pyramid before we were joined by our animals.

Doug thumped his chest and caught Rusty in mid-leap, laughing and twisting his face from side to side as Rusty tried to lick every square inch of it.

Then I was too busy petting Shadow to pay attention to the others. It was then, as I held the purring cat in my arms and felt tears well up in my eyes, that I realized just how frightened I'd been. That I'd never see her again. That I'd never get out of that tree. That I could maybe even die in there.

I took several deep breaths and smiled when Shadow leaned over and licked my cheek. Just once. The rough surface rubbed warm against my skin, and something that had been tight and cold inside me relaxed. I hugged her gently and set her down, feeling ready to go on.

I'd survived the tree the month before, and this morning had been a piece of cake. Things were looking up.

-xXx-

We passed the three houses on the edge of town with no discussion and continued down the road to a small stone bridge that spanned the wide stream below in a graceful arc.

"I thought magical people can't cross water," Faith said.

"Where did you hear that?" I tried to remember if Ronny had said anything about crossing water.

Faith stopped and turned toward me, surprised. "It was in the books about Merlin. The ones by Mary Stewart," she said. They'd been favorites of ours in middle school. One of the benefits of Mom being a Librarian; she could recommend good books, even if they'd been written long before I was born.

"I don't think Mary Stewart actually knew any magic people," I told her, grinning. "I think she made him violently ill when he crossed water to make the story more interesting."

"Okay, fine." She sighed. "I know you're probably right, but I plan on asking Ronny."

"Can we get on with it?" Doug had so much exaggerated patience jammed into his voice, he sounded like he was about to choke. "Can we, *please,* get on with it? Or do you want to stop and discuss *all* of your favorite books first?"

Olivia rolled her eyes, but I said sweetly, "Why, no. I think we're done for now. But we'll let you know if we want to stop and talk about sparkly vampires."

He glared at me under furrowed brows. I grinned back. I'd just scored big; he hated the Twilight books. Monsters, he liked to say, should be scary not friendly. Olivia and I grinned at each other as he turned and stomped onto the bridge.

"Are you sure bridges are protected the same way roads are?" Faith asked hesitantly, hanging back.

"Of course I'm sure," Doug bellowed over his shoulder. "Now hurry up!"

I let the others go first, basking in the knowledge that I'd actually riled Doug up. It didn't happen often, so I was determined to enjoy it. Unfortunately, I couldn't bask long. As soon as I stepped on the bridge a rumbling growl rose from somewhere below us. It started low, then grew in force and volume until the entire stone span shook.

The bridge had a low flimsy wooden edge, no more than three inches high. And there were no guard rails.

I staggered and nearly pitched into the dim shadows below. For a brief moment, I struggled then managed to get my feet back under me. I looked around and saw Brady grab Olivia's arm. He yanked her away from the edge where she'd been teetering, on the brink of plunging over.

We were at least twelve feet above the dark wet boulders that filled the shallow stream below. The shadows made it hard to see, but there was something down there. Based on the strength of its rasping grunts and mind-numbingly loud growls, it was big. And it sounded…hungry.

I gulped. If we survived falling onto those rocks, we'd probably be sorry we did.

I didn't see him move, but Doug was suddenly at my side. He grabbed my arm as something slammed into one of the pillars supporting the bridge. Everything started shaking. My stomach flipped as several rocks broke loose from the edge of the bridge and tumbled down into the water. I didn't know if the whole thing was swaying, or if it was just me. I grabbed onto Doug's arms and held on.

Faith screamed, high-pitched and shrill. A large dirty hand, with three long, gnarled fingers, reached up over the edge. Then cracked, yellowed claws that tipped each finger bit deeply into the thin wood, making it splinter and groan. The back of the hand, down to where it disappeared under the bridge, was covered with thick ropy veins and straggly black hair.

A deep voice rasped out incomprehensible words, raising the hair on the back of my neck.

I asked Brady out of the corner of my mouth, "Did you understand that?"

He shook his head, a look of deep concentration on his face.

The voice came again, this time in English. If anything, it sounded even deeper, more a growl than a voice. "Who dares cross my bridge?"

Doug's hand tightened on my arm. He kept his voice low. "So the protections on the road don't apply to bridges?"

"No," I hissed back. "That can't be right. Ronny would have warned us."

"She hasn't exactly been herself lately." His voice was still low, but now it was…kind. "She may have forgotten."

I opened my mouth to protest, but the bridge shuddered and jerked as the hand grasping the edge flexed, the muscles bulging. A huge, misshapen head slowly rose over the side. I gulped at the mottled scalp, covered with green scabby blotches and a few strands of greasy black hair. That unappealing sight was followed by a bulging forehead and two narrow, deep-set eyes. One was definitely lower than the other, set in folds of skin above a wide twisted cheekbone. A bulbous, pendulous nose, so darkly red it was nearly purple, hung over the thick upper lip. Gaping nostrils flared wide, then the monstrous thing sniffed. Repeatedly. It raised its head and waved it slowly back and forth, inhaling deeply.

It lowered its head and growled again. Louder. It opened its mouth and screamed as it shook the bridge once more. Faith stumbled to one knee, right next to the wide, hideous mouth. It was filled with a few long, crooked, grey teeth. Faith shuddered and turned away, gagging.

That raspy voice sank even lower. "I can't see you, but I know you are there. And I am going to gobble you up."

Faith's head jerked up. She glanced quickly at Olivia, who was standing next to her, then stared at the thing intently. She choked out, in a very small voice, "Oh no. You should let me go by, Mr. Bridge Troll. I'm too little. Wait until the next one comes. She is *much* bigger."

Olivia spluttered indignantly. I couldn't be sure what bothered her most; that Faith had suggested the troll eat her instead, or that she'd said Olivia was so much bigger. I gritted my teeth in disbelief; how could Faith sell Olivia out like that?

What had happened to our promise —*All for one and one for all*?

The troll nodded impatiently and said, "Be off with you."

And suddenly I remembered. I recognized Faith's brilliant inspiration. I was the daughter of a Librarian, after all. It might have taken a minute longer, but I recognized *The Three Billy Goats Gruff* when I heard it. The goats had stopped a bridge troll from eating them and after that it never bothered them ever again. I just had to remember what the heck they did.

I held my finger to my lips and gestured so Brady knew I wanted to go around him. He nodded shortly and moved aside, careful to make no sound. When I got next to Olivia I whispered urgently, "Just say, 'You don't want me. The next one is much bigger'." She shook her head, and I whispered frantically, "Trust me!"

She didn't move for a moment and I had to nudge her forward while Faith scrambled safely off the other side of the bridge.

The troll repeated, "I can't see you, but I know you're there. I'm going to gobble you all up."

Olivia gulped audibly, but said in a quavery voice that sounded convincingly small, "Don't eat me!" She glanced over her shoulder at me; her voice was a bit more forceful and rather snotty when she said, "There's someone *much* bigger coming after me."

The bridge troll gave a long-suffering sigh. "Very well. Be off with you."

And at that moment, I remembered the ending. I motioned frantically for Brady and Doug to stand next to me. I whispered, "In *The Billy Goats Gruff*, the largest goat knocks the troll off the bridge into the stream. After that it never bothers them again."

Doug spun me around and dug into my backpack. I hissed, "What are you doing?"

He ignored me. Of course. When he finally stopped fumbling inside my pack, I turned in time to see him holding his sling shot in one hand and a bottle of his favorite carbonated water in the other. Instead of finding something to put in the sling shot, he held up the bottle and shook it vigorously.

Once again, he ignored me when I whispered, "What are you doing?"

Instead, he turned and spoke directly to the troll. His voice was deeper and more powerful than I'd ever heard it. "Listen here, Bridge Troll. I'm bigger than you. And I'm going to blow you right off this bridge."

He took a deep noisy breath, and aimed the top of the bottle at the troll. Then he ripped off the cap.

Water sprayed out and hit the troll squarely in the face. It jerked back reflexively. Hard enough to loosen its grip on the bridge. As it flailed for balance, Doug put the half empty bottle in the cradle of his sling shot, pulled back so hard the rubber bands creaked in protest, and let the bottle fly.

The troll screamed and grabbed its face with both hands, then continued screaming as it fell off the bridge and landed with a sickening thud onto the rocks in the stream below. It hit so hard, water splashed up over us, leaving us dripping.

Doug moved carefully to the edge and glanced below. He grinned fiercely and said, "That'll teach it to mess with us."

I hoped he was right. That the troll was dead, or at the very least, couldn't hurt us. I almost opened my mouth to wish that, but bit back the words before they could escape.

I wrapped my arms around my waist as a shudder chased down my spine. When did wishing become so scary that I'd rather risk a bridge troll coming back?

Chapter 7/February/Chimera

Static!

Brady stepped to the edge of the bridge next to Doug and looked down. I, on the other hand, had no desire to see what happened when a large ugly body fell on a bunch of rocks. Faith and Olivia, who had both left the bridge already, started yelling to hurry up. I started in their direction, but stopped when Brady said, "Clearly, the composition of a troll is significantly different than that of a human being. We'd have been seriously injured by that fall, but that must not be the case for bridge trolls."

"What are you talking about?" I asked.

Doug swung around and grinned at me. "Why don't you come see for yourself, Taylor?"

I glared at him, but reluctantly moved over to the side, angling over so I was standing next to Brady.

I looked down, braced for disgusting carnage, then gasped and grabbed Brady's arm. There was no blood, no broken body parts, no sign anything had ever fallen there. The troll had disappeared.

"What are you doing?" Olivia protested.

"It's gone," I yelled back. The skin between my shoulder blades was prickling and I whirled around, momentarily sure it had climbed onto the bridge and was creeping up behind us. The sight of the empty stones behind me did little to slow the racing of my heart.

"What do you mean, it's gone?" Olivia called back.

"It disappeared." I yelled. When she merely frowned I continued, "As in missing. Absent. Vanished. AWOL. You know, gone!"

Olivia and Faith both whipped their heads from side to side, peering around intently. Clearly I wasn't the only one picturing that thing skulking around, ready to grab us.

I hurried off the bridge, calling back over my shoulder, "Come on, you guys. Let's go."

Shadow followed me down the road, her tail held high.

Doug and Brady hesitated a moment more. Doug sounded plaintive as he told Brady, "We should climb down and look for it." Rusty barked several times and I was pretty sure it was his not-a-good-idea bark. I was glad Rusty agreed with me.

I didn't even turn around as I yelled, "No way, Doug!"

I ignored Brady's mutters about weight and impact and trajectories and bone density. I didn't really care why it wasn't lying there. The only thing that concerned me was what it intended to do now.

Brady pulled out the map. "Now that we're across the bridge, we need to decide where we are going to look next. A very large building appears to exist behind those hedges on our right. That may be the South mansion that Ghalynn made reference to. It seems unlikely we'd discover anything there; Ghalynn certainly didn't succeed in doing so. Therefore I propose that we look at the houses to our left. We can work our way around town from left to right."

"I don't care where we look," Olivia said, foot tapping impatiently, "just as long as we look somewhere."

"How many houses do you think we'll be able to get through?" I asked, doubtfully. I could see a lot of houses.

"Since I have no way to determine the types of furnishings and paraphernalia we'll need to go through, I have no way to estimate the likely duration," Brady said. "However, I'll mark each house off on the map as we complete our investigation. That way we'll know where we left off and where to resume our search the next time."

"Okay then." Faith said, and squared her shoulders. "Which one first?"

We were on a slight rise where I could look down over the town. To our right, where Brady had pointed first, tall hedges lined the road as far as I could see. On our left, I could only see houses. Houses of all shapes and sizes and descriptions.

Those closest to the edge of the road were one story, crowding next to the neighboring houses. Beyond those, the houses looked bigger. And taller. And further apart.

It was as if different designers had split the town into small neighborhoods then filled each neighborhood with different types of houses. Some looked like small estates, built of stone with slate roofs. Others looked modern, full of glass and wood and sharp angles. Farther away, some appeared to be mini-castles, complete with pennants and tiny moats. That should make Olivia happy! Beyond those were cottages, taken straight out of a fairytale, topped with thatch roofs.

I didn't say it out loud, but I still didn't like the idea of being under thatch.

Olivia pointed in the direction of the compact castles and said, "See, Brady. Castles!" She looked like a cat that had just stolen a bowl of cream.

Brady ignored her and gestured to the nearest group of houses. These were fairly non-descript wooden houses, none very large. Best of all, they had wood shake roofs. Not a single bit of thatch in sight.

We turned onto a narrow path that led from the road and wound between four matching houses. I couldn't help wondering if the path was protected like the roads. That thought made my palms sweat, but the people who lived here must have protected themselves. It wouldn't make any sense to protect the roads, but not the paths that led to their houses. Right?

I rubbed my hands on my jeans and told myself not to be ridiculous.

The path was so narrow in places that we had to go one at a time. Doug went first, followed by Faith, then me. Olivia came next, with Brady last.

Olivia and Brady were arguing. Again.

Olivia: "Did you remember to bring a pencil?"

Brady: "What is your sudden interest in my ability to produce a writing implement?"

Olivia: "You said you were going to mark the houses on your super-map. That will be pretty hard if you forgot to bring," her voice changed as she tried to imitate Brady's voice, *"a writing implement."*

After several steps with no response, I began to breathe easier. Maybe they were going to stop. Then Brady cleared his throat and I cringed.

Note: to self — Don't walk near Olivia when she's close to Brady.

Brady: "You should know that I never leave home without a writing implement. After all, you've had to borrow one from me on several occasions."

There were times I hated the intense silence in Chimera. No engines, no birds, no sound of people. But right now, I actually missed silence.

Olivia: "Maybe once or twice, but—"

Brady: "I know you don't have an eidetic memory like mine, but really—"

Olivia: "Now you're going to brag about your miraculous memory, like that makes you special—"

Brady: "I never claimed that it makes me special—"

Olivia: "'Cause it doesn't—"

Brady: "What it does is allow me to remember that you've borrowed a pen or pencil from me on at least fifteen occasions in the past two and one half years. So it is obvious that you know I always have one—"

Olivia: "Errgghhh! Your memory sucks. No way did I borrow *a writing implement* from you fifteen times."

I was tempted to turn around and yell at them to zip it. I had to grit my teeth together to keep back the words. Even then, it was a near thing.

Brady: "I can tell you the exact dates and times if that will assist your memory. But perhaps today you're worried that I finally ran out? Since you've never returned one."

Olivia: "So now you're, what, accusing me of being a thief as well as having a crummy memory?"

Brady: "I have never once said that you are a thief. I—"

Olivia: "Oh, so you've thought it, you just haven't said it?"

I never found out what Brady would have said to that. The footpath had widened and I hurried forward, grateful to get away. I caught up with Doug just as we reached the houses. I honestly didn't care what we found today, as long as I didn't have to listen to the two of them sniping at each other for awhile.

Our familiars gathered outside one of the houses. I turned to Doug and grinned. "I think we should look in that one first."

He glanced at Rusty, then grinned back. "Works for me."

Doug and I stepped onto the porch together. He reached for the doorknob while I peered over his shoulder, wondering what we'd see. There was a sizzle and flash of light, and the air between us sang with energy. I could feel static dance over my skin, tingling painfully, raising the hair on my arms. Even the ends of my hair lifted off my shoulders. Doug jerked his hand back, shaking it vigorously, and the feeling died.

I bit my lip. How in the world were we going to check out the house when we couldn't get in?

I looked back at our animals and burst out laughing. Rusty's tail went down and Shadow flattened her ears. Those two were the worst. Rusty's fur might have been short, but every bit of it was standing out. Shadow looked like she'd stuck her paw in an electric socket, and she wasn't happy about it. Foxy's tail was puffed out to twice its size. Pyg looked like a round ball of feathers. Only Fangface looked normal.

Doug hadn't noticed. He was glaring at the door. "It shocked me," he said, still shaking his hand. "What happened?"

Brady moved onto the porch next to him, and I had to back over to the edge to get out of his way. "If I had to speculate," Brady said, "I'd say there is a defensive spell on this door." He looked at it carefully, then pulled a handkerchief out of his backpack and wrapped it around his hand. He saw my confusion and said, "It's cotton."

Which cleared up absolutely nothing.

He asked Doug to spray some water on the door and Doug held out his hand to me. I ground my teeth together, slipped off my backpack, and opened it. There were two more bottles of carbonated water in my pack. No wonder it weighed so much. Annoyance flooded through me and I raised my chin. I was going to have a serious talk with Doug about using my backpack. Not right now, of course. But soon.

I handed one of the bottles to Doug without a word. He shook it and sprayed it on the door.

Brady turned to me and said, "Cotton is neutral; it doesn't generate static electricity. And moisture decreases it." He reached out and tapped his handkerchief-wrapped knuckles against the door knob twice. The first time there was another jolt of electricity, though much smaller than the first. At least there was no flash of electricity through the air that time. The second time he tapped it, there was no reaction at all.

He reached over, confidently twisted the knob and shoved open the door. Then he stepped back and punched Doug's shoulder. "Science wins again!"

Doug laughed then stepped cautiously over the door jamb and into the dark interior of the house.

Chapter 8/February/Chimera

Statues, Statues, Everywhere...

As soon as Doug stepped into the house, lights came on. I crowded in next to him as he gave a nearly soundless whistle.

The house looked like something out of a museum. The furniture, lots and lots of furniture, had curved, spindly legs. It was painted white with gold trim on the edges, while the chair seats and couch were covered with thick brocade fabrics in pale gold and white. The wooden floor had been white-washed. Ornate chandeliers of faceted glass hung from the ceiling, mirrors adorned the walls, and cut glass bowls and golden candlesticks stood on every open space. Light flashed and sparkled off every surface.

The walls were a brilliant white, covered nearly floor to ceiling with paintings. Lots and lots of paintings. I'd seen some of them in pictures of real museums. I didn't know much about art, but even I could recognize Van Gogh and Degas and Monet. Then I saw Monet's Water Lilies; the one with the Japanese Bridge. It was my most favorite painting. And it absolutely, positively shouldn't be there. For one very long moment, I was tempted to pull it off the wall and take it home with me.

"I'm afraid to touch anything," Faith whispered.

"Someone actually lived here?" Doug asked skeptically.

I pointed to the ornately bound leather book sitting open next to the couch, as though waiting for the owner to return and sit down for some more heavy reading. "I'd say yes, although it doesn't look exactly comfortable, does it?"

Brady wished to see anything hidden by Ghalynn or objects of significance, but nothing showed up on the map. "We can't be sure the map will show us everything," he reminded us.

"Let's check inside the drawers and cupboards for anything that looks atypical," He turned and winked at Faith. "Which means touching them."

She grimaced, but headed to the large elegant side board, where she began pulling out drawers and resolutely looking through the contents.

I quickly followed Olivia into the bedroom. Hopefully that would keep her and Brady apart for a while. 'Cause I might end up committing friend-icide if I had to listen to them arguing again anytime soon.

Olivia opened the ornate wardrobe and exclaimed in pleasure. Dozens of elegant gowns hung inside, made with satins, velvets, and brocades, glowing with deep jewel colors – ruby, topaz, sapphire and amethyst. She reached out to pull one off its hanger and I snapped, "Olivia! We don't have time to play dress up."

She glared at me. "I wasn't going to do any such thing!" She dropped her hand, and after one more wistful glance at the beaded shoes and belts and purses tucked carefully into the bottom of the wardrobe, she reluctantly shut the doors.

We finished the dresser quickly and met the others back in the living room. I looked at them all hopefully, but everyone shook their heads. No one found anything that qualified as unusual.

"Well, onward," Doug said, motioning to the door. I shot one last longing glance at the Monet before decisively turning my back. I hoped we'd find something more useful —and less tempting — in the next one.

As we left the house Brady conscientiously marked it off on the map, and we greeted our animals where they waited patiently. At least their fur and feathers had settled back down while we were in the house. Pyg flew over and settled on Olivia's shoulder.

"We didn't find anything," she told the small owl and reached up to stroke her head. Pyg hooted, then flew off in the direction of the next house. The other animals headed after her and settled once again in a loose circle around the porch. It only took a few moments for the rest of us to get there.

This one was a bust, just like the first, and so was the one after that. By now it felt like we'd spent hours looking through drawers and cupboards and closets, and we had nothing to show for it. Were we doomed to spend months poking through other people's houses? And what exactly were we looking for, anyway? We still had absolutely no idea.

I just hoped we'd be able to recognize anything important. The other objects had certainly been ordinary looking.

As we came out of the third house, Olivia pointed where a chest-high stone wall surrounded…something. "Should we check that out next?"

"We should check out the houses," Doug said decisively. "That's where we'll probably find something important. We can check out that thing before we leave."

Olivia grumbled something about being surrounded by dictatorial guys, but turned obediently to follow Doug toward the next house.

I caught up with Brady and asked, "You are remembering to ask the map to show anything Ghalynn might have left us, right?"

He opened his mouth to answer me, but before he could speak Olivia said, "Why would he?" She turned to him and asked, "You're not wasting our time, standing around asking questions are you?"

He opened his mouth again, but I narrowed my eyes at Olivia and spoke first. "Ghalynn could have left something for us, no matter what that Sylph said."

Brady spoke up quickly, "It is accurate to state that we don't know whether Ghalynn left anything for us in town. In addition, we don't know if there is anything else we should find that could provide data required to calculate what occurred here in Chimera. We have nothing to tell us where we might find significant information or important clues."

His voice was becoming more and more officious and Olivia was looking increasingly irritated. "That is why I always ask the map to show us anything from Ghalynn and anything that might be of interest to us, each time we enter a house. It's the only intelligent thing to do." He raised his eyebrows and narrowed his eyes, staring right at Olivia. Daring her to argue with him.

Olivia rolled her eyes but didn't say anything else.

We went through the next house as quickly as possible. Unfortunately, it also held nothing exciting. It was just a house. An ordinary house. Well, except for the lack of anything electronic. And the magic lights that came on as soon as we entered the living room. That was pretty cool.

We met back in the living room and I could tell the others were starting to feel as discouraged as I did at the moment. We'd checked four houses today and hadn't found a single thing to help us. I followed Doug to the front door, allowing my feet to scrape despondently against the wooden floor. I had my eyes down, not on Doug, and walked straight into his back.

"What's up?" I asked, gloominess making me sound cross. "Why are you just standing there?"

"The door won't open," Doug said. *His* voice was curiously flat.

"What do you mean, it won't open?" I crossed my arms over my chest and said. "Of course it will open. Just turn the knob."

He shot me a disgusted glance, grasped the knob and turned it firmly, first one way, then the other. Nothing happened.

I stared at the knob. Something about it seemed strange, but I wasn't sure what was bothering me. Maybe...

Faith interrupted my thoughts. "You must not be turning it hard enough. Try again."

He shot Faith that same disgusted glance, which she proceeded to ignore just like I had. This time, he grabbed the knob with enough force to turn his knuckles white. He twisted it so hard the tendons in his neck stood out and his face turned red with effort. He let go and panted a moment, then did the same thing, trying to turn it in the opposite direction.

This time when he released the knob, he shook out his hand and I could see angry red marks on his palm.

"What now?" Olivia asked, staring at Brady.

He rolled his eyes. "Why do you expect me to be knowledgeable about operating the locking mechanism on this door?"

"You seem to know everything else," Olivia said snidely.

"I've never heard of a door that locks from the inside," I said slowly. "Why would someone do that?"

"Even better," Doug said, "how do you lock a door that has no place for a key?"

We all stared at the featureless knob. Doug was right. Unlike most outer doors, there was no place for a key. There was no thumb latch, no combination lock, no bolt. No lock of any kind.

Brady leaned over and examined it closely. "If I had to venture a guess, I'd have to say it is locked by a spell."

That made me grin. Brady had changed over the past few years. He no longer went around Chimera muttering "not scientifically plausible," "irrational," "breaks Newton's law," or "contradicts Einstein's theory." Of course, he still liked to say things like "scrutinize variations," "extrapolate differences," and "interpret meanings." I was actually getting pretty good at all the geek-speak.

What theory would he expound upon now?

"There doesn't appear to be a locking mechanism in this door, therefore there's no lock that we can force open. However, the door hinges are on this side, which means we can pry them open and remove the door altogether. I need someone to find a hammer or a reasonable equivalent."

He shrugged out of his backpack and pulled out a screwdriver.

It was Brady; why did that even surprise me?

Doug grabbed a heavy silver candlestick off the nearby table. After pulling out the candle, he held it toward Brady.

"A moment," Brady told him, and worked the tip of the screwdriver into the small space between the edge of the pin and the metal hinge. He grabbed the candlestick and used it to give a few sharp blows against the handle of the screwdriver. The pin rose slowly out of the hinge, then popped out. Brady grunted in satisfaction, then knelt down and went to work on the bottom hinge. This one took more effort, but eventually the pin popped out as well.

Brady and Doug grabbed the loose hinges and tugged. The door creaked and groaned, then reluctantly opened.

Faith and I cheered, making Brady flush. His coppery red hair clashed horribly with the color staining his cheeks. At least he'd shed most of his freckles over the last year. Those used to stand out like someone had splashed small bits of paint all over his face. He swept a low courtly bow and said, "Once again, science prevails over magic."

A ripple of unease worked its way down my spine. It had worked well this time, but there were so many types of magic in here. I somehow doubted science could always prevail.

Some magic was merely annoying, like the knife-sharp grass that had stabbed our ankles when we walked by. Others were unsettling because we'd never knew what to expect. Like the spells that kept the roads safe but meant we could be lost forever if we stepped off them. Some spells had set off earthquakes and opened deep fissures under our feet. Other spells went horribly wrong, like the one that created the magic rock slide that killed Ronny's father and still crushed anyone who walked by.

There were parts of Chimera that seemed to overflow with magic. Like the hideously cold, greasy yellow fog we'd encountered. *It* had no trouble crossing the roads. It had covered several as it continued to slowly spread out from the center of Chimera where the magic of this world was contained.

I must have been standing there lost in thought longer than I realized. Faith poked me in the shoulder and hissed, "Earth to Kat."

I glanced around; Faith and I were the only ones still left in the house. The others were outside, staring back at me with varying levels of impatience. "Sorry," I said, and hurried out of the door-less house into the bright sunshine.

"Now can we go see what that thing is?" Olivia asked, planting one hand on her hip and pointing impatiently to the stone wall in the center of the houses.

"Yes," Doug said, like he was telling an impatient child she could finally have a piece of candy. "Now we can check it out."

-xXx-

In the space between the houses, scattered around the four foot wall in the center, were statues of people. As we got closer, I counted ten; some sitting on the wall, others standing next to it.

"What's with all the statues?" Olivia asked. "Didn't Ronny say they didn't do statues in here?"

"Yes," I said, feeling strangely uncomfortable. "She said they could be used against you. Like a voodoo doll."

"Sympathetic magic," Faith said, nodding.

"She was gone for months before we came here," Doug said. "Something may have changed after she was banished. Exiling the only child of a high ranking Council member is bound to have an effect on society."

We were taking Sociology this year, but I had no idea Doug had applied any of it to Chimera. I said, hesitantly, "We know people started vanishing at some point after Ronny was banished. If they didn't vanish all at once, the ones who remained might have built statues of the people who disappeared. You know, like memorials."

"That's actually quite intelligent, Kat," Brady said and gave me a big smile. He made it sound so complimentary; he obviously didn't realize he'd just implied I didn't act intelligent most of the time. And he didn't recognize the fact that I was glaring at him, tight lipped. I was pressing them together to hold back the words crowding my throat, eager to get out.

I smiled at him with those tight-pressed lips and said, "Why gee, thanks Brady." Olivia and Faith both snickered at the sarcasm I'd layered onto those words.

Doug snickered too. "I thought you wanted to check this place out, Olivia."

We crowded around the wall and I gasped in astonishment. The space looked far bigger on the inside than it had from the outside.

It must be at least twenty feet long and three feet wide, shaped in a sinuous 's'. Water filled the bottom, which varied in depth, but most looked about four feet deep. "I guess it's a fountain," I said.

Glass floats of every color drifted on the still water. Extending above it were strange tubes of different heights and sizes, some of shiny metals and some of glass. I wasn't sure what it was all for, but it looked beautiful. Very steampunk.

"It must do something," Olivia said, walking around, staring at it. "I wish we could see it."

There was a moment of stunned silence as we all waited to see if her wish would bring a new disaster down on our heads.

With a groan from the pipes that made the ground vibrate beneath our feet, things began to happen. First came a discordant spluttering. Then water of different colors surged over the top of the pipes. It flowed down the metal and glass tubes and entered the pool in swirls.

Colors mingled where they touched; red and blue into a thin line of purple, red and yellow into a thin line of orange. Other colors that I didn't recognize combined into dizzying patterns. And accompanying the water was sound. Each tube emitted high ringing tones like a tympani. Each of the tones fit together into perfect, ever-changing chords.

The water began to swirl faster, moving in ripples down the entire length of the fountain. The glass floats began to circle, and whenever they touched there were flashes of light so bright they hurt my eyes. Then the colors and the tones settled into a pattern, forming a song. I didn't recognize it, but felt like I should.

Decorative posts set around the edges of the courtyard burst into life. Glowing balls of light appeared on each, washing the entire area in a warm golden glow.

It looked — and sounded — like something that belonged at Disneyland.

"I want one of these," Olivia said and leaned against the wall, enthralled. "George would love this. We could spend hours—"

"Sorry, you don't have hours," Brady said shortly, glancing at his watch. "We need to head back."

Olivia tipped her nose in the air and sniffed. "Fine. Let's head back." She turned to look at Pyg who flew over and perched on her shoulder. She said, in a voice meant to carry, "Brady always likes to spoil our fun, doesn't he pretty Pyg."

Pyg made a cooing noise and nibbled a strand of her hair, as if commiserating.

I scooped up Shadow and buried my face in her fur. I didn't know whether to be irritated or amused by Brady and Olivia. But at the moment I was leaning toward amused.

Brady rolled his eyes and turned the way we'd come. He pulled the map out of his pocket and pushed his glasses higher on his nose as he scanned it carefully. "I don't see any signs of the Rejects, so it should be safe."

Doug reached down and rubbed his leg before squaring his shoulders and heading back toward the tree.

Chapter 9/February/Santa Ramona

Don't Cut Off Your Nose To Fright Your Face

We covered the distance to the tree quickly, and didn't spend long on goodbyes with our animals. Even so, the sky was darkening as we emerged from the tree into the cemetery. That meant there wasn't any time for talk. We all needed to be home before full dark.

I called Ronny and told her we'd be over after school on Tuesday. She sounded so tired it worried me.

The rest of the weekend dragged by. Homework and cleaning my room only took so long. I was worried about Ronny and felt restless and irritated at being cut off from my friends. Usually Olivia and I could hang out on Sundays, but she was babysitting her younger brothers and sisters. The twins were sick so Olivia's mom didn't want anyone else there. She said I might be too big a distraction for Olivia. Which was really insulting. Sure, we'd gotten sidetracked a few times in the past, but we'd be sixteen in a few months. It wasn't like we were little kids any more.

Mom noticed how preoccupied I was and suggested I help her around the house, which only felt like adding salt to my wounds. I ended up dusting the living room, doing the dishes and folding the laundry.

There's nothing like chores to make you look forward to school.

-xXx-

My eyes flew wide and I lay very still, afraid to move. My room was pitch black, so it was way too early to be awake. I held my breath, listening for whatever might have woken me. I nearly felt grateful; being awake was better than dreaming about faceless angels crowding around me, slowly forcing me toward the tree in the cemetery. They'd reached for me, expressionless, so I couldn't tell if they were trying to help me or hurt me. I'd woken just before the first hard cold marble hand, twisted into a grotesquely clawed shape, had touched me.

A sudden flash of blue lit my room as lightening speared through the sky. It was followed by a crack of thunder that shook the entire house. Now I understood what had caused that dream. *I* knew those angel statues moved during the magical blue lightning storms even if the others refused to believe me.

I wanted to go back to sleep but the storm raged outside my window for hours. It was still dark when it finally died away, but I got up and dressed, obsessed with the idea of checking on those angels before school. To see if any had moved again.

I left a note for Mom, telling her I had to leave early to work on a project. After leaning it against the coffee maker, I crept out of the house and hurried to the cemetery. I tried not to be too obvious about skulking down the street, but I kept to the shadows hoping no one would see me. I had only one moment of alarm as I got near the cemetery. What if the gates were locked? I couldn't get over the high stone fence surrounding it. The stones were like cheese graters; there was no way to climb in without taking off most of your skin.

By the time I got close enough to see that they were open, my hands were damp from nerves. I saw a gardener's van in the parking lot, and realized there were people around. I'd have to continue to be careful. I really didn't want to try to explain what I was doing there.

The cemetery always felt creepy, even with all my friends. Even in full daylight. In the dark, with no moon, it felt like something out of a horror movie. Patches of low-lying fog only made it worse. Gravestones and mausoleums suddenly loomed up in front of me, sometimes looking as though they'd deliberately leapt into my path. I was glad the others weren't there to see me hopping around like Olivia, trying to avoid stepping on anything, and ducking behind headstones at every sound.

By the time I got to the back of the cemetery I was shaking and wanted, more than anything, to get out of there. But when I reached the first of the faceless statues I stopped, horrified. If I hadn't known what to look for, I might have missed it. But I could see faint drag marks where the statue had moved at least a foot from its previous position. I shuddered as I realized it had been heading straight toward the tree.

Like in my dream.

I took a few pictures, determined to prove to the others once and for all that I was right, and turned toward school.

-xXx-

We were too busy avoiding the Rejects to talk any sooner, but at lunch I spoke up as soon as we got seated.

"There was another magic storm last night," I said.

Olivia shook her head. "No way. I wouldn't have missed that."

"I saw it," Faith said, and Brady and Doug nodded.

Olivia crossed her arms over her chest and narrowed her eyes.

"I dreamt that the statues in the cemetery moved," I said. "I— "

Doug didn't let me finish. "You have those statues on the brain, Taylor. When are you going to get over it?" His impatient tone set my teeth on edge.

"You're such a know-it-all, Doug. You think you know *every*thing." I didn't try to disguise my anger. "It just so happens that I went to the cemetery this morning, and I was right."

"How could you do something so stupid?" Doug sounded way past angry. He sounded appalled.

"You went to the cemetery by yourself?" Olivia sounded just like Doug. "What were you thinking?"

"The Rejects could have hurt you." Faith was clearly horrified. There actually was a slight but significant difference between appalled and horrified.

Before Brady could stick his two cents in, it was my turn to sound impatient. "You guys are missing the point!"

They all stopped and stared at me. Okay, my voice might have been a bit louder than I'd meant it to be. But really, how else could I get them to listen? "The statues moved," I said flatly.

"How far did they *appear* to move?" Brady asked. I noticed he was being careful to keep his voice neutral. But I also noticed his emphasis on the word 'appear'.

I glared at him, my eyes narrow and fierce. "They didn't *appear* to move. They *did* move. More than a foot."

Olivia's voice was soothing, like she was verbally patting me on the head. "How could you possibly tell one of them moved a foot?" I was wrong. It wasn't soothing, it was patronizing. "I had no idea you'd measured where each of them was."

A growl of frustration erupted from my throat. I kept my teeth clenched as I said, "I paid attention since none of *you* believed me." Brady opened his mouth as if to comment and I shook my head at him. "There were tracks," I said, emphatically.

I pulled my cell out of my pocket, careful to keep it under the table. It was breaking the school rules to use phones at school except in an emergency. No way did I want a teacher to confiscate it now! There was no way showing pictures of statues in the cemetery would count as an emergency.

I opened the picture I'd taken that morning and passed my phone to Olivia. "There. See the drag marks behind the statue?"

She stared at it, and cocked her head to the side, then shrugged. "I guess I see marks, but I don't see how you can be so sure they're drag marks."

I rolled my eyes and felt like throwing something. "Really?" I pointed to the obviously bent and torn grass the same size as the bottom of the statue. "What exactly do you think made that?"

Brady looked over her shoulder and said, "Actually, that could be damage that occurred during the storm. Or it may have been moved when they performed maintenance in that area. Or more likely, it could be an optical illusion based on the angle of the sun reflecting off the grass. It could even have been caused by someone playing a practical joke. It doesn't prove your theory that the statue moved itself."

"Drag marks don't prove my theory? I see." I felt discouraged, but asked, "Just what would I need to show you to prove my so-called theory?"

Brady looked regretful. "I would have to see them actually move. Otherwise there are too many plausible causes."

I snatched my phone back and stuffed it in my pocket. "Fine. Don't believe me. But if you're smart, you'll stay away from that cemetery during magic storms. And that's *not* a theory."

"We'll see," Brady said placatingly, then turned to Olivia. "Are you still meeting George after school?"

Olivia looked at him as if he'd lost his mind. "Of course. Why wouldn't I?"

"Just making sure," he said. "If something had changed we might be able to go to Ronny's today instead of tomorrow, that's all."

"Sorry to disappoint you," she said, not sounding sorry at all.

The rest of lunch passed in near silence. Brady didn't say another word and neither did I. I wasn't sure what was up with him, but I was brooding and the others knew it. When they did speak, they did so carefully, like they didn't want to say anything to upset Brady or me.

Which suited me just fine.

-xXx-

I knew Olivia had met George for a soda after school on Monday just as they'd planned. She'd texted me several times about how nice he was, how funny he was, how happy she was. And it only took one peek at Olivia's face Tuesday morning to know we were going to hear nothing but *George said this* and *George did that* and *George is so perfect* all day.

I couldn't help wondering if perfect George would have believed me about the angel statues...

Doug took one look at her. "So, you had a good time with George?" Wow, even Doug could tell how excited Olivia was.

Before she had a chance to start waxing all poetic about her new boyfriend, Brady announced that he was busy with a project, so we wouldn't see him until after school. Olivia stared after him as he all but ran down the hall, then turned back to begin the first of her George-is-wonderful speeches. Fortunately, the bell rang.

I felt lucky that Tuesday. We didn't really have much chance to talk. Better yet, we hardly saw the Rejects at all.

After school, we met up and headed to Ronny's. I was busy worrying about her, and didn't join in the conversation. Ronny had sounded pretty bad when I'd checked with her last night. I'd mentioned it to Mom and she said Chris was concerned about her, too.

I followed the others up the steps onto the porch and Doug knocked. Instead of Ronny, Chris opened the door. Ronny was sitting in her chair, wrapped in a blanket even though the room was warm. Shame squirmed in my chest; I'd been so upset about angel statues, I'd forgotten how much magic storms affected her.

As I stepped past Chris he muttered, "Keep it short, Kitty-Kat."

I glared at him in disbelief. How could he use that hated nickname when he was asking me for a favor? He knew I was irritated, but didn't apologize. Instead he merely added, "Please," in a strained, harsh voice. That finally brought home how serious he was. Because Chris never begged.

I gave him a quick thumbs up, and he brushed past me and perched on the arm of Ronny's chair.

As I sat down, I got a closer look at her and felt shock stab through me. Ronny had never been so pale. Her face was drawn, with a slight frown of pain or exhaustion between her eyes. And for once there were no cookies waiting for us. She'd never forgotten to make us a treat before. I could definitely see why Chris was so worried.

To break the silence, which had stretched too long, I told her, "One of the houses we were in had lots of famous paintings. Paintings I know are in museums. So were the ones in Chimera forgeries?"

Ronny smiled tiredly. "Not forgeries, really. They are exact duplicates, created by magick."

"I nearly took one," I told her, thinking of those beautiful water lilies. "But I was afraid I'd be accused of being in an art heist."

That pulled a short laugh out of her. "Do not cut off your nose to fright your face, Kat." That drew a snort of laughter from Faith, which I tried hard to ignore. "You could not take any of those paintings out of Chimera."

When I looked puzzled, she explained, "It requires a significant amount of magick to sustain duplicates. So if they are removed from Chimera, they would collapse into nothing more than colorful dust."

"Oh," I muttered in disappointment. Not that I'd actually steal anything from Chimera, but, well, darn it anyway. I flopped back against the couch and looked at Brady.

He leaned forward and pulled the map from his pocket, spreading it on the coffee table, and turned it to face Ronny. "We found some sort of water feature, here." He pointed to the map where the houses we'd searched that Saturday had been crossed out. "I couldn't help wondering if it had a specific purpose or was merely decorative. Once it began operating, I noticed that several columns around the area lit up. What caused that?"

Ronny smiled faintly. "Those columns have been enchanted to light up whenever the luminstropasphere—" She broke off and shook her head, then pinched the bridge of her nose. "There is no similar word in your English. You would say it is a fountain, I believe, though that word does not provide it justice. It is a spell. It causes the columns to light up while it operates. It is so beautiful..." She sighed and the corners of her mouth turned down. "There is nothing like that here."

I rounded on Chris. "Haven't you taken her to Disneyland?"

He shook his head. "We talked about going later this year," he glanced at Ronny quickly, then away. "But it may have to wait."

I turned to Ronny. "You have to make him take you there. You'll love it. They have a whole lake full of dancing water and lights. And there are rides, and things to see. It's as close to magic as you can get."

Chris laughed and for a moment the worry tightening the corners of his eyes lightened. He picked up Ronny's hand and squeezed it gently. "You'll have to forgive Kat, my love. Disneyland is her happy place."

Ronny had been smiling at me, but at that her smile faltered. "Chimera was my happy place." Then she smiled apologetically at Chris. "But you are my happy place, now."

I'd planned on discussing my idea that the statues we'd found could be memorials created as people went missing, but Ronny looked so tired and dejected I couldn't bear to remind her of what she had lost.

Besides, she was busy. She cupped my brother's cheek and looked at him intently. At that moment, I don't think either of them remembered the rest of us were there. "You must not look so sad, my Christopher." She glanced briefly at the curio cabinet in the corner. The one that held all the clues and objects we'd found in Chimera over the past three years. From here, it didn't look like much. The small chest holding several musty old papers. The heavy old-fashioned key. The tarnished lantern. The small, plain metal compass that didn't work properly. And a bunch of cryptic riddles about a quest.

Looking at all that useless stuff made me feel tired. We still didn't know what else we were looking for. And we didn't know what to do with all of it if — when — we found it.

Ronny smiled and grabbed the pendant around her neck. She turned back to Chris and said, "I would not trade my life with you for anything."

Chapter 10/March/Chimera

Holo-Dragon?

We left after that, promising to see them after we made our next trip into Chimera.

"So," I said, as we neared the large hedge at the corner of their street, "do we have a plan for next month?"

"Yes, we'd all like to know the answer to that. Just where *do* you intend to go next time?" The deep, angry voice came from the other side of the hedge. I stepped back in surprise, directly onto Faith's foot. Instead of jumping out of my way, she grabbed my shoulders and held on tight.

Ray rounded the corner, followed by Andrew and Arnold. It would be five against three if they started anything, but the fact that it was *those* three made the air feel leaden inside my chest.

Doug glanced quickly at Faith, Olivia and me, then glared at Ray. "We're not looking for trouble, Tate."

What was up with him baiting Ray like that? And what was up with that glance? Could he be acting so tough because there were three girls present? Seriously?

Note to self – Convince Doug not to act so macho! If only to protect him from himself.

I pulled out my cell, ready to call Chris if necessary. We were still only a few houses away, so he'd be here quickly. I held up my phone so Ray could see it and grinned. A very nice be-careful-what-you-do-next grin. Okay, maybe it wasn't very nice. Maybe it was snide. Taunting. Mocking. It certainly made Ray grit his teeth and glare.

Score.

But he must have remembered the time Chris and Ronny had come to our rescue once before. Because he cleared his throat, deeply, and spat at Doug's feet. Then he shrugged and gave a half smile that didn't reach his eyes. "Who says we're looking for trouble? Sounds like a personal problem, Geller. We're just out for a walk."

I gave a silent sigh of relief and started to slip my phone back in my pocket, but stopped when Arnold flashed a sudden, scary grin. "We would really like to hear where you plan to go next month. You're going to share, right?"

"Not a chance," Doug said. "Now if you'll excuse us, we have more important things to do than hang out on a corner with Rejects."

Ray flushed a deep, angry red and I tightened my fingers on my phone. But my hands began to shake as Arnold pulled his sunglasses down his nose to stare at us. I clutched the phone to my chest, afraid I'd drop it. Ray and Andrew both looked furious, but Arnold was horror-movie-villain scary. His pale grey eyes were so cold they made my teeth chatter.

Ray's eyes focused on something behind us. "Yeah, we've got better things to do than look at your ugly faces." He jerked his head toward the other side of the street.

I glanced back and saw that Mrs. Rodriguez had come out to check on her beloved roses. *Thank goodness.*

We didn't say anything on the rest of the short, silent walk home.

-xXx-

I couldn't believe we made it through the rest of the month without being ambushed by the Rejects. Not that they didn't want to talk to us; they tried several times. But one of us must have had a guardian angel looking out for us, because teachers always showed up every time they tried to make us to tell them where we planned to go in Chimera.

I'd like to believe the teachers had caught on to the Rejects and were protecting us. But they always greeted Ray and Andrew with pleasure. At least it forced the Rejects to stop and talk to them, giving us time to get away.

On the full moon Saturday, the damp cold wind off the ocean seemed to soak into my bones, making me shiver. I pulled my hood up then tucked my hands into my pocket and stamped my feet to keep them warm. Doug and Faith did the same thing when they met me there. Brady was wearing a dorky button-down sweater when he came running up. I thought it belonged in the trash, but I knew it was his favorite. I glanced at my watch and groaned. Olivia was late again. I could swear my lips were turning blue by the time we saw her coming.

We didn't wait for her but started out quickly, too cold to talk. I spent the whole trip to the cemetery planning how I could convince the others the moving statues weren't just my imagination. I was sure they were important, even if I couldn't explain why. When we got near the tree, I pushed ahead. The long mark, like the statue had been dragged through the grass, was still there. Forgetting all my well-thought out arguments, I stabbed my finger at the obvious track. "Are you still going to tell me this statue didn't move?"

Doug heaved a deep sigh and folded his arms across his chest. At least Brady came over to look at it. He got a curious expression on his face, a puzzled speculation. I'd only seen that expression a few times; usually when he didn't have any ready theories to explain something different or strange. I felt a surge of hope.

Then he looked at me and said, "I don't have an hypothesis at this time. I still don't accept the idea that this statue moved under its own power, but I will grant you that the circumstances do appear to be unusual."

It was not an apology or an agreement that I'd been right all along, but it was better than nothing. It meant he was going to start creating and discarding potential theories. And when he ran out of them, he'd be left with the only possible answer. I smiled at him and said, "Just let me know when you finally realize I was right."

Not wanting to argue about it anymore, I turned and stepped into the tree.

I'd been in such a hurry I forgot to take an extra-large breath, so it was fortunate this was one of the shortest trips I'd ever made. I'd only counted to 48 when I was expelled from the tree into Chimera.

Brady and Olivia came through last, a few minutes after Doug and Faith. Olivia came through first but didn't say anything to us. Her eyes were so tight they were half closed and her hands were fisted by her sides. Clearly she'd been sniping at Brady again.

Note to self —Make sure you don't leave them alone next time!

Olivia whirled around, planted her fists on her hips and began speaking the second Brady appeared. "What *I* believe is totally beside the point." Her tone was lofty, her nose raised at an uncomfortable angle, and she was wearing her this-isn't-about-me-you're-the-problem smirk. She tipped her head to one side and said, "What really matters is what *you* do about it."

"*I* am going to run soil tests, get Kat to send me a copy of the picture she took, and take measurements. In other words, perform a scientific analysis of the situation." He gave her an answering smirk. "What are *you* going to do?"

"You are such a geek, Brady! Never mind." Olivia turned her back to him, dropped her backpack, yanked her sweater off, and stuffed it in her pack. She spun around and began stomping down the road toward the town. There was a tense silence as Brady motioned us ahead then followed after her, brushing out our footprints. Being careful to keep several feet of space between them.

The rest of us shed our sweaters and sweatshirts as we headed down the road. As usual this time of year, the temperature in Chimera had to be at least twenty degrees warmer than the cold misty morning in Santa Ramona.

No one said anything until our animals showed up. Then we got really busy welcoming them. After a few moments, the thick tension eased.

I scooped up Shadow and gave her a hug. "Do you guys fight when we're not here?" I asked in a whisper. I laughed when she reached out and gently placed her paw against my face. I could swear she was saying, 'silly human, we don't fight'.

Rusty danced around Doug's feet, barking and giving him cute doggy grins, his tail wagging so hard I was surprised it didn't fall off.

I glanced at Olivia and managed to bite back a laugh. Pyg was on her head, clutching her hair tightly. She was bouncing up and down as Olivia's feet slammed into the dirt with each step she took. She was walking so hard she was leaving a trail of small dirt puffs behind her.

Faith's fox slunk along the road behind us, shy as always, while Brady's bat swooped overhead, letting out contented squeaks.

Brady occasionally squeaked back, but he kept his head down looking intently at the road. Maybe he was looking at our foot prints; he was diligently dragging the small branch behind us, wiping out all signs of our presence. But I was sure he was trying to avoid looking at Olivia, too.

Just another day in Chimera.

-xXx-

Brady pulled the map out of his pocket and checked it quickly. A brief smile flashed across his face. "No sign of the Rejects yet."

He'd stuffed the map in his pocket before I could catch up to him. "So where are we going today, Brady?"

He sighed, then pulled the map back out. He pointed to a group of houses a bit farther down the road than we'd been last time. Before I had a chance to do more than glance where he pointed, he shoved the map away. Apparently all of us were getting the silent treatment.

Doug came up and stated, "I think we should split up. We'll get through all these a lot quicker."

My mouth fell open and I stared at him in amazement. He thought it was a good idea to split up? In here?

Apparently only Olivia and I were getting the silent treatment. Brady shook his head and told him, "It's possible that one of us would overlook something relevant. Multiple pairs of eyes will enhance our potential to perceive items of importance."

Olivia was standing right behind me, so I heard her mutter, "I hate geek speak!"

Doug opened his mouth as if to argue, but Brady said, "It would be…awkward to be the one that missed something important. I think some of us," he cut his eyes toward Olivia then looked quickly away, "could hold that against you."

Instead of glancing at Olivia, Doug looked at me. He nodded once and turned away, making me wonder what that was about.

When did *I* hold something against him? I hadn't even yelled at him about stuffing my backpack full of his…stuff. Not yet, anyway.

We followed Brady down the path, past the houses we'd checked the last time, and emerged near a place that would have been at home in Malibu. Everything was all modern glass and wood and concrete, with strange sharp angles and second stories that were set 45 degrees off center.

I wondered how they would look inside. I pictured stainless steel appliances, and minimalist, angular furniture. Then I remembered there wouldn't be any appliances.

We crowded into the first of the houses, and I shut my eyes tight before reopening them in amazement. This didn't look like some modern minimalist house; it looked like a Victorian nightmare! Everything was oversized and puffy, covered in yards of fabric, crammed in next to large oversized hutches and sideboards and dressers of dark wood. Every square inch was covered with fussy china figurines in pale pastel colors. My eyes kept bouncing around the room; there was so much furniture shoved into that small space I didn't know what to look at first.

"How could someone live like this?" Olivia asked, looking slowly around, shaking her head.

"Never mind that," Faith sounded dumbfounded as her gaze roved over all the drawers and shelves. "How are we going to find anything in here?"

Brady sighed. "Nothing has shown up on the map. So this will require being systematic, of course. Faith and Oliva should take opposite sides of this room. Kat should take the kitchen. Doug and I will check the bedroom."

He sounded so sure of himself, I was in the kitchen before I had a chance to think about it. Being in here made me sigh; for months now I'd been coming to the realization that the kitchen was not my favorite place. Mom claimed I allowed myself to become easily distracted, but I hated my failures. Undercooked potatoes, hard-as-a-rock cookies, and burnt toast. Especially the burnt toast! The smell took forever to get out. I just found the whole cooking thing…boring.

No wonder I got distracted.

I poked unenthusiastically through the cupboards and drawers. Instead of a stove, there was a large fireplace with a huge cooking pot suspended in it. Some cupboards were full of cups and plates and glasses just like at home. One was filled with heavy iron pots and skillets that were nearly too heavy to lift. Thank goodness Mom hadn't gone through with her plan to replace our pots and pans with cast iron.

There were spice racks and sealed jars filled with vegetables and sauces. Bowls filled with the shriveled remnants of garlic and potatoes. Drawers loaded with silverware and cloth napkins. It was nearly as crammed full of stuff as the living room.

It had everything except the slightest hint of a clue or magical object.

I stomped back to the living room, glad to see the others there. Everyone was waiting while Faith finished looking in the bottom drawer of a massive sideboard. Finally she shoved it closed and straightened up. When she saw us staring at her, she shook her head. "I got nothing."

"On to the next then," Doug said in a disgustingly cheerful voice. Next time he could check the kitchen!

-xXx-

After striking out in the next three houses, I was getting pretty tired of Doug's hearty, "On to the next then." How could he sound so cheerful when we weren't getting anywhere? It was exhausting looking through someone else's stuff, trying to be careful not to miss anything important. And it still didn't feel right to be rummaging around through someone else's private stuff. I couldn't stand the thought of my *friends* doing that to me, let alone a bunch of strangers.

I was also tired of poking into every possible space where something could be hidden. Couldn't we narrow it down? "Hey Brady," I called. "Are you sure we can't ask the map to show us everything we needed to find? You know, like we did in the past."

Brady squashed that hope. "You've heard me ask the map to show anything we should know about. And anything Ghalynn might have left for us. However, we don't have sufficient data about what actions cause items to show up. Don't forget, Ghalynn set up everything for us before, but the Sylph said he wouldn't be able to leave more clues. So if nothing shows up, we have no way to ascertain if that means there is nothing to find, or if there was no um… no magic prepared to cause it to display."

"Erghhhh." I had to clench my teeth to stop the sound of my disappointment.

Brady's lips quirked but he managed not to grin at me. "Even if some items did show up, we couldn't know if *every*thing important did."

I hated when Brady went all logical on me. Of course, that was pretty much all the time.

We hadn't seen a hint of anything on the map, but Brady kept asking in each house. I was getting tired of that moment — the breathless anticipation, waiting to see if anything showed up — followed by disappointment when nothing appeared.

As we left the fourth house, I nearly tripped on the uneven steps and realized I was just plain tired.

"Are we nearly done?" I asked, then grimaced. Even my voice sounded tired.

Brady pulled the map and held it out to me. "As you can see, there are two more domiciles that I selected for review today."

This time I didn't try to hide my groan. I turned and walked onto the porch of the next house. I'd gotten so used to just walking into each house, I didn't even think about magical booby-traps. Big mistake. The door came to life as Doug pushed past me and touched the doorknob.

The door shook itself, rattling in its frame, then began to swell and bulge. We backed down the steps as the bulge grew larger, covering the entire door.

"What did you do?" I asked Doug.

"Nothing!" he said.

It swelled like a giant, pulsating blister, the wood grain slowly transforming until it resembled a thin membrane stretched over something…scaly. Then, with a deafening pop it burst, spewing a watery-brown putrid liquid over the porch.

From inside the tattered remains of that blister, a long sinuous neck covered with horns and spikes emerged, topped by an enormous head with glowing red eyes and long dagger-like teeth. The nostrils flared as if it could smell us.

I recognized that head all too well. It was a dragon.

My breath began to hitch as two short thick dragon legs followed the neck out of the door, slamming to the ground hard enough to make it shake beneath my feet. Each leg ended in wickedly curved claws that gleamed like polished metal as the sunlight hit them.

We were too close. There was no chance to get away, even if we tried to run; dragons are just too fast.

Olivia and Faith crowded next to me, standing shoulder to shoulder. I reached out, grabbed their hands and held on tight. Thankful to be with my best friends in this or any other world.

I was torn between the need to shut my eyes so I wouldn't have to watch death coming for me, and the urgent need to see what was happening.

The need to see won. Sweat broke out on my forehead as I remembered the other dragon from a few months before. The one that nearly succeeded in burning down Chimera with us in it.

This one looked frighteningly familiar. Dark grey cheeks narrowed into a sharply pointed flat beak. A black tongue, forked like a snake's, shot out and moved slowly through the air as if tasting us. Behind the tongue, buried deep in the back of its lower jaw were sharp curved tusks, sharpened to dagger-like points, longer than my hand. Beyond that were glowing red and gold flames fading into blackness.

Dragon fire.

Fire born of magic, burning hotter than anything in our world. Fire that could shoot a dozen feet into the air, roaring and shrieking like a living thing. Fire that changed directions, launching long swirling gouts of flame toward you no matter where you ran. Fire that could singe and burn everything it touched.

I started to shake as a sudden thought struck me. Did the Salamander have anything in common with dragons? And would it be as freaking scary as a dragon? I'd have to ask Ronny.

If I lived through this.

A strange hissing chuckle came from its throat and the beak opened into a wide hideous grin. Brady straightened up, staring as if fascinated by that gaping maw. A deep growling voice that echoed through my bones declared, "Begone, interloper. You shall not pass."

Next to me, Brady muttered, "Who does it think it is, Gandalf?" I managed to suppress a hysterical giggle, wondering if Brady could suddenly read my mind.

Olivia, Faith and I didn't say anything. Instead, we all very sensibly stepped back. I felt a moment's desperate hope that we'd be allowed to leave without any screaming or burning or dying.

Doug's reaction didn't surprise me. He held his ground, obviously not ready to give up, but his shoulders slumped.

It was Brady's reaction that was beyond strange. He threw back his head and laughed.

"Are you crazy?" I hissed.

"Oh, come on," he said and laughed again. "You can't possibly be afraid of that illusion. It's well done, I grant you, but unquestionably an illusion none the less."

Olivia's voice came out higher than normal when she snapped, "You know there are dragons here. How can you be sure it's an illusion?" Her voice was as confused as I felt. More irritated maybe, but equally confused.

Brady shook his head and spoke in a condescendingly patient voice. "If you'd paid attention, you would have noticed that it has flames in its neck."

"It's a dragon; they have flames inside!" I asked, impatiently, itching to get away.

Brady looked at me pityingly. "Firstly, the pattern of those flames keeps repeating. And beyond the flames, it is black and empty. There is no fire burning deep inside that thing." He shook his head and added, "I can't believe I'm saying this, but according to legend a dragon dies once its fire goes out inside."

I started to protest but he continued, "Secondly, in case you haven't noticed, this supposed dragon is just sitting there. And it spoke. Once."

This time I managed to make myself heard, "So?"

His lips quirked. "So, ob-vi-ously," he drew that word out very long, his form of sarcasm, "it's a magical hologram. I'd love to know how they created it. Other than the flames being in the wrong place, it's a remarkable construct." He stared at me intently, watching me think that through, then asked, "Okay?"

Olivia sprang forward and I nearly lost my balance as her shoulder collided with mine. She looked at Brady challengingly, one eyebrow raised so high it disappeared under her bangs. "Okay? Hah! If you're so sure it's not real, you go in the house first."

Brady shrugged. "Sure." He turned and walked calmly toward the house. Faith and Olivia each tightened their grip on my hands. I sucked in my breath and fought the temptation to shut my eyes. If I was watching this in a movie, I'd have both hands in front of my face, fingers nearly touching, leaving just enough room to peek between them. Instead, my heart began to pound in time with each step he took as he marched upon the angry dragon.

Then my heart stopped for a moment as he walked through the dragon, gripped the door knob, threw the door open, and disappeared inside

Faith, Olivia and I released our hands, first staring at each other, then turning back to the open door. Where the dragon still sat, waiting.

Doug moved forward before I could. He straightened his shoulders and climbed the porch with a sure step, disappearing through the dragon into the house. Which meant it was my turn. I took a deep breath and began walking. The sight of the huge creature filling the doorway made my skin crawl and my breath hitch in my lungs. Sure, I'd seen Brady and Doug go through it safely, but what if third time was the charm, or something like that? When I got near it, I closed my eyes and burst into a run. When I stopped and opened my eyes, I was in the living room of an ordinary house.

Well, ordinary for a house with no electricity. One at a time, Olivia and Faith crowded in after me. Faith asked, "What, exactly, was that thing, Brady?"

"I told you, it was some form of illusion." Brady seemed positively buoyant. He grinned widely. "It was a very good one." I think he was trying to make her feel better, but mostly he succeeded in sounding condescending.

Olivia grumbled, "Fine. You were lucky this time."

Brady's lips compressed and his satisfaction drained from his eyes. Then he turned away, hiding his expression. I poked Olivia in the side with my elbow and muttered, "Be nice."

She rolled her eyes, but didn't say anything else.

Faith, Olivia and I started searching the bedroom together, leaving Doug and Brady to search the kitchen and living room. Olivia was dragging drawers open and rummaging through everything impatiently. Whenever she finished checking a drawer she slammed it shut. I sighed, wondering how long she was going to stay mad at Brady this time. Faith and I headed into the hall, leaving her to it.

It didn't occur to me to tell Olivia to be careful, but maybe it should have. I heard the sound of the last drawer, the one on the bottom being yanked open. That was followed by a jarring thud and a loud pop.

I glanced at Faith, not sure if I should be alarmed or not and met her concerned eyes. I shrugged and said, "I'll go and see."

I was nearly back to the bedroom when the scream came.

I burst into the room and came to an abrupt stop. The entire room was filled, floor to ceiling, with billowing clouds of fine white powder. I felt it settling on my face and hair and blinked rapidly to keep it out of my eyes. I peered through it frantically, trying to find Olivia. Instead, the powder seemed to coalesce into a human shape.

I yelled, "Olivia?"

The powder monster opened its mouth and screamed. I screamed back before I realized I knew that scream. It was Olivia. I rushed up to her and hugged her then both of us whirled to face the door as Faith burst in. She took one look at us and let out a horror-movie scream.

Before we could explain, the sound of frantic footsteps pounded down the hall. Doug was yelling, "Stupid, helpless girls. You can't leave them alone for a minute." He and Brady burst into the room and smashed into Faith, who staggered and started to fall.

I darted forward and caught her. Olivia scooped a handful of the powder off the floor and advanced on Doug. "Stupid, helpless girls?" she demanded, then hurled the powder into his face.

Brady sounded shocked, "What are you doing? You don't know what that powder is. It could be anthrax for all you know."

Olivia smirked at him. "Well, well, well. Mr-know-it-all *doesn't* know everything. But I know talcum powder when *I* smell it."

"You can't be certain of that. Not without running chemical tests," he told her, impatiently.

"Actually," she told him with a tight-lipped smile, "after taking care of four younger brothers and sisters and rubbing it over all of them, I *can* be certain."

Doug had been making outraged noises during this. Finally, he gave a loud growl. I looked over and nearly laughed out loud. His face was thickly smeared with powder. Only his eyes and lips looked normal. Then he yelled, "Why did you do that?"

"Probably 'cause we're stupid, helpless girls," I told him with a cocky smile, then reached down and grabbed a handful of the powder and tossed it at him as well.

There are some disadvantages to having a powder fight. By the time we were finished, all of us were sneezing so hard that tears were running down our cheeks, leaving long trails in the white powder that coated every square inch of us.

One by one we staggered out of the room and collapsed on the living room floor, trying to get our breath back. Every time I looked at the others, I giggled uncontrollably. They all looked completely ridiculous. *I* thought I might never stop until I looked at Doug just as he reached down and rubbed his leg like it was hurting him. Then I felt my laughter die inside me.

Brady sat up and pulled off his glasses. He blew at the powder coating them, then reached into his backpack and pulled out a small square of cloth. It took him several tries to clean them. Then he put them back on before asking, "Did anyone find anything of interest?"

We all shook our heads, and my shoulders slumped. Once again we'd found nothing. No clues, no objects, no Salamander. How many more houses would we need to search? I reminded myself we'd only been in the town three times. We couldn't really expect to find anything right away. But I still felt disappointed.

Brady climbed to his feet and said, "We've got one more to check today. We should go."

Apparently we had one more chance to find something before heading back home.

Chapter 11/March/Chimera

Mirror, Mirror, On the Wall

Doug climbed painfully to his feet and staggered out first. I didn't think about how strange we would look to anyone — or anything. I don't think any of us did. But as we emerged from the house, our animals went berserk.

Rusty backed up several steps and started barking hysterically. Shadow's fur stood on end, making her look nearly twice her normal size. She arched her back and hissed at us. Pyg flew from branch to branch in the trees around the house, hooting with agitation. And there was no sign of Foxy or Fangface.

Doug called out, "It's alright, boy. It's just us."

Rusty fell silent, but whined and refused to come any closer.

I sat down and held out my hand to Shadow. "I'm sorry we scared you," I told her. "It's just powder. It'll come off."

Then I turned to Olivia in alarm. "It will come off, right?"

She laughed and pulled the sweater she'd been wearing that morning out of her pack. She scrubbed it over her face and arms, and soon looked like she normally did, at least if you ignored her powdery white hair. I pointed at my own hair then back at her. She looked blank for a moment, then her mouth dropped open and she quickly rubbed the sweater over her head.

It took a few minutes for the rest of us to get cleaned up, but I was pretty sure all of us would be finding powder in unexpected places for days.

I bit my lip to hide a smile at that thought as we headed for the next house. Our animals followed, slightly aloof, as if they found the whole head-to-toe powder thing disgraceful. They sat to one side as we climbed the porch, a silent row of disapproval. I looked back and smiled at Shadow, then stiffened. Behind her, at the edge of the trees that grew around the house, was another statue.

Just how many statues did they put in here?

Remembering the dragon at the last house, I hung back and let Brady and Doug go inside the wood and glass structure first. I had no desire to set off an illusion or shocking static, or who knew what. So of course, this time there was no reaction when Doug opened the door. Which made me feel ridiculous. Darn it.

I stalked past the others, feeling out of sorts, and started checking the living room. Faith quickly joined me, and Doug sighed and headed for the kitchen. That left Brady and Olivia to check the bedroom. I had just enough time to think that might not be a good idea when the first argument began.

"Under the mattress? Really?" Olivia's voice was filled with scorn. "What, you think a princess slept in here? And someone left a pea under that, what, one foot thick mattress?"

"Left a what?" Brady sounded clueless.

"A pea. You know. The Princess and the Pea?"

When he didn't respond, she said, "The fairytale?"

Brady cleared his throat, and I didn't have to see him to picture the red climbing into his cheeks. He responded in a flat voice, "My parents weren't big on fairytales. Guess I missed that one."

After a long moment of silence, Olivia said brightly, "At least there aren't many places to look in here. There's absolutely *nothing* interesting in the wardrobe."

I grinned at her disdainful tone. Obviously she hadn't seen anything she wanted to try on this time.

Faith and I finished in the living room, and I wandered over to the doorway to the bedroom just in time to see Olivia stop before the large ornate mirror hanging on the wall. She stared at herself, raising her hand to fluff her hair, then wet her lips and tilted her head.

Even though his voice was hushed, I clearly heard Brady. "Mirror, mirror on the wall, who's the fairest of them all."

I nearly jumped out of my skin when the mirror grew cloudy and a disembodied voice said, "Since there are no others here, it would have to be her, my dear."

Olivia whirled around, her face dark with betrayal. "You're always making fun of me, Brady."

Brady's eyebrows drew together even as his color rose. "I was just repeating a line from one of your fairytales."

"I thought you didn't know any."

"We saw *Snow White* together, remember? Besides, everyone knows that phrase. It just seemed...appropriate, under the circumstances." His voice dropped slightly as he said, "You know perfectly well that you're aesthetically pleasing. Everyone knows that."

"So why did you say I look good because there's no one else in here?"

"That wasn't me. Ventriloquism is not one of my competencies. Besides, no one could throw their voice across the room like that. It's physically impossible."

Olivia stamped her foot and glared at him. "Then whose voice was it?"

I cleared my throat, figuring it was time to join this conversation before it got any farther out of hand. "It was the mirror."

Both of them spun around and stared at me like I was crazy.

Brady shook his head and said, "That is also an impossibility. Mirrors only speak in fairytales, not in reality."

I rolled my eyes. "We're in a world created by magic. Do you really believe that mirrors can't be enchanted to speak?"

That shut up Brady, but Olivia got a speculative look on her face. She turned around slowly and looked at the mirror again. "Mirror, mirror on the wall, show me where the Rejects are."

The mirror remained a normal mirror. No swirling clouds, no strange echoing voice.

Olivia turned back to me and said, "So what did I do wrong?"

I shrugged, but Faith spoke behind me. "It has to rhyme."

This time Brady rolled his eyes, but I felt excited. "Of course. Why else would everyone talk to mirrors in rhymes all the time? I never understood that!"

Olivia chewed on her lip a moment, then grinned. "We all know the Rejects are the creepiest things that ever lived, so how's this?" She faced the mirror again and said, "Mirror, mirror on the wall, show me where the Rejects crawl."

I let out a breath I hadn't known I was holding as the mirror clouded and the voice rang out again, "Though those you seek do not crawl, they can be found inside this hall."

The mirror cleared and showed the five Rejects walking down a short hallway. As we watched, they crossed through a living room and out a doorway.

Behind me Faith said, "They're in town." She sucked in a deep breath. "They'll find us."

"How did they find this place?" Olivia asked. "We've been so darn careful."

"Obviously not careful enough," Faith said. Her shoulders slumped and she shoved her left hand in her pocket.

"They're in town, no matter how," I said. "The question should be, where in town are they?" I felt suddenly cold. I rubbed my hands rapidly over my arms but didn't feel any warmer. Probably because it wasn't the room that was cold.

Brady leaned forward and bounced on his toes. "I know where they are. That was the first house we entered. At the edge of town."

"How can you be so sure?" Olivia asked. "They all look alike."

I felt like kicking Olivia for asking such a stupid question and wondered what Brady was going to say to that.

But he didn't say anything. Without a word, he pulled out the map and wished to see the Rejects. Five red dots showed up outside one of the small roughly drawn houses. He was right. They were outside the very first house we'd checked.

"How did you do that?" Olivia asked.

He gave her a disgusted look. "Eidetic memory, remember?"

I spoke up quickly. "I knew you could remember things you read and hear, but I wasn't sure it applied to things you see."

"Exactly," Olivia said, sounding smug. Apparently nothing I said was going to help.

Brady turned red again and I felt sorry for him. He muttered, "Yeah, it's basically everything."

"Your brain is going to explode from all the information you keep stuffing into it," I told him.

"There are large parts of the brain that are unused by most people," he said. "I should have plenty of storage space." He took a quick glance at the watch on his wrist. "It's getting late. We should go."

Doug grabbed his arm. "Wait. Check to see if the Rejects are moving. We don't want to walk into them."

Another quick glance at the map showed they had left the house and turned toward a side road, not the road we needed to take back to the tree.

Faith gulped loudly. "It might be safer to wait and give them a chance to move further away."

Brady nodded and pointed to a place nearby that seemed curiously empty. It was surrounded by thick hedges or trees. "We could take a moment to check that out."

"Why?" Olivia asked. Then, perhaps realizing how abrupt that sounded, she added, "I mean, why look when the map shows clearly there's nothing there."

Brady nodded. "I remember seeing a large building, possibly the mansion Ghalynn spoke of, on the map in the past. I believe it's worth investigating."

He stuffed the map back in his pocket and headed for the door. As we followed him out, I wondered if the mirror was just a spell or if it was somehow sentient.

Brady walked past the houses we'd already explored, heading farther away from the tree. I glanced back and smiled at Shadow, pleased to see all our animals a short distance behind us.

After walking another ten minutes, Faith pointed at two houses on the right side of the road. They looked derelict; boarded up, falling apart, paint peeling, dead leaves covering the porch, weeds in the yard. Except for Ghalynn's cabin that we'd found our first year, these were the first houses that actually looked deserted. Even though all of the houses had been abandoned, most of them looked as if their owners had simply stepped away a few minutes ago.

Why did these look so different?

Brady didn't give me time to think about it. He led the way around the outside of the tall hedge that encircled the blank space on the map. The space Brady was sure was hiding a mansion. He kept muttering that someone had to have planted the hedge, and must have had a reason. Well, that's what he meant. Of course, the words he used took much longer to say.

We finally saw a thin area in the hedge and Brady pushed his way inside. I was cursing him under my breath by the time I made my way through after him. The hedge was filled with small twigs with sharp pointy ends. They poked through my shirt and pants, and scratched every inch of bare skin.

"There'd better be something good in here, Brady," Olivia said through clenched teeth. I looked back; her face was red and sweaty, and a thin line of blood marred her make-up near her left eye. Between rooms filled with powder and hedges filled with sharp pokey bits, this hadn't been a good day for her.

Brady finally got out the other side of the thick hedge. I stepped around him to see why he'd stopped there, head back, staring. There was a huge house inside that hedge, at least three stories high, and as long as four other houses we'd checked.

Olivia was too busy plucking twigs and leaves out of her hair to notice. "What was worth getting snagged and poked like that?"

I waved my hand in front of her eyes to get her attention. "You might want to look around."

"Oh fine." She stopped brushing at her clothes and looked up. Then her jaw dropped as she stared at the house. "What is that place?"

"Looks like a mansion to me," Doug said. "We should definitely check it out."

Brady glanced at his watch and frowned. "Darn it. We literally have only minutes to spare if we intend to get home before dark."

Doug clapped him on the back. "That's the spirit. Can you see a door?" He began pacing toward the far end of the building.

Faith fell into step with me as we followed. She muttered, "He really thinks it'll only take a few minutes to look through *that*?"

I laughed and watched as Doug searched for a door. But several minutes later it was my turn to mutter to Faith, "It doesn't look like size will be an issue. Not if we can't find a way in." We were half way around the house and there was still no sign of a door or a window.

By the time we made it back to the beginning, we were all tired and discouraged. What kind of house has no doors or windows?

Brady stared at it, deep in contemplation, humming slightly under his breath. Faith said, "We should get going," but he waved her off and continued staring. Finally he said, "I wish to see the door."

I sucked in my breath, my eyes roving over the exterior, waiting for a door.

Nothing happened.

Then he said, "I wish to see the way inside." That was followed by more staring.

Finally Olivia poked him in the side. "Aren't you the one who said we need to head back if we want to be home before dark?"

Brady started and glanced at his watch. "I…yes, we do. Need to get back."

He turned and headed toward the hedge. I sighed — I wasn't looking forward to going through that again.

-xXx-

We were getting near the tree when we heard yelling. Fortunately, the road went up a short hill and made a slight turn to the left. Otherwise, the Rejects would have seen us.

I realized it was Arnold who was yelling. There was no mistaking that low, cold voice. This time, it was edged with anger; sharp as the blade of a knife. I was fervently grateful he wasn't using that voice on me.

"...*not* a matter of 'getting along,' Ray. And tell your girlfriend to back off."

What the heck had Ray and Polly done to get Arnold so upset?

"I can't stand anything about them, and I won't try to *get along* with them." My nails dug into my palms as I urgently hoped he wasn't talking about us. "I don't *tolerate* snakes."

I slowly released the breath I'd been holding.

Ray muttered something I couldn't hear and Arnold's voice grew even colder. "I'm not afraid of them, you ass. I despise them. I loathe them. I don't care if someone told you these animals can help us. Nothing could make me care, not even if it started laying solid gold eggs. Nothing is worth making nice with a reptile."

Ray's voice came again, even fainter than before. This time there was just a touch of heat to Arnold's words. "I consider snakes proof there is no god. No so-called loving creator would permit something like *that* to exist."

I heard his foot scuff in the dirt, then something hit the branches of one of the trees beside the road.

"Whoa, man. What's the matter?" Ray's voice was loud enough to hear now. His words implied concern, but there was none in his voice. If anything he sounded amused. "You dizzy?"

"I'm fine." If Arnold ever sounded like that when he spoke to me, I'd know I was about to die. I wondered if Ray realized just how angry Arnold was. His voice made my skin feel like it was being brushed with frost when Arnold said, "You just worry about yourself."

The sound of their footsteps moved down the road away from us. I crept to the top of the short hill and Shadow followed me. I peeked over in time to see them near the tree, their four animals — Polly's pink pig, Andrew's small…um, donkey, Ray's huge rat, and Arnold's snake — following dejectedly behind them. They appeared to be deliberately keeping their distance. Hopefully the Rejects would never find out how helpful they could be. I reached out and rubbed Shadow on her favorite spot between her ears, and she purred contentedly.

Faith came up next to me and asked, "What do you think Arnold did that made Ray so happy?"

"If I had to guess, I think he kicked his snake into a tree. He probably lost his balance for a moment." The Rejects had disappeared into the tree, so I got to my feet and headed in that direction. "It should be safe now, and we need to hurry. It must be pretty late."

"We'll need to be careful," Olivia said. "Since we can't trust Brady to keep an eye on the map."

"We almost walked right into them," Faith said, and shuddered.

Brady flushed and shoved his glasses higher on his nose. "Sorry. I was busy thinking about the house with no doors or windows. It doesn't make sense."

Olivia looked like she was going to keep talking but off to our right, from somewhere in the woods, something hissed in the shadows, then gave a low rumbling growl. It was a reminder, not that I really needed one, that the Rejects weren't the only things to worry about in here.

After that, none of us felt like dong any talking.

Chapter 12/March/Santa Ramona

A Time Between

Even though we'd hurried back to the tree, we were almost late. The sun was just slipping below the horizon as I entered my house. Mom came out of the kitchen right away. Clearly she'd been lying in wait for me.

"Where have you been?" she asked.

"With my friends," I said, surprised. Why would she even ask that? She knew we spent all of our time together.

Then a feeling of dread made my throat feel tight. She couldn't suspect we'd been in Chimera, could she? Well, not in Chimera exactly. How could she? But somewhere she wouldn't approve of? The tightness in my throat spread to my stomach, then dropped toward my toes like a lump of lead.

Mom sighed like she was…tired? Sad? No, more like wistful. "I was just hoping we could sit down and have a bit of girl talk tonight. I never get to see you anymore."

"Well." I said, being careful to keep my relief out of my voice, "I do have a couple hours of homework. But we could talk after that, I guess. Uhhh…what do you want to talk about?"

She laughed and shook her head. "I don't want to talk about anything too specific." There was a strange look in her eye when she said that. And what did *too* specific mean? She smiled at me and said, "Mostly, I'd just like to spend some time with you. Let's talk after dinner."

Mostly she'd like to spend some time together? Waiting until after dinner was going to drive me crazy, but I was all in favor of procrastination in this instance. "Okay, sure. When's dinner? I could go upstairs and start on my homework now."

"You cut it very close tonight. Dinner will be ready in a couple minutes," she said. "So right now you need to set the table."

I stared after her as she went back into the kitchen, biting my lip, wondering what this was about. We never sat down and had 'girl talks'. It sounded like something you'd hear on a talk show: *So Ms. So-and-so, your mother wants to know what classes you prefer at school this year and why? Is there any truth to the rumors that you have a friend who is dating even though her mother wouldn't like it? Has that affected your friendship? Are* you *seeing any boys?*

Oh no. Mom wasn't going to ask about boys, was she? That thought kept me worrying about our *talk* through most of dinner.

As usual, Dad left the kitchen once we'd finished eating. I could hear him rummaging around the living room as Mom sat down across the kitchen table from me. She smiled and I smiled back tentatively. Then the phone rang and I sagged back in my chair with relief when she got up to answer. It was a struggle to look properly concerned when she hung up and said there'd been a water leak at the library, threatening to damage some of the books. She was sorry she had to leave, but she had to supervise the clean-up.

She sounded regretful when she said we'd have to talk some other time. I was fighting an odd mixture of pleasure at the delay and guilt about the books, so my assurances that she should go take care of things came out a bit too fervent. She didn't seem to notice; she was smiling as she dropped a kiss on my head on her way out.

Dad wandered in as she left. "What did your mom want to talk about?"

"Um…not sure. Maybe boys," I said.

He looked horrified. "Boys?" He looked at me warily and asked, "Uh…you don't feel the need to talk to me about boys, do you?"

I burst out laughing. He looked like someone had asked him to stick his hand into a beehive. "No, that's okay Dad." He looked doubtful, like he thought he was supposed to offer to talk about *something*. "No, really, everything's okay," I assured him. "If it's all right with you, I'll just go upstairs and do my homework."

As I left the kitchen, I'm not sure which one of us was more relieved.

-xXx-

On Monday, Olivia arrived at our corner practically glowing. "George," she turned to me and grinned, "you remember him, right?" She waited until I nodded then announced smugly, "He's asked me out a few times, but last night he asked me out to a nice dinner, not just Johnny's, *and* a movie." She made a high-pitched squeeee sound and danced in place. Faith and I congratulated her, but Brady made a strange sound in his throat and turned away.

For the rest of the way to school, Olivia and Brady sniped at each other about everything and nothing. I was sure neither of them could have said what started it. By the time we got to school I was done with it. Completely and totally done. Brady must have had enough too, because he stalked off down the hall without a word.

Olivia watched his receding back and asked blankly, "What did I say?"

Faith and I looked at each other, then shrugged. It could have been too many things to hazard a guess.

Olivia sniffed and said, "Well, who cares about him anyway."

I was glad he was too far away to hear her.

Olivia and Brady continued being snarky to each other every time their paths crossed. At lunch, they made sure they were sitting as far apart as humanly possible. Neither one said anything directly to the other, although Olivia made a few pointed comments that I was sure were aimed at Brady.

The bell rang, and as we stood up to leave Olivia managed to get in one last comment. "The problem with science types is they think they're so smart. While they may get along with test tubes, they don't have a clue how to get along with human beings." She never looked at Brady while she said this, but he reacted like she'd addressed him by name. A dark flush climbed slowly up to his hairline; even the tops of his ears turned red.

I put my hand on Brady's arm and asked him to stay a moment. When everyone else hesitated, I said, "Go ahead. We'll be right there." Olivia looked at me questioningly, one eyebrow raised. I smiled and waved her away.

Brady said, "I really need to get to class, Kat." He shifted his weight from foot to foot. "Can't this wait?"

I narrowed my eyes at him and glared. "If you walk away from me, I swear I'll yell my questions at you all the way across the cafeteria."

That earned me a startled glance. At least he looked like he was paying attention now. I decided I'd better start talking before I lost it again. "What's up with you and Olivia?"

His hands balled into fists. "Maybe you should ask her."

"I would, if I thought it would do me any good," I told him. "I've asked her more than once over the past few years why she acts like that toward you. She's never given me a straight answer." I gave him a tight smile. "So now, I'm asking you."

"I…" Brady shook his head slowly from side to side.

"Look," I said. "The two of you are driving me crazy. Whatever it is, you need to resolve it. Like, now."

His shoulders slumped and he sat heavily on the chair he'd vacated a moment before. That didn't look good. Maybe this was something I didn't really want to know.

Then he blurted, "I hate that Olivia chose someone else. Again."

I'm not sure what my face did, but Brady stopped abruptly, staring at me. I cleared my throat nervously and asked, "Why are you telling me that?"

"You wanted to know. And who else can I talk to?" he demanded. "Besides, you're Olivia's friend. If anyone can help me, it's you."

"Okaaaay." What could I say? He reminded me of a puppy seeking reassurance after accidently scattering kibble all over the floor.

"I know it's all a mess," he said. "I've tried, but I haven't been able to design a strategy that's been successful with her. I don't know what to do; none of my science books describe how attraction works, other than pheromones."

Now *I* didn't know what to do. I knew what I'd tell Olivia or Faith, but this was Brady. What could I say to *him*?

I fought to keep my face interested rather than shocked. Or amazed. Or completely dumbfounded. "Uh... Have you... That is... Um... I don't..."

"I can't stand it when she talks about George," he said, his voice rising. "Oh, I know it isn't logical to think a girl like her might pick a guy like me. But knowing that doesn't change the facts; I want her to choose *me*."

I took a deep breath and tried again. This time I aimed for coherent. "Does Olivia know you like her? Like her like *that,* I mean?"

There was no way! None.

"I mean, *I* had no idea, Brady," I added.

Wow, no kidding Kat. Understatement of the year.

He stared straight into my eyes. Even through his glasses, I could read the misery in his. He shrugged, and when he spoke his voice was very low, not much above a whisper. "I don't know the answer to that."

Then his gaze switched from dejected to expectant. He grabbed my arm tightly, and I tried not to flinch. "So how do I make her think about me as boyfriend material?"

Boyfriend *material*? Like, what, an ingredient in a freaking science project?

"Well, you need to let her know you're interested."

"I can't do that!" He straightened and looked at me like I was some strange, rather disgusting bug. "She's seeing someone else. She thinks I'm a hopeless geek. She tells me that to my face. She likes making fun of me. Why give her something else to tease me about?"

And Olivia didn't think he understood human beings. Silly girl; he certainly had her nailed. So what could I tell him?

"Well, you really can't be sure she'd make fun of you." I ignored his sarcastic glance. "We've all been friends a long time, Brady. She's probably never considered you or Doug as boyfriend *material*." My throat tightened and I had to swallow before finishing, lamely, "And, well, she probably never will think of you that way if you don't let her know she's more than a friend to you."

He shot me an agonized glance, and I said, "Look, whatever you've been doing isn't working, right?" He nodded reluctantly and I said, "Isn't there a scientific principal of something. About if you keep doing the same thing and don't like the results you get, you need to try something different?"

He stared at me for a very long moment, then smiled. "You'd make a good scientist Kat. You're absolutely right. I need to try something different. I need to make her see me as a viable option."

He'd thought of something, I could tell. But I was pretty sure it didn't involve letting Olivia know he liked her. If I was this surprised, how would Olivia feel? What would she do? Would it stop their arguing, or just make it worse?

I shuddered at that thought.

I didn't get to ask about it because the final bell for class rang and we both took off like startled rabbits. Fortunately, Ms. Gates was pretty lenient, so I probably wouldn't be in trouble. But from the look on Brady's face, I didn't think that was going to be true for him.

-xXx-

For the rest of that day and all the way home I kept an eye on Brady. He wasn't really acting different, but he didn't look as gloomy as he had the last few months. That had to be good, right?

We'd nearly reached our corner where we'd each go our own way, when I realized what had changed. Not surprisingly, Olivia had thrown out a couple snarky comments. They were so normal, I barely paid any attention. The difference was Brady wasn't responding to them. Or when he did, he sounded cheerful. Like he'd completely missed the hidden slight in her words. By the time we said good-bye, Olivia was tight-lipped and baffled by his lack of response.

Note to self – Brady's on to something. If you want Olivia to stop snarking at you, pretend she's being nice. Who knew?

I was grinning as I waved goodbye to the others and turned toward my house. I didn't even have time to shrug off my backpack before my cell rang. It was Ronny. I was so surprised I almost dropped it. Ronny still didn't feel comfortable with a lot of electronic stuff, though she'd taken to the radio and television easily enough. I don't think she'd ever called someone before.

She rambled on a bit about nothing in particular. I finally pieced together that Chris was out of town on one of his paranormal investigations and Ronny was lonely.

"I'll have to get back for dinner," I said hesitantly. "But I guess I could ask Dad if I could come over. Or maybe you could come here."

"Oh, no, there's no need for that. I will be fine. I just wish magick worked better in your world. I could project myself to Chris and we could spend some time together, even if it was in my astral form."

That whole sentence really freaked me out. First, she was still referring to this as *my* world, not *her* world. Even though she'd been banished here for the remainder of her life. But it was the second part, the idea of sending part of yourself, without your physical body, to be with another person that really gave me the creeps. I mean, what if you couldn't get back to your body? Nothing would be worth risking that!

I said quickly, "Well, Chris will be home soon, right? You can both be together in your, um, real forms then."

Ronny sighed heavily. I heard the rustling of cloth and could picture her grabbing onto her pendant. She was doing that more and more often these days. She sounded very tired when she said, "It does not matter. I should just let weeping frogs sigh."

I managed to get off the phone before bursting into giggles. That had been a great Ronny-ism.

Chapter 13/April/Chimera

Oh…Spit!

Olivia kept us waiting five minutes before our next trip through the tree. Which for Olivia wasn't really late. We'd had to wait longer in the past, but today Brady acted like he was in a tearing hurry to get to Chimera. In a hearty, un-Brady-like voice, he said, "I don't understand your propensity for being late, Olivia. Perhaps you need to ensure that the time on your phone is accurate. It's not considerate to make people wait for you. It's a real, what do you call it, pet-peeve. For some people."

By *some people,* he obviously meant himself. The way he waited, arms crossed over his chest, foot tapping impatiently made that clear. He straightened and his voice took on a self-congratulatory tone. "*I* always plan to be two to three minutes early. Being on time is important. To me." He followed that pronouncement with a benevolent smile at Olivia.

Based on how he felt about her, I was pretty sure he was trying to brag on his punctuality in order to impress Olivia. But from the sound of her grinding teeth, it wasn't having anything close to the effect he wanted.

Olivia scrunched up her face like she'd smelled something bad. "Well, excuse me! Some people think taking an extra minute to be presentable..."she ran critical eyes up and down Brady's over-sized plaid shirt, rumpled gray corduroy pants, and plain white sneakers, then shook her head, "…is considerate."

Brady's smile faded as he realized his epic fail. Poor Brady.

I needed to pull him aside and suggest he study some fashion magazines and maybe watch *Clueless*. I'd tell him to think of it like a science project —the study of things important to Olivia. After that, he'd either realize the two of them were totally different, or he'd know how to relate to her better.

I just had to make sure Olivia never found out I referred to her as a science project!

Olivia spun on her heel, nose raised, and marched toward the cemetery at a fast, very un-Olivia-like pace. I glanced at Brady and his crestfallen expression made me determined to have that talk soon.

When we reached the tree, Olivia glared at Brady then smiled at the rest of us. "See you soon," she said and leaned against the smooth grey bark.

This time, the trip was almost instantaneous. I was so surprised at being thrust into Chimera after counting to just 18 that I stumbled and fell to my knees. I barely got out of the way in time to avoid being tripped over by the others.

Everyone was exclaiming how fast it had been that time. I realized the last three times had been pretty quick. Why couldn't it always be like that?

Our animals ran up in a barking, purring, squeaking horde and we took a couple minutes to greet them before heading toward town. I scooped up Shadow and spent half the trip petting her and telling her how glad I was to see her. That way I didn't have to listen to anything Brady and Olivia might say to each other.

We made good time to the town, even with Brady brushing out our footprints and frequently, almost compulsively, checking the map. We made it all the way to the tall hedges that surrounded the mansion when he said, "They're here. The Rejects are heading toward the lake!"

"If the Rejects can't bug us for a while, we should try to figure that place out." Doug gestured toward the hidden mansion. "No one would build a house with no way inside."

I bent over and set Shadow carefully on her feet. When I straightened, I said, "I'm sure Ronny could explain it." I frowned and bit my lip. "I was going to ask her about it the last time we saw her. But you saw how bad she looks. And it feels like everything upsets her these days." I looked at my feet for a moment then admitted, "I'm getting worried about her."

Doug glanced at me then away. His voice was curiously gentle. "No worries. It'll wait till next time."

"So where are we heading today?" Faith asked brightly.

Brady lifted the map and pointed to an area deeper into the town. A cluster of five larger houses was drawn there, with a road leading right to them. He stuffed the map back in his pocket then started walking.

I settled my pack more comfortably on my shoulders and set off after him, with the others, and our animals, following behind.

As we drew closer, it was obvious these houses were different from the others we'd seen. These five were mini-mansions, built of smooth grey stone with shadowy slate roofs. Everything about them appeared dark and forbidding. The narrow windows looked shadowed and furtive. They seemed to peer at us like the soulless eyes of dead things.

Too many horror movies, Kat.

Our animals weren't acting all freaked out, which made me feel better. I told Shadow to stay there as we headed inside the first house. I glanced back and saw all of them sitting there, waiting patiently.

I relaxed when we found nothing remotely scary in the first three houses. They were much larger than the others we'd been through; two stories tall, and full of rooms. But they were light and cheerful inside, if a trifle cool. And most rooms didn't have a great deal of drawers or cupboards, making the search easier than some we'd done.

By the time we got to the fourth house, I was feeling as comfortable as I ever was in Chimera. But as soon as we got the door open we all froze.

The eerie sound of music drifted on the air, not loud, but jarring after all the silence.

"Someone's here," I whispered, and felt my stomach twist. This was what we'd been trying to find for over three years. And now that it was here, I was ashamed of the fear crawling up my spine.

Who could still be here? And why were they alone spared?

"We'll have to check," Doug said, nearly soundless. He squared his shoulders and started steadily up the staircase toward the sound of harp music. I managed to smother my instinctive cry for him to stop. I knew he was right; we had to check. But watching him climb those stairs was tying my twisted stomach into knots.

The harp played a slow and mournful tune that spoke of loneliness, and isolation, and a need for companionship. It was sad and sweet and heartbreaking.

How else would the only person left in Chimera feel?

I couldn't let Doug face it…him…her…alone. I sucked in a deep breath and squared my shoulders just as he had. I kept close behind him, noticing briefly that I could probably remain completely hidden behind him now. His shoulders were surprisingly broad.

I felt remarkably safe, walking behind him like that.

The others followed. Faith and Olivia were taking the steps at the same time, with Brady trailing after them. He had a strange look on his face and it took me a moment to realize he looked skeptical. I wasn't sure why he doubted we'd find someone, but I was suddenly convinced there must be something, other than a person, to explain the sound.

Which meant that Brady and I were the only two who weren't surprised when we got to the top of the stairs and looked to the end of the hallway. There, on a pedestal, with a glow of light shining in a halo around it, stood a harp. A golden harp. Playing by itself.

When we got nearer, the mournful tune changed abruptly, as if the harp was aware of our presence. Now the music was upbeat, welcoming.

"Hello," I whispered, wondering if it understood English.

The music didn't change, so I guessed it didn't.

Doug got close and looked it over. "It's not connected to anything I can see." He tried to lift it off the pedestal but it wouldn't budge. "Maybe it's hooked up to something inside the base."

"Or maybe," Faith suggested, "it's under a spell and will continue to play until the spell is removed."

"Whatever the reason," I said, "it sounded lonely. I'd take it with us if it wasn't attached to the house."

We split up and started hunting for clues or anything from Ghalynn. This house was even more minimally furnished than the others. We were back downstairs in about fifteen minutes.

"One more to go," Brady said, checking the map. "And the Rejects are still at the lake, so we don't need to worry about the four of them."

"I'm not worried," Faith declared, making us all stop and stare at her in amazement. "What?" she asked, then grinned. "Oh, all right. I've decided they aren't as scary as I believed, that's all."

"Why would you decide that?" Doug asked. He merely sounded curious. I felt something nearer to incredulous.

"Arnold is afraid of snakes," she said and grinned. "He's a total coward about them. So..." she reached into a bulging pocket on the side of her backpack and pulled out a long, and at first glance highly realistic, rubber snake. It had been crammed in so tightly, it looked like she was a magician the way it kept emerging from that pocket.

She waved it in front of her and said, "I'm carrying this everywhere with me. If they try something, I'm going to heave it right in Arnold's face. Bet *that* slows them down!"

I laughed out loud. Faith actually sounded ready to kick Reject butt.

It took her several minutes to cram the snake back in her pack, then we headed for the last house. I glanced up the stairs as we left. The music was lonely to the point of desolation now.

Shadow started twining between my legs as we made our way to the next house. At first it seemed sweet but when I almost tripped over her I yelled at her to stop. She meowed back at me and I really wished I understood cat-speak.

Rusty started jumping up and down, barking, just as Brady started up the steps to the last house for the day. I was so busy feeling grateful that we'd be done soon that I actually forgot about possible spells, like holo-dragons, and mega-static, and self-locking doors.

My mistake.

As soon as Brady's fingers touched the doorknob, the large, metallic, lion-head door knocker came to life. I hadn't noticed its eyes were closed until they snapped open. What should have been white was the same metallic bronze as the rest of the knocker, but the pupils were deep black holes that looked as though they had no end. Back. Bottom. Whatever.

Now I understood what Shadow had been trying to say. When it was too late.

The mouth opened, filled with incredibly long, sharp bronze teeth inside a darkly red, wet mouth. "State your business." Everyone took an involuntary step back. Not only was a wickedly fanged doorknocker speaking to us, it had a snooty English-butler accent.

When none of us responded, it growled softly and demanded, "State your business or begone. Before I take measures."

Doug took a step closer and stated in a confident tone, "We've been sent by Ghalynn and Rowena Lenora Danaan to discover why all the inhabitants of Chimera have disappeared."

The growling, hissing laugh that erupted from that mouth was hideous. It scraped along my nerves, making the skin on my back twitch. Then it said, "Rowena Lenora Danaan is banished and has no power here. Ghalynn should crawl into a cave and take up the title of resident hermit. We have no interest in helping either of those individuals." As it spoke, the cultured English tone began to slip, turning to something deeper, something thick and raspy, with a strange lisp on the letter 's'. By the end of that statement it sounded as far from a cultured butler as possible.

"Now go." Those last two words came out as more of a growl than words; a tone any actor playing the Phantom of the Opera would give his right arm to produce.

Doug merely snorted. When Olivia and Faith began to edge down the steps leading to the house, he said, "Don't be ridiculous. It's a door knocker. It's attached to the door. It's not going to jump down and eat you."

Apparently it didn't like Doug's tone. And it didn't need to jump down. Instead, it pursed its lips and blew a stream of something that looked like spit. But where it touched the stone steps it sizzled and smoked and left a shallow pit in the rock.

All of us jumped back, just in time to avoid the next stream that hit directly where Brady had been standing a second before. Several more streams shot toward us as we continued to back away. They bubbled, hissed, steamed and created small holes in the hard ground.

"Think you can get away from me?" The knocker panted, then took a very deep breath and spit more of the acid in a high arc. We had to scatter away, and Olivia screamed as a single drop landed on her sleeve, burning through the fabric in seconds and eating a tiny hole into her arm. She clamped her hand over it and gritted her teeth.

"Is it bleeding?" I asked, quickly fishing a small first aid kit out of my backpack.

She reluctantly moved her hand away, twisting her head so she couldn't see. Bile burned up the back of my throat and I swallowed convulsively. I kept my voice cheerful as I told her, "Good news. There's no blood."

Actually, I didn't think it was good news at all. The skin around the edges of the hole looked blackened, and there were white, scaly patches down inside. I quickly slapped on a bandage, hoping it would look better by the time we got home. Maybe, if we were lucky, Ronny would know what to do about it. I resolutely refused to think about Doug's leg. Just because she hadn't been able to make that go back to normal didn't mean Olivia's arm would be the same.

Olivia let out a shaky breath and said, "So, Brady, how are you going to get us past that?"

Brady was staring at the bandage on Olivia's arm, his face pale and covered with a sheen of sweat. I was pretty sure he hadn't even heard her question. Olivia snapped, "Well? What are you going to do?"

Brady shook his head briefly, then focused his gaze on her derisive face.

He didn't sound like himself at all when he said, "I have no idea how to get us past it."

Olivia crooked her uninjured arm and stuck her hand defiantly on her hip. "If you think, for one minute, that I'm going to get hurt like this, and then we're not going to get inside there, think again. No way did this happen to me for nothing. No freaking way!"

"I suppose you think George could do better?" Brady compressed his lips so tight they went nearly bloodless.

Olivia flipped her hair behind her shoulder and smiled, "Maybe, but he's not with us, is he?"

"Fine," Brady said, and straightened his shoulders. "Give me a minute. I'll think of something." He paced away from us, muttering. "There must be some substance we can use to neutralize it." He turned and paced back. "Judging by its color, smell and action, it would appear to be a corrosive acid, probably in the Inorganic Oxidizing Acid or Inorganic Non-Oxidizing Acid family."

"How do we figure out which?" I bit my lip; that had come out a bit more freaked out than I intended.

"Hmmm?" He looked at me, his gaze somewhere else, then blinked. "Oh, we don't need to determine which family it is. The treatment would be the same. A weak neutralizing agent should do it."

I started to ask why he'd brought it up, then, but Faith spoke up first. "Why would you want it to be weak? Shouldn't you use something strong to stop it?"

His shook he head so hard he had to push his glasses more securely on his nose. "A strong acid mixed with a strong base can cause a violent reaction. I believe we may be able to counteract it with sodium bicarbonate or calcium carbonate. Hmmmmm." He rummaged in his backpack and pulled out a small box of baking soda and a piece of chalk. He turned to me and said, "Let me see Doug's sling shot, Kat."

"What do you want my sling shot for?" Doug asked suspiciously.

Brady rolled his eyes. He whispered, as if the knocker could hear and understand him, "I will use it to make my counteragents contact the mouth of the knocker."

"Baking soda and chalk?" Olivia asked skeptically. "What good are those going to do?"

"They are both alkaline. Base agents. If I can get them inside that mouth, one or the other should counteract the acid."

I pulled out the sling shot, but before I could hand it to Brady, Doug held out his hand. "I'll do it," he said. When Brady looked like he was going to argue, Doug said flatly, "It may have been your idea, but I'm the better shot. Just tell me where you want it."

Brady frowned, then shrugged his shoulders. He pulled a plastic cup out of his pack and poured a small amount of baking soda into it. Then he crushed about half a piece of chalk and added that to the baking soda. He bit his lip and stared into the cup a long moment before saying reluctantly, "I can think of no other options. This is not the method I would prefer, but I guess it can't be helped."

"What can't be helped?" I asked, feeling anxiety dance down my throat at the uncertainty on his face.

He looked up and gave me a weak smile. "I need to bond these loose powders together so they can reach and penetrate the target. But we don't have any appropriate binding materials."

"What about using water and forming a paste?" Olivia didn't sound like she was making a suggestion; she sounded… superior. "You know, like turning a cake mix into batter?" She might as well have said she couldn't believe he hadn't thought of something so obvious.

Doug managed to speak up before Brady got his mouth open. "Even I know using water with an acid can be dangerous. Not all acids react as expected when mixed with water."

Brady nodded at Doug then turned to Olivia. "Doug is correct about the danger. But you're right. The only way we can make this work is to form this into a paste." He gestured at the cup and shrugged. "I'll use just the minimum amount of water and hope it provides the anticipated result."

"So, like muffin batter," Olivia said, a haughty edge to her voice. "You want to barely dampen the dry ingredients. In muffins, too much stirring will make them tough."

Brady grinned at her, ignoring her tone completely. "Sounds like you know what you're doing. Why don't you mix it?" He thrust the cup into her hands and said, "Kat, give her a bottle of water. Don't forget to use the least amount of water possible to make the powder stick together. But the bond must be sufficient for Doug to launch it from his sling shot."

Doug grimaced, no doubt picturing the mess that would create, but didn't argue.

Olivia sat cross-legged on the ground and leaned forward over the cup. She tipped the bottle back and forth as if getting a feel for it. She caught her bottom lip with her teeth, then carefully tipped the water bottle, letting only a couple drops land in the powder. She gave a careful stir then tipped the bottle again. She kept working a couple drops into the cup at a time until she'd formed a thick, barely damp paste.

She sat back and grinned. "Tah dah!" She handed the cup and the bottle of water to Brady. "All yours."

He pulled about half the mixture out and formed it into a ball the size of a large marble. He handed it ceremoniously to Doug. "All yours," he echoed.

Doug shook his head and said, "How do I get this in the mouth?"

Brady looked surprised, then said, "I'm going to get it talking. As soon as I do, you shoot."

Brady moved a few steps closer and called out, "We are all impressed with your range and accuracy. I noticed that you are fixed in place, but still able to aim in various directions. I would be very interested to hear how you accomplish that."

The sculpted eyebrows on the door knocker lifted for a moment, looking intrigued by the question. Then it frowned and clamped thin bronze lips together, displaying its disinterest in explaining itself to interlopers.

Brady took another step forward and tried again, "Do you create that acid each time, or are you able to draw upon a reservoir as needed?"

Again it showed a brief moment of interest. Before it could decide to ignore him again, Brady took another step forward so that his feet were only inches from the farthest reach of its acidic spit. "We were discussing it." Brady pointed to the pitted ground where the acid had eaten into the dirt in front of his feet. He tipped his head to the side and said. "I think you can do more than this, but the others don't believe you have the capacity to reach any farther."

I hoped Brady knew what he was doing, because from where I was standing he looked like a sitting duck.

At least he'd finally got the reaction he'd been looking for. The face on the door knocker glowered at the rest of us, then opened its mouth. I'm not sure what it planned to say because from behind my left shoulder came a thwanging sound, and the thickened ball of alkaline powder flew past my ear and hit the knocker on the side of the head.

It began to curse and howl. "Miserable simple-minded deceivers! Impudent mealy-mouthed tricksters! Foolish pathetic worm-meat!"

Brady quickly threw the cup to Doug, who scooped out the remaining paste. He pinched it quickly into a semi-round shape and let loose again while the knocker was still cursing.

This time his aim was dead on. The ball flew directly into the mouth, causing it to sputter and swallow in surprise. I sucked in my breath, hoping this would work. And if it did work, I wondered how that thing would react. And how long we'd have to wait before we knew.

Not long. Like nearly instantaneous. It began to choke and gasp, sounding worse by the second. A dark mist issued from its nostrils. The bronze face first dulled then turned a pitted green. It gave a long, shuddering groan before its eyes rolled back in its head. A blackened, swollen tongue suddenly and violently protruded from between sharp teeth that now looked half rotted. With a final gurgle, it stilled.

Brady started to climb up onto the porch. Doug pushed past me and caught Brady's arm. "It could be faking. Be careful."

Brady nodded quickly and hurled the bottle of water into the knocker. Part of the cheek shattered and fell in small chunks onto the porch. There was no other reaction so the two of them moved forward. Brady paused to pick up the half full bottle and handed it to me.

"Eeeeow. You're not going to drink out of that are you?" Olivia asked, horrified. "After it touched that thing?"

Brady gaped at Olivia for a moment like he couldn't make sense of the question. Then he said, "We don't have to drink out of it. But I'm not leaving any plastic bottles lying around in here. The mess we're making in our own world is bad enough."

"Oh. That's, ah…that's good." I'd never heard Olivia at such a loss for words and almost laughed out loud.

He merely shrugged, then reached out and opened the door. I was wondering what could possibly be kept in a house with such an elaborate defense system, so I entered hesitantly and took a minute to look around.

The first glimpse left me unsettled; relieved and uneasy at the same time.

Chapter 14/April/Chimera

Signs

The walls were covered with strange signs I couldn't read. Some looked very old; the inked shapes faded, the paper yellow and cracked. Others looked relatively new, or at least extremely well preserved. All of them were in fancy gold frames decked out with ornate carvings.

Brady yanked the map out of his pocket and wished to see anything Ghalynn wanted us to find or anything else important. When nothing showed up he sighed. "The rest of you see if you can find anything important in this place." He waved his hand at one of the walls. "I'll start translating all this."

He shrugged out of his pack and settled cross-legged on the floor. I started to offer him a pencil and paper, but caught myself in time. He didn't need to write anything down. He had an eidetic memory. Duh. He'd remember everything he looked at.

I moved off into what looked like a guest room. Fortunately, it was sparsely furnished with no pictures or signs. I was done with it and the next two rooms in maybe half an hour. When I started to go into the next room, Doug bumped into me as he came out of it. He grabbed my arm and said, "It's okay, the rest has all been checked. Let's see what Brady's found."

Brady was sitting where we'd left him. Exactly where we'd left him. I could swear he hadn't moved.

"Anything cool?" Doug asked.

"The houses we've been searching today belonged to the Council members," he answered and waved at an ornate plaque by the front door.

"The people that banished Ronny?" I asked, feeling a nearly overwhelming desire to destroy something in their houses. Just like they'd tried to destroy Ronny's life.

Before I could actually act on that thought, Rusty barked and his claws scrabbled on the door. It popped open far enough for Shadow to push her way inside. She moved a few feet to the side of the door and made several gagging sounds. Then she threw up a large wet mess on the floor. She met my eyes and I could swear she was grinning. Then she turned, tail held high, and sauntered back outside.

Doug asked what that was about, clearly mystified, but I burst out laughing. Shadow had understood what I wanted even without my making a wish.

Brady spoke up and stopped my laughter. "Apparently there are seven Council members, one of whom is…was…Ronny's mother."

"Is," I said emphatically. "I know she's missing, but until we know why, we're going to say *is*, not was."

Brady opened his mouth. He had on his logical professor look and I was sure he was about to argue with me. Then he looked at my face and said, "We can call it whatever you want. Whatever tense you use doesn't change reality."

I decided I didn't want to know what he meant by that.

Doug asked, "What's the rest of this stuff say?"

"Most appear to be mottos of different kinds." Brady said, switching off his logical professor face with a grin. "This one reminded me of you, 'A chain is no stronger than its weakest link'."

Doug laughed, "Right back at you."

"There are several I've heard before. For example: 'Desperate times call for desperate measures.' Then there's 'Straight from the horse's mouth'."

Faith clapped her hands. "I've heard those. Are there more?"

Brady grinned and shot a quick glance at Olivia. "I'm happy to oblige. Guess my work on translations is finally paying off?" The words should have been a statement, but he said them like a question. Probably because Olivia had given him plenty of trouble over the years about how slow his translations were. Olivia merely rolled her eyes and Brady's grin grew wider. Well, if it had been anyone other than Brady, I'd have said it was a smirk.

"There are some I've never heard before," Brady admitted "Like 'Put not your faith in Echoes'."

"Are any of them useful?" Faith asked.

"Some of the language is extremely archaic," he told her. "I think some are based on sayings from the 16th and 17th centuries. There isn't anything particularly useful, unless you count being told 'Swamps can cause night chills."

Olivia snorted. "Ugh! Not even!"

"But that one," he gestured to a large, elaborate sign that took up most of one wall, "you will all recognize."

As he began speaking, my blood iced, making me shiver. I wrapped my arms around my waist and wished he'd stop. Even worse, Doug's wristband, the one we'd found in the dragon cave, gave a quick flash of blue-green light as Brady spoke. I'd seen it do that a few other times and still had no idea why.

Time shall come when silence rules
Echoes of what was remain
East and South dark MALICE pools
Set loose as protections wane.

Two worlds WITH one dire test
With the entrance breached by man
Mundane MAGICK marks the quest
Fate awaits the final plan

Only clear to those with Sight
Direction is necessity
Paths revealed within the Light
Resolution is the Key

Greed with evil SPELLS entwine
Without courage faith will quail
Magick and Mundane COMBINE
For one without the other fail

ANNIHILATION

He put the emphasis in the same places where the words had been carved deeper and heavier into the cave wall where we'd first seen them. Three years ago.

Brady took another quick look around, then shrugged. "I don't think there's anything else for us here. I guess we should head back."

I still felt chilled at finding the Annihilation Prophecy displayed on the wall. Leaving sounded like a great idea. "Yeah, let's get out of here!"

Chapter 15/April/Santa Ramona

Lightning

On the way back to the tree, I noticed a single house sitting alone. It was a small wooden structure without the same well maintained look of the other houses we'd seen. Instead it looked…forlorn. "We haven't searched that one yet," I said, pointing.

Brady stopped and pulled out the map. "It's not indicated on the map," he said, frowning. "In fact," he looked at the house again and glanced up and down the road near it. "In fact," he repeated, "there has never been a house here before."

Now that he mentioned it, I didn't remember seeing it before either. Of course, Olivia tried to argue with him. "You're, what? Trying to say the house was invisible before?"

He looked at her and said, "I have no idea if it was invisible, hiding on another plane of existence, or if it moved here from some other part of Chimera. What I'm saying is I haven't seen it here before."

Olivia snorted and muttered, "Other plane of existence." But I noticed she didn't say anything else.

"Should we check it out?" Faith didn't sound excited by the idea and I didn't blame her.

Olivia moved as if she was going to place her hands on her hips, then winced. She touched the bandage on her arm and gave a tight smile. "I wish this didn't hurt," she said, so quiet the others didn't hear. But I did. I opened my mouth to remind her not to wish in here, but her expression stopped me. She looked amazed, then excited, then grateful, and ripped off the bandage.

She touched her arm, gently at first, then harder.

The charred skin had turned the healthy, shiny pink of new scar tissue, and the pitted hole had mostly filled in, leaving a shallow dent about the size of a pencil eraser. I was worried the small scar would bother her, but she was smiling. A real smile.

"No," Doug bit out, "I may not have a special watch, but I can tell it's getting late." He was staring at Olivia's arm suspiciously. He hadn't heard her wish but must have suspected something.

Brady glanced at his wrist then said what I think started as a curse. But he glanced at Olivia, and it merely came out a strangled mess. "Oh, shee-no-dar-um-heck. We've got to go!"

Faith and I were fighting giggles over that one, but Olivia actually smiled at him. We started down the road, Rusty and Shadow moving ahead while the other animals followed or flew over us. I was grateful they never listened to the call of nature while flying over our heads.

Although Pyg *had* purposefully pooped on the Rejects on more than one occasion. Just to make Olivia happy.

We made good time back to the tree, and crossing into the cemetery went quickly. Which was good and bad. I was really glad I hadn't gotten stuck in the tree for a long time. But there was nothing to distract me, and I kept worrying about the Annihilation Prophecy. Something was nagging at me. Something Brady had said while we were in the house. I just wished I could remember what it was.

In the cemetery, the feeling in the air made me forget everything. There was a distinctive buzzing, like the air itself was filled with electricity. And directly overhead dark clouds were gathering, low and thick and oppressively dark.

Doug yelled, "Let's get out of here. It feels like a magic storm."

I could swear the angel statues near the tree were watching us. There was nothing creepier than knowing, bone deep, that a trace of dark intelligence lurked behind those featureless faces. I whipped out my phone and took several pictures in rapid succession, then realized I might have made a serious mistake.

One blank face turned, ever so slightly, in my direction. It was watching me.

I didn't bother saying anything to the others. I just ran.

No one questioned my headlong rush; it had begun to sprinkle. I did consider mentioning what had happened, but was sure they'd just dismiss it. Somehow, I needed to prove that those statues could move. I had to find something that not even skeptical Brady could ignore. Maybe another magic storm would prove my case once and for all. Knowing I was hoping that would happen made me feel slightly guilty. Okay a lot guilty. But the others *had* to stop ignoring those statues.

-xXx-

They say you should be careful what you wish for. The storm raged that night and all day Sunday. Blinding torrents of rain. Massive gusts of wind that rattled the doors and windows and howled under the eaves. Sudden bursts of golf-ball sized hail, pounding against the roof like they'd been shot from a canon. I cowered in bed with the pillow over my head and curled into a fetal position during the long hours of the night.

The worst part was the massive strikes of blue lightning. They punched out of the sky and slammed into the ground with explosive force. Where they crashed into the ocean, they sizzled and hissed, producing huge geysers of steam that shot skyward with a roar. Even from blocks away, I could hear it.

I slept fitfully and was up in time to witness what should have been the dawn on Sunday. The thick clouds darkened the sky, but enough light entered my room that I was fairly sure I'd be safe from any possible beast-monster beneath my bed. I stood up and bounced on the mattress a few times, then took a flying leap that carried me halfway across the room. And even though I'd never been attacked anywhere other than next to my bed, I covered the distance to the bathroom in mere seconds.

When I got back to the doorway to my room, I hesitated. I was still tired and eyed my bed longingly, but decided I'd have to be a complete and utter idiot to risk getting close to it while the storm still raged outside. If anything, the storm was growing worse.

I went downstairs and found a note from Mom on the refrigerator.

I've gone to the Library. The leak is back; worse than ever.

There's not enough staff available, so I've taken Dad to help shift some of the books to a safe location. We'll probably be gone several hours, but I'll have my cell phone if you need to reach us.

We love you, sweetie.

P.S Stay in the house; no going outside in this storm.

I glanced out the window and sighed. Who wanted to go outside in this, anyway?

I poured myself a bowl of cereal, then sat on the couch to read. The sounds from the storm outside kept growing louder and more violent. I jumped at a tremendous crash and rushed to look out at the backyard. A large branch had broken off one of our trees, narrowly missing the glass-topped patio table.

As I stood at the window I watched in amazement as bits of debris, empty cardboard boxes, roof tiles and small signs went flying over the house, held aloft by the furious winds. Then something dropped without warning, barely missing the sliding-glass window where I was standing. I decided it was high time to back away from all that oh-so-breakable glass.

Every time lightning flashed and thunder drummed through the sky I cringed. I managed to lose my place in the book so many times I finally tossed it aside. There was no point trying to read during this.

I picked up my phone and tried calling Faith, but there was no ring. Instead, there was a deafening burst of static. Only, it wasn't just static.

My fingers tightened involuntarily around my phone. I'd heard this before. There was something under that crackle-rasp-hiss; something that made a crazy jumble of sound. Roaring, muffled grunts, screeching, high-pitched laughter, distant screams. And coming over everything else, ear-piercingly loud, were howls. Just like angry trolls make. I knew that sound.

And buried down deep, under all the other noise was the hint of words being chanted. Indistinct and guttural. Not quite human.

I turned my phone off and set it down so quickly it bounced on the table and nearly fell onto the floor. Okay, it might have been more like tossing it rather than setting it down. But I didn't want to so much as touch it, not until the storm was over. My heart was still beating so hard I pressed my hand against my chest. As if that could prevent it from pounding its way out.

-xXx-

The storm didn't slacken until it was too late to go to the cemetery to check the angel statues on Sunday or before school on Monday. Besides I'd decided that this time I shouldn't go alone. Considering how bad the storm had been, I was seriously freaked out about going to the cemetery by myself. Though if anyone else said so, I'd deny it. They already thought I was over-reacting.

I might have been a bit on edge that morning — who could blame me. And yes, I might have overreacted when Mom told me my skirt was too short right as I was heading out the door for school. What was up with that? It was a totally normal length; just how everyone wore skirts! But she refused to listen, so I finally stormed out of the house. By the time I met up with the others, I was absolutely determined *they* were going to listen. After some argument, they agreed, reluctantly, to go to the cemetery with me after school. Before we went to see Ronny.

At lunch, Olivia kept snarking at Brady, but he managed to stay pleasant. Or at least polite. As we left the cafeteria, I whispered to Faith, "Do you have any idea why Olivia keeps sniping at Brady? It's giving me a headache."

She grinned and shook her head, then whispered back, "No kidding. I have *no* idea. Maybe you should ask her."

I'm not sure what my expression did, but it made Faith laugh and add, "Yeah, better you than me!"

The rest of the day passed in a blur. I kept wondering what we'd find when we looked at the angels that afternoon. Had they moved again? Would the others finally be able to see what I saw?

Were they finally going to admit I was right?

I was practically jittering with a disturbing mix of excitement and trepidation when we met up after the last bell that afternoon. But then Doug said, "Why do we need to waste our time going to the cemetery? We should go straight to Ronny's." My resentment must have been clear on my face, because he said quickly, "It's just that I have a sh—um, significant load of homework tonight."

I gritted my teeth together so hard they felt like they were going to crack, but my irritation spilled out anyway. "I don't ask for much, right? But right now I'm asking, make that begging, for you to come to the cemetery with me."

I heard Olivia groan behind me and turned on her. "I'll make it a Blood Sister request if I have to."

She cocked her head to one side and stared at me for a moment before asking, "It's *that* important?"

"Absolutely," I assured her, meeting her eyes with what I hoped was a look of steely determination.

It must have worked. She turned to Faith and lifted an eyebrow. Just one eyebrow — I still didn't know how she did that. Faith sighed but turned to Doug and Brady. "We're going to the cemetery. What are you guys doing?"

Doug rolled his eyes. "I guess we're visiting the cemetery. This better be good, Kat."

I passionately wished I'd taken the time to check out those statues this morning, raining or not, but it was too late now. We walked fast, knowing Ronny was waiting, and made it there in less than fifteen minutes. I managed a small smile as Olivia leapt about; she still couldn't bear to walk over graves.

Brady had been watching her too. "You know," he said, "it's not uncommon for the ground to shift in cemeteries. Bodies become offset and end up to one side or the other rather than directly in line with headstones."

She froze, one foot lifted off the ground, ready for her next leap. She wavered there, gaping at him in horror. "Why are you so mean, Brady?"

He frowned in confusion. "What do you mean?"

She carefully lowered her foot and said, "What do I mean? I mean that you're mean! Why would you say something like that to me? Now I won't know where to step."

"Oh. Uh...well...it's not like they care anymore. Scientifically, either life ceases altogether when you die, or your spirit, being a form of energy, leaves the body and goes somewhere else. Regardless of which is correct, there's no evidence that something hangs around after death, worrying about someone stepping on their grave."

"You obviously haven't seen enough horror movies," she told him, her nose tilted up in an I-know-more-than-you-do attitude. "Everyone knows you should avoid stepping on graves."

"Horror movies? You don't step on graves because you believe the movies?" Brady stopped, his mouth opening and closing like a fish. He seemed to be literally speechless. I had to turn away to hide my grin.

Faith linked arms with Olivia. "Don't worry, we'll go together. I actually agree with Brady, but just in case, nothing's going to take both of us on."

After that, it took only a couple minutes to get near the tree. I slowed down and tightened my hands into fists, sure the others were going to tell me I was imagining things again.

I needn't have worried. Brady exclaimed, "How did *that* happen?"

There was another trail of broken grass and disturbed mud leading from the statue's previous location. It was two or three feet closer to the tree than it had been on Saturday. And it had turned nearly 90 degrees; now it was facing the tree. I felt suddenly chilled and shivered even though I was wearing polar fleece.

Note to self – A picture may be worth a thousand words, but a picture can't beat seeing something in person.

"*Now* do those angels freak anyone else out?" I couldn't help the fierce grin that flashed across my face, but managed to keep my voice low. Even though they were carved from stone, I couldn't bear the thought of them hearing me.

"Don't talk about them," Olivia said, her voice so low I could barely hear it. "They might be listening."

Should I feel grateful I was not, finally, the only one worried about that? Or should it creep me out even more?

Brady didn't look grateful *or* creeped out. In fact, he was looking at Olivia in disappointment. He cleared his throat and said, "They are pieces of rock that have been carved to represent Biblical figures. They are not now, nor have they ever been, alive. And they certainly can't hear us."

Olivia shook her head. "You're so close-minded, Brady." She pointed at the tree, just a few feet away. "They're right next to a magic door, remember? What if they're magic too? What if they're, how would *you* say it? Awake? Aware? No, I've got it. Sentient."

Brady's voice was stiff as he replied, "That would be the correct word, but your concept is inconceivable. Stone isn't magic; it's inanimate. It is scientifically impossible for stone to become sentient."

I'm sure that was normally true, but Brady had forgotten we were talking about magic, not science. The whole idea of magic bothered him. He'd only started talking like it really existed in the last few months.

"I think we need to ask Ronny," Faith said in a hushed voice.

I bit my lip; that was a good suggestion under normal circumstances. But lately, Ronny's circumstances had been anything but normal. "We have to play that by ear. She may be too sick. You know Chris doesn't want us to upset her."

Even though this would be a good time, I couldn't bring myself to talk to the others about my argument with Mom. She'd stopped me on my way to bed and told me not to bother Ronny. She'd actually suggested we should cancel our visit after school. I'd tried to explain that Ronny wanted us there, but she wasn't listening. So I'd finally yelled that Ronny had asked us to come. When that didn't work I told her she didn't know anything about it and stomped out of the room.

I hoped *I* was right, and Mom and Chris were just being over-protective.

Chapter 16/May/Chimera

Need A Magic Cloak? A Cauldron? How About A Wand?

By the time we got to Ronny's, I was sick of talking about those statues. Maybe I shouldn't have dragged the others to see them. What was the point of discussing them ad naseum? None of us knew how, or why, they'd moved.

Faith kept suggesting they were probably nice, like they were trying to protect the magic doorway.

Doug and Brady were sticking to Brady's 'maybe someone just snuck in and moved them' theory.

Olivia seemed torn. I think she liked that theory, but didn't want to agree with Brady. I merely snorted when she told me, for the second time, "Think about it, Kat. That's all I'm saying. There might be nothing creepy about them after all!"

I'd pretty much decided nothing was creepier than listening to the four of them talking about those statues. And it was all my fault. I was the one who'd dragged them there and insisted they look. I'd only wanted them to acknowledge what was happening.

Note to self – Mom was right. Be careful what you wish for; you might just get it!

When we finally made it to Chris and Ronny's, it was Chris who answered the door. And he wasn't happy to see us. He frowned at me and snapped, "Keep this short!"

One look at Ronny made it clear we weren't going to talk about creepy angel statues today. I could see a small heater next to her chair, blasting out heat. Even so, she was in sweat pants and a t-shirt, a blanket wrapped around her, though it must be close to 80° in the living room. She had her hands wrapped tightly around a steaming cup of tea and looked half asleep.

What was doing this to her? She was growing worse by the day. And, I realized, a ball of selfish misery dancing around my stomach, I wasn't just worried about her and Chris.

There might be a day we wouldn't be able to talk to her anymore. What would happen to us then? Could we visit Chimera with no one to help? Or would we have to give up? I'd come to count on her giving us information. Encouragement. Giving us a reason to keep going...

Brady explained how we'd checked the Council's houses and hadn't found anything important, other than the Annihilation Prophecy on one wall.

Ronny gave a weak smiled that flickered then died. Her voice sounded hoarse. "That must be Council Member Serenitrekwars. He has every famous saying, good or bad, ever written." She gave a wistful smile. "Mystic was a marvelous place to grow up. People were so polite. Of course, I realize now that the Mimps running around town may have had something to do with that."

"Mimps?" I hadn't heard of those before. Was there something else we had to avoid in Chimera?

"Singly, they are not imposing," she said. "Not with their small, pale green triangular bodies and stubby arms and legs. But they travel in groups." She coughed twice, and held her hand to her chest as if it hurt her. When she spoke again her voice was lower, and scratchier. "Mimps must never be harmed. They are connected to the magick of Chimera, though no one knows exactly how. It is speculated that they were born of the magickal residue from its creation."

"Why would someone harm them? Will they try to hurt us?" Faith clasped her fingers together, but kept her hands in her lap.

Ronny managed a brief flash of animation when she answered, "They hate all arguments and raised voices. You must never yell near a Mimp. They race en masse toward the one who is yelling, waving those little arms, uttering high-pitched screeches loud enough to make your ears ring. And all the while, they giggle maniacally."

She smiled, then fell silent for a moment. "They hurl anything within reach at the ones who are arguing. Due to their small stature, they do not cause serious damage. Normally." She started to laugh then coughed hard and long, a deep, harsh sound that left her struggling for breath.

I jumped to my feet. "Well, that's all we've got for now. We should get going." I flashed a quick smile that felt awkward and phony. Hopefully she wouldn't notice. "Good seeing you. I hope you feel better next time!"

We made it out of that house in under a minute. Chris' voice, a faintly whispered, "Thank you," floated quietly behind me.

What had started as a pleasant place to visit was rapidly becoming something else. It felt like visiting someone in the hospital who might never leave there. The five of us stared at each other. None of us said it, but we all knew we were pretty much on our own now.

-xXx-

For once school didn't include the usual desperate attempts to avoid the Rejects. Ray wasn't there. He'd gone to France for a two week 'educational' vacation with his parents. And lo and behold, the others lost interest in harassing us without Ray there. I couldn't help wishing that Ray's family would just decide to stay there. Forever.

The next two weeks went by way too fast. I practically felt like *I* was the one on vacation. It didn't help that I was dreading the next Saturday. We'd be going back to Chimera without being able to count on Ronny for anything. And, of course, Ray would be back in time to go too. It was probably useless to hope that his parents wouldn't want him to be gone his first day home.

Worse than that, we'd have to walk by the statues in the cemetery. By the one that moved and turned to face the tree. That was freaking me out. What if they were like *Dr. Who's* weeping angels? What if there was something horrible hidden behind those blank faces?

When Saturday came, I was nearly hyperventilating by the time we got near them.

I hung back, profoundly relieved when everyone walked in a wide arc around the one closest to the tree. I'd hoped, though I knew it was unlikely, that it had moved less than I remembered. But if anything, it looked even worse this time.

If we weren't back in the oldest part of the cemetery, the part where no one but us went anymore, someone would have noticed. But back here, I didn't think anyone ever would.

-xXx-

This passage was a bad one. I'd known it from the instant I sank into the cold, clammy darkness inside the tree. I was so frightened by that feeling, I forgot to start counting. And not knowing how long I'd been trapped made it so much worse. My chest was making small involuntary contractions, fighting against my knowledge there was *no air*. My lungs were sure they should try to breathe, no matter what.

My mind knew it would be so much worse.

When I was finally propelled from the tree I bent over, hands on my knees, sucking air into my starved lungs. I wasn't the only one; the others were all gasping as they stepped into Chimera. I managed to quip, "Brady, you have to create some way for us to breathe in there."

He lifted his head a few inches and glared at me from the corner of his eye. "What makes you think I haven't tried?"

Excitement welled up; I opened my mouth to ask him to explain, but he shook his head and let it droop against his chest. "Do I look like I've had any luck with that?" he asked.

My shoulders slumped, as excitement leaked out. Then he added, "I have no intention of abandoning my analysis of the phenomenon, I assure you. If successful, you all will be the first, figuratively speaking, to be informed of it."

Olivia's voice was hoarse, as if she'd been screaming in the tree. "You'll be my best friend if you can make that easier." She straightened slowly and rolled her neck in a circle, eyes closed.

Which meant she missed the fleeting look of longing on Brady's face. He turned away and muttered, "Yeah, coming up with helpful ideas is what I'm good for."

His voice was so quiet I barely heard it, or the thin edge of pain it held. Olivia was far enough away that she didn't hear it at all.

I turned to her and whispered, "Why are you so mean to Brady?"

She raised her eyebrows and muttered back, "I don't know what you're talking about."

"Yes, you do," I insisted, fighting to keep my voice down as Faith glanced over. Of course, it was really Faith's fault I'd started this. She'd told me to ask.

Olivia glared at me a moment, but maybe my anxious…serious…hopeful expression won her over. Or maybe it was nearly thirteen years of friendship.

"I don't know," she growled. "Something about him rubs me the wrong way. He makes me feel…twitchy."

"Twitchy?" My voice rose and I coughed when she glared at me again. I whispered back, "Uh, okay then. I guess."

She snorted and turned away.

I was glad when Shadow distracted me. She leapt into my arms and rubbed her head against my face, purring madly. I wondered if she knew how hard that trip had been.

I heard the others greeting their animals. I put Shadow down when Brady pulled out the map. He pointed to a group of houses near the far end of Mystic. "That's where we're heading." He grabbed a branch and cleared our foot prints from the road.

I choked briefly when he got a bit over enthusiastic with the sweeping, creating a small cloud of dust.

"How many kinds of houses do you think are in here?" Olivia asked. "We've seen fairytale cottages, ultra-modern ranch houses and McMansions. What else could there be?"

Brady closed his eyes for a moment, then began reciting. "Roman, Gothic, Renaissance, Baroque and Tudor. Georgian would certainly be possible. However, if the people living here traveled extensively in the United States, they could have also been influenced by Spanish, Cape Cod, Antebellum, Craftsman, or A-frame styles."

He was so busy talking, it took him a minute to realize we'd all stopped to stare at him. "Is that all?" Olivia asked, and a smile tugged at the corner of her mouth.

"Oh no. There's also saltbox, shotgun, brownstone," he caught sight of Olivia's smile, which had gotten out of her control and blossomed over her face. He finished lamely, "And…uh….numerous other styles of architecture."

Doug clapped him on the back. "It must be fascinating to be in your brain."

Brady's cheeks flushed a bright crimson and he grimaced. "Not really. It's obviously full of too much useless information."

I rushed to fill the sudden silence. "You can't know that it's useless. It might all be important…someday."

He grinned weakly. "Thanks Kat."

Doug started walking, throwing over his shoulder, "Enough with the Architectural Digest lesson. Let's go."

I rolled my eyes, but fell in behind him. After three years, Doug still liked to act like he was the boss. Clearly I hadn't done enough to convince him otherwise.

After a short distance, Brady handed Doug the branch and took the lead, map in hand. He held it closer, then shoved at his glasses which were slipping down his nose. He led us over the bridge — still, thankfully —with no hint of the bridge troll, and past the houses we'd already checked. He finally turned off onto a well-worn path that ended in a small cluster of buildings.

It took me a minute to realize they weren't houses. They seemed to be small shops; a cross between ToonTown and Diagon Alley. There was something off about them, like the perspective was wrong. Some leaned toward each other, or out over the street. Some appeared larger on the top than the bottom. Most were two stories, though some seemed more like two and a half on one side or the other. The doors weren't perfect rectangles. One was nearly circular in shape. None of the corners on the windows were squared off. Some were closer to 45 degree angles rather than the normal 90 degrees. But all of the windows, no matter their shape, were filled with colorful…stuff.

Chapter 17/May/Chimera

Mystic Alley?

I was fascinated to see what types of things a magic town would have for sale. I couldn't get Harry Potter out of my head, and caught myself humming snatches of the movie soundtracks. I sucked in an excited breath as we entered the first, then let it back out again.

It was some kind of herb shop. There was a short counter on one side, a long bench covered with gardening tools on the other, and a wobbly stack of cauldrons in one corner. The ceiling was difficult to see since it was at least two stories above us, but it looked fuzzy. It took me a moment of peering into the dim shadows to understand why.

Strange plants hung upside down from every square inch of the ceiling. Some were green — lots of weird shades of green — while others were covered with flowers. I'd have liked a closer look at some of them, but one large bunch looked like they were covered with shiny black beetles. Those I had no desire to see any closer.

The small shop was filled with a heavy, nearly overpowering scent of rosemary, lavender, gardenia, jasmine, lemon and sage. Faith's eyes began to water and Doug began sneezing uncontrollably.

"Wait outside," I said, motioning for the others to leave. Fortunately, there was only one small drawer in the counter and it took only seconds to check it before I could join them outside in the clear air.

I laughed as soon as I got a look at Doug. Rusty was alternately washing Doug's face and sneezing all over it. When Doug heard me, he quickly set Rusty down and turned away to wipe his face on his t-shirt.

"Maybe we should take our animals into the shops with us," Olivia said, petting Pyg's feathers where the owl perched on her head.

"I can't believe you suggested that," Faith said. "Don't you remember what happened in the first house?"

"Maybe we should let our animals decide which shops they need to enter with us," I said thoughtfully. After all, they *were* there to help us.

Doug considered this then nodded slowly. "I think we could trust them to decide if they need to go inside."

"They are very intelligent. I've said that before. But to expect them to decide when they should enter a shop isn't logical." Brady looked tired for a moment, like the need to keep explaining logic to us exhausted him. "They don't have the capacity to weigh alternatives and make informed decisions."

Olivia sniffed. "Why can't you ever remember that this is a magic place?" She turned and smiled at Doug. "I agree with Doug. And Kat."My name sounded like she'd tacked it on as an after-thought. My questions about Brady *had* upset her.

"You know my position," Brady said. "So do not blame me if Rusty gets over-excited and knocks things over."

Doug bent over and scratched behind Rusty's ears. "You won't make a mess, will you boy." Rusty barked enthusiastically and Doug laughed.

We were a bit hesitant when we got to the second shop. It was made of whitewashed bricks, with patches of paint missing here and there, showing the brown brick underneath. The windows were filled with bottles and jars and cauldrons, hanging glass globes of all shapes and sizes, and strange brass objects used for who knew what. A black sign, chipped and weathered, stated *Magickal Equipment* in elegant gold paint.

"Think this is a place that sells magical cooking implements?" Faith asked.

"We'll see soon enough," Olivia said and turned toward the door. I followed her, and noticed that our animals chose to stay outside. I hoped that was a good thing.

Inside, the room was dark and musty, with dust motes swirling through the few shafts of light entering the high windows. There was something wrong with that but it took a moment to figure out. This was one of the only places I'd seen dust anywhere in town.

Half the building was about one story tall, but the other half was far taller. Hanging from the ceiling in the tall end were long strings of black and copper cauldrons, some tarnished, some shiny, while the rest of the space was filled with shelf upon shelf of…clutter.

"What is all this?" Faith lifted a jar filled with a pale pink liquid. It swirled with hints of bright silver every time it moved.

I picked up a tall bottle shaped like Mom's salad dressing carafe. This one shot out pale beams of light when I moved it, spilling a warm glow onto the floor and ceiling. "No wonder they kept it so dim in here," I said. "This stuff is beautiful in the dark."

Olivia stopped by a jar filled with deep cobalt blue spheres. She picked it up, lifting it to eye level, then shrieked. It fell from her slack fingers, landing back on the table with a thud. I stepped back quickly and gagged. The jar was filled with eyeballs. They'd all opened and stared intently at Olivia. But when I moved, they all swiveled to peer at me. Looking at the variety of colors, those eyeballs were clearly not human. Or, at least, not all of them were human.

"Don't pick up anything on the shelves," Brady ordered. "Just examine the drawers and cupboards. It's improbable that anything of importance to us would be stored in plain sight."

"Maybe," I groused. "Though we still have no idea what we're looking for."

Other than my brief mutter, no one said anything. We tip-toed around that space, careful not to touch anything. That was easier said than done since several aisles were so narrow I had to turn sideways to get through. A couple times, I had to drop to my hands and knees and crawl.

That actually began to seem like a very practical way to get around. Until I bumped into a table leg.

Everything above me clattered, clanked, rocked, and jiggled, sounding like it was all about to rain down on my head. I rolled into a ball, hands clasped behind my neck, and gave a quick prayer nothing would topple off. It seemed to take forever before everything settled back into place.

When I slowly climbed to my feet, everyone was staring at me, wide eyed. "What?" I asked, nervously. I glanced down and saw that one bottle had fallen on its side. The cork in the top had come loose and a thin line of black liquid had run from the bottle, snaking across the table and ending only a fraction of an inch from the edge. Right where my head had been.

I felt first hot, then cold. Very cold. The wooden table top was smoking everywhere that liquid had touched. A pale green smoke that smelled like singed wood, scorched sugar and burnt popcorn.

"Everyone stay still," Brady ordered. He opened the map and wished to see anything we needed to find in this shop. His shoulders slumped; obviously nothing had appeared this time either.

At the far end there were only a few drawers and cupboards to search, which didn't take long. I shut the drawer I had looked through harder than I meant to. The map had been right; there was nothing useful in here.

It took much longer than it should have to make our way back to the entrance, dodging carefully through the stacks and shelves, but we made it without further incident. I glanced back one last time, and caught sight of the eyeballs inside the jar. They'd all closed again, looking like nothing more than innocent blue circles.

The sun felt warm and clean against my skin when we got outside. I'd just squatted down to pet Shadow when I heard slamming, crashing sounds. I straightened up and turned in time to see layers of bricks, wood and metal — some shiny and others tarnished — closing over the windows and the door. Some layers slammed down, others across, still others diagonally. They didn't just slam. Some crashed while others banged, thumped and crunched.

There would be no getting back into that place.

No one spoke until, at last, everything fell silent. Then Faith shoved her hands into her pockets and bit her lip before blurting, "What would've happened if we were still in there?"

Brady shook his head. "There's no point in speculation. It didn't occur and it is my belief that whatever spell was triggered did not intend to trap us in there."

"That sounds like wishful thinking, not scientific reasoning," Olivia said.

"No, it's not conjecture, it's a theory based on a review of the available facts. We were in there for twenty-seven minutes. We," he glanced quickly at Olivia and then at me, "dropped things or knocked them over. We weren't quiet or stealthy. Therefore, there was a substantial opportunity for a spell to take effect. It would be a fairly useless one if it was meant to trap us in there, but took so long that we were able to exit successfully." He shrugged. "Therefore, it is a reasonable hypothesis that the intent was to lock up after us."

Olivia opened her mouth to respond, but Doug spoke quickly. "Let's not stand here arguing. We have several shops to get through before we leave."

There was only one more on this side of the street, and two, no, make that three, on the other. The third was a short distance away from the others, and looked completely different. The shops were rough stone or brick, this other place was smaller and made out of wood. It looked…shabby. And next to it there were several more statues.

"Hey," Faith exclaimed, "isn't that the same house we saw before?"

"Don't be silly," Olivia said. "Houses don't move."

Brady gazed across the street, then stiffened and looked more intently. "That is the same house," he said. "Or one that is identical down to the scratch in the paint by the front door."

We all stared at it. "Maybe we should check it out next," Doug said.

"Not next," Brady said, shaking his head. "We need to finish checking the others first."

I could see where being all scientific and logical could be useful. There were times that Brady had figured out important things the rest of us might have missed. But no one would call Brady spontaneous. Not ever.

I followed him to the next building and sighed, wondering what horrors waited for us here as we slowly, carefully, entered.

-xXx-

This shop was completely different. It sparkled. Really sparkled. The sunlight streaming through the windows cast glittery splashes of color across the walls and ceiling and ran in dazzling rivers over the floor. The space was filled with small tables, and the walls were lined with crockery of all shapes, sizes and colors. One wall, behind a low counter, was filled with jars of what appeared to be different types of teas.

"I love tea," Olivia said, and stepped behind the counter. Before any of us could tell her to stop, she snagged one of the jars, twisted open the top, and took a deep sniff. A beatific smile crossed her face and she let her breath out in a long, slow sigh of pleasure. She passed the jar to me and I took a small, cautious sniff. The aroma of apples and cinnamon and honey and a dozen other bakery scents I couldn't make out combined into a smell that made me want to crawl inside the jar and live there.

I passed it to Faith just in time to catch the next jar Olivia thrust at me. She looked a bit like her cat when it had been into catnip. "Oh, George would really like this."

This jar smelled like blueberry pancakes and maple syrup and butter. And even though I'd had a good breakfast before leaving home that morning, my stomach growled and I suddenly craved a blueberry pancake.

I passed that jar to Faith and turned back in time to see Olivia take a whiff out of the next jar. She gagged and turned green, looking unsteady on her feet. She cleared her throat but still sounded half strangled. "Do not smell this one. Seriously. I don't know what it is, but it's nasty."

Faith plucked it out of her hand, made sure the lid was on tightly, then turned it over. That was the first time I realized there were descriptions listed on the bottom of the jars. Looking over her shoulder I read, "Goblin tea – Not for human consumption!"

Faith set it on the counter and said, "Maybe we'd better leave off smelling the merchandise."

Olivia coughed and rubbed her throat. When she spoke again, her voice was *far* lower and rougher than normal. "Yeah, no kidding." She clapped her hands over her mouth, looking appalled.

"What's wrong with your voice?" Faith asked.

Olivia cleared her throat and croaked, "I don't..." Now she looked frightened and I saw a hint of tears glaze her eyes. She cleared her throat again, so hard I was afraid she was going to damage it. But at least this time when she spoke, she sounded nearly normal. "I think it was something in that tea." She shot it a baleful glance. "Whatever you do, don't open it again. Not while I'm in here."

I giggled in relief, but Olivia must have thought I was laughing at her. She shot me a scathing look of annoyance and before I could apologize, she turned her back on me.

Brady stepped around the counter and said, "There's just the one drawer here, and it's empty. We can cross off this location." He pulled out a pencil and placed an 'x' over the store. Only he pressed a bit too hard and the pencil skittered across the paper, leaving a long jagged line of graphite.

A shiver went through me, though I wasn't sure why. "We should get out of here, before something else goes wrong."

Now I'd somehow managed to offend Brady. He turned his back on me as well. How had I managed to upset them both in one day? Heck, in less than five minutes. My shoulders slumped dejectedly as Olivia spun away and headed toward the entrance.

I followed her outside and scooped up Shadow, taking comfort from the feel of her soft fur as my mind raced over how to convince the two of them I hadn't meant to offend them.

We crossed the street, with me trailing slightly behind the others. Olivia and Faith gave exclamations of interest as they entered the next shop, but Doug and Brady were strangely silent. I followed them inside and understood why.

One wall was covered with hats. Mostly traditional witch hats. Well, the shape might be traditional, but the hats came in every color of the rainbow. Interspersed among the tall pointy hats hung cowboy hats, fedoras, fezzes, straw hats, and hats I couldn't begin to name. The next wall was covered with robes that looked like they'd been stolen from a Harry Potter set, although these also came in multiple colors. Vests covered a third wall. Velvet vests, satin vests, brocade vests, embroidered vests, striped vests, herringbone vests, and of course, single color vests in dozens of colors. The last wall was covered with scarves. Again, there was a distinctive resemblance to Harry Potter, but these were a wild mix of strident colors.

Bins stood in one corner, filled with knit gloves and socks in colors to match the scarves. I couldn't imagine what a large group of people, wearing all those colors, would look like. And sincerely hoped I'd never have to see it.

Faith walked over and picked up one of the most vile of the bunch – striped in what Mom called chartreuse green and fuchsia pink. It made my eyes cross if I looked at it too long.

Faith wrapped it around her neck and said, "It's too bad it's so short. I wish it was about twice as long."

I sucked in a breath, terrified by what might happen, but Faith laughed delightedly. The scarf doubled in length in seconds.

"Actually," Faith said, "I'd like it about four feet longer." My eyes nearly popped out of my head as it began to grow again, stopping when both ends nearly reached the floor.

"How did you do that?" Olivia sounded as surprised as I felt. "You didn't wish that time."

Faith laughed and pointed to a small sign covered with different languages; one of which was English. It said *Scarves - Pick Your Own Length.*

Olivia reached out and touched one. "I'd like you to be as long as you can get."

"No," I yelled and began edging towards the entrance. My mind was spinning with images of the scarf multiplying in size until it filled the entire shop and crushed us against the walls.

It did continue to grow for what seemed like an incredibly long time. The rest had followed me toward the door before it finally stopped. Olivia picked up one end and began folding it in two foot lengths. By the time she reached the other end, I guessed that it must be thirty feet long.

"Take that, Dr. Who," I said. Actually, an over-sized scarf was kinda cool; certainly better than weeping angels. I shuddered and fought that image out of my head.

Faith picked up another scarf. It wasn't really white, or cream, or any color I could lay my finger on, it was just…blank. "What do you think this one does?" she asked and handed it to me.

I shrugged and put it around my neck. Instantly, the colors began to change, until it matched my plaid shirt. Exactly. Down to the exact placement of the stripes. I pulled it off and held it out at arms-length. Instantly, the colors began to fade until it was once more just a blank scarf.

Doug came over, crossed his arms over his chest and tapped his foot impatiently. "While you all were playing dress-up, Brady and I checked this place out. There's nothing here." He turned away and said over his shoulder, "Let's go."

Olivia and I both hung the scarves we'd been holding back on the wall. Faith however, kept hers.

The next shop made me think of a Target. Or it would have, without some of the merchandise. The first hint that things were different was the carpets. The *flying* carpets. They zoomed and swooped around the ceiling, looking like something straight out of Aladdin, with fringe trailing behind them. I stopped and stared fascinated. So did Doug. "I'd love to ride one of those," he said. And unlike his dragon obsession, this time I agreed with him.

As we made our way deeper, parts looked perfectly normal. One section of the store held towels and sheets. Another was filled with cups and plates. Toward the back, there was a furniture section filled with chairs and couches of every style and color. The one thing they all had in common was how soft and inviting they looked. Doug flung himself down in one of the chairs. He laid his head back and closed his eyes, a look of utter delight on his face. As I watched, I could swear the chair snugged in around him. And did he sink a couple inches deeper?

Faith grabbed my arm. "Come on," she said and towed me to a particularly inviting couch. We sank into the corners and I sighed with pleasure. It felt like heaven. And I might have been right about the chair arranging itself around Doug. I could swear the couch was adjusting to me, some parts growing softer, others firmer, until it cradled me, perfectly.

I hadn't realized that I'd closed my eyes, totally blissed out, until Olivia spoke right next to me. "My turn. You've been hogging that couch for five minutes."

"Get your own couch," I grumbled.

"Not a chance. I want to try whatever is making you look like you just took a giant bite of hot fudge brownie topped with vanilla bean ice cream."

I reluctantly climbed to my feet, my muscles feeling like they'd forgotten how to cope with gravity.

Faith got up so Brady could take her spot. As soon as the two of them were seated, Olivia let out a surprised hiss. The couch was moving, slowly. It was growing shorter, bringing Olivia and Brady closer together. My mouth popped open as they ended up so close their knees were touching. Olivia scrambled further into her corner, pulling her legs up and wrapping her arms around them.

"Stop that, Brady," she said crossly.

"Stop what?" He sounded confused.

"Stop playing with the couch," she said, starting to sound angry.

"I'm not doing anything to the couch. I thought you were." There was a crease between Brady's eyebrows. The one he got when confronted by something that puzzled him.

"Of course I'm not doing this. Don't be ridiculous." She burrowed farther back as the couch grew shorter than a love seat and crossed into very wide chair territory. "It has to be you."

Brady jumped up and said furiously, "I don't lie. If I tell you it wasn't me, it wasn't!"

He stomped off toward the other side of the store and I watched fascinated as what Ronny had described as witch lamps turned on in that side of the shop. Clearly Brady had entered the lighting section.

We quickly split up and checked out the remaining parts of the shop. When we met back near the entrance, we all shook our heads. None of us found anything important.

"One more place," Brady said, "that we can cross off our list."

"One more place where we didn't find anything," Olivia muttered, an irritated frown wrinkling her forehead.

Well, that was certainly one way to look at it.

Right before we got to the door, Brady said wistfully, "I always wished I could ride on a flying carpet when I was a kid." I shot a quick glance at Doug and grinned. That made three of us. Brady turned toward the door so he didn't see the carpet swoop down from its place near the ceiling. It circled over his head then dove toward the back of his legs.

I yelled a warning, but it wasn't necessary. By the time it reached him, the carpet had slowed and merely tapped the back of his ankles gently.

"What was that?" Brady demanded. He whipped his head around to look behind him and his mouth fell open. The carpet reared back, then tapped against him once again. When he didn't react, it moved up and pushed against the back of his knees.

Brady shot it a look of amazement tinged with… disappointment? Then he said, "I'm sorry. I'd love to try you, but not today. We have to leave."

The carpet shuddered for a moment then stilled. With a look like a little boy that had been scolded by his mother, edges drooping, fringe dangling limply, the carpet slowly ascended toward the ceiling. After one more incredulous look, Brady turned and headed toward the door.

How could Brady refuse to try it? I don't care how big a hurry we're in, if I wanted to do something that much, I'd do it. I glanced at Doug again and amended that thought. Well, as long as it wasn't trying to ride a dragon, of course.

After a last wistful glance at the doorway, Brady grabbed a pencil out of his backpack, pulled the map out of his pocket, and crossed off that shop. Then he straightened his shoulders, turned his back on temptation, and said, "Well, there's just one more, then we can go home."

Chapter 18/May/Chimera

When You Can't Just *Read* A Book...

The next store made me smile; it was filled with books. Even without seeing the shelves of books, I'd have recognized it as a book store or library. It was filled with the scent of old paper and ink, mixed with leather and cloth and glue. I inhaled deeply, feeling right at home. Not surprising, really, since my mom was the town's librarian.

Once all of us were inside, the lights in the store, clear glass globes floating a few inches above decorated pillars, flared to life. Every square inch was brightly lit, leaving no shadows.

In addition to books, there were several shelves with beautifully arranged brightly colored pots of ink. I wandered over to check them out but was frustrated by the Chimeran words on the labels. I grabbed Brady as he walked by and asked him to translate.

He rolled his eyes but complied, pointing at each bottle as he did so. "Midnight blue, spring green, lemon, sunset, polka dot—"

"Polka dot ink?" I could hear the skepticism in my voice.

Brady shot me an exasperated look. "I'm just telling you what it says. I can't speculate about what it means without more data." Somehow I managed not to roll my eyes at that. "Are you ready to hear the rest?" he asked.

I nodded quickly and he began reading again. "Autumn leaves, fern and buttercup stripes, disappearing/reappearing ink—"

"Wait!" I glared at him skeptically, convinced he must be trying to pull a fast one on me. "What did you say?"

He grabbed a bottle of black ink and carefully opened the cap. He grabbed one of the quills and dipped it into the bottle. "Pass me one of those pieces of parchment, will you?"

I picked up a piece of paper. It was thin, nearly see-through, and a pretty cream color. He took it from me and started writing. As soon as he finished he handed it to me. I snorted as I read, *This is Disappearing/Reappearing Ink.* Then, in what would have been the blink of an eye — if I'd actually had a chance to blink — the words disappeared.

I held it out to him and asked, "What good is this? You can't read it."

"I'm sure there's a spell that toggles on and off the disappearing function." He capped the bottle carefully and tucked it into one of the side pockets on his backpack.

I knew that ink was destined for extensive experimentation.

Doug wandered over to the towering bookshelves that covered one entire wall. He reached for a book and there was a quick flash of blue-green light from his raised wrist. He hesitated then pulled back his arm. When he touched his wristband, I knew he'd seen that brief flash too. It didn't happen often, even though he'd worn it since finding it in the abandoned dragon's cave three years before. The wristband had kept growing as he did, so that it fit his wrist as well at nearly sixteen as it had when he was twelve.

Doug stared at it, twisting his wrist back and forth. It looked like it always did; intricate Celtic patterns burned into the heavy leather band, with a small blue-green stone fastened in the center. It wasn't the first time I'd seen a flash of light from it. But this time, I could tell the flash had come from somewhere inside the stone. And even though there was light from the lamps around the room shining on it, no amount of twisting and turning coaxed another flash. Then Doug slowly reached back toward the book he'd planned to touch before and when his hand was about six inches away, the stone flashed even brighter.

"What do you think it means?" Doug kept his hand in the air, still six inches away from the book. "Is it telling me to touch it, or to keep away from it?"

"Um…that could be incredibly important," I blurted. "What if it's what we've been looking for? This could be it!"I felt my heart accelerating, a thrill of excitement sing though my blood. Even my toes felt energized.

Brady sighed, and I felt some of my excitement falter. "Let's accept Doug's premise, at least for the purpose of discussion, that the flash was caused deliberately by an inanimate wristband." The twist to Brady's lips made it clear *he* didn't believe that premise. "If that's the case, we should be able to test whether it is a warning or an invitation."

"How do you propose we do that?" Olivia asked and crossed her arms over her chest.

Brady looked thoughtful, then smiled. "First we need a base line. Doug, start at the beginning of that row of shelves. Keep your hand that same distance — I make it six inches from the books — and begin moving along the shelf. Watch and see if the stone reacts again."

Doug shrugged and did as Brady said, only he started with the top shelf and worked his way down. There was no reaction at all for the first few shelves and Brady began to smile an I-thought-so smile. Then on the third shelf, about half way across, the wristband flashed again.

Brady yelled, "Stop."

Doug froze. Brady reached past him and used the eraser end of a pencil to tug the book out of line from the others. Then he nodded at Doug to continue. By the time he'd moved past all the books, there were ten that made the wristband glow. Brady carefully tugged them all out a few inches so we could find them again, then carefully stepped back and viewed them.

"I must admit that there was a clear reaction from your wristband next to these books. However, there was no discernable pattern." Brady had an interested yet puzzled expression on his face. He tipped his head to one side then said, "None of those books has any writing on the spine and they are some of the oldest volumes."

"How do you know that?" Olivia asked skeptically.

I was close enough to hear Brady's quiet sigh, but he answered patiently enough. "The binding on those books is leather, not paper or cardboard or cloth. The leather is worn and cracked, and looks dry at the top and bottom edges. Leather holds up well to repeated use, therefore, these books must be old, hence the dry leather, and must have been used on many occasions, resulting in cracks and wear on the binding."

"Oh," Olivia said, biting her lip. I think she was disappointed he'd had an answer.

As if Brady would have mentioned it in the first place if he didn't have an answer.

"Where was I. Oh yes, first we need to determine what, if anything, these books have in common." He turned to me. "Sorry Kat, but with this many books, I think we can rule out the theory that we've found the last object."

I nodded, the last of my excitement dying with a quick, almost painful fizzle.

"So what do you think it will be?" Faith asked, sounding cross. I guessed she felt as let down as I did.

Brady sighed. "As I have told you before, it is pointless to waste time in conjecture. We lack the necessary data to make such a determination with even a remote possibility of success."

Faith and I both sighed, loudly, then looked at each other and grinned. Olivia laughed and linked her arm with Faith, who reached out and linked her arm with me.

"Okay," I said to Brady. "Then what do these books mean?"

He began tapping his cheek with his finger, staring at them. Finally, he said, "There's nothing else for it."

Before anyone could react, he reached out and grabbed one of the books. I gasped. It sounded much louder than normal since Faith and Olivia gasped in unison. I'd have liked to take a big step back away from that book, but my arm was held tight in Faith's grip.

Fortunately nothing happened when he pulled it off the shelf, so I started to relax. He hefted the book in his hand as though trying to judge its weight, then without warning, opened the cover.

Nothing happened. My shoulders, which had clenched themselves up near my ears relaxed back to normal.

Brady read the title page out loud, with no hesitation, even though it was written in Chimeran. "Major Mundane Storms - 1150 to the Present."

"I wonder what they considered to be *major storms,*" I mused.

Brady shut the book and turned it so the back cover faced up. Then he opened it to the last page, which was blank. He turned to the next, which was also blank, then kept turning blank pages one at a time. Finally, he grabbed several pages and flipped them over together.

A huge spinning tornado erupted from the page. My hair began to whip around my face and I was knocked off my feet into the bookcase. Doug was lifted partially off his feet, then thrown to the ground.

Brady slammed the book shut, and instantly the howling winds died away.

Doug climbed slowly to his feet and for a long moment, we all stared at each other in stunned amazement. Then I said, "I wonder if all of those books act out what's inside. And if so, what kinds of things they contain." I could almost hear the sound of three descending notes: dum, dum, dum.

The sound we liked to use when things were about to get intense.

"Well, there's only one way to find out," Doug said. Unlike the rest of us, he didn't look disturbed or anxious or even hesitant. He looked eager. It was his I-always-wanted-to-ride-a-dragon look. The only problem with that — just a few months ago it resulted in half of the forest burning down, almost taking us with it.

I started to protest but Doug reached past Brady, grabbed another of the books that made his wristband flash, and flipped it open.

When nothing happened, my lungs started to function again and I asked impatiently, "What's it say?"

"Who knows?" he said, and held it out to Brady.

"I do not recognize some of these words. I believe we should take this one with us so I can translate it later," Brady said. He shrugged out of his backpack and placed the book inside.

"What about this one?" Faith asked, letting go of Olivia and me, and pulled the next book off the shelf. I relaxed as it and the two books that followed were filled with writing, not tornados or something even worse. They were written in Chimeran of course, and Brady insisted on taking them with us as well.

Doug pulled the next one down before Brady had time to close his pack. Doug opened it then frowned. Instead of a title page, there was a hand-drawn picture of a man hunched over a table, writing with a feathered quill pen. The page the man was writing on had the number 101 printed at the top.

Doug moved like he was going to shut the book, but Brady plucked it out of his hands. He turned to the next page and read, "One Hundred and One Tales." Then he hesitated like he wasn't sure he should open any more pages.

"What's it about?" Olivia asked impatiently. When Brady still hesitated, Olivia reached over his shoulder and flipped to the next page. Brady only had time to say, *"Eye of the Storm,"* before everything went crazy.

All around us clouds boiled up out of thin air. They massed around us like giant cotton balls that slowly darkened as though something was rubbing them with soot. Then they began rotating around us, slowly at first, then faster. And faster. Lightning speared down over our heads, followed by the crash of thunder. Around the room, winds grew in intensity, pulling things off the tables and shelves in the far corners of the room. Rain pounded down in torrents. In mere seconds, puddles became small trickles of water which gathered together with others. Chaos poured down all around us. But where we were standing, nothing happened.

No rain, no wind.

Not yet, anyway.

I watched in horrified fascination as water began creeping across the floor toward us.

"Shut the stupid book!" Faith screamed.

Olivia started, then jerked her hand off the page just in time. Another second and her fingers would have been squashed as Brady smashed the book shut.

And in that instant, it was all gone. The clouds, the lightning, the thunder, the water. All of it. There was not so much as a drop of water left on the floor.

My heart was pounding and I had to swallow twice before saying, "Do we really need to check the others?"

"Yes," Brady said, with unshakable certainty. "But we should do so with extraordinary caution."

The next book did nothing and went directly into Brady's backpack. That left just three more.

Faith picked up the first and opened it, then screamed and dropped it to the ground. I didn't understand at first, even when she began swatting at her hand. Then I realized something was crawling on her.

Ants.

Well, ants formed from the letters on the page. They swarmed from the book, up her fingers and onto her wrist. Dozens, *hundreds* of ants, poured from the open pages.

Faith screamed again and tried to knock them off with her other hand, but only managed to have dozens transfer to it as well. Now she had them teeming up both arms, heading toward her shoulders.

Faith choked out, "They're biting me!"

I watched in horror as small red welts began to rise on her skin. Tears of pain streamed down her face.

Olivia squealed and stepped back, with me right beside her. Brady quickly scooped his foot under the back cover and used it to shove the book closed.

Thankfully, the ants disappeared the moment it shut. I wasn't sure what we'd have done if something came out and didn't leave.

"Cool," Doug said, looking at Faith's now ant-free arms. Perfectly normal; not a hint of a welt. Only the tracks of tears on her face remained. I could have kicked Doug for his lack of sympathy.

He picked up the next book. Nothing happened when he opened the cover, but he flipped through several pages and stopped at one with a large, black rectangle taking up most of the space. He reached out and touched it, and I watched in horror as his fingers sank through the black square, slowly disappearing inside. More and more of his hand disappeared into the page, even as he gritted his teeth and pulled against the book.

"Doug, get your hand out of there," I yelled.

"Are you blind, Taylor?" Doug's voice came out in a snarl. "What do you think I'm trying to do?"

"Well, try harder!" Panic clawed at my chest as his hand slid deeper into the book, resisting his efforts to get loose.

Doug let out a fierce growl and yanked harder, sweat beading his forehead. Even the muscles in his jaw were tight with strain, and he spoke through clenched teeth, "Brady — ideas?"

"I'm considering," Brady said, face blank with concentration.

"Consider faster," Doug said, trying to sound casual. But his grunt of pain pretty much ruined that attempt.

The book closed around his wrist, and right before his wristband started to disappear from view, the stone began pulsing. Blue-green light flashed out, spearing through the bookstore. I felt a swell of hope. As the light flashed, his hand pulled back out of the book an inch or so.

Then it slid inexorably back inside.

My hope began to die as this repeated again. And again.

Flash. Gain an inch. Sink back in to the wrist.

Flash. Gain an inch.

The muscles in Doug's shoulder were bunched and straining with the effort to drag his hand out. Panic was beginning to show in his eyes. When it spread over his face, my heart began to race. "Can't get away from it," he bit out, his voice tight. "And I can't keep this up."

The rest of us grabbed the edges of the book and tried to rip it off him.

It didn't move so much as a centimeter. *How could a book be stronger than five people?*

Terror welled up inside me as the edge of his wristband slipped inside. I redoubled my frantic tugging, not sure if it was fear or effort that had my breath coming in short pants. Maybe both.

What if we couldn't stop it? Could it swallow up all of him?

Doug cried out, a long harsh sound that was somehow worse than a scream. He strained wildly against the book; head thrown back, neck corded with effort. Finally, with a squelchy, sucking sound, his hand jerked free. It was mottled red and purple, like his circulation had been cut-off, and there were splotchy areas where blood had puddled under the skin. Otherwise, he looked mostly unhurt.

"What did it feel like?" Brady asked. He had on his oh-good-another-scientific-puzzle expression. How could he stare at that bruising skin and feel nothing but science-techno-geek interest?

"Hot. Wet." Doug shuddered, looking slightly sick. "Like dozens of mouths were sucking on my hand."

I was seriously thankful there was only one more book to check. I'd have suggested we just leave it there, but what was the point? Brady would only argue.

This time it was Brady who reached out and gingerly pulled the book from the shelf. A spark flew into the air and Brady's hair seemed to lift straight up, like he'd touched something full of static. Then his hair settled into place and he relaxed his shoulders.

He ran his finger over the title page and quoted, "Magickal Curses." He opened the book to somewhere near the middle, and before he could start reading, there was an ear piercing howl. I clapped my hands over my ears hoping that would cut through some of the sound. Or if not that, at least relieve some of the painful pressure on my eardrums. Brady dropped the book, which stayed stubbornly open to that page. His left hand was clasped tightly over his left ear, but when he stooped down, he had to use his right hand to force the book closed.

In the immediate silence that followed, my ears rang. A loud, high-pitched buzzing that was, frighteningly, the *only* thing I could hear. Even more frightening, a slim trickle of blood had emerged from Brady's right ear. The one he hadn't been able to cover.

Faith opened her mouth, and her lips moved. I was pretty sure she was talking, but I couldn't hear anything except that annoying, ringing buzz. She dashed her hands over her eyes and I realized she was crying.

I'd have liked to cry, but felt too shocked for tears.

Olivia was the only one of us who kept her wits. She tugged off Faith's scarf —the one she'd taken from the store, what felt like hours ago now. She used it to wipe the blood off Brady's neck, then dropped it on the ground. She tugged Brady's arm, heading toward the entrance.

Faith shot an annoyed glance at her scarf before turning after Olivia. Doug and I followed like Olivia was the Pied Piper. Although none of us would have heard a pipe playing. As I walked outside, I couldn't hear the intense silence that blanketed Chimera. I couldn't hear anything. Not even the pounding of my own heart.

Brady pulled the map from his pocket and marked off the shop. The other one, I noticed, the one that looked so different, had disappeared. I wasn't sure what to make of that, but was too tired and scared to care at the moment. At least there was no question of checking it out.

The only real question was when I'd get my hearing back.

I squatted down, rubbing my hands over Shadow's soft fur as Brady pointed back to the tree drawn on the map. Doug gave a thumbs-up gesture with his uninjured hand, and the rest of us nodded.

I could feel Shadow's rumbling purr under my fingers before I straightened up. For once I hadn't been able to hear it. That, somehow, made everything seem so much worse. I turned my head away for a moment so the others wouldn't notice the tears that welled into my eyes.

We'd survived other frightening and dangerous things in Chimera. Doug had been injured so badly he'd quit the basketball team. Even now I could see him limping as we made our way back to the doorway. But somehow this felt worst of all. What if our hearing *never* came back? I'd never hear my favorite tunes again. I wouldn't be able to go to the movies. I sniffled as my nose threatened to start running, knowing the others wouldn't be able to hear me.

It seemed to take much longer than usual to get back to the tree. Half way there I had to admit that I totally sucked at sign language. Olivia and Brady seemed to understand each other well enough, while Faith and Doug mainly kept themselves to shrugs, nods and head shakes. I was the only one who wanted to communicate but kept failing. Abysmally.

I quickly grew tired of the others staring at me in puzzlement when I tried to pantomime something. I mean, how hard is it to ask if the others were getting their hearing back? Or, more important, for Brady to check the map for the Rejects?

Fortunately, there was no sign of them.

The closer we got to the tree, the more Shadow began driving me crazy. She kept twining around my ankles, nearly tripping me, until I finally picked her up in self-defense. Once I was holding her, she stretched up and licked both of my ears. I don't know if it was just a coincidence or not, but it seemed like my hearing started to improve. I could hear, albeit incredibly muffled, by the time we reached the tree.

I grabbed the others before they could go through the tree and pantomimed picking up their animals. Thankfully, they understood me this time, though their expressions ranged from puzzled to annoyed. Maybe they finally did it because their familiars were circling them in a frenzy. But one by one they knelt down and picked them up and each of them got their ears licked. And one by one, their miserable expressions lightened. I could tell when each one began to hear again.

-xXx-

The trip through the tree wasn't too bad, fortunately.

As soon as we exited from the tree, Faith demanded, "Why…you ruin… scarf?"

"What?" Olivia asked, and cupped her fingers around her ears.

"…scarf?" Faith stamped her foot and waved her hands in the air, frustration clear on her face. She turned and marched around the angel statue, giving it plenty of space. I couldn't help but notice she was stamping her feet with every step.

By the time we neared home, my hearing was nearly back to normal. The others hadn't improved quite as much; I could only hope more time would fix that. And that the others could hide the fact they couldn't hear until they'd recovered.

What could they say? Sorry Mom, I lost my hearing when I opened a magic book in a secret land, but I'm sure it'll be better soon?

Who'd believe them if they did?

Chapter 19/May/Santa Ramona

Land of the Lost...Make that the Missing

When we headed toward school on Monday, I asked how the others were doing. Fortunately, we hadn't suffered long-lasting damage. Except for Brady. He was still having trouble hearing out of his right ear. The one he hadn't been able to cover.

"It's getting better," he said, starting at twice his normal volume. I shushed him and he dropped his voice until I could barely hear him. Olivia opened her mouth – I was pretty sure she was going to ask him to speak up – but I shook my head at her. Better to miss part of what he said than to risk the whole school hearing.

He continued and I was suddenly glad he was speaking quietly. "My theory is that my tympanic membrane was ruptured by acoustic trauma." At our blank looks, he sighed and said, "That sound ruptured my eardrum. Fortunately, the eardrum is able to heal small perforations of this type."

Olivia opened her mouth but he kept talking, slightly louder, "I have researched this condition extensively." *Of course he had.* "I'm sure I will have the majority of my hearing return to optimal levels in a few weeks."

"How are you going to get through class unable to hear?" Faith asked, her brow furrowed.

"Firstly, as you can tell, I am able to hear some sounds." He reached into his pocket and pulled out a note. "I complained to my father that my allergies have been acting up so much my Eustachian tube has become congested." At our puzzled looks he sighed and said, "Fluid in my ear is making it difficult to hear."

"Wait a minute," Olivia said, her eyes narrowing. "What allergies? You don't have allergies."

His face flushed slightly but he answered readily enough. "My father is unaware of that particular fact. He believed me."

Brady had made a few comments over the past three years hinting that his family wasn't as close as mine. But this made it all too real. His own father had no idea whether Brady had allergies. What kind of home life was that?

The warning bell rang then, and we said hurried goodbyes before heading off toward class.

"Let's hope Brady's note works," Faith said as we entered our first period classroom.

When I sank into my seat, I had time for one last thought before Mr. Kline began talking. *Let's just hope his ear gets better.*

Mr. Kline seemed to drone on forever, and I was glad when we were able to escape to second period. When we settled into our seats, Mr. Harper wasn't there. Instead, 'Ms. Loyd' was written on the board and she introduced herself as our substitute for that day's history lesson.

I nearly groaned out loud. At least I knew what to expect from Mr. Harper. What would Ms. Loyd be like?

It was probably the strangest class I'd ever had. It *was* history, of a sort. I'd never really been a big fan of history, but this class was different. Ms. Loyd started by asking if any of us had been following the news this year. I glanced around and saw about a third had their hands up.

"Normally, I encourage my students to pay attention to the news," she said. "What happens today becomes the history of tomorrow, after all. This year is a bit different, however. For those of you who have been paying attention, there have been several mentions about Santa Ramona. One of the darkest parts of our history is having a greater number of missing persons per capita than any other comparably sized town in California."

There was an agitated whisper around the classroom. Ms. Loyd waited a moment to let us settle, then continued, "This is part of our town's history. I want to take time out of our normal World History curriculum to discuss the history of what you may be hearing on the news."

I sat up straighter in my chair. This kind of history interested me.

"It is estimated that Santa Ramona, in some form, was first established sometime in the late 1600's. There are, unfortunately, no written records from that time. There are, however, tales going back to when the indigenous peoples, thought to be part of the Chumash tribe, lived in this area."

She looked over the class and said drily, "As you should already know, this was before the coming of American pioneers, even before the Spanish missionaries. But many of our town's legends have their roots much further back. Many believe these roots actually go back to October 1347."

Again there was a rumbling through the classroom. How could the roots of our town go back to 1347? Columbus hadn't come over until 1492. Ms. Loyd again waited for the chatter to quiet before she continued. "In that year, twelve Genoese trading ships docked at Messina after a long voyage through the Black Sea."

The Black Sea? What did that have to do with Santa Ramona?

"Most of the sailors on those ships were dead from an unknown fever; the beginning of the plague, also known as the Black Death. Though it is estimated to have claimed up to 75 million lives since its introduction, 20 million were lost in the first five years. Don't forget that the estimated world population in 1347 was only 450 million."

Again there was a ripple of sound through the room.

"With the coming of the Black Death, so-called witches became known as plague-spreaders, and in 1486 the Malleus Maleficarum was published by the Catholic inquisition. Less than sixty years later in 1542, Henry VIII introduced the first English statutes addressing witchcraft. Persecution of witches skyrocketed around 1550, which was also known as the Burning Times."

I gasped, instantly remembering the pages Ronny had left for us before we met with her the first time. Nearly three and a half years ago now. They were pages from her mother's journal. Not having Brady's eidetic memory, I couldn't remember everything, but some things felt burned into my brain.

The world of men has turned against us.

For 50 years, the book condemning witches, Malleus Maleficarum, was used by the church to instruct witch hunters and inquisitors.

In Europe, many tens of thousands were burned for witchcraft.

It was a time of darkness referred to by many, Magickal and Mundane alike, as the Burning Times.

I snapped back to the present when Ms. Loyd said, "Such things were not peculiar to Europe alone. Of course you have heard of the Salem Witch trials in 1692. That is taught throughout the United States. But only in Santa Ramona is there any talk of witches being killed on the West Coast. And that is not taught as part of history."

There was a lot of rustling when she paused and people in class wiggled in their chairs. We all knew what was coming. Ms. Loyd smiled as if those reactions were what she wanted. "There is a long-standing cultural myth, the scientific term for a local legend, about our cemetery."

Now it was totally silent as everyone sat transfixed. I don't think any of us really believed she would bring this up.

"It is the oldest known in this part of California. That has always been a claim to fame for this town. But it has always had a strange reputation, including the tale of a witch who came here to escape persecution. Tales have been documented about the death of a suspected witch. According to our legend, she was executed — some have said slaughtered — in our cemetery. It has been said that she was buried there with a book, purportedly a book of spells." She flashed a smile and said, "I'm sure this is no surprise to any of you."

She looked around expectantly and a titter of nervous laughter erupted and was quickly suppressed. She nodded and smiled. "Have any of you participated in a witch-book hunt?"

This time the room was silent as only a few people nodded. Ms. Loyd smiled again as if that was the answer she expected. "I'm sure most of you will have a chance to do so next year. That seems to be a rite of passage for the senior class in this town. "

She perched on the edge of the desk and pulled off her glasses, briefly massaging her eyes before replacing them. "So what, you may be asking, does this have to do with World History, and how does it relate to Santa Ramona?"

Again a pause as she looked at us. No one moved, but it was clear she had the attention of everyone in class. She looked disappointed when no one answered. "Come now, this is not difficult."

When the silence continued she said, "It could be speculated, could it not, that if the Black Death had not happened, the war against witches might never have started. Or at least it might not have been pursued as vigorously. Correct?"

She waited for a few nods before adding, "If that were the case, some who came to this country seeking freedom of religion might not have come. Additionally, the Salem Witch trials might never have happened if hysteria against witches was not so prevalent. Are you following?"

Again she waited for a few nods. "If those parts of World History had changed, it is unlikely there would be a legend of a witch dying in our cemetery." She paused as a wave of chatter burst out, smiling at our interest. "And with no witch, there would be no witch-book hunts by our high school seniors."

That earned her a full-fledged laugh. Her smile faded as she added, "Perhaps if none of that had happened our town might never have developed its strange reputation. And without its strange reputation it is unlikely we would become known as the town with the highest number of missing persons in California." I wasn't the only one who sat up straighter at that. I'd love an explanation that made sense of that. Unlike the town's weekly whitewashed newspaper.

She stood and began pacing. "I don't know if anyone has told you this, but our Police Department believes this reputation has been perpetuated by people who utilize our town's reputation for their own purposes. For those who wish to disappear from their existing lives, they choose to come to our town first to confuse their trail."

She stared around the room, eyes hesitating on several of us. "Let me assure you, there is nothing to indicate someone has been lurking around town for more than one hundred and fifty years kidnapping unwary visitors." I glanced quickly at Olivia just one seat away. Her eyes looked as wide and startled as mine. Both of us could think of not some*one,* but some*place,* that might have been responsible for kidnapping a few unwary visitors. If those visitors had seen something they shouldn't.

Ms. Loyd said, "And don't forget that sixteen years ago Santa Ramona became known as the town with THE-STRANGEST-YEAR-EVER." I cringed; not that! She continued, "That fact, combined with our recent unusual weather phenomena, has caused this town to become the center of a media frenzy." She stopped pacing and faced the class. "Therefore, you must *never* underestimate the importance of historical events on the present day."

The entire class was silent, then there was a smattering of applause. I'd bet it was the strangest, most interesting history class that had ever happened. Ms. Loyd smiled. "With that in mind, your assignment, due next Monday, is to describe one other way that World History is having a direct effect on the present." The applause died as if someone had flipped a switch.

As the bell rang, she stood up and said, "Class dismissed."

Chapter 20/June/Chimera

Tag, You're It

The rest of June seemed to drag by, but I didn't complain. Under some circumstances I decided, boring was good. As in not being chased by Rejects. As in not hearing about THE-STRANGEST-YEAR-EVER. As in getting all of my homework, even the History paper from Ms. Loyd done and turned in on time before school let out.

As in Ronny not appearing to be any worse — though she certainly wasn't any better. At least she'd tried to look interested when Brady told her about the books we'd taken from the bookstore in Chimera. He'd pulled them out of his backpack and showed them to her, but she hadn't reached for them. In fact, she didn't tell us anything about them, just asked Brady if he'd had a chance to read them. He told her he hadn't yet, but would go through all of them and share anything he found.

Before we could talk to her about anything else, Chris came in and basically kicked us out. Oh, he was polite about it, but he was obviously determined to get us out of there.

Right up there on my boring can be good list was the surprising absence of drama when Olivia met George for burgers and sodas. Three times. Of course there might have been more drama if she'd noticed the sad-puppy-dog look on Brady's face every time she mentioned it.

But all in all, it was a *nice* boring month.

Then it was the Saturday of the full moon, and I could only hope things would stay boring, not like last month. At least Brady's hearing had finally come back. I kept the hope for nice and boring in mind all the way to the cemetery.

Then we went through the tree.

Going through this time wasn't as quick and painless as our more recent trips. I hated feeling like I was being shoved through the cold and damp. That first part seemed painfully drawn out this time. At least the whole I-can't-see and I-can't-breathe part seemed fairly short, but I'd counted to 108 by the time I popped into the complete stillness of Chimera. Maybe I'd gotten out of practice with longer trips through, because my heart was pounding and my gasping breaths seemed startlingly loud as I stumbled out.

I deliberately relaxed my shoulders and took a very deep breath of the sweet air, trying to relax. Then my stomach rumbled, even though I'd eaten breakfast right before leaving home. Being in a place that smelled like a bakery had convinced my stomach that being full was completely immaterial. *It* wanted whatever smelled so good.

Shadow ran up and rubbed against my legs, meowing and purring excitedly. I scooped her up, just in time to prevent Rusty from bowling her over in his race to get to Doug.

Brady stuck his hand in his pocket. I expected him to bring out the map, but he held up his hand when Pyg and Fangface swooped in. They both circled while Pyg hooted loudly, only growing quiet when she finally landed on Olivia's shoulder. Fangface could have been squeaking at Brady, but any sounds the bat made were drowned out by the little owl. Then Fangface darted down and snatched something off Brady's hand.

"What was that?" I asked, startled. It had looked like Brady was being attacked!

"Freeze-dried crickets," Brady said with a grin.

Olivia gagged and turned her back. Fortunately Brady was watching Fangface enjoying the dead bugs and didn't notice.

Foxy came over and sat down in the dirt by near Faith's feet, her red coat glowing in the sunlight. Faith leaned down to pat her timid familiar as Brady reached in his pocket and pulled out the map. He pointed to an area near the stores we'd visited last month.

According to the map, there should only be four houses in that area. Thank goodness. I still couldn't bring myself to enjoy looking through other people's drawers and cupboards. It might be different if we kept finding cool — as in exciting, *not* scary — magical objects. But looking through a stranger's plates and socks and bits and pieces felt…icky.

We were nearly all the way to town when Brady announced that the Rejects had entered Chimera. "They're heading this way," he said, and we increased our pace. The town held far more hiding places than this empty stretch of road.

We hurried over the bridge and as we stepped off the other side, I had a brief wistful memory of the bridge troll. It might have scared the Rejects off if it was still hanging around, but we hadn't seen it since that first time. Of course, if it was still hanging around it might decide to scare us off, too. My wistful memory popped like a soap bubble that hit the low splintered edge of the bridge.

Okay, maybe not.

We followed Brady to the cluster of four houses that reminded me of Disney's original *Cinderella,* with white-washed plaster crisscrossed with dark wood. They looked larger than the small cottages we'd searched. At least they were smaller than the Council's huge houses.

We approached the first hesitantly. Who knew if this one had been booby trapped? I wasn't sure if Brady had enough chalk and baking soda left, in case we met up with another acid-spitting door knocker. I felt my shoulders hunch up near my ears as Doug reached for the door knob. Then, my breath came out in a whoosh as the door swung open soundlessly.

I shot a quick glance at Doug's wristband. It had reacted to some of the books at the bookstore. I wanted to know if it reacted to anything in here. I was torn between relief and disappointment when it didn't do anything.

We made short work of that house. The inside furnishings were rough and minimal with few places to store something important. When we met back in the living room, Brady checked the map again and smiled. "The Rejects are checking out one of the side roads right now."

"If we're lucky," Faith said, "they won't *ever* come this far."

Brady led the way to the next house, and our animals followed behind us. They lay down in the shaded garden surrounding it, looking calm and relaxed. That made me feel good. And thankfully, the house didn't react when we entered. But after one look, I still almost ran away screaming.

It was dim inside, with little light entering the windows. At first glance you'd think the lush garden outside was blocking the light. But that wasn't it. The windows were covered with dozens of matted grey strings that resembled a disgusting, tattered doily. Thick sticky ropes of cobwebs festooned the ceilings. They blurred the corners of the room and covered every surface.

I kept very close to the door. I had no desire to run into any more Chimeran spiders! Brady, on the other hand, reached out and touched one of the webs. It was a mistake. The web stuck to his finger and resisted his efforts to break loose.

Stupid science-geek! Note to self — Don't touch spider webs in Chimera. Scratch that. Just don't touch spider webs. Ever.

Brady jerked his hand one way then the other with increasing violence. Doug grabbed his arm and tried to help him pull loose but the web merely stretched tight. It made a high-pitched whine that set my teeth on edge, but showed no signs of breaking.

Doug grunted with effort and told Brady, "Dude, do something."

"Stop playing around," Olivia said, worry leaking through the sarcasm in her voice.

Finally, Brady reached his free hand into one of the side-pockets on his backpack and grabbed his Swiss army knife. He handed it to Doug. "Can you cut it?"

"Sure thing," Doug assured him and quickly hacked the web into small sticky bits.

All of this made the entire web shake. As if to announce to its maker that it had caught something very large.

I looked around, terrified that whatever had made those webs would come to investigate. There was no sign of a spider, but signs of the spider's victims were all around us. Bugs of all shapes and sizes and colors – some the size of a pea, others the size of a dinner plate. They were hanging, trussed in webs or dangling by a single creepy little leg. In one corner, something vaguely cricket shaped was spinning lazily in small circles, dangling from an antennae.

This was intensely creepy! Any normal person would think so. But once he finished picking off bits of web, Brady kept exclaiming excitedly. Like a bunch of dead bugs was the best thing ever.

I wanted to look away, but couldn't. It was the colors. Vivid greens and blues. Some with streaks of yellow or patches of pink and orange. Some iridescent purple. All of them should have looked gorgeous. If they weren't bugs.

"Um, I'm not going in there," I said, my voice far more hesitant than I liked.

Doug grinned and knocked his shoulder against mine. "Come on, Taylor. You're not going to let a few little bugs stop you."

"Oh, yeah!" There was no hesitation in my voice now. I continued, strongly, "First that's not just a few bugs. Second, some aren't exactly little. You feel free to check it out, and I'll just wait here."

"I'll go." Brady's voice sounded eager. *No surprise there.* "This structure is fairly small. It shouldn't take long to search it."

"I'm right behind you," Doug said cheerfully, giving my shoulder another bump as he passed me.

"I'm not," I called after his retreating back.

Faith looked around, then shrugged. "I think I'll help."

I gaped at her and I could feel Olivia shudder next to me. Faith followed the guys into the other room, ducking and twisting out of the way to avoid dangling bugs smacking into her face.

Time seemed to stretch longer and longer as we waited for them to return.

Note to self — Waiting takes a lot *longer than looking.*

Olivia's foot was thumping out a rapid impatient beat and I'd begun eyeing the floor for a web-free, bug-free space to sit down in by the time they returned. Their empty hands and discouraged faces made it clear they hadn't found anything.

Faith shook her head and said, "Probably a good thing you didn't go. It's even worse in the other room."

That was an understatement. All of them had bits of sticky grey web clinging all over them. Faith kept swiping her hands over her hair and shoulders, as if to clean it off. I didn't have the heart to tell her it wasn't working.

I was just glad I hadn't gone. Even when Doug started making chicken noises when he drew closer. The creep.

Olivia had the door open and stepped outside before they could get anywhere near her. I followed on her heels, leaving the others to finish making their way across the bug draped room.

I took a very deep breath of the sweet fresh air. I hadn't realized how stale and musty the house had been. "Where now?" I asked, hoping fervently that the next place would be web and bug free.

Brady pointed to our right and led the way. I smiled as Shadow and Rusty took turns chasing each other in circles, keeping just ahead of us.

Chapter 21/June/Chimera

Brady-ella

As we emerged from the path and climbed the stone steps to the front door of the next house, I sighed. "I keep expecting to hear Cinderella talking to mice."

Everyone stopped to stare at me, and I felt an embarrassed flush crawling up my cheeks. "Because of the house." Olivia raised her eyebrow at me. Just the one.

"These houses look just like fairytale cottages, like the ones in *Cinderella*." I explained. "Um, the animated version."

"I preferred *Sleeping Beauty*," Faith said. "But the live-action *Maleficent* was pretty awesome."

"Yeah, that was cool," I told her, deliberately ignoring Doug's gathering frown.

"*Beauty and the Beast* is better," Olivia stated, as if that should be the end of the discussion.

"*Cinderella* is best," I said, decisively. "I loved how her step-mother tried to intimidate her, but she—"

"You like stories about mean step-mothers?" Brady's voice grated out, far deeper than normal. As if the words had been dragged from him.

I took a half step back, startled. I'd never heard that tone from Brady. "Well, it's just that—"

"Step-mothers don't have to lock you up or treat you like a servant to be no good," he said, eyes narrowed behind his glasses. I was surprised he'd been able to speak; his jaw was clenched so tight the words had been spit out between his teeth.

"I never said that," I told him carefully, feeling like I was walking on eggshells. "Lots of step-mothers are nice." Out of the corner of my eye I saw confusion on Faith and Olivia's faces, so I wasn't the only one that didn't understand what was going on here.

"Don't worry about it," Doug told Brady in a quiet voice. He looked like *he* understood what was happening. He raised his hand to give Brady his favorite everything-will-be-okay shoulder punch, but Brady shoved Doug's hand away. He didn't even look at Doug. He was too busy staring at me.

"It's not okay to treat step-mothers like a joke. You're right. Most of them are probably very nice, but when they aren't, it's not a laughing matter."

My throat felt tight and I cleared it before trying to answer. "I'm not laughing Brady. Cinderella's step-mother was horrible. She turned her into a servant in her own house, then lied about her living there."

"There are worse things," he said, bitterness congealing his voice, making it come out thick and stiff. I suddenly remembered hearing him sound like this once before. A few years ago. I tried to remember how it started, but the memory slipped away from me.

I made sure my voice was low and gentle. "You…um, have trouble with your step-mother?" At his nod, I asked, "Do you want to talk about it?"

I saw refusal gather in his eyes, but before he could say no, Olivia blurted, "What does she do?"

"Do?" he asked, his eyes shadowed with some emotion I couldn't make out. When he spoke again, his voice was flat. "She doesn't *do* anything."

Okay, that was confusing. If his step-mother didn't do anything, why was he so upset?

His eyes were slightly unfocused behind the thick lenses of his glasses and he was breathing heavily. He'd grown several inches during the last year, and he'd been taking Tae Kwan Do for a while now. When he clenched his hands into fists, he suddenly looked buff and angry and slightly dangerous. I shook my head, trying to get rid of such a ridiculous image. This was nerdy Brady I was talking about.

I tried to pick my words carefully. I didn't want to make him any more upset. "So you and your step-mother don't get along with each other?"

"My step-mother and I don't do *anything* with each other." Behind his bleak, angry voice, I noticed a muscle jumping in his cheek and misery darkening his eyes.

And just like that, I remembered when he'd sounded like this before. It happened nearly three years ago. Olivia had ignored him while he was trying to tell her something important. She'd turned her back and walked away from him and Brady had said it was just like at home. That nobody listened to him.

Brady sucked in a breath then blurted, "My real mother moved away after the divorce. She's only managed to send me a couple birthday cards in the last five years. Dad and I were pretty close for a while, and I didn't miss her much." His voice dropped and his mouth tightened in disgust. "Then he met Judy."

"I was happy for him at first," he said, and shook his head. "Then they got married and she moved in. Her and my step-sister, Margie." His lips twisted when he said his step-sister's name. "It didn't take long for Dad to take Judy's side on everything. Dad said," now Brady's voice dropped still lower. His voice changed, as if he were imitating the sound of his father's voice, *"My family is my whole world, Brady."*

He relaxed his fists and gazed at his hands expressionlessly before saying, "As if I wasn't a real part of his family anymore."

He looked at me and in that imitation father voice said, *"We have to make her happy, Brady. You need to stop arguing with her, Brady. I don't care if you proved scientifically that you're right, Brady. Stop complaining, Brady. I make sure you have a roof over your head and food on the table, what more do you want from me, Brady?"*

He snorted. "No one listens to me at home. Margie keeps asking why I can't act like I'm *normal* instead of a character in some nerd movie. My step-mother calls me an embarrassment."

He shoved his glasses higher on his nose and glared at me. "Who cares about being treated like a servant! Being treated like you don't matter? Being told you're a waste of space? That's worse than any stupid fairytale."

I shook my head, not knowing what to say. But he was right. Cinderella might have had it much easier.

Brady turned away and muttered, "I just wish everyone would stop telling me how much I must enjoy being part of such a great family." He kept his back to us and kicked a rock. Then spoke so low I almost didn't hear it, "I don't think of them as my family anymore. You guys are my family."

There was a moment of silence. I don't know about the others, but I had no idea how I felt about this. My brother frequently annoyed me. Dad and I didn't talk very often. And Mom and I seemed to be arguing a lot more often lately. But I knew all of them loved me. And I loved that. So maybe I did know how I felt. Being considered family by Brady was pretty cool. Something to be proud of.

Then he added, "You guys, and my grandfather Chuck. He's the only one left in my real family who cares about me. I don't get to see much of him since Dad remarried. He and Dad have been arguing for years, but Dad was furious when Grandpa Chuck told him they weren't treating me right."

He lifted his arm and stared at the watch he always wore in Chimera. He turned around slowly and looked nearly back to normal; his misery under tight control. He gave a weak smile and said, "Did I tell you Grandpa Chuck gave me this?"

I felt a stab of confusion. "I thought it was your Dad's watch."

Brady grinned and glanced back at it. "Grandpa knew I'd been borrowing it from Dad. I didn't know it before, but it really belonged to Grandpa Chuck. He told me it was mine to keep if I wanted. That made Dad even angrier. But Grandpa said Dad had locked it away in a cupboard and never looked at it, so Grandpa could give it to anyone he wanted."

"Cool," Doug said. "You deserve it."

Brady glanced up then. "I told you it's similar to one that my Great-grandfather Arthur invented, right?"

When we all nodded, he said, "Grandpa Chuck still says Arthur would have been a world famous inventor if he hadn't disappeared all those years ago. According to family history, Arthur completely lost it when his wife died. He got more and more strange after that and finally handed Grandpa Chuck over to his sister who lived here. I mean, in Santa Ramona."

He laughed. "If my Great-Grandfather hadn't disappeared, I'd probably have been born in Long Beach. Instead, Grandpa Chuck got raised by his aunt and I was born here."

"If you were born in Long Beach you wouldn't be able to go into Chimera," Faith said, sounding like she was unsure if that was a good thing or a bad thing. I knew she was still ambivalent about having the ability to come in here.

"You wouldn't have been able to help us," I said, making sure he could tell I was glad he was there.

"We'd never have met you," Olivia said. Her tone was, if anything, even more ambiguous than Faith's.

Brady squared his shoulders. "Well, being born here, during THE-STRANGEST-YEAR-EVER, is intriguing. From a scientific point of view." He looked around at all of us, an apologetic smile on his face. "Can we finish checking this cluster of houses now?"

-xXx-

The next two looked like Cinderella had been hard at work inside. No spider webs, no dirty fireplaces, no signs of bugs or mice or birds inside. And they were also empty of anything of interest to us.

When we came out, Olivia grabbed my arm and pointed over in the direction we'd just come. "Look what's back there!"

I tried to see where she was pointing. It took a second, but I saw it at the same time that Doug let out a sharp whistle.

"That house wasn't there," I said, staring in disbelief at the shabby wooden house we'd seen twice before.

"I always hated playing hide and seek," Faith grumbled. "Should we go back and check it out?" Then she glanced to our right, toward the last house we were supposed to check today.

I was relieved, though I wouldn't have told him so, when Doug said, "Why bother. It seems to be following us around. I'm sure we'll see it again next month."

Brady's mouth tightened momentarily, then he sighed. "There is a certain logic in sticking to our original plan. But perhaps we should check that building out first the next time we see it. There must be something significant about it."

"Absolutely," Faith said, with a decided lack of enthusiasm. She didn't sound any more interested in entering a disappearing/reappearing house than I was. "Let's check it next time — if you're sure we can't disappear along with it."

Doug turned toward the house Brady had originally indicated. A small grove of trees lay between us and the house. At the edge of the trees I could see another statue. When we got closer, I could see it was a bent old woman, her boney hands on her hips, her hair straggling around her face. That seemed strange —why would anyone make a statue of someone looking their worst?

I was distracted by the realization that the path we'd been following was circling way out of our way. It headed through the center of the grove, when it would have been quicker and easier to go straight along the edge. That was strange, too.

Even stranger, our animals disappeared the instant we entered the trees. I started to point that out to the others, then forgot all about them. I stopped in amazement. Frozen in wonder. Enchanted.

Different types of trees filled the grove; some had trunks of shining bronze. Others were copper or pewter. I thought it was beautifully colored bark until I tripped over a small stone, causing it to bounce against one of the trees. A deep metallic ping made it clear these weren't ordinary trees.

The copper trees had leaves of thin bright gold. These leaves were pointing up to the sky, as if attracted to the sun. They were so delicate, they danced and quivered with a slight metallic rustling as I passed underneath.

Next to those, the bronze trees were topped with leaves of the finest silver. These looked more substantial than the golden leaves –

they drooped down, as if they were too heavy to point upward. These didn't move when I walked by.

From a distance the pewter trees looked nearly normal. At least their leaves were green. But when I drew closer I could see they weren't normal at all. They were long, thin emeralds, only vaguely leaf-shaped. Here and there among the leaves were clusters of white gems, similar in shape and size to magnolia blossoms. But the white gems sparkled in the sunlight like diamonds.

I was startled when a voice came from behind me. I'd forgotten anyone else was there. "Are those what I think they are?" Olivia asked. Her voice was very low and quiet, as if she was afraid something, or someone, would hear her.

I glanced around and felt like I was waking from an incredible dream. And not particularly happy to be woken.

"Doug, can you grab some of the leaves and one of the flowers?" Brady asked slowly. Doug shot him a questioning glance and Brady explained, "I'd like a closer look."

Even though Doug was the tallest, there was no way he could reach any of the leaves without jumping. As Doug gathered himself, I wanted to shout no. I didn't want him to touch my jewels.

Besides, I remembered Doug saying it hurt when he over-used the leg Arnold had injured. That's why he'd quit basketball. Looking at the height of the leaves over his head, I was suddenly sure he'd try too hard and injure his leg again. But I bit back the word. The pleased look on Doug's face stopped me. He wasn't worried about how much his leg would hurt. He was excited to be asked to do it. And if he did get some of the jewels, I was sure I could convince Brady to let me have them.

I held my breath as he launched himself up four times, grabbing different leaves and one of the flowers. Each time he pulled one loose, his wristband flashed blue-green in the dim light filtering down through the trees. The last time he landed, he landed hard, and sprawled on the path with a pained grunt. I sucked in my breath, not sure if I was more worried about him or the gems. When he climbed to his feet, even though pain showed in the lines around his eyes, he wore a broad grin. He handed his captured wealth to Brady, but his hand lingered on it before he let go.

Brady ran his hands over the leaves, held them to the light, manipulated them between his fingers and finally tipped his head to the side, his eyes focused inward.

"Well?" Olivia snapped. "Are they real? Are we all going to be rich?"

"I really need to do a chemical analysis to ensure they are genuine rather than some sort of magical construct," Brady said. "But under my cursory examination, they appear to be quite real."

There were several ragged sighs at that. They were really gold and silver. Those were real diamonds and emeralds. This was better than finding a buried treasure! Better than tripping the Rejects in school. Better than anything! I looked quickly around the grove of them. There were dozens and dozens of trees. Too many to count. I was going to be rich!

"Let's hurry up and check that last house," Faith said. "We need to get back so Brady can do his chemical tests."

"Maybe we should just skip the last house," Olivia said, practically bouncing on the balls of her feet.

"We should probably finish before going home," I said, trying to be practical. But my eyes were fastened on all of the precious metal and gems glittering in Brady's hands. *My* treasure.

"The house would wait," Doug said and rubbed absently at his leg. "We could check it next time."

"Yeah, next time," Faith echoed.

"We'll be too busy collecting leaves and flowers next time," Olivia said dreamily, craning her neck to peer up into the trees. "We'll have to bring a ladder so we can reach the top branches. These don't look like good climbing trees."

I reached over and touched one of the tree trunks. "It's really slippery. Without a ladder, we'd just slide off if we tried to climb."

"Kat's right," Brady announced. I was glad *someone* was listening to me. I needed their cooperation when I asked for those jewels. All those beautiful, shiny gems and precious metals.

"We should finish what we started," Brady said and I started. I'd forgotten he'd been talking.

"Mom has a small folding step stool I could probably sneak out," Faith told Olivia.

"We should finish that last house today," Brady said.

"There's no way I could sneak my ladder out," Olivia said glumly. "It's huge. Everyone in town would see us dragging it in here."

"How tall is your step-stool?" Doug asked Faith.

"We need to follow the plan," Brady said, nearly speaking over the top of Doug. I felt like I was giving myself whiplash looking from one to the other as they spoke. "Then we need to get back home. Testing, remember?"

"It's about three feet tall," Faith said. "I can reach the back of the highest shelf in the pantry."

"Three feet should be enough," Doug said, visually measuring the distance to the lowest branches. "I just need to be able to get onto that branch."

"The logistics can be worked out over the next four weeks," Brady said, voice raised impatiently. He was frowning at Doug and Faith and Olivia where they were still talking about step-stools.

Who needed step-stools? The four of us could boost Doug into the tree so he could pull down more of those lovely things for me.

Olivia sniffed and turned away, heading down the path that would take us back home. Doug and Faith moved after her, arguing about what they would do with hundreds, thousands, make that millions of dollars.

I'd just started to turn after them when Brady spoke up again. "*I* am going to check the last house."

I swung back around. Brady hadn't moved, other than to cross his arms over his chest in defiance.

He glared at Doug, who turned back to face him. "You know I'm right," Brady insisted.

Doug glared back. "Why don't you just give me those leaves? After all, I was the one who got them. I can take them back with the rest of us and you can go check out that house by yourself."

That startled me out of the fantastically extravagant pictures clouding my mind. An immense 3D Curved UHD TV taking up one whole wall in my room. Being inundated with incredible surround sound. Scrolling through several brand new cell phones and lap tops, each better than the next. All while sitting in the middle of a huge, gorgeous, canopy bed.

Those things all disappeared without a trace. Because we couldn't leave Brady in here. We were never supposed to be in Chimera alone. That was the rule. We'd all sworn…

The leaves over my head gave a seductive metallic rustle.

I saw a low-slung sports car in my driveway, with a license plate that said KAT. Right next to a jet pack. How awesome was that? Or better yet, an actual jet. I could fly to France for dinner, or to Africa to pet a giraffe. Then the picture of a giant closet filled with awesomely cool clothes popped into my head.

Wait. Clothes? Where did that come from? That was something Olivia would like.

Although, why should it just be Olivia? Why couldn't I look cool too? I could have a whole room with nothing but clothes and cosmetics and perfumes. And shoes. I could have a whole room with nothing but shoes. I could look even better than Olivia.

Suddenly, Brady's voice intruded on my lovely vision. "No, Doug, I'll keep hold of them," he said, implacably. "You do whatever you want."

I focused on Brady, and realized his voice was growing fainter. He'd turned and was making his way toward the next house. He was leaving us behind.

And he was taking my treasure!

All of us surged down the path after him. Olivia and Faith were protesting angrily. Doug wasn't saying anything, but his jaw was tight and his mouth was compressed into a thin white line. I wouldn't want to be Brady when we caught up with him.

Maybe Brady knew that. He managed to keep out of reach until he entered the house. It was two stories tall, and when we got there I heard his feet on the floor above us. We pounded up the stairs after him and tore through the house like a demolition team, trying to find him.

It was probably the most thorough search we'd ever done.

Brady must have hidden until he thought it was safe to sneak back down. I realized he was searching downstairs when I heard something heavy thump against a wall.

I raced down, the others behind me, just in time to see him disappear out the front door.

We were nearly back to the troll bridge before we caught up to him.

"What do you think you're doing?" I demanded.

"We're supposed to be a team," Faith said bitterly. "How could you just ditch us like that?"

"Why shouldn't I?" Brady demanded. "You guys were going to ditch me."

"Our motto is *All for one,*" Olivia told him, "not *One who's out for himself.*"

He stopped and glared at her. "You've made it very clear that only applies to the three of you girls. You wish I wasn't here at all."

"I've never said any such thing." Olivia sounded particularly sanctimonious, and managed, somehow, to look down her nose at him. Even though he was taller.

"Honesty is critical, to me. If I could buy just one thing, it would be honesty." Brady met her eyes and added, "You should try it some time."

Olivia got very red in the face. "I can't believe you would throw that in my face. You know I've sworn to only tell the truth. All of the truth. I can't believe you would accuse me of lying to you."

"Oh, you may not have said, *Brady, I wish you weren't here* in so many words. But I know that's what it means when someone is sarcastic and ill-tempered all the time. Which is exactly how you treat me!"

He sped up and Olivia fell back a pace. Brady was right; that was how Olivia treated him. But Olivia was right, too. He shouldn't have taken my treasure! How dare he?

Faith caught up with him. I couldn't hear what she said, but whatever it was, Brady didn't like it. His shoulders hunched up, then he whirled around, tugged the sleeves of his button down shirt into perfect alignment around his wrists and said something to Faith that had her stuffing her hands in her pockets and falling back.

Doug nearly knocked Faith off the path in his rush to reach Brady. Doug grabbed his arm and yanked Brady around to face him. The two of them were nose to nose, shouting something, nearly incoherent with anger. Spit was flying from Doug's lips and if looks could kill, they'd both be dead.

We were *supposed* to be friends. What was happening?

Why was Brady hoarding my treasure? And why was Doug trying to take it for himself?

I ground my teeth together and growled low in my throat. If Doug hadn't been bigger and taller than me, and Brady trained in Tae Kwan Do, I'd have rushed over there and taken those lovely things from both of them!

At least Faith and Olivia were no threat. They were hanging back, probably afraid of getting any closer to those two angry, scowling guys.

Doug's wristband glowed a steady, intense blue-green. That seemed wrong to me, but I couldn't decide why. I looked around for Shadow, thinking I'd like to hug her and realized I hadn't seen her in a long time. That seemed wrong too. When had I last seen her? I almost had it, but the thought of adding an entire room to be my own personal library intruded.

Why the heck were we standing around here? We couldn't waste time arguing! We needed to get home so I could start spending my money.

"Let's go," I yelled. "Brady needs to check those leaves and find out how much they are worth, while the rest of you figure out how to trade them in for cash."

And just like that, Doug stepped away from Brady. Without a word, we all began rushing headlong toward the tree. The rest of the trip was made in grim silence. I don't know about the others, but I was too busy thinking how I'd spend all of my lovely money without having to put up with the rest of them.

-xXx-

For once I didn't even notice the trip back through the tree. I was too busy picturing the mansion I would live in, complete with dozens of servants. And all of the fantastic parties I would throw. All of my favorite actors and singers would come. Everyone would want an invitation to Kat's.

That's how I'd be known. Just *Kat*. I would be so famous I wouldn't need a last name.

I was thrust out from the safe darkness of the tree, where my mind could fling itself into amazing dreams of the future. Instead, I found myself huddled in the misty heat of the cemetery. Surrounded by creepy statues and the four other people I'd been wishing I'd never have to see again.

The memory of all those thoughts began churning in my gut, curdling into a painful ball. I rolled onto my hands and knees, and threw up a small stream of bile at the feet of one of the statues. I'd been so busy worrying about gold and silver and emeralds, I hadn't even touched the lunch I carried in my backpack.

I flopped over onto my back and wiped my mouth on my sleeve. What had happened to me? Rooms full of clothes and make-up and shoes? Wanting to out-do Olivia? That wasn't me! I didn't want any of those things. Wild parties and being famous? I'd always made fun of people who lived like that. For the last couple hours, I hadn't been me at all.

I hadn't even seen Shadow to say good-bye. Hell, I hadn't even thought about it.

I was afraid to look at the others. I couldn't remember if I'd said something nasty to any of them. In fact, I couldn't remember exactly what anyone had said to me. Just that it had been ugly.

Olivia sank onto her knees. Her voice was shaking as she asked. "What just happened?"

Faith groaned, and rubbed her temples. "I have no idea. I feel like someone drugged me. With something *bad*."

I sat up and looked around. Everyone looked tired. Like up-for-thirty-six-hours-after-running-a-marathon tired. Doug and Brady sat down between Olivia and me. Brady had to lick his lips before he could get his voice out, and when he did speak, his voice was hoarse. Like he'd been shouting. "It started with the leaves."

For a moment I remembered him and Doug standing toe to toe, bellowing at each other, then the image disappeared.

"The leaves?" Faith echoed, puzzled.

"When I asked Doug to pick some of the leaves from the trees," Brady reminded her.

"The trees?" Olivia said. "What are you talking about?"

In the back of my head, faintly, I heard *my treasure*.

"It's when everyone forgot why we were in Chimera. When everyone started arguing with each other. When I started dreaming of the laboratory I'd build, complete with beakers and chemicals and the most modern, expensive lab equipment ever made. And some I had created just for me."

"Yeah, that sounds like you," I said, and managed to give him a small smile.

"Then I started thinking of all the things I could make in my lab. How famous I'd be. How I could come up with ways to save the world. And how they'd declare me to be King of the Lab." He gave a wry grin, acknowledging how crazy that sounded.

"I was going to have a whole room full of shoes, and be able to out-dress Olivia," I admitted, and gave a weak laugh.

Olivia snorted and said, "Never gonna happen."

"I was going to be Captain of my soccer team, then President of the women's soccer league. I'd have my name in the Guinness Book of World Records as the highest scoring player in the history of the game." Faith laughed and flopped down next to me, wrapping her arms around her knees.

Now all of us laughed and told her how perfectly it suited her.

"Well, not really," she admitted. "I bought out any team that did better than mine and fired anyone who might possibly become better than me."

"What about you, Doug?" For some reason, I couldn't wait to hear what he'd dreamt of.

He shook his head, then said, "I don't want to talk about it."

"Oh come on, we told you," I teased.

"I don't remember," he said decisively, and stood up. "You're right, Brady. It had to be those leaves. I think we should get rid of them."

Brady shrugged out of his backpack. "I tucked them in here where they'd be safe. I'd suggest incinerating them if possible, and burying the ashes where no one will find them."

"Sounds good to me," Olivia murmured fervently, and I wondered what she'd dreamed of. Then decided it was probably better not to know.

Brady gingerly dug his hand in one of the outside pockets of his backpack, his expression grim. Then it slowly turned to puzzlement. When he pulled his hand back out, instead of gold and silver and emeralds, he was holding small bits of gravel and sand. He grasped his pack and flipped it upside down, shaking it until there was a smile pile of grit on the ground and the pocket was completely empty.

He scrubbed his fingers in the grass, probably harder and longer than really necessary. I wasn't surprised. I wouldn't want any of that on my fingers either.

We looked at each other wordlessly. I think the others felt like I did, unsure what to say after everything that had happened. Brady had called us his family today, which had felt really good. Then we'd all turned on each other, ready to do who knew what. How could it all have changed so fast? So much? How could that have happened to *us*?

Was there some way to be sure it never happened again?

Then Olivia stretched her hand out, looked straight at Brady and said, "This is for *all* of us. One for all..."

We all reached out and waited for Brady, then laid our hands over hers. At the same time, we declared, "And all for one."

Chapter 22/June/Santa Ramona

Translations

Brady called me Sunday night and said, "We should see if we can meet with Ronny tomorrow."

For the first time, I hadn't called her to meet with us after Chimera. And she hadn't called to ask what happened. I remembered how Chris all but pushed us out last month.

"You know how sick she's been," I told Brady. "I don't think we should bother her. Not until we have something new to tell her."

"She needs to know what I found in the book I just finished translating." Brady sounded…concerned? Worried? Scared?

I hesitated, then agreed. When he cut the connection, I called Ronny, but Chris answered the phone.

"Can Ronny meet with us tomorrow afternoon?" I asked. There was a short pause, and even though Chris hadn't said anything, I could tell he was going to say no. I said quickly, "Brady thinks she needs to hear the information he translated in one of the books we found last month."

There was no sound on the other end so I added, "It's just one book. He really thinks Ronny should know what it says."

There was another pause, then Chris sighed, "Okay. I think it will be okay. We'll see you tomorrow."

I realized his days of lurking in the hallway were over. He planned to be in the room with us the whole time. I couldn't blame him of course, but I was going to smack him over the head if he called me Kitty-Kat.

-xXx-

The next day, the five of us were almost back to normal around each other. We did a lot of laughing and teasing on the walk to Chris and Ronny's. My relief lasted up until we got into the living room. Chris had pulled one of the dining room chairs up next to Ronny. He placed his hand on her arm, as if to give her strength.

Brady sat forward. "Do you remember last month when I told you we'd taken some books from the book shop?"

Ronny nodded and Brady said, "We took the books that Doug's wristband reacted to."

Ronny frowned and straightened in her chair. Her voice sounded rusty when she said, "What do you mean, his wristband reacted?"

I interjected, "You remember Doug found a wristband in the dragon cave a couple years ago?" Ronny looked momentarily confused then nodded, her eyes fastening on Doug's wrist.

"I remember," she said. "But I do not understand what you mean about reacting to books."

"When I get near things that are dangerous or magical, this," Doug pointed to the blue-green stone, "begins to glow."

Ronny's cheeks turned grey and her hands begin to shake. "Do you have those books with you?"

Brady said, "No, but I know their names." Without hesitation he began reeling off a list of titles. I got lost after the first two.

If anything, Ronny grew paler. "I know a few of those books. They are filled with great and often dangerous magick, and may have spells upon them that will prevent you from opening them. Others, I have never heard of before. Which makes me think they are, perhaps, even more dangerous."

"I opened all of them," Brady said, sounding momentarily diverted. Then he gave his shoulders a quick shake and said, "I've only managed to translate one so far. It's about the events leading up to the creation of Chimera."

Ronny reached up and grabbed her pendent, holding it so tightly her knuckles turned white. Her voice was hoarse as she said, "I remember. Mother told me of that time."

Ronny's phrasing was still a bit stilted, but I realized suddenly that it had been months since she used one of her mangled sayings. I missed them.

Brady leaned further forward. "The book talks a lot about your family."

He paused and for a moment there was no sound except Ronny's ragged breathing. I saw Chris tighten his grasp on her arm and a brief smile flitted across her lips though her attention stayed on Brady.

He said, "I'm very sorry about your grandmother."

Ronny swallowed convulsively. "What did this book say?"

Brady hesitated. "I don't think— "

"Tell me," she demanded, more life in her voice than I'd heard for some time.

Brady glanced briefly at Chris. He glanced at Ronny's tense face, then nodded for him to continue.

"It spoke of your grandmother, Gloriana. It confirmed exactly what you've told us. That she was renowned throughout Europe for her healing gifts. That people sought her out and praised her. That she was known as a white witch."

Ronny smiled wanly and nodded.

"It spoke of the monk who swore an oath to suffer no witch to live. How he came to Gloriana's village in 1571 for the specific purpose of destroying her and her children. That would be your mother and your aunts, right?"

Ronny nodded, then bowed her head, one hand still clenched around her pendant.

Brady's voice sped up slightly, like he was trying to get through this as quickly as possible. "No one in the village paid him much attention for most of a year. That unbalanced him, producing various demented behaviors. The monk grew so enraged, he supposedly shook and frothed at the mouth and spoke words that no one could understand."

I couldn't be sure, but it looked like a tear fell from Ronny's bowed head into her lap.

"He spread terrible lies about Gloriana and your family. Accusing her of sickening babies in the surrounding villages so she could use those that died in evil ceremonies. Accusing her of murdering them as sacrifices. If any stood up for her, he threatened to accuse them of witchcraft as well."

This time I was sure I saw a tear fall. Ronny began to rock gently, her head still bowed.

"Then two of her daughters, Brigana and Morgana, were caught tormenting a Mundane family. And that's when the favor of the village changed."

A small sound escaped Ronny and Brady stopped. He asked anxiously, "Would you rather I not finish?"

She kept her head bowed but said, "No, continue please."

"The villagers wrapped your aunts mouths so they could speak no spells, and tied their hands so they could make no gestures. They dragged them in front of the village and the monk read a long list of crimes." He glanced at Ronny's bent head then added, "It's obvious they couldn't have done everything they were accused of, but the villagers became even more enraged. They prepared to burn the two of them at the stake."

Brady stopped and it was Olivia who said, "Tell us what happened, Brady."

"Ronny told us that part. Gloriana was angered by what her daughters had done, but couldn't bear to watch them die. She went to the monk and told him it was she who had magic. That she had cast the spells and ordered her daughters to use them against the Mundane family. She promised to come quietly and let him do with her as he wanted as long as he let her daughters go. The book implied that she threatened to do something very unpleasant to him if he did not accept this offer." A brief smile crossed Brady's lips and I wondered just what type of unpleasant things she'd threatened.

"Why didn't she just do something unpleasant to whoever stood in her way, grab her daughters and leave?" Olivia demanded.

Ronny cried, "Do you remember nothing I have told you?" Her grip tightened on her pendent and this time it was too much. With a snapping sound, the chain broke, leaving the pendent in her hand. Ronny stared at it dully for a moment, then placed it with great care on the table next to her. She drew in a deep breath and lifted her head to look at Olivia. "I have explained to you that using magick against others will cause it to return against the user three-fold. There was nothing she could do. To have used enough magick against the village to save her family and get away would have been to destroy them utterly. Her only hope for her daughters' future was to bargain for them. And the only bargain she could make was to sacrifice herself."

Brady cleared his throat. "The book said the monk lied to your grandmother. He agreed to release her daughters, but once your grandmother was bound and unable to use her magic, he ordered them all to stand trial. Your mother, Glenna, and the youngest daughter, Titiana, tried to break the others out. They must have done something that terrified the monk, for the next day it was announced that Brigana and Morgana had been found innocent. The book said your mother and your aunts promised your grandmother to leave town. Your grandmother insisted on that."

Ronny nodded, then laid her head against the back of her chair. Chris dropped his hand onto her knee and squeezed gently.

"According to the book," Brady said, "they didn't leave. They were still there, hiding in shadows they created so the town wouldn't see them. They planned to stay and save Gloriana, no matter what the danger was to them. But she knew them well. She knew they would risk everything to save her and all of them would be destroyed." He swallowed audibly and glanced at Ronny. She didn't move.

"Your grandmother cast a geas on them, so they couldn't use magic against anyone in town. They could do nothing to stop what happened. The book said Gloriana had a plan to save herself, but when she chanted the geas, the monk thought she was casting a curse on him. He threw a rock at her head; she wasn't knocked completely unconscious, which would have been a blessing, but she couldn't do anything to save herself. Her daughters were forced to watch, helpless to stop it, when Gloriana burned."

"She could have been unconscious," Faith said, glancing at Ronny.

Brady gulped audibly and looked nearly as grey as Ronny. "The gag burnt away before she died. She was screaming as the fire destroyed her."

When Faith opened her mouth again, Brady shook his head. "I'm not going to describe any more. The book was very explicit. Believe me, you don't want to hear it. This is one time I'd give almost anything to lose my eidetic memory."

Ronny shifted restlessly in her seat and he added, "As Ronny told us, the geas broke at the moment of Gloriana's death. The book said she wanted her daughters to live with the Mundane in peace. But that's not what happened."

"No," Ronny said dully. "That is not what happened. At first they enjoyed wreaking vengeance upon the Mundane. They took pleasure in destroying their homes, crops and belongings." Ronny's eyes looked haunted. "It was Mother who first renounced revenge, saying their actions dishonored their mother's memory. My aunts however, refused to listen. And that eventually destroyed the relationship between them and Mother. Just as the fire destroyed my grandmother."

Ronny reached over and touched her pendant. "They were never untied as sisters again. My aunts would not stop, and Mother believed their actions did much to increase the anger and violence directed toward those of magick."

"Which is why she came up with the plan to create Chimera," I said.

"Yes." Ronny turned her head to smile at me. It wasn't much of a smile, mostly just a slight upward curve to the corners of her mouth, but it *was* a smile. "Mother became convinced there would be a war between the Magick and the Mundane if things continued as they were. And if that happened, the Magickal world would be destroyed utterly. Chimera was her answer."

Brady said, "The book emphasized, several times, that none of your aunts renounced their acts of vengeance against the Mundane. Ever."

Other than Ronny's swift intake of breath, there was no sound in the room. She straightened and said, "Tell me, exactly, what this book said."

"It was written by someone close to all of them. His name was Naryeth."

Ronny stared at Brady. "*I* knew Naryeth. He was a good friend of my father's."

"Yes, he said that," Brady agreed. "He approved of much that your aunts had done, but when your mother explained her reasons for Chimera he saw the wisdom of it. He loved the idea of a world without the Mundane. He explained this to your aunts but they weren't interested."

"Most of what I've told you has been no surprise. I'm glad." Brady gave her a strained smile in return. "But there's something you don't know. It's why I said I needed to talk to you." He glanced quickly at Chris, then back to her. "You consider Naryeth as a reliable source, correct?"

Ronny looked puzzled but nodded in agreement.

Brady took a deep breath. "According to his book, your Aunt Morgana swore vengeance upon your mother for abandoning their crusade. She told him, repeatedly, over hundreds of years, that she would destroy your mother for forsaking them. He said she swore an Oath of Requirement." He leaned back and said, "I'm not sure I understand what such an oath entails."

Ronny stared at him, seeming to shrink into herself. For a moment, I was afraid this would be the news that destroyed her. "You must have read that wrong," she told him weakly.

"No," Brady said, finality in his voice. "She swore an Oath of Requirement. Based on Naryeth's reaction I can hypothesize, in general terms, that this is something like an unbreakable vow."

Silence settled thickly around the room.

"You are trying to say that whatever has gone wrong in Chimera has been caused by Morgana," Ronny said slowly. "That in trying to destroy my mother she destroyed everyone."

I started shaking my head. After all, Brady hadn't said anything like that. My lungs froze painfully, as if I'd been hit in the solar plexus, when he nodded. "You understand me," he said. "Yes, after reading everything in that book and re-reading some of the messages we've received from Ghalynn, that is my theory."

Ronny closed her eyes and reached out for Chris. He clasped her hand tightly in his, her fragile hand nearly disappearing inside his strong grasp.

Brady said, "I have three more books to read. Perhaps one of them will include information that will change my mind. But for now, when we return to Chimera I will be looking for clues about what Morgana was up to. Don't forget, Ghalynn said the same thing. Remember?"

When Ronny didn't speak, he closed his eyes and began quoting.

"Morgana hates you, Glenna. She hates that you married one of the enemy. Arthur's death was no accident. Morgana killed him. That trap was also meant for you. She wants you dead. Morgana had been plotting against Rowena as well. She tried to convince Rowena to spend most of her time in Santa Ramona. That would make her Mundane half grow old."

He opened his eyes and looked at Ronny. "He wrote one last thing to your mother.

"I beg of you, do not trust Morgana."

Ronny was crying openly. Chris patted her hand, then stood up. "I can see why you felt the need to share that information, Brady. But I think you need to leave now."

We said quick, subdued good-byes and hurried out the door, followed by the sounds of quiet weeping.

-xXx-

The rest of that month dragged by. School was out, Faith was at soccer camp, Olivia had to take care of her four younger siblings. And Brady's Dad made him go to sports camp. His step-mother had been only too glad to get him out of the house.

Mom kept getting on my case for moping around, but there was really nothing interesting to do without them. I'd read my favorite books and re-watched my favorite movies and looked up all of my favorite stars on IMDb. I thought a bit of moping was definitely in order.

Doug and I got together a couple times, but things seemed…different…between us. A bit strained. Not distant, exactly, but not…comfortable. I kept trying to figure out what I'd done to upset him, but when I asked he brushed it off and said I was imagining things.

Nearly two weeks had passed since the last time anyone had come over. As in one week, three days and nineteen hours. But who's counting.

I was in the kitchen, poking through the cupboards and refrigerator, trying to decide if anything sounded good for lunch. Mom and Dad were at work and I was home by myself, as long as I didn't do anything they wouldn't want me to do — like too much moping.

I almost dropped the sliced turkey when someone pounded on the front door.

I looked through the peephole and was pretty sure I recognized who it was. At least, I was pretty sure I recognized the back of Doug's head. I opened the door, then gasped. Loudly.

Doug snarled, "Don't make a big deal about it, Taylor, or I'll leave and take care of it myself."

His nose was bleeding profusely and one eye was swelling shut even as I watched. I opened my mouth to say…something, but couldn't think of an adequate response.

"Are you going to make me stand here and bleed all over your porch, or are you going to let me in?" His voice sounded much rougher than normal, but the words were perfectly understandable. Even so, it took a moment to make sense of them and step out of the way so he could enter.

He brushed past me into the house and I could see the back of his shirt was torn and dirty. Through a large hole I could see a bruise forming. I could also see blood gumming up a silver-dollar sized patch of hair on the back of his head. This time I knew what I meant to say when I opened my mouth. I was going to ask him what the heck had happened! Then I realized I already knew. Not every detail, but the important part. So instead I said, "You met up with the Rejects."

He headed for the kitchen, and by the time I shut the door and followed him, he'd grabbed a paper towel and was pinching his nose with his head tilted back. I grabbed some ice, wrapped it in a wash cloth and placed it in his free hand, then pushed him gently into a kitchen chair.

After a few moments, he lowered his head and tentatively let go of his nose. I was shocked by how much blood stained the paper towel, but it seemed to have stopped bleeding. He carefully held the ice up to his eye and groaned. I wasn't sure if it was in relief or pain, but either way, it surprised me. Doug liked to be stoic when he was injured.

"Mom's going to kill me when I come home with a black eye," he said. "She warned me three years ago that she'd better not find out I'd been fighting."

"You could say you tripped or walked into a door or some other stupid excuse," I suggested.

"My parents aren't going to believe that," he said, shaking his head.

"Well, I think you should try it." I looked him over and bit my lip. He looked pretty awful. Maybe he could say he'd been attacked without provocation. Of course, then his parents would make life miserable for Ray and whoever else had done this. And nothing would save us if his parents made trouble for the Rejects. If that happened, what they'd done to Doug today would seem like a love tap.

"Um…" I hesitated, then blurted, "You're not going to tell them you were attacked by Ray and Andrew. Are you?"

"No, I won't tell them that. You're right, I guess. I'll probably tell them I fell. They won't believe it, but what can they do about it?" His shoulders slumped and he muttered, "Other than ground me, take my cell phone away, and make me wait before I can get my driver's license."

I ignored his pity party. "Are you going to tell *me* what really happened?"

He stared at me for a moment, then snapped, "What happened? I got stupid, that's what happened. I wasn't paying attention and walked around a corner right into Ray and Andrew."

"They just attacked you? Without saying anything?" I frowned. That didn't sound like Ray. Not the fact that he attacked Doug. But he usually liked to make threats and ask questions before getting around to the attacking part.

Doug's mouth twisted. "You're going to keep asking questions, aren't you?"

I nodded vigorously, and he sighed. "Fine. But I was startled. So it wasn't exactly my fault."

"What wasn't your fault?" I asked, and narrowed my eyes at him.

He didn't look impressed by my what-kind-of-stupid-thing-did-you-do face. "They were just standing there, you know? Staring at me. Mouths hanging open. So I told them they'd better shut them quick or they'd attract flies. They didn't seem to like that."

"You said that? While it was two against one?" I knew my voice was raising, but I couldn't help it. "What the heck were you thinking? That's the most stupid, brainless, idiotic, thoughtless, irresponsible, doofus thing you've ever done." I'd never really spoken to him like that before and he was staring at me, eyebrows raised. But all I could think was, thank goodness Arnold hadn't been there. Things could have been so much worse.

How could Doug have been so careless?

He gave me a look I didn't understand and a wave of color darkened his cheeks. "They kept pounding on me, wanting to know why the gold and silver they found disappeared when they got home."

My legs started shaking so hard I staggered back and grabbed onto the counter to steady myself. "They made it into Mystic? They made it all the way to those trees?"

He nodded and tightened his jaw. "I would've been fine if it was just one of them," he growled and tightened his hands into fists. "And you should see them. They'll think twice about cornering me like that again!"

He glared at me as if I was arguing with him, then gave a nasty grin. "I managed to outsmart them. I convinced them I didn't know what the hell they were talking about."

"Okaaaaay," I said, not sure where this was going.

"It shut them up," he said, like I was being deliberately obtuse. "They didn't want me to know they'd found gold and silver in there. Like I'd try to steal it from them." He sighed and gave me a crooked smile, though it looked like it hurt him. "So then they let me go."

"They let you go," I repeated numbly.

"Yeah." He closed his eyes and pressed the ice against the one that was already bruising.

"Well, good." I wasn't sure what else to say.

"No, it's bad," he said. "It means they'll be hanging around Mystic from now on, making our lives miserable."

Chapter 23/July/Chimera

Payback Is A …

Remembering what Doug had said about the Rejects, I was nervous when we entered Chimera on Saturday. I kept asking Brady to check the map to make sure they weren't already there. And to make sure they didn't enter after us. Brady was patient about it, but Doug finally said, "Give it a rest, Kat."

"They're out of control, Doug." I glared at him. "Have you forgotten what they did to you?" I tried to raise one eyebrow like Olivia did, but ended up with both of them climbing half-way up my forehead. I leaned forward and hissed, "And to your *nose*?"

He glared right back, squinting a bit in the bright sun. The doctor had forbidden Doug from wearing sunglasses until his nose healed. So obviously there was no way he could've forgotten. His eye was still slightly swollen, surrounded by fading shades of green and yellow and purple. And even though his nose didn't look nearly as bad as his eye, it had been *broken*.

Doug's mouth firmed into a hard line. "Ray and Andrew are going to be sorry. I'll make sure of that!"

Uh-oh. Things were going from bad to worse. Doug sounded more interested in payback than in keeping away from them.

Our animals ran up and gave us an exuberant welcome before we headed toward town. I was sure we'd be seeing the Rejects at some point. They'd be heading back there now that they'd found the town. And the trees.

Those trees had made *us* angry and greedy. What would they do to people like the Rejects, who were already like that?

Even though we had to stop several times to allow Brady to check the map, we made good time getting to the group of houses he'd selected. I was pleasantly surprised the Rejects hadn't entered Chimera yet. And although it was probably a waste of energy, I couldn't stop myself from hoping they wouldn't come today at all.

"So how many houses do we need to check this time?" I asked. I shrugged my shoulders, trying to settle my backpack into a more comfortable position. The quicker we checked them, the sooner we could head back home. The sooner we got home, the sooner I could take it off. And the less time I'd have to worry about bumping into the Rejects.

"There are only four of them," Brady said, and pointed them out on the map. I smiled. Only four houses, and still no sign of our adversaries.

I was surprised to see that this group of houses looked like log cabins. Really small shabby cabins. In fact, they looked one step up from a lean-to. Why would magic people, who could apparently make their houses look any way they want, make them look so…so…dismal?

Our animals lay down or perched in a wide half circle, clearly settling in to wait for us. They didn't look worried. I guessed that was a good thing.

It was true there were no dragon attacks. Or static shooting out of door knobs. But I still came to a shocked halt when we opened the door to the first house. Obviously I'd have to work on making assumptions based on appearances! Olivia had to shove her way past me while I stood there and gaped. The outside and inside were *nothing* alike.

Understatement of the year.

The inside was like the throne room of a palace: Two thrones sat at the far end of the long narrow living room. It was filled with highly polished marble floors, elaborately carved columns that speared up to stone arches, walls covered with tapestries on the right, and stained glass windows on the left showing scenes of King Arthur. And everywhere I looked, there were gold accents and purple velvet.

Fortunately, there didn't seem to be anywhere we needed to check in that huge space; no shelfs, no drawers, no cupboards.

We made our way down the length of the room to the arched doorway leading to the rest of the house. Olivia and I took the bedroom. The canopy bed nearly had Olivia drooling. She spent the entire time we were in there muttering that she'd get one of those beds if it was the last thing she did.

I almost laughed out loud, but managed to keep my amusement to a few twitches at the corners of my mouth. Even if Olivia's mom allowed her to get a huge canopy bed, which she wouldn't, it would never fit in her small bedroom.

Doug was still in the next room when we were done checking the dresser and closet. There was really no reason for him to be in that room at all. There were no drawers or cupboards. But there were weapons displayed on every square inch of wall space. They seemed to have placed Doug in some sort of trance. He was slowly moving to each of the display cases, taking a moment to tug on each of the glass doors. Every single one. The fact that all of them were clearly locked did nothing to stop him.

When he reached the last case, he slapped his hand against the glass in frustration. Then he turned and brushed past me, cursing under his breath. I began whistling, loudly, so Olivia wouldn't be able to hear what he was saying. Her mom would ground her for years if she slipped up and said one of *those* words in front of her four younger brothers and sisters. Although they weren't really so young any more.

It didn't take long to finish checking the rest of the house. The next we entered was similar, though instead of a throne room it had a huge indoor swimming pool filled with flotation devices rather than couches and chairs.

"Do you think this is the home of a mermaid?" Faith asked, eyes alight with wonder.

Brady snorted, clearly not on board with mermaids.

Olivia rolled her eyes at Brady, then turned to Faith. "How would a mermaid get to this house? And why would she even need a house if she lived in the water? Think about it."

Faith smirked. "Didn't we watch *The Little Mermaid* together? She might get to use legs part of the time."

Brady made a sound like he was choking on something.

We ignored him.

Then Doug asked, "Why does it have to be a she?"

"What?" Faith wrinkled her forehead in confusion.

"Why can't it be a merman?" Doug insisted, looking at Faith irritably. "Why is it always a mermaid?"

"Okay fine," Faith told him. "Maybe *he* gets to use legs part of the time. Satisfied?"

"Sure," he said blandly. "Glad you see it my way."

Olivia rolled her eyes again, but she was fighting a grin.

When we left that house, I looked around for the next, then turned to Brady. "I thought you said there were four houses to check out here."

Brady pulled out the map, though I was sure he had no need to. "There are four on the map, but we have to go down there." He pointed to a barely discernible path.

Olivia sounded concerned. "That path looks pretty narrow. Are you sure it's safe?"

"Firstly, we've been on constricted paths before and had no trouble. Secondly, we haven't heard anything around town. I would postulate that this area is most likely one of the safest we've been in while inside Chimera."

As we headed toward the path Olivia muttered, "He'd better be right. If something jumps out of there and eats me, I'm going to kill him."

We rounded a bend in the path and stopped directly in front of the third house.

Things were different in this house. Oh, the living room was still far larger than it looked from outside, decorated a la early Robin Hood, with rough bent wood chairs, fur rugs, swords and crossbows — fastened tightly and unmovably to the wall as Doug quickly discovered — wooden tables with the bark still on them, and a large fire pit in the middle of the floor. Of course, that room wasn't any stranger than the others we'd seen that day. It was down the hall that things got…interesting.

A burst of energy warmed my chest at the sight of the closed door. After all, most people leave the doors inside their house open. What was so special that it had to be kept in a closed room? Maybe we'd finally find…something. Something useful. A spurt of excitement made me grin. One could certainly hope so. I just wished I knew what it was that we were looking for.

Other than a flaming lizard.

Faith sounded as interested as I was feeling. "What do you think they're hiding in there?"

"It might be locked," Olivia cautioned, and I felt a momentary impulse to stick my tongue out at her. Why wasn't she enthusiastic like Faith and me?

My breath caught in anticipation as Doug shoved against the door.

Olivia was wrong; it definitely wasn't locked. Instead it bounced off the wall and rebounded against his shoulder. I started to tell him to be careful, but got distracted.

Once upon a time, that space had been a bedroom. But someone, or something, had taken up residence.

I was leaning toward some*thing.*

The back wall of the room had collapsed at some point, leaving a fairly large opening to the outside. If it had opened onto a protected road, it probably wouldn't have been a problem. Unfortunately, there was a dark forest just beyond that wall. The trees pressed close up against the house. Very close. And something that had been living out there had decided that staying in a house was much better.

Maybe it *had* been better, but not now. There were corpses of small animals in various states of decay scattered over the floor and piled in three of the corners. From the last corner came an outhouse reek; clearly whatever lived here had never learned to use indoor plumbing. In the middle of that chaos stood what had probably been a beautifully carved bed. Now it was crusted with grime and covered by a mess of dirty sheets and blankets that were twisted into a disgusting, smelly nest.

A very *large* smelly nest.

I took a couple steps back. "I really don't think we want to be here when…whatever…comes back."

Doug pointed to a small dresser against the far wall, the room's only place where we might find something. He strode over, carefully avoiding the bones and filth, then jerked the drawers open, riffling through the jumble of clothes and other bits that had once belonged to the house's true owner.

He shook his head and started to turn away. Olivia hissed, "Shut the drawers. We don't want…whatever…to know we were here."

He shoved them closed and we all backed out of the room, watching the opening until we got the door closed once more.

"In the future," I told him, "we should be a bit more careful when we open doors. They might be closed for a reason." I was keeping my voice down, half afraid that something was going to walk into that room and yank the door open. I tried to console myself we only had one more house to check this trip.

Which was a good thing, because my backpack was beginning to feel really heavy.

I ended up next to Brady as we crossed the path to the other house. I tried to talk to him, but behind us I could hear snatches of Olivia's conversation with Faith. George's name came up with surprising regularity. And Brady kept growing more and more quiet.

When we got to the last house, our animals were all there. Foxy, Shadow and Rusty were sprawled in the dirt like they'd been waiting there all along. As we climbed onto the porch, Brady pulled out the map and said, "I wish to see any monsters inside this house." Nothing showed up on the map. I started to relax, then stiffened. "How sure are you that nothing showed up because there aren't any monsters in there? I mean, could that wish just not have worked?"

Brady stared at the map a moment then looked me in the eye. "I believe I am quite good at constructing the most appropriate wording to achieve my desired outcome. So I think the most likely hypothesis is that the lack of an indicator denotes an absence of monsters. But I can't exclude the possibility that my phrasing could be off, now or in the future, and generate no response on the map." He flashed me a half smile. "I guess we'll find out."

I didn't smile back. I just wasn't feeling very reassured.

Imagine that.

Chapter 24/July/Chimera

Nearly Back to the Beginning

Hopefully this last house would be quick and easy. I tugged at the straps on my backpack, trying to make them stop digging into my shoulders.

The front porch was huge and all of us were able to crowd onto it before Doug reached for the doorknob. I followed him inside with the others pressed close behind me. I had only a moment to realize there was a strange resistance as I crossed the threshold. Then the door slammed shut behind us and I realized the house was no more than a hollow shell…

Everything began spinning around, like the house was one of the Disneyland teacups being turned maniacally by a super-Energizer Bunny. I tried to grab onto the wall to keep my balance, but it was ripped from my hand. All around me I could hear the panicked sounds of my friends, but I couldn't see them. I had to keep my eyes shut — when I tried to open them I felt sick. Next to me I could hear the sounds of retching and was pretty sure it was Faith.

It was growing harder and harder to stay on my feet. The whole world felt like it was tumbling, with me in the middle. Like being trapped inside a huge clothes dryer.

Then, just as suddenly as it had started, everything went still. We were still standing in the living room, but it was not the same room we'd been in a moment before.

"What the heck happened?" Faith asked. She gulped and wiped the back of her hand across her mouth. "Because whatever it was, I don't ever want it to happen again." I believed her. There was a faint sheen of sweat on her skin, and her face had a greenish tinge.

I glanced around. The house we were in now looked familiar. Outside the window, I could see thatch hanging from the roof. The floor was wooden and rough, and thin gauzy curtains that seemed to change color from soft yellow to peach to pale raspberry covered the windows.

"I think there's something more important," Olivia snapped, "like, where the hell are we?"

I gaped at her, amazed. She'd used a forbidden word.

Brady cleared his throat. "I think they are both equally valid questions—"

"Haven't we been here before?" I knew I'd interrupted Brady, but didn't care if they were equally valid. I just wanted to know where I was.

Doug looked around curiously and said, "Actually, I think you're right, Kat."

He didn't have to sound so surprised. Like he could hardly believe I'd thought of it.

"Gee, thanks," I told him sweetly, then shot him a glare.

In the meantime, Brady had been looking around. "This is the third house we visited," he stated. I opened my mouth to ask how he could be so sure then remembered; this was Brady. I closed my mouth so quickly my teeth made an audible click.

I looked around and felt a momentary spurt of amusement when I realized what had seemed so incredibly strange before – the lack of TVs, Blue-ray players, or anything else electronic – looked pretty normal to me now.

"Okay, let's say for a minute that I buy it. I still want to know how we got here!" Olivia glowered at Brady as if he should know.

"I hypothesize that something we did in the other house triggered a teleportation spell or something similar." Brady shoved his glasses up and blinked thoughtfully. "We'd have to go back and try again to be sure, of course."

"You want to do that again?" Faith sounded incredulous. "It was horrible. I'll just stay here and wait for you, okay?"

"I'm not—"

I had to clap my hands over my ears to shut out an abrupt deafening peal. It was an overwhelming noise, as if my head was inside a giant bell and someone had struck it with a huge metal mallet. The sound kept reverberating around us, while other matching peals sounded in the distance. Howling came from the woods outside town, raising the hair on my arms. Who knew there could be that many trolls out there. Finally, slowly, it died away, leaving only silence behind.

I knew that sound. The question was, which pyramid had it been and who, or what, had set it off? Before I could ask, Brady yanked the map from his pocket and wished to see the Rejects. He glanced at it then his eyes widened behind the lenses of his glasses. "Damn!"

Olivia shot Brady an accusing glance; he'd cursed.

For once Brady didn't even notice Olivia. He was staring at the map, lips moving as he said something under his breath. I could only make out a few words. "Move..." "Which way…heading?" "Likelihood…intersection…" He glanced over at the road only a few feet away from the house and frowned. He opened his mouth as if he was going to actually talk to us, rather than the map, then paused. "Ahhhh. That should be sufficient…"

I couldn't stand it anymore. "What are you muttering about, Brady?"

A look of alarm flashed over his face and his voice was the barest whisper. "I haven't had sufficient time to calculate the probable distance that the sounds of our voices could travel from here." At my puzzled glance he added, quietly, "The Rejects are at the pyramid just down the road."

He muttered something about feet and speed of sound and I'm not sure what else. Then he nodded and spoke slightly louder. "The Rejects were at the pyramid. They're leaving now; heading back toward the tree. We should definitely be out of earshot…" His lips moved again as he calculated under his breath, then spoke in a normal voice, "Now."

"So the Rejects caused all that?" Olivia asked, peering around Brady, trying to see the map.

He pointed to the four red dots hurrying away from the metal pyramid toward the tree. Unfortunately the pyramid was all too close to us.

If they hadn't hit the pyramid, if they hadn't turned back, we could have run right into them. That had been far too close.

Our familiars came running down the road to us. I guessed they hadn't been thrown half-way across town like we had, so they had to follow us all the way back here. As soon as she reached me I scooped Shadow up, telling her how smart and soft and beautiful she was. I'm not sure she understood all that, but she was purring so loud Doug asked, "What are you doing to that cat?"

That made me laugh. "Wouldn't you like to know," I told him, and turned to make my way back toward the tree, feeling better than I had in a while.

Then Olivia decided to mess with my mood. "Doesn't it bother anyone that we haven't accomplished one thing so far? No messages from Ghalynn. No special objects. No clues buried in strangely bad poetry." She raised her eyebrow and stared at the rest of us like she expected an answer. "We've found bupkis."

I spoke up quickly, "Just because we haven't found anything yet doesn't mean we won't. You can't give up."

She rolled her eyes at me. "I'm not talking about giving up. I'm talking about what the Sylph said. That Ghalynn couldn't leave us any more clues. It feels like we're just bumbling around in here. We don't even know what we're looking for."

"I've felt the same," Brady said. "And now, we haven't searched that last house. I don't know if there is any way to circumvent the actions that prevented us from searching it. I dislike moving forward without more information. How am I supposed to devise a realistic search grid in such a large place without more data?"

Olivia lifted her eyebrow at him, but he didn't seem to notice. "Well, Brady," she said. "I think you'd better get to work translating everything we've found so far. Maybe that will give you more…data."

Brady stared at her for a moment, expressionlessly. I wondered what could be going on in that mind of his. Then he nodded decisively. "You are correct. I do need more data. In the meantime, we've cleared nearly six sections of town. Only five remain, so we've assessed more than half of the potential locations where the last object could be hidden." He turned and began stomping in the direction of the doorway and muttered, "Remaining optimistic in the face of repeated neutral results is imperative for a scientist."

The rest of us followed him toward the tree and home.

-xXx-

On Sunday night, I woke to the sounds of another raging magic storm. Blue lightning strikes pelted the town unmercifully for half an hour.

School started that Monday, and we were officially in 11th grade. I hated being subjected to a full day of rumors about hundreds of fish falling from the sky and snakes boiling up out of cracks in the ground. I cringed at all the TSYE talk in the halls, and could only feel grateful the news channels hadn't heard about it in time to send out any crews. At least the rest of the world wasn't talking about how weird Santa Ramona was getting.

For now.

Chapter 25/August/Santa Ramona

Can Anyone Plug a Leaky Tree?

None of us had planned to bother Ronny, but Chris called the week before the full moon and asked if we could come over. He had several investigations that he couldn't put off any longer, and he wanted us to come by before he left. So after checking to be sure everyone was available, I told Chris we'd be there after school.

Brady was dragging a guitar when we met after our last class. I asked if he wanted to drop it by his house first, but he shook his head, emphatically. "Dad said I was hopeless at team sports, so he ordered me to learn a musical instrument."

"Why do you have to do that?" Faith asked, frowning.

"Because *she* announced how worried she was that I was such a one-dimensional person. Because, according to *her*, it's not normal to have such an obsessive interest in science." Brady kicked a rock off the sidewalk and glowered.

Wow, his step-mother really didn't get him at all. Poor Brady.

I was dreading what we'd find at Chris and Ronny's, but when Chris opened the door, I came to a dead stop. Ronny was sitting up straight in her chair, not slumped over. Her eyes were bright. Her skin had a faint pink flush to it, rather than the frightening grey she'd had the last time I'd seen her. Best of all, she looked really pleased to see us.

"I have been so looking forward to seeing you and finding out what has been happening in Chimera," she exclaimed.

We crossed to our usual seats. Olivia pushed the pillows and the colorful throw out of her way and curled her legs up under her. Faith and Doug looked relaxed as they sat back on the long couch. But it took Brady a moment to get comfortable. He finally leaned the guitar awkwardly against his legs and leaned back gingerly.

"What happened to you?" I asked Ronny, then realized that hadn't come out right. I added, "The last few times we were here you looked pretty bad."

More like terrible!

She gave me a small smile. "I am not sure why I have felt so much better lately." Her fingers fumbled at her throat, and finding nothing there, she glanced at the pendant still sitting next to her chair. Her smile grew wistful at the sight of it.

"I think I can fix that so you can wear it again," I told her. I was pretty sure I could figure out some way to make it wearable. And if I couldn't, then probably Brady could.

"No, thank you." Ronny shook her head, but smiled to be sure I wasn't upset by her refusal. "I find I enjoy looking at it. And I could not see it when it was around my neck."

Then her expression changed, becoming serious. "I am sure all of you are aware of that terrible magick storm Saturday night."

"It's all over the local news," Doug said. "Several houses were damaged."

"Too bad it didn't get Ray or Andrew's house," Faith mumbled.

"What was that?" Ronny asked.

"Oh, um, never mind," Faith said quickly. We all knew Ronny wouldn't agree with her, since magic mustn't be used to harm others.

Ronny shrugged and looked at me. "Do you realize how much the magick has been growing in strength? And how it is escaping more often, and for longer periods of time?"

"I…" Now that she said it, I realized the thought had been rattling around in the back of my head for a while now. I could understand why I'd never stopped to think about it. The thought of it now made my skin crawl. Because if it was happening more often, just how often could it happen in the future? And if it was getting stronger, how much stronger could it get? These magic storms had already started damaging houses and causing strange things to happen in town. So just how bad *could* it get?

Ronny leaned forward. "I must assume you have not found anything of significance or you would have let me know right away. But have you found anything?"

Brady cleared his throat and reached into his backpack, pulling out one of the books we'd found. I noticed uneasily that he had a metal band fastened to the cover and it was closed with a padlock. He'd made sure nothing could accidentally open that book.

He held it up so Ronny could see it. "This book."

Doug reached toward it and the stone in his wristband cast a pale blue-green glow around the room. I heard Ronny gasp and out of the corner of my eye, I saw her face twist in amazement. For a moment everyone froze.

Doug turned to Ronny. "Do you know what this glow means?"

She shook her head slowly. "I have never seen anything like that. When does it happen?"

"I know it reacts to things that may be dangerous," he told her. He hesitated, then added, "There's also the possibility it shows when there is magic nearby."

Ronny reached for the book, then turned it in her hands, eyes closed, as if she was trying to feel something from it. I knew she'd been able to sense…vibrations…or something from other items we'd brought to her.

Finally, her brow scrunched in confusion, and she hesitantly said something in her strange Chimeran language. There was a flash of clear blue light, followed by a crackling sound. Something left the book and hit her hands; something that resembled a small bolt of lightning. She hissed in pain and dropped the book. There were several more of the crackling flashes that fizzled out before touching anything.

"Are you all right?" Chris asked. I hadn't seen him enter the room, but maybe he'd been there the whole time, hovering nearby, trying to be sure we didn't tire Ronny out.

"I'm fine." She held up her hand and waggled her fingers at him, perhaps to show there were no lasting ill effects. If that had been her intent, it backfired. Her fingers moved a bit too slowly, out of sync with each other. She quickly tightened them into a fist and dropped her hand to her lap. She bit her lip then said, "I have never had magick react in such a fashion. I believe it may have to do with the amount of magick leaking from Chimera. It has become so strong, I can sometimes feel it licking against my skin. It has begun interfering with the little magick I have left."

She turned in the chair until she faced Chris. "This cannot go on," she told him. "If it continues to escalate at this rate, I believe it could do more than cause another of your Strangest Ever years. It could cause real damage to your world."

"More damage than hitting houses with lightning?" Olivia sounded appalled. "*I* don't call that minor."

"I am talking about more than a few houses," Ronny said quietly. When Brady and Olivia started peppering her with questions, she held up her hand. "I need to think about what it could mean and what could happen. For now I have no clear answers for you." She smiled thinly. "There is no point worrying about something that may not occur. Do not cut off your nose to fright your face."

It had been so long since I'd heard Ronny mangle a saying it almost didn't register, then I had to turn away to hide my grin. She was trying to be serious; I didn't think she'd appreciate me laughing in her face.

And when I thought about what she'd said, I really didn't feel that much like laughing anyway.

Brady shifted as if he was uncomfortable and adjusted the angle of the guitar leaning against his legs. Ronny looked at it and said, "That seems far too large for a lute."

"A lute?" Doug asked, puzzled by the unfamiliar word.

Brady spoke up quickly, "That was an instrument that became popular in the fifteenth century. The guitar is a modern ancestor, if one can refer to an instrument as having ancestors.

"Can you play it for me?" Ronny asked. "I loved when my father played."

Brady's mouth twisted in consternation. "I haven't been taking lessons for long."

"It matters not," Ronny assured him, and gave him a smile so beautiful that I smiled too.

"Come on, Brady," Olivia said, and nudged him in the ribs. She must have done it pretty hard. He made a huffing sound as her elbow connected, then nodded.

He strummed the first few chords of *Dueling Banjos* then offered the guitar to Ronny. She didn't reach for it at first, eyeing it like it might bite her.

Brady stood up and waved the guitar at her enticingly. He grinned and said, "I'll show you the chords. We can take turns." He waved it again. "Go ahead," he encouraged.

Chris patted her arm. She grasped it gingerly and awkwardly placed her fingers where he pointed. Her first strum was so tentative I could barely hear it. But that didn't last. Soon the two of them were passing the guitar back and forth with her playing nearly as fast and well as he did.

"I thought you'd never played a guitar," Olivia told Ronny. "Why are you so good if you haven't done it before?"

"Done what?" Ronny sounded totally distracted, busy playing the next set of chords.

"She means the guitar," Faith spoke up.

"Yes she does," Chris agreed. "Perhaps we should get you one."

"You play it really well," Faith told Ronny.

Ronny looked up and met Faith's eyes. "Well, it is true I have not played a guitar before. But my father was very musical. He played the lute and spoke often, with great longing for something he called his sacks." Ronny sighed. "I do not know how you turn a sack into a musical instrument. He never told me that."

"I believe he might have been referring to a sax," Brady said.

"Yes, as I said, his sacks." Ronny smiled. "Do you know how to make this instrument?"

"Um, no. It's spelled S-A-X," Brady told her. At her puzzled expression he said, "It's short for saxophone. A metallic instrument that is played by blowing into a mouthpiece with a single reed. You press keys on the body of it to produce different tones. My great-grandfather, the one that went missing, he had a saxophone. My Grandfather Chuck still has it. He said his father could have been professional, but was too busy conducting experiments." Brady smiled crookedly. "I got his interest in science, but I'll never be a famous sax player!"

"Well I have never blown into a metallic instrument," Ronny told him, "but playing a stringed instrument is not unknown to me. I suppose playing one has stuck with me." She looked momentarily nostalgic. "I find I like being able to do something that reminds me of him."

They continued playing for a few more minutes, but it was obvious that Ronny was starting to tire. What didn't make sense was the speculative looks Brady keep sending her. So it shouldn't have surprised me when he set the guitar down and asked abruptly, "Tell us more about your father."

"What is it you would like to know?" Ronny looked surprised but willing enough.

"How did he and your mother meet?" That seemed to be a strangely un-Brady-like question. Then he asked, "Why did he end up in Chimera?"

"My father?" Confusion clouded her face for a moment, and Chris sat up straighter next to her, eyes on her face. "My Aunt Morgana brought him to Chimera. You know he was born in Santa Ramona?" When we all shook our heads, she smiled.

"Aunt Morgana claimed he had seen her leaving our tree in the cemetery when he was visiting family here. It took her some time to hunt him down since he had moved away from here to a lengthy shore." Ronny didn't meet our eyes as she continued, "Aunt Morgana forced him to come to Chimera."

She locked her hands in her lap and stared at them intently. "Mother said he pined for his family and his home for a few years. She felt sorry; it had been years since someone was kept in Chimera against their will. He was furious at first, yelling abuse at everyone who tried to speak to him. If the magick in Chimera had not been so strong, Mother feared he would harm someone. Instead I think he only hurt himself. He punched the walls of the room where he was kept so hard that he made holes in them."

Ronny must have heard my shocked gasp, but merely smiled so deep a dimple winked at the corner of her mouth. "I have seen that wall. He is lucky he did not break his hand. Mother had to enchant the entire house so he could do no further harm to it or to his skin. Finally he calmed enough to listen, and she explained about Chimera, about the need to keep it safe. About the rules that no Mundane who knew it existed could be allowed to live in the Mundane world. He claimed he had not seen Aunt Morgana leave the tree in the cemetery. But she could only apologize, because by then the damage was done."

It was so quiet you could have heard a pin drop. I actually jumped when the refrigerator rumbled to life with a low whine. Ronny didn't seem to notice. "I was just ten years old when he and I first spoke of it. He said what started as the very worst thing that ever happened to him ended up being the best. He fell in love with Mother and she with him. It was frowned upon by the rest of the Council, and Aunt Morgana was furious, but Mother and Father chose to become handfast and insisted the Council recognize it."

"Handfast?" Olivia asked.

It was Faith, our resident expert on all things myth and legend, who answered. "It's a ceremony where two people who have no priest or minister available, swear to take each other as husband and wife. It often involved making a small cut on each wrist and binding them together. So they were literally one blood." She looked thrilled, like it was romantic to bleed on each other.

How could someone like Faith, normally so grounded in what was real, be so fascinated by myths and legends? I leaned forward and asked, "So they were like blood sisters, uh blood brothers, uh blood partners then?" I hoped my face wasn't as red as it felt after botching that up so badly.

"Yes, that is an important part of the ceremony," Ronny said, smiling in what looked like commiseration. Maybe my face *was* that red. Darn it.

"What's eating you, Brady?" Doug suddenly asked.

"Nothing important," Brady said. I could only see the side of his face, but thought he looked confused. Or maybe disturbed. Then he looked away from Doug and seemed normal. Maybe I'd imagined that strange look.

Wrong.

Brady leapt to his feet, knocking the guitar to the floor. "What gave Chimera the right to force people to live there? It wasn't just your father. According to Ghalynn at least three important people from our world were taken there. There must have been others. So what possible justification did you have for disrupting their lives?"

Ronny looked startled by the sudden accusation in his voice. I was too. What was wrong with Brady's eidetic memory? Ronny already explained this to us. It was part of the whole protecting-themselves-from-being-burned-at-the-stake thing.

Chris opened his mouth, probably to remind Brady to be civil, but Ronny spoke first. "You must not think we did it randomly. And certainly we did not do it often. It would do us no good to have the Mundane world searching for ours because too many had disappeared. The purpose was always to keep Chimera secret. To keep it safe." She moved restlessly in her chair then continued, "At first, when there was still magick in this world, we could simply make the Mundane forget they had seen us. Once the magick faded, there was no other way to protect ourselves."

"Didn't you say your father denied seeing your aunt?" Brady sounded like he was angry with Ronny. Like she'd done something that hurt *him*. He was actually glaring at her. "That means she dragged him to Chimera for no reason."

"Brady," I said, worried about the angry flush darkening his face and the growing pallor on Ronny's, "what's this about?"

"I've been thinking of the myths and stories, where people were supposedly stolen or lured into the world of fairy. I've been wondering how often that really happened. Because it's not right." He glared at me. "You should agree with me, Kat. Ronny said they might have made your brother disappear in there."

I sucked in my breath and shuddered. How would I feel if Chris had been trapped in Chimera? Furious! But only because he was my brother. What was making Brady so angry?

Ronny shook her head at Brady. "Those stories occurred long before Chimera was created. I do not believe the land of fairy still exists. It has been years since anyone from my world has heard from the Fae. Those of the fairy folk did not wish to leave the Mundane world when we did."

"It still doesn't explain how you people could think it was acceptable," Brady insisted. "It would be like being in prison."

Ronny pressed herself against the back of her chair, eyes wide. She didn't say anything, only began shaking her head slowly back and forth. Chris bent down and murmured something I couldn't hear into her ear.

Olivia muttered, "Nicer than any prison around here."

Brady ignored that. He stared at Ronny and demanded, "How could you countenance such a thing?"

Chris straightened again, but Ronny patted his hand and answered, "It was the Council that made those decisions," Ronny said slowly. "I was not part of their discussions on these matters. In fact, it all happened before I was even born. It has been more than eighty years since a Mundane was taken." She shifted in her chair, brows drawn tightly together in thought. When she spoke again, it was almost as if the words were being dragged from her. "Actually, my father was the last."

Brady stared at her a moment, then said, "I still don't think it's right, forcing people to stay there. Away from their life. Away from their family."

I hadn't realized how stiffly he was holding his shoulders until he slowly relaxed. "I just don't agree with it."

The flush faded from his cheeks. He looked at Doug and said, "It's time I went home."

I jumped to my feet and looked at Chris, perched on the arm of Ronny's chair, holding her hand tightly, frowning at Brady. I thought again about how close Chris had come to being forced to live in Chimera. I agreed with Brady on this; I didn't think it was right either.

Our goodbyes were quick and subdued.

-xXx-

It was only two days before the next full-moon Saturday when the new student was introduced, even though classes had already started. As usual, we'd been avoiding the Rejects and they must have been feeling deprived. Why else would they pick on the new girl? Although it might have something to do with how hesitant and nervous she acted. That probably appealed to Andrew.

We were in the hall when Andrew reached out his foot and tripped her. I knew just how it felt to fly through the air and crash into the lockers, books and papers sliding from the backpack she'd slung half open over her shoulder.

Next to me, Olivia snapped, "That's it!" I'd never heard her sound so angry and determined.

She stalked down the hall, stooped down beside the girl, and said, "My name is Olivia. I apologize, but we have a turkey infestation in this school. I'd like you to know not all of us are like that."

Faith and I hurried to her side; Faith stood with her arms crossed over her chest, eyes watchful. I began grabbing books and papers and helping the new girl shove them into her backpack. It only took a couple minutes, but I kept expecting Ray and the others to come after us, so it felt like hours.

Olivia helped the girl, who looked far too young to be in high school, to her feet. She stuttered, "I'm B-B-Brenda."

"You're all a bunch of stuttering freaks," Ray growled. He brushed past Faith and stopped in front of Olivia. "What do you think you're doing, O-li-li-li-via?" He was glaring at her as if he'd like to tear her apart.

She just smiled sweetly, pretending not to see the promise of pain in his eyes. "I'm just welcoming our new student." She turned to the girl and said, "You should get to class."

The girl didn't waste any time. She practically ran down the hall, backpack swinging down by her side, glad to get away.

Faith and I flanked Olivia, standing with her shoulder to shoulder. Under her breath, too quiet for Ray to hear, she muttered, "I wish George was here."

I wished *someone* was here. Three of us against Ray, Andrew and Polly didn't seem like good odds. But neither Doug nor Brady, or even George were around right now. The only saving grace was that Arnold wasn't here either.

Ray looked us over contemptuously then turned away. He called out, "Better watch your step, you freaks. Wouldn't want anything to happen to you."

I stared after him, grinding my teeth. We'd just been threatened in the middle of school and there was nothing we could do about it.

Chapter 26/August/Chimera

Electricity!

Going through the tree this month was bad. It reminded me of being caught under strong, crashing waves at the beach. Bitterly cold waves that crush you under the surface, toss you in circles, and give you no idea of which way is up. Give you no chance to breathe. The kind that make you question why you ever wanted to swim in the ocean. The kind that have you struggling blindly, flailing about in desperation as your lungs scream and your mind begs you to do something. Anything.

The kind where you begin to wonder if it was worth dying for.

I exploded out of the tree, flung from the spinning water onto a distant shore. Except I was, of course, completely dry. Chilled to the bone, but dry. I lay on my belly in the dirt, greedily sucking in deep breaths of air. Still not sure if this was worth dying for or not.

At the moment, I was leaning towards…not.

Then Shadow was by my side, licking my face with her rough tongue. It was only then that I realized there were tears on my cheek. This one had been bad. But as Shadow climbed onto my neck, her rumbling purr spreading through me, her little chirps of welcome warming me, I decided Chimera was worth a few minutes of terror each month.

Probably.

I sighed and told her, "I need to get up, girl."

As if she understood me, she stood up and jumped to the ground next to me. I climbed to my feet and began brushing vigorously at the dirt covering my shirt and pants.

My hands faltered as Faith asked, "Is it my imagination, or is that doorway getting worse every month?"

Olivia stopped petting Pyg long enough to say, "Not every month, no. But when it does get bad this year, it seems a lot worse."

"Ronny said magic seems to be escaping Chimera more and more often." Brady looked contemplative, like he was looking at something I couldn't see. Then his brows scrunched like he'd thought of something. "Yes. Perhaps there is a correlation. If so, I may be able to extrapolate the rate of deterioration."

He pulled the map from his pocket and wished to see the Rejects. He gave a startled exclamation and for a moment I thought they must be close by.

Faith turned in a circle, trying to see what had caused that reaction from normally calm, collected Brady. Seeing nothing she looked at me and shrugged.

Doug stepped up and peered over Brady's shoulder at the map. He tilted his head to one side, then the other. "What has you so spooked? I don't see anything unusual."

Brady pointed at the edge of the map. "There."

Now we were all peering at it, clustered in a tight circle around Brady. And all of us looked completely clueless.

"Why don't you tell us what the heck you're talking about, Brady?" I didn't need Olivia's snarky tone of voice to know she was losing her patience with him. Her pinched lips and narrowed eyes made that clear.

Plus she'd said heck out loud.

"I acknowledge that I have viewed this map in significantly more detail than the rest of you. And of course, my memory of what it used to look like is exact, so I have an advantage. However, it is disconcerting that none of you can recognize what has happened to the boundaries of Chimera."

I looked again and realized some of the land drawn on the edges of the map looked…fuzzy. And there were a few places where it appeared to be missing altogether.

"What could cause it to disappear like that?" I asked. Seeing the worry on Brady's face made my stomach clench. Whatever he thought this was, it wasn't good.

"It might not worry me if that was all. That could have several causes, such as the ink fading with age and use." He glanced again at the map, as if wanting to confirm what he had seen. He swallowed audibly and said, "Some parts have changed shape. Something is altering Chimera." He stabbed his finger to one corner of the map. I looked closely, but didn't see anything different. However, I had no doubt Brady knew what he was talking about.

"We'll have to ask Ronny," I said, trying to sound more optimistic than I felt. "I'm sure she'll have a reasonable explanation."

Brady stared at me, eyebrows raised uncomfortably high, for a long moment. Then he said, "We need to see her as soon as we get back. I suggest we make this day as short as possible."

Brady turned and set a rapid pace toward the town. All of us, even Faith, were panting and though Doug didn't say a word, I could see he was limping heavily by the time we reached the first of the houses Brady wanted to check. For once, Rusty wasn't bouncing around exuberantly, knocking into Doug every few steps. Instead he walked close beside Doug's bad leg, looking almost…protective.

These houses didn't really look like houses at all. Instead, they were mini-castles, complete with turrets and pennants. Next to me, Olivia sucked in a wondering breath, then exhaled a long, low "Ahhhhhh." She turned to Brady and said in satisfaction, "Castles!"

In the center of the 'castles' lay a small park. I noticed two statues; a woman sitting on the wide stone edge of a flower bed, and a man standing next to her. His hand was on her shoulder, looking down at her with a loving expression. I could understand why they'd put up *this* statue. It was nice.

Brady led us to the closest house. For the first time in months, Rusty acted like he was going to follow Doug inside. Doug sounded apologetic when he told the little dog he needed to wait. When I looked back, our familiars were all standing in a clump, watching us forlornly.

It would have been nice to take them inside with us. If I wasn't so worried about the havoc they might cause.

I was watching my feet, still thinking about how we could bring them with us when we stepped inside. Maybe we could just tell them to be careful. They were smart after all—

"It's a good thing we left them outside," Doug said fervently.

I glanced up, curious, then gasped. Good thing was right!

Brady's muttered, "Why is there always three or seven?" barely registered. I was too busy looking around in fascination.

I'd never seen so much glass in my life. Delicate, paper thin glass vases. Faceted bowls that shimmered like diamonds. Goblets perched on threadlike stems. Solid glass mermaids with hair as fine and curled as real human hair. Spun glass castles taller than me, dwarfed by rearing dragons. And everywhere, fantastically hand-blown animals: Pegasus with wide-spread translucent wings; unicorns with long, twisted horns and tails flowing in unseen breezes; gryphons with strong lion bodies and delicately detailed feathers covering eagle heads. Plus dozens of other fantastical creatures I couldn't recognize.

Every square inch of that room was covered with glass. I felt a momentary stab of envy. I'd like to take all of it, or half of it, or just one tiny corner of it home with me. My fingers actually twitched with the desire to pick up just one thing. After all, the person who owned it wasn't here anymore. It wasn't like anyone would miss it.

Right?

As my fingers touched a tiny castle, an exact replica of this place, a ripple of guilt ran through me. It was true no one had been here in the past three and a half years, but it didn't mean they would never come back. How would I explain to them, or to Ronny, why I'd taken something that didn't belong to me?

Reluctantly I pulled my hand back and curled my fingers tightly into my palm. I wasn't going to open my hand again until I was away from temptation. It was pulling at me even now.

Fortunately, we made short work of searching the house. And none of the other rooms had any glass pieces. I was careful to keep my eyes on the floor when we walked back through the living room as we left.

Outside the house, I scooped up Shadow and held her tightly, running my hands over her fur, trying to get the feel of the glass out of my head. I breathed deeply, listening to Shadow's purr and felt myself relax. Hopefully nothing else would ever appeal to me like that again. I wasn't even sure what had made me want those bits of glass so badly. They were beautiful, but I'd never wanted to own something like that before. It was almost as if they'd been enchanted.

I shuddered. It suddenly felt too much like the horrible metal forest.

What would have happened if I'd grabbed an enchanted object and tried to take it out with me? So many houses in Mystic were booby-trapped. What if that had been another?

I set Shadow down reluctantly and followed the others toward the next house.

Nothing happened at that house or the next. I'd have liked to relax but Brady kept pushing us to hurry. He *really* wanted to get back and talk to Ronny. But these were big houses, and there were eight of them he wanted us to get through. By the time we'd finished checking the third house, I was ready to tell him to back off.

Olivia beat me to it. "Maybe we don't try to get through all eight today if you're in such an all-fired hurry! Who cares if we wait until next time to finish?"

"I've studied the map extensively and determined the most logical use of our time." Brady sounded like a teacher giving a lecture. "There are eight houses in a tightly clustered group in this area. They are separated by the road from other houses. It makes sense to finish these as a group. So that next time we won't have to come this far."

Olivia rolled her eyes, but didn't argue. Brady turned and stomped off, with the rest of us rushing to catch up.

The next house also seemed empty of anything interesting. Until we got to a back room, filled with unidentifiable objects in varying stages of completion. It looked like the laboratory of some half-crazed inventor.

Brady would probably feel right at home.

Shelves on the left wall held a number of beakers and flasks that may once have been filled with liquids. There were no fluids in them anymore, but strangely colored residues could still be seen on the bottom of some containers.

To the right, a beautifully carved wooden cabinet was filled with dozens of drawers of varying sizes. Brady began pulling them open, glancing inside, and closing them in rapid succession. Finally he finished peering into the last drawer and closed it slowly.

"Well?" Doug asked.

"They're filled with screws, washers, nuts, wires, screwdrivers and wrenches. The kind of stuff my dad keeps in his garage."

If that was so boringly normal, why did Brady look so puzzled? He began walking toward the back of the room, then stopped so fast I almost walked into him.

"What is it?" I asked, looking at the bench in front of us, covered with twisted copper wires inside metal cages.

Brady had his hand pressed tight to his chest and his voice shook when he said, "Tesla coils."

"Like those weird lightning machines they showed on *Mythbusters*?" Olivia asked, amused.

Brady coughed. Actually, I think he nearly choked, but was trying to hide it. He said, "That is certainly one way to describe them. Nikola Tesla invented them the 1890's. And they shouldn't be here."

"Why? What are they used for?" Faith asked.

"They are electrical resonant transformer circuits that produce high-voltage, low-current, high frequency alternating-current electricity."

"Whoosh," Faith said, and ran her hand a couple inches over her head. "Sorry I asked!"

"Don't you understand what this means?" Brady asked, his voice high. He bounced back and forth, from one foot to the other, like he couldn't bear to stand still.

Olivia crossed her arms over her chest. "Ummmm. That would be…no."

"Someone was trying to generate electricity." He looked around expectantly, and when none of us got excited, he added, "Electricity. Here, in Chimera. The place where nothing electrical or battery-operated can work."

Doug let out a low whistle. "You think someone in Chimera, someone who either wasn't good at magic, or perhaps someone who couldn't use magic at all, wanted to find a way to make electricity? They would have to know how it works."

"This is just speculation, but it is based on logical facts. Magic users would have no need for it, since they are able to make things operate with…magic." There had only been a slight pause before he used the '*m*' word. I knew it still bothered his logic-craving brain to acknowledge that magic really existed.

Brady's brow creased. I knew that look. He was going into techno-science-geek guy mode.

"How do you know so much about this stuff?" Olivia asked. Her arms were still crossed.

"Grandpa Chuck liked to tell me about my great-grandfather, Arthur. He used electricity with a number of his inventions. There are still some of his experiments boxed up in Grandpa Chuck's attic. I think I should ask to see them. It might be possible to extrapolate what this person was attempting to accomplish."

He walked from one end of the bench to the other, looking carefully at everything. The way his brow was scrunched in concentration, I could tell he was trying to make sure he got everything stored away in his photographic memory.

At the end of the bench, he reached out and picked up some papers, looking at each carefully. He took so long I was tapping my foot impatiently before he finished. Then he placed papers to one side and picked up a thin book they had been hiding. He flipped through dozens of pages covered with cramped Chimeran writing.

"Um, didn't *you* say we're in a hurry?" Olivia's voice was very sweet, like she was talking to a small child.

"What?" Brady didn't even look up. When Olivia cleared her throat, loudly, he finally looked at her, then blushed. "Sorry. I got carried away I guess. But it's an inventor's journal." He said it like that explained everything. When she kept staring at him, he said, "Um…I'll just take it with me and read it later."

As he swung his backpack off his shoulder, his grip on the book loosened momentarily, and a hand-drawn picture fell from between the pages, unfolding as it drifted lazily to the floor. Brady leaned over to pick it up and froze. He stayed bent over, head cocked to one side, like he'd been turned to stone.

"What is it?" I asked, puzzled by his reaction.

He picked the paper up gingerly, holding it by one corner, then gently laid it on top of his palm. We gathered around, interested to see what had caught his attention like that.

It was a map of Chimera and of the cemetery. It was drawn in vivid detail, in a birds-eye view of this world and part of ours.

Brady turned the drawing this way and that, then held it out at arm's length. He squinted at it and turned his head from one side to the other, then sighed.

"There's something hidden here," he said. "A pattern, or clues to something, I'm sure of it. Unfortunately, it will take more time than we have right now to determine what it is." He re-folded it and placed it back inside the book, then carefully placed it in his backpack.

He also grabbed the other papers and laid them on top of the book. "I'll have to analyze all of this later. I can interpret Chimeran with significant accuracy now, but it can still take some time and concentration." He shot a look at Olivia and added, "More than we can spare now."

Doug led the way to the next house, trailed by our animals. Brady was walking slower, wearing an abstracted expression, lips moving as he tried to work through something. He kept running his hands through his collar length hair until it was sticking out in different directions. Not a pretty sight. And it was no use asking him what was going on in his head. He probably wouldn't hear me if I tried.

Once inside that house, Olivia made a retching noise and groaned. I barely stopped myself from making that same sound.

The walls of the living room were covered with the remains of dead bats and a number of undefinable creatures. They'd been dissected, pinned to boards, and turned into some kind of disgusting wall art. Fortunately, there were no cupboards or other hiding places in the living room. We were able to work our way rapidly through the other rooms, each filled with dried bits and pieces of bugs and animals. I just wanted to get the heck out of there.

"One last door," Doug exclaimed and threw it open. We crowded around him, gazing at the stairs that plunged down into a black space below.

Next to me, Faith gulped, but I didn't look over to see how she was doing. She was on her own. I was too busy trying to convince my stomach there was nothing down there to tie it into knots. That the musky, musty smell wafting up was perfectly normal for a closed up basement. My stomach wasn't buying the pep talk. It continued to feel like a fish pulled from the water, flopping around on the land. I *really* didn't want to go down there.

Brady dug candles and matches out of his pack and passed them around. Then Doug led the way down into the darkness, and the rest of us followed close behind.

The candles flickered and cast small circles of light. Enough to see our feet on the worn stone steps, but not enough to show the next step ahead. There was no hint about what existed farther down in that space.

When we got to the bottom, we moved slowly across the floor, sticking together. I held my candle high, trying to throw more light, then wished I hadn't. The space was filled with cages and small locked cells. And they weren't empty. The creatures inside those cells were mere pitiful dried skin stretched tightly over bone. Some had scraped all the skin off their arms and legs, trying to force their way out.

In one of the cells, the occupant had been desperate enough to try to force its head through the bars. It almost succeeded. It had gotten as far as partially scraping off one ear before becoming hopelessly stuck. Its body dangled in a painfully twisted position.

"Why would someone just leave these…these…whatever they are, to die?" Faith sounded appalled and turned her face away so she didn't have to look.

I couldn't tell what they had been, but at least it was obvious none had been human. I thought I might have recognized one —tall thick bones, bits of bristly black hair, shriveled warty shapes on some of the remaining skin. I was pretty sure it had, at one time, been a troll.

"I bet these were going to be more specimens for the walls," Olivia said, sounding shaken. "Why do you think they're still down here and not on display?"

Brady cleared his throat and when he spoke his voice was strangely gentle. "I think these…creatures…were in here when everyone disappeared. There was no one to feed them or let them out…" His voice trailed off and his gaze grew distant.

"What is it?" I asked, sure he'd thought of something.

"We've never really talked about it," he said slowly. "But I think it's time we gave it some thought."

"Give what some thought?" Faith demanded.

"Why it is that all of the people are gone, but the monsters aren't."

-xXx-

We were silent as we made our way to the next house. We'd all known there were no people in here. And we'd all seen spiders and trolls and ogres. We'd just accepted that there were monsters in here. Maybe because there are always monsters in fairytales. Chimera was a magical place, just like something out of a fairytale.

Of course there were monsters, right?

But now that Brady had asked the question, I didn't have an answer. Or even a guess. Why *were* there monsters in here, but no people? What could only get rid of people? My mind kept circling around that question. That, and one other. If it had happened once, could it happen again?

I crowded onto the porch with the others, glad to have something else to think about. Hopefully this next house wouldn't throw anything weird at us. I wasn't in the mood to deal with any more weirdness.

Chapter 27/August/Chimera

Lions and Tigers and Bears!

At first glance, this house had a terribly ordinary living room for Chimera. Filled with comfortable chairs and couches. Large, beautifully detailed paintings, full of vibrant colors on the walls. Faith wandered over to look closer. When she made an awed, "Ooooooo" sound I went to see what had her so interested.

I was momentarily distracted by Rusty. Somehow our animals had followed us inside, and Rusty was standing in front of one of the paintings, growling. Shadow was near him, her back arched, hissing loudly. That set off the others; the room began to ring with squeaks, growls, barks and hisses. It made my head hurt.

"Stupid dog, it's just a painting." Irritation roughened Doug's tone and Rusty stopped barking. But growls kept rumbling from somewhere deep in his chest.

I ran over and scooped up Shadow. I wasn't sure what had her so angry, but she was puffed up to nearly twice her normal size. I carried the hissing, squirming cat to the front door, while Doug tugged Rusty across the floor, nails digging into the wood as he tried to escape from Doug's grasp. I noticed his wristband flash once and wondered if it was reacting to whatever was making our animals act so strange.

Once we had Shadow and Rusty outside, the others followed and we were able to shut the door with them outside. We stared at each other in amazement in the silence that followed.

"What was that about?" I asked.

"No idea," Doug said, and stared at the door as if it could give him a clue.

Faith had gone back over, staring at the painting that had upset Rusty so much. I couldn't understand why he didn't like it. It depicted a jungle with vivid shades of greens and browns, filled with inky shadows between the trees, under luxuriant vegetation. It was so detailed and realistic, I almost believed I could step right into it.

But as I stared at it, despite the fact that it was astonishingly beautiful, I suddenly had no desire to try to get inside. Because something was peering out of the deepest of those shadows.

It was so well-camouflaged, it took me a minute to make it out. It reminded me of a Beverly Doolittle painting, where the artist deliberately tricks the eye. But once I saw the tiger's face I knew I'd always be able to see it. It glared out of the darkness, eyes blazing, top lip drawn back in a frozen snarl, exposing long, sharp teeth. I was grateful it was just a painting.

I'd never want an actual tiger looking at me like that.

Why would someone want it in their living room, staring out at them? Watching them. Hating them.

I stepped away slowly. For some reason, I didn't want to turn my back on it until I was several feet away. Then I turned around and hurried across the room, glad to leave it behind. There was another painting on the other wall. Perhaps it would be more appealing.

This one was a sweeping African savannah, with a few sparse green trees in the distance. A scattering of zebras and giraffes stood near those trees. At the far right, a hint of water glimmered. The mid-day sun beat down, blurring the views in the distance, but shimmering where it touched that hint of water. This was even more realistic than the other painting. I looked carefully for the artist's signature, interested in trying a Google search when I got home, but couldn't find one.

That search did reveal something else. Make that five somethings. On the left, disguised by the tall grass, a large lion reclined along with four lionesses. All but one was looking at the zebras in the distance. The other had its head turned to look out of the painting. Now that I saw it, I could feel its eyes on my face, like a weight. That gaze made me so uncomfortable I moved several feet to the right.

I'd heard that the Mona Lisa keeps looking at you even when you move around the room. This lioness was the same. Those eyes watched me in an unwavering, unblinking stare. I wanted to laugh at that thought. Of course the eyes were unblinking. It was a painting, after all. But I couldn't shake the thought that they *could* blink.

They just didn't want to.

I very deliberately turned my back and walked into the middle of the room, as far away from the walls and the other paintings as possible and resolutely kept my eyes turned away. Faith came over and stood next to me. She didn't mention the tiger or the lioness, but she was keeping her eyes away from the walls as diligently as I was.

Brady said, "I don't see anything useful in here, but let me check the map." He pulled it from his pocket. "I wish to see anything we should be aware of or that Ghalynn left for us."

Nothing showed on the map, but Doug's wristband let out a bright flash of blue-green light. It was followed by a growl to our right. A deep, angry, tiger growl.

"Maybe we should learn to listen to our animals." It was hard to force those words out with the spit drying in my mouth.

"It's just a painting," Faith said angrily.

"What's a painting?" Olivia had to raise her voice to be heard over the next growl which was lower pitched, yet louder than the one before.

Before Faith could respond, there was a loud snarl to our left. A very lion-ish snarl.

From the wall in front of us, from one of the paintings I hadn't wanted to see, came the distinctive sound of a bear making loud huffing noises. Angry bear huffing noises.

Even worse, from the wall behind us came the sound of tearing canvas, like something was trying to rip its way out. I grabbed Faith and shouted, "We've got to get out of this room!"

There was no way we could make it back to the front door, so I rushed toward the only other door in that space. It opened onto a hallway, which struck me as odd. I'd never seen a house with a door separating the living room from the hall. But as Doug followed the rest of us out, I was never so glad to slam a door in my life.

Doug reached over my head and shot a thick metal bolt into the door frame just as something heavy hit the floor in the living room.

Another deep growl reverberated through the house, rattling the door we'd just shut.

"What the heck happened in there?" I demanded. My heart was pounding so loudly I wasn't sure I'd be able to hear if anyone answered.

"The paintings," Faith whispered. "They came to life."

Darn it. I heard *that.*

"Don't be ridiculous," Olivia told her. "Paintings can't come to life." Her voice didn't sound nearly as sure as she probably meant it to. She dug a small pack of beef jerky out of her pocket and started chewing a piece, trying too hard to look nonchalant.

"We've seen plenty of defensive measures on other houses. Are you forgetting the holo-dragon?" Doug asked her. "This is another defensive spell. We made it through all those other traps. We can handle this."

He was right; we'd made it past plenty of strange scary stuff over the last few months. His certainty helped me relax. My heart began to slow, and I was able to take a deep breath. We'd escaped the paintings. We'd get out of here. Somehow.

Olivia pulled out another piece of jerky and put it in her mouth.

Which is when the house went crazy.

Something heavy, something that roared in frustration, began crashing against the door. The flimsy wood rattled and creaked. Then the floor began to ripple, becoming softer, almost muddy underfoot.

Thick, sticky mud.

We pushed our way down the hall, which I would have been willing to swear, was growing longer with every step we took.

It wasn't until Doug stooped in front of me that I realized the ceiling was lowering. And the walls, with a series of jerks and groans, were closing in on us.

We were going to be crushed by the house if we didn't get out of there!

"Shut down all the garbage mashers on the detention level!" I yelled, knowing I sounded ridiculous. But it managed to pull a chuckle out of Doug, which made me feel better. He wouldn't be chuckling if he really thought we were going to die in here. Would he?

There was a narrow bathroom on the right side, about halfway down. It had no windows and no way out so we kept going. Only one other doorway led off the hall, at the far end, on the left. It felt very far away. The walls were changing around us. Morphing into something wet and red and pulsating. Something that was making hungry grunting noises.

We were all trying to hurry now, the floor sticking to our feet, making it harder and harder to move. Olivia tripped and Brady grabbed her arm, hauling her back to her feet in one quick movement. She cried out as her grip loosened, and the pack of jerky slipped from her fingers, striking the floor with a wet plop.

She started to reach down for it when something vaguely tongue shaped, though far too long and pointed, lashed out of the muddy surface of the floor with a thick slurping noise, wrapped around the package and pulled it out of sight.

Brady jerked Olivia's arm. "Run!"

We hurled ourselves down that sticky, clinging hallway. That slurping sound kept erupting just behind our feet, and once I felt something hot and wet glance against my ankle. I screamed and forced myself to move even faster.

How could this be happening to us? I didn't want to die like this!

Normally I wouldn't enter a room in Chimera before checking it out, but this time all of us flung ourselves through the open doorway without a pause. I glanced back the way we'd come. The beef jerky pack — torn and crumpled — erupted from somewhere inside the floor with so much force it hit the ceiling before bouncing back down and sinking under what used to be hard wood planks.

Brady slammed the door shut, cutting off my view of the hall. This door was thicker and heavier, with bolts near the top and bottom. Olivia stooped down and shoved the bottom into place just as Doug got his done at the top.

We stood still for a moment. I was panting and dizzy and drenched with rank fear sweat. So were the others.

"The house. The house..." Faith's teeth were chattering and her eyes were a bit wild. "It was trying to *eat* us."

No one answered. After all, what was there to say?

Chapter 28/August/Chimera

Mimps!

There was a small window on the far side of the bedroom. Doug stayed next to the door, listening for pursuit. But nothing was pounding, thumping or scratching on the door, so the rest of us quickly riffled through the dresser and closet, jerking things out and dropping them in our hurry. There was no way we were ever coming back inside this place!

When we didn't turn up anything useful or interesting, and nothing appeared on Brady's map, we took turns squeezing out through the window. I was nervous about standing in the flowerbed, away from the safety of the road, and hissed at Doug to hurry up. We edged around the house and finally reached a well-defined path that ran between the road and the porch of this death trap.

I didn't relax until we all reached the safety of the road. Seeing Shadow hurrying toward me made me smile. We'd all survived.

Everything was going to be okay.

Ear piercing sounds from the metal pyramids blared out, accompanied by the usual howls. Only this time, I could swear there were at least twice the number of monster throats uttering them; an overwhelming number of voices. They layered one on top of another, until the air rang with them, coming at us from every direction. They obliterated everything else, nearly drowning out my own thoughts. I slapped my hands over my ears, digging my knuckles as far into my ear canals as possible. Even with the slight barricade that provided, I wondered if I was going to have any hearing left when this was over. Brady kept one ear pressed to his shoulder, covering the ear he'd damaged last month with his free hand. His other was busy shaking the map open so he could find out which pyramid the Rejects had set off this time.

To our left, off the road, the sound of trees being shattered and flung about added to the cacophony. With a crash that shook the ground beneath my feet, a huge branch, one end broken and jagged landed on the road only a few feet from Olivia. She jumped back and huddled close to Faith and me, staring at the branch in horror. It had flown from the trees with tremendous force. It could have killed her if it hit her.

With the howls all around us, there was no way to tell which direction was safe. We all drew close together, our animals pressed up next to us. Faith was shaking so hard it reminded me how fearful she'd been last year. Then without warning, she stepped forward and screamed, "Stop it!"

There's no way anything could have heard her over the howling and ringing that inundated the air around us. Yet, as suddenly as it had started, the sounds died away. Until once again, Chimera was silent.

I squeezed Faith's shoulder, then whispered, "Where are the Rejects?"

We should be far enough away that they couldn't hear me, but several trolls were in the woods near us a moment ago. They shouldn't be able to hear us, either. The roads should protect us from being seen or heard, but I wasn't willing to take any chances.

Brady was standing there, strangely still, staring at the map.

"So where are they?" Olivia nudged him, probably harder than necessary.

When he didn't answer, I felt my heart begin to sprint. I'd read a theory once, that everyone has a certain number of heart beats available for their lifetime, and once you reach that number your heart stops. It was foolishness of course, but I couldn't help thinking that if it was true, Chimera was making me use mine way too fast.

Doug grabbed the edge of the map and tugged it away from Brady. His hands shook briefly, and his voice was hoarse as he said, "The Rejects aren't near any of the pyramids. There's no sign of what set them off. The Rejects are in one of the houses we checked out a few months ago."

"That's not what bothers me," Brady said, staring at the map.

"So, what set off the—" I didn't get to finish my question, I thought knowing what set off the pyramid was pretty important, but Olivia spoke over the top of me.

"How could you let them get so close, Brady?" Olivia sounded furious.

"How could *I* let them get so close?" He asked. "Really?" When Olivia lifted a yes-I-absolutely-did-mean-that eyebrow, Brady looked like he was going to explode. "Things were a bit crazy, don't you think? Do you really expect me to ignore everything going on around me to stare at the map all the time?" Brady didn't seem to have my concern about being heard. He was nearly shouting.

"Yes," Olivia said, unreasonably. "I do expect that." She'd raised her voice as well. "I expect you to do whatever it takes to keep us safe."

The flush of anger was already fading from Brady's face when the sound of low-pitched maniacal chuckles and giggles, punctuated with shrill ear-piercing screeches, began coming toward us.

"Shut up, both of you," I said as calmly as I could manage. "Ronny's Mimps must've heard you. Whatever you do, stop yelling."

I held my breath as the sounds grew nearer. Then they began to quiet; the harsh, disturbing chuckling dying away. Well down the road from us, I glimpsed a dozen or so strangely short pale green triangular creatures. They burst into views, flapping surprisingly short arms, milling about on stubby little legs. The five of us didn't utter a sound while they twisted and turned their bodies, listening for the sounds of raised voices. Finally, the whole mass of them turned back the way they'd come.

I whispered, "Doug said the Rejects were in one of the houses, but you said that wasn't what bothered you, Brady. So what's the problem?" I was having trouble picturing what could be worse than the Rejects being here in town.

"It should be obvious," Brady said. "Firstly, what caused the pyramids to go off? Secondly, whatever the cause, it seems to have had a significant effect on Chimera."

He plucked the map from Doug's hand and I squinted at it, trying to make out what was bothering him. I finally shrugged in defeat.

"You don't see it?" When the rest of us shook our heads, he said, "There's a price to pay for having an eidetic memory. I remember the smallest of details. Like the shape and size of the blank area in the middle. It has grown larger since this morning." He pointed at it, careful not to let his finger touch the paper at the spot where nothing showed. The last time he'd touched that blank area, his finger had gotten a mild case of frostbite.

Then he moved his finger, tracing along the outer edge of Chimera. "See there? The boundaries of this place have changed again. At least, this representation of the boundaries indicates change. Some sections are far less distinct than they were previously. In addition, some have altered significantly." His finger hesitated over a place on the map.

I guessed it was possible it had changed since that morning. But just how perfect *was* Brady's memory? It really did look the same to me.

Doug let his hand fall on Brady's shoulder, making Brady jump. Doug bent toward him and kept his voice low, but I heard what he said. "We have a bigger problem right now. That branch that nearly hit Olivia? It's blocking our way."

I felt as though the temperature had suddenly dropped twenty degrees. Doug was right, the branch was huge and completely blocked the path. It was far too big and unwieldy for us to move or climb over. It actually resembled a large tree that had been broken off near the base rather than a mere branch.

It left us two options, neither one pleasant. We could leave the path, cross around the branch inside the forest, and hope we could find the road again on the other side. Of course, based on previous experience, that seemed highly unlikely; we'd risk being lost forever. Plus, we'd be vulnerable to attack from trolls and other creatures out there. The other option was to try to find a road that would take us back around to the last two houses Brady wanted us to check today. That would take much longer.

Maybe we should just rethink this.

"I understand your plan Brady, but maybe we shouldn't try to fit all the houses in this time." I used what I thought was a very reasonable tone. "There's nothing to say we can't check them out next time we come here. When we have more time."

Brady stared at me, eyes narrowed. He looked like a doctor who was about to tell a patient they only had a month to live. "I don't believe that is necessarily a true statement, Kat."

I felt a spurt of irritation. "What do you mean, not a true statement?" What was he accusing me of? "Of course it's true." When his expression didn't change, I narrowed my eyes back at him and gritted my teeth. "Do you have a freshness date that's going to expire or something?"

From over my shoulder I heard Olivia snicker. Brady closed his eyes, ran the fingers of one hand up under his glasses, and massaged them a moment before looking back at me. "Haven't you been paying attention? The center keeps expanding. The boundaries are disappearing and where they aren't disappearing, they are pulling back. *I'm* not the one with an expiration date. I think Chimera is."

Okay, that shut me up. I took a quick step back and felt someone's foot under my shoe.

"Owwww!" Only one person would make such a high pitched yelp. I'd stepped on Olivia.

"Sorry," I muttered yanking my foot off hers, but I didn't take my eyes off Brady. His face was solemn, his normally pale green eyes dark with worry. He wasn't joking around. He really thought our time in Chimera was limited.

Doug glanced at the map in Brady's hand, then up at Brady's face. He apparently came to the same conclusion I had. "I guess we'd better go check the last two houses. Do you have a suggestion how we can get there?"

"We'll have to follow this path back around." He indicated the long narrow trail we'd have to take and my backpack suddenly felt far heavier.

I could see the roof of the house we needed to check next. It was so close I could probably hit it with a rock. Instead, we were going to have to walk away from it and go all the way back the way we'd come. I looked at Shadow who'd come up and was sitting calmly by my feet. "Too bad you're not a pony," I told her. "Then you could carry this pack for me. I have a feeling it's going to weigh a ton by the time we get there."

I looked at Doug, thinking this would be a good time to tell him not to treat me like his personal pack mule, then felt ashamed. He was holding his injured leg at an angle, massaging the muscles where they'd been damaged by magic and never really healed. That leg obviously caused him a lot of pain, though he'd never admit it. How much worse was all this walking going to be for him?

I shifted the straps of my pack, trying to get them placed more comfortably and said, in as cheerful a voice as I could manage, "We'd better get going. Brady still wants to talk to Ronny today."

We turned and headed down the narrow dirt path, away from the branch, back the way we'd come. It seemed to take twice as long even though we didn't stop to check any of the houses again. I was starting to feel really tired, and I might not have been paying enough attention to my feet. Which would explain why I set my foot down on a small rock. It turned under my weight, twisting my ankle, sending a jolt of pain through it.

"Ouch!" I hopped on my uninjured foot and began cursing under my breath so Olivia wouldn't hear me. Because the words I was using would definitely get her grounded, big time. Unfortunately, my 'ouch' had been pretty loud. And something in the woods right next to the path seemed to notice. So much for hoping monsters in the woods couldn't hear us.

There was a loud thrashing just off the path. I couldn't see what was causing all the damage, but there were flashes of something big in there. Something the color of a pale, bloated fish belly moving between the trees, flailing about as if looking for the creator of the sound. I got a brief glimpse of something huge and shaggy, with a long rounded nose, like a squash, hanging from the middle of a broad face covered with saggy grey skin and purple warts.

A troll!

We froze, afraid to move. And had to stand there while the all too familiar sound of breathing grew nearer. Hair-raising sniffing, snuffling sounds, punctuated by eager grunts. Like something was *smelling* us. We'd heard those sounds before.

Faith, standing closest to me, breathed, "Are you okay?" It was the barest whisper of sound and fortunately the thing sniffed loud enough to cover her words. After gingerly testing my ankle, finding it tender but useable, I motioned that we should keep moving. I don't know about the others, but that was the slowest and stealthiest that I'd ever moved. Bit by bit we inched away until the sounds faded from hearing.

I felt weak in the knees when the last two houses we needed to check finally came back into view. On the far side of the last house, I could see where the branch, which still completely blocked the path, lat over the road. Where we'd been standing what felt like hours ago. Well, for all I knew, it might have been hours ago.

"We made it," Faith said. Even she sounded tired and dispirited, and she ran for miles every week to keep in shape.

That made me feel surprisingly better.

Doug rubbed his face and turned toward Brady. "There's something else changing in here. The monsters, creatures, whatever you want to call them, are becoming more aggressive. And it sounds like there are more of them."

Brady hesitated a moment then nodded. "I think the evidence is fairly clear on that point. Another thing to discuss with Ronny." He gave Doug a lopsided grin and turned up the short path leading to the next house.

Doug had slowed and his limp was more pronounced. I knew I wasn't the only one who would be glad to be done for the day. I couldn't help myself; I murmured, "Let this be a nice house." I repeated it quietly, like a mantra, matching it to the rhythm of my steps.

"Oh, stop muttering," Olivia said crossly.

-xXx-

As soon as we entered, I knew something was off about this house. Nothing tried to eat us or attack us or spit poison on us.

Nothing howled. There was absolutely nothing I could put my finger on. But something was definitely off.

Most of the living room was in shadow and felt unpleasantly dark. At the far end of the room, light streamed in from a single window, lighting several objects in glass boxes. The contrast between the darkness at this end and the light at the other made it difficult to make out what we were looking at.

We made our way cautiously down the length of the living room. It was far larger than it had appeared from the doorway. Faith was the first to recognize the objects deliberately displayed in the sunlight. Her loud gasp was followed by a sound of disgust in the back of her throat. I glanced where she was looking but wasn't sure what had upset her.

Olivia stepped next to her and put a hand on her arm. "What's wrong?"

Faith pointed, her finger shaking slightly. There was one chair in the living room, facing the display cases, as though the occupant liked to sit there and contemplate those items on a regular basis.

The most obvious were displayed high on the far wall; six rather lopsided hand-made shirts. I couldn't begin to guess what kind of fabric had been used. It was an unattractive lumpy green, and one of the shirts was missing a sleeve.

"That shirt isn't even finished," Olivia said. "Why would someone put it on their wall?"

Through clenched teeth, Faith said, "That fairytale is one of my least favorites." At our blank looks, Faith sighed. "There once were six brothers and a younger sister—"

Doug interrupted. "You stand there talking about made-up stories if you want, but Brady and I are going to go do what we came for." His tone clearly meant that we should stop talking and start searching too. I smiled and waggled my fingers in a go-ahead motion, then turned back to Faith. "So what happened?"

She grinned, then looked back at the wall and grew serious. "Their mother died and their father, the king, remarried. Their stepmother didn't like reminders of his previous marriage and didn't want any of them to inherit. She cursed the six brothers, turning them into swans. They could only take human form for a few minutes every evening. Their sister found a way, just *one* way, to break the curse. She had to make six shirts out of stinging nettles, twisting the nettles into cloth by hand."

"Ewww," Olivia said, wandering over to a china hutch with several drawers. She pulled one open and looked through, it then turned back. "Who would want to wear such nasty things."

I ignored her, too busy recalling the feel of the stinging nettle I'd touched once. I shuddered and rubbed the palm of my hand, remembering the burning, itching pain. "Ouch!"

Faith nodded and gave me a grim smile. "It gets worse. She couldn't speak or laugh for seven years, otherwise her brothers would stay swans forever."

"No talking or laughing for seven years?" Olivia sounded appalled, and slammed the drawer. She opened the next one and peered inside it as my mind boggled at the thought of Olivia not talking for seven years. That made me grin. She wouldn't be able to do it for seven hours, let alone seven years.

Not surprisingly, Olivia sounded outraged when she asked, "How was she supposed to do that?"

"It's a fairytale, remember?" Faith told her. "The evil stepmother tried to deliberately create so many impossible conditions that the spell could never be broken."

I hadn't realized he'd come back into the room until Brady muttered, "Evil stepmother. Of course."

Faith ignored that and continued as if he hadn't spoken. "But she hadn't counted on the determination of their sister. She refused to speak, even when a King saw her and insisted they be married. She didn't speak when the king's mother, who didn't like her, stole her child. The King's mother accused her of *eating* her own child and she still refused to speak. She didn't even speak when she was condemned to death for killing that child."

"Are you kidding me?" Olivia burst out and whirled around to glare at Faith. "Tell me this has a happy ending."

"Well, sort of. This part is not my favorite." Faith walked over and started looking through the last drawer, then shut it firmly. She glanced at Olivia and said, "As she was led to the pyre where they would burn her, she carried the six shirts. They were all done except the last which was missing a sleeve. As they got ready to light the fire around her feet, her six brothers, still in swan form, flew in and landed near her. She threw the shirts over them and each in turn completely regained his human form. All except the youngest. He still had the wing of a swan where the sleeve had been missing."

I glanced up at the shirts on the wall and decided this wasn't one of my favorite stories either. I bit my lip then asked, "Was the youngest brother angry about his arm?"

"The story doesn't say," Faith said. "But it did say they all rejoiced together, the six brothers and their sister. And now that she could talk, she was able to tell her husband that it was his mother who had stolen their child. In the end, it was the king's mother who was burned."

"That's not a nice story," I told her.

She pointed to a case in the corner, where the shaft of sunlight illuminated a pair of red shoes. "You know that story, right?" The shoes were gorgeous. And they were dancing, all by themselves.

I took a step forward, wanting to get a closer look. Olivia grabbed my arm and held me back. She said, "Oh, I know that one."

"There's a fairytale about red shoes?" I asked.

"Oh yes. Mom knew I'd be interested," Olivia told me. "Because, you know, shoes."

"Okay, everything makes sense now." I grinned at her. "So, which of you are going to tell me this one?"

"This one is also not my favorite," Faith said. "An orphaned peasant girl was adopted by a rich old lady and became vain and spoiled. She got a pair of red shoes that she loved and she wore them everywhere, even to church. One day a strange man said the shoes would never come off or stop dancing. The girl couldn't resist dancing a few steps, but once she started, the shoes kept dancing and wouldn't come off."

"She never got the shoes off her feet?" I decided this story was even creepier than the last.

Faith shook her head. "A few other things happened, but in the end the shoes wouldn't stop. And they wouldn't come off.

Olivia muttered, "What's wrong with dancing? They're gorgeous red shoes."

Faith rolled her eyes. "What's wrong? They kept dancing, night and day, through wind and rain, through meadows and fields, with brambles and thorns tearing her skin. Finally, the girl danced by the executioner's house. She begged him to cut off her feet—"

"She did what?" Now I felt sick.

Faith sounded like she was losing her patience. Her tone lost that dreamy fairytale quality and she finished quickly. "She begged him to cut off her feet, which he did. The shoes, with her feet still in them, danced away."

I glanced at the case with the dancing shoes. Fortunately, the angle made it impossible to see inside them. I *really* didn't want to know if her feet were still in there. "What kind of sick story is that?"

Olivia elbowed me, gently. "It's supposed to teach children not to be vain about clothes and shoes."

"Well, it certainly didn't work for you," I told her, and we grinned at each other.

Faith moved a bit closer, then pointed to another of the cabinets. "These are all things that represent the bad parts of stories. Look, that flute has the word Hamelin on the side. The Pied Piper of Hamelin used a flute to lead the town's children away, never to return, when the town tried to cheat him."

Then she pointed to another case. It took a minute for me to make out that the strange blond braid, coiled several feet high, was human hair. The case was labeled *Rapunzel*. If I remembered right, there'd been something about the Prince being blinded, and years wandering in the desert in that one. In the far corner, a beautiful spinning wheel sat behind glass. The light glinted off its extremely long, extremely sharp needle. There was no name on that case, but I was pretty sure I knew the story behind that one.

Above the spinning wheel, a beautiful red cloak with a large hood was draped across the wall. Near the hem were several long gashes. Like those you'd expect to see if a huge wolf slashed its claws through the material.

I wandered a little closer and saw the skin of an animal folded up. That one had a card that said *Selkie*. Next to it was a bowl full of beans and an axe, and the story of Jack and the Beanstalk jumped into my mind. Things had ended up okay in the end, but it had been a very near thing.

Against the back wall, underneath the six nettle shirts, was a glass coffin. It was quite beautiful. But inside it was a perfectly preserved apple with a single bite missing.

"You're right," I told Faith. "This is like a museum of things that caused harm to people."

"To the Mundane," Doug said, his voice coming from right behind us. I jumped and felt my heart rate quicken. We'd been so busy talking, I hadn't even heard him return. Brady was right behind him, clutching several leather journals to his chest. He looked sickened.

"What's up?" I asked, unable to take my eyes off Brady.

"This was Morgana's house," Doug said.

That got my attention off Brady. "You mean, Ronny's Aunt Morgana?"

Brady spoke up. "That's the one. Ronny told us she kept hurting the Mundane. These disgusting bits of memorabilia belong to her."

I remembered Ronny saying Morgana took pleasure in being known for every evil female character in all the fairy tales and legends. I'd never really thought about what that meant before. But looking at her little collection of misery, I was getting a much better idea.

"We found her diaries," Brady said. "From the little I translated, I'd theorize that no one knew just how much hatred she harbored. And not just toward the Mundane; toward her sister Glenna and Ronny as well. I'll need more time to understand everything in here, but I'm afraid it's going to be seriously…" Brady's mouth twisted, then he said, carefully, "…unpleasant."

Doug motioned toward the door, "We're done here."

"You don't have to ask me twice," Olivia said, and headed out into the sunshine.

When we got out of that house, even though I knew we were supposed to be in a hurry, I leaned over and ruffled Shadow's fur, feeling as if some lingering trace of darkness was being cleaned off with each stroke of my hand. Shadow turned around and licked my fingers, and I welcomed the rough rasp of her tongue against my skin.

Then Doug stalked past me, heading for the last house and I gave Shadow one more pat before heading after him.

Chapter 29/August/Santa Ramona

Where Is the Fun in the Funhouse?

We'd already entered the house when Brady began cursing. It was really quite inventive, since he never used any words that Olivia's mother wouldn't like. Things like, "Addlebrained idiot." "Wretched ignoramus." "Stupid-a…donkey." "Complete and total waste of space." It took a few attempts to get him to explain why he was so upset.

Finally I yelled, "What the heck is the matter with you, Brady?"

He stopped and stared at me for a moment, then said, "You shouldn't curse around Olivia."

"Fine. I won't curse around Olivia." I glared at him and said, "Now tell us what the heck is wrong."

Without a word he thrust the map at me. His hands were shaking so it took me a minute to realize the Rejects were practically on our doorstep. If we went out the way we'd come in, they'd catch us. We had to find another way out. One that didn't involve making us leave the road. If there was one.

"Rejects," I said when everyone started clamoring for information.

"It's not like they know we're here," Faith said. She was obviously hoping we'd agree with her.

Brady shook his head. "We were in a hurry. We didn't wipe out our footsteps."

There was a moment of stunned silence, then Doug pulled the map from my hands. He took a quick look and said, "Bar the door."

Without a word, Faith, Olivia and I grabbed the edges of the large couch and with a lot of lifting and shoving, we got it to partially block the door. It wouldn't stop them for long, but it would slow them down.

While the three of us did that, Doug and Brady looked through the room. Then Doug said, "Leave it. Let's check the rest before they track us here."

The changes started as we walked down the hall. The floor seemed to ripple up and down, like waves passing gently under foot. Then the walls undulated like funhouse mirrors. In the rooms on either side of the hallway, doors and windows opened and slammed shut. I kept turning from one side to the other, afraid something was going to come shooting out. Books and other items flew around, some landing in the hallway. None, fortunately, hit any of us, though Faith let out a yell as a book was flung just past her head.

We bunched inside the room to our right, and things stopped whizzing through the air. I felt a momentary sense of reprieve and had just enough time to see that the room was strangely empty. No windows, no bed, no shelves. And no furniture except for one beat-up old dresser.

That seemed weird.

Then the floor began to spin, slowly at first but growing faster and faster with each revolution until I thought I was going to be sent crashing into the wall. Around me everyone was flailing around. Olivia was teetering off balance, shrieking. I could swear I heard curse words but wisely didn't comment.

I took a chance and jumped off into the tiny space at the room's edge. It seemed to be the only spot that wasn't spinning. It was near enough to the dresser that I could open the drawers and check inside them.

The others were all yelling at me to hurry up. There wasn't enough room for them in my little corner and they were clinging to each other, trying to keep their footing.

I felt like screaming when I got to the bottom drawer and realized I had risked jumping for nothing; the dresser was completely empty. I gathered myself and yelled, "Don't let me fall."

I jumped back onto the spinning floor. My feet were pulled sideways before the rest of me began moving in the same direction. Doug grabbed me and held me up while I got my balance.

"Thanks," I told him and grinned. I would have stepped away, but his hands were still gripping my arms. I blew the hair out of my eyes to see his face.

I only got a quick glimpse before he let me go and turned away. I wasn't sure what the expression in his eyes had been, I'd never seen it before.

"Let's go," Brady said, and timing it carefully, jumped back through the doorway. He crashed into the opposite wall, and had to fight to remain on his feet. Then one by one, he told the rest of us when it was safe to jump and helped to catch us as we flung ourselves through the open doorway.

Only a few steps farther, the entire hallway – floor, walls, even the ceiling, began revolving around us, as if we were in a large barrel turned onto its side, rolling wildly down a hill. Only there was no hill, just a nasty, dark, disorienting hallway.

I only managed two steps before ending up on my knees. Around me, the others were tumbling to the floor. Doug clutched his leg and let out a deep groan. Brady grabbed Olivia and tried to boost her to her feet, but she toppled back, landing on his outstretched arms. For once she kept her mouth shut, closed her eyes and held on. Faith and I took turns trying to pull each other to our feet.

Every time I thought we'd make it, we ended back on the floor. My head felt like it was spinning in time with the walls, and my stomach was starting to complain. I'd completely lost my sense of balance. Even sitting on the floor was making me dizzy.

I looked at Faith; she was a pale, sickly green and had one fist crammed against her mouth. Considering her habit of losing her lunch on the Teacups at Disneyland, I was surprised she'd managed to hold on this long.

I closed my eyes not wanting to see her struggle and felt marginally better. "Brady, do something," I croaked, eyes still shut, knowing I wasn't being fair, but not caring. We had to make this stop and Brady was the most likely to figure something out.

I slitted my eyes and glanced over at Doug. His face was tight; it could be from pain in his leg, which he was still rubbing. Or he could be having as much trouble as I was with the whole equilibrium thing. Maybe both.

Then Brady said, "Stop trying to walk. Stay on your hands and knees, keep your eyes focused on the floor in front of you, and crawl."

We'd made it a few feet down the hall when, as abruptly as it started, the rolling motion stopped. Everything was still. Completely normal. I'd forgotten how much I loved normal.

We staggered to our feet and kept moving. After a few more steps, sections of the floor began to move; some went right, some left, while others rose or dropped half a foot or more. I had no idea which way my foot was going to move from one step to the next. Even worse was when my heel went one way while the floor did something entirely different under the front of my foot.

I was jerked painfully back and forth, somehow keeping on my feet. I couldn't imagine how awful it would feel beneath my butt. Several more groans were wrenched from Doug and in the moment I managed to focus on his face, he looked white and grim.

There were several minutes of chaos as we bounced off the walls and each other. This time I was sure I heard a really nasty word out of Olivia when I crashed into her back, my head banging painfully into hers. I'd nearly bitten through my tongue and couldn't have cursed if I wanted to.

Somehow we made our way beyond the crazy floor. I glanced behind and realized the movements were becoming increasingly violent. We'd made it through just in time.

I spat out a mouthful of blood. Fortunately, it felt like my tongue had nearly stopped bleeding. I could only hope this house didn't have anything else to throw at us. Doug was limping so badly I was surprised he could still walk. I was bruised and exhausted and had a sore knee. The others didn't look much better.

"One good thing," I said. "If the Rejects try to follow us through here, they'll have an even worse time than we did." It didn't make me feel completely better, but it helped.

As we got to the next room, there was a huge rush of air from behind us. Now all the debris that had been blown into the hallway hurtled around in billowing gusts. The intense streams of air blasted up from the floor and out from the walls. Even as I watched, one of the books rose up off the floor, then knocked sideways hard enough to embed itself into the wall.

Hopefully if the Rejects saw that, they *wouldn't* try to follow us.

Only one more room remained. My poor stomach clenched, then tied itself into knots at the thought of what might be behind that door. Somehow, whatever it was, I was pretty sure it would be worse than anything I could imagine.

When we entered, it didn't seem so bad. Not at first. We were confronted with dozens of identical doors. Which, I realized, meant there could be something horrible behind each and every one. My hand was shaking so hard it was difficult to grab onto the doorknob of the one next to me. My breath escaped in a relieved whoosh at the sight of a blank wall when I wrenched it open.

Faith opened the one opposite mine and found a blank wall as well. We both flung several more open with the same result.

"They don't go anywhere," I said flatly, managing to keep a tired whine out of my voice.

"Are we trapped?" Olivia asked, her voice small.

"No," Brady said. He reached over and opened the door opposite the one where we'd entered. This led into a small room with six doors, counting the one he'd opened.

"How did you know that one would lead somewhere?" Olivia demanded.

"It's a logic puzzle." When she merely raised her eyebrow at him, he said, "It was the process of elimination. It was logical that one of them had to lead somewhere. The others didn't. Therefore this one would."

Olivia turned away. "Therefore this one would," she muttered in imitation, but quietly. I didn't think he heard her; his face gave nothing away. Then I noticed his shoulders twitch ever so slightly.

The sound of banging and shouting at the front of the house made all of us twist around. As if we could see through the doors and down the hall to the living room. Faith clutched my arm tightly. I winced but didn't try to shake her off. In fact, I was tempted to grab onto Doug who was standing right in front of me.

Although their voices were faint and muffled, I heard Ray yell, "They're in there…"

Several more bangs and thumps echoed down the hall, followed by a string of curses from Andrew.

Ray's voice came again, angrily, "Stop acting like a baby and get that door open."

There was a splintering sound and Doug, who'd been checking out the door we came through groaned. "I wish there was some way to lock this da… darn door."

A split second of silence was interrupted by an incredibly loud click.

Doug twisted the knob then said blankly, "It locked."

"You wished," Olivia accused him. "How could you do that?"

"I forgot," Doug told her defensively. "And it's a good thing, don't you think?" He turned his back on her and told Brady, "Let's get going."

Four more times we went through the process of entering a room and trying several doors until one lead on to another small room. Some rooms were round, others rectangular or square. The worst was completely off-kilter. The walls and ceiling came together at strange angles, and I felt like I was going to fall on my face. Brady came up between Olivia and me. He grabbed my right arm and Olivia's left. "It's an optical illusion," he said calmly. "Commonly known as a funhouse effect. Just keep walking."

I was momentarily distracted by screams and shouts from the hallway. It was easy to tell where the Rejects were just from the sounds they were making. I tried very hard not to hope that they'd get trapped forever in that hallway.

I was beginning to panic, suddenly very sure we were just going in circles. That we would never make it out of this maze. Then Brady opened a door that led into a larger room. A real room, with a bed and a bedside table and a dresser.

"We don't have time to check in here," Faith said, heading toward the long thick curtains covering what I hoped was a window on the other side of the room.

"We're not coming back here," Doug told her. "We need to check it. All these precautions could have been set up because there is something important hidden in here."

"But the Rejects could get here any minute," she said, voice high with distress. She flung open the curtains and light flooded into the room. She turned to face Doug and fisted her hands on her hip, looking ready to argue her point.

I was glad no one asked my opinion, because I agreed with both of them. I felt nearly paralyzed with indecision.

Doug kept his voice calm and patient. "They'll have to make it through that hallway, check for us in all the rooms, and get through the door I locked. Then they'll need to open all the doors in here, just like we did." He turned away and opened the bedside table nearest to him as he added, "I made sure all them were shut behind us."

For some reason, this decided me. I was closest to the dresser, so I started opening drawers, rummaging through socks and underwear and nightgowns and jewelry. Brady came over to help and we'd finished in no more than two minutes.

By the time we were done, Faith had begun tugging on the window. For a minute, I thought it was stuck. We could break it of course, but the sound would give our position away. Olivia joined Faith and said, "On three, okay?" The two of them counted and on three shoved with all their weight on the window. With a long, loud, haunted-house-groan, it slowly swung open.

Note to self — Sometimes just breaking the glass is better.

As we scrambled out, we could hear the Rejects shouting behind us. They were flinging doors open probably just one or two small rooms away. I felt relief flood through me as my feet landed on a path running along the edge of the house.

"Hurry," Doug said. "We need to be out of sight by the time they reach this window."

The five of us fled down the path to the main road and headed back toward the tree, our animals following behind. Brady kept his eyes on the map and kept reassuring us the Rejects were still in the house until we were just a few steps away from the tree.

I took a deep breath and took a moment to pick up Shadow and give her a long hug goodbye before setting her down and stepping into the tree.

-xXx-

It was close to dinner time when we crowded into Chris and Ronny's house. Even before sitting down, Brady said, "We'll have to come back after school on Monday to finish talking, there's just not enough time for everything right now. But there's something I must ask."

All eyes were on him, but I don't think he was even aware of anyone in the room except Ronny. He jerked the map from his pocket and handed it to her, standing close by her chair. "Do you notice anything that worries you?"

Ronny glanced at the map, then her hands began to shake. "Oh no," she whispered. "If this continues, you will not have a peg to land on." As I tried to puzzle that out she looked at Brady, eyes dark with fear and said, "This should not be possible."

"And yet it *has* happened, therefore it is possible." Brady sat down and said, "What factors could cause the boundaries of Chimera to warp and disappear altogether, and the center to keep expanding like this?"

Ronny's shoulders slumped and her voice was dispirited as she answered, "I have known for some time that more magick is escaping from Chimera, as if something in there has been growing in strength. To me, it is as if opposing spells are creating an imbalance. Like during the wars the year you were born. Only this time is worse. I can feel the effects. What little magick I have is becoming more unpredictable." She looked at her hands and fell silent for a moment. None of us spoke; it was clear that she was thinking intently. She looked up and said, "If I am right, it is possible your ability to use wishes when you are there may become compromised." She looked over at Brady."To answer your question, since Chimera is made from magick, I believe this imbalance is growing so strong it is affecting Chimera itself."

Faith leaned forward and cleared her throat. "Can you tell us any defensive spells we might be able to activate? Obviously we wouldn't want the magic to rebound against us, but we were nearly caught by the Rejects today."

Brady opened his mouth as if to argue. I'm sure that wasn't what he wanted to talk about. But Ronny said, "Since the magick is becoming unpredictable, I am not sure. I will have to give that some thought."

Faith sat back, clearly not satisfied, and Olivia spoke up quickly, "So what do the edges of Chimera look like? Are they like the painting of the sky in *The Truman Show*?"

Ronny laughed. "You are not far off. There are avoidance spells around the parameter of Chimera. It prevents those who live there from getting near the edges of the world. Otherwise you could fall out into the void between dimensions."

Brady's eyes lit in interest and he opened his mouth, ready to ask a bunch of off-topic questions. That seemed un-Brady-like, since it sounded more like something out of a fantasy novel than a scientific possibility. Brady seemed to realize it too, and changed the subject. "I found some diaries from your Aunt Morgana."

There was a moment of tense silence, then Ronny leaned forward. "I would be interested to see what she wrote."

"No, I don't think you will, actually." Brady gave a decisive shake of his head. "I didn't have much time to read, but I did see some things she wrote about you and your mother."

Ronny's laugh sounded more uneasy than amused. "When Aunt Morgana was in a bad mood, she often made rash statements. You cannot put too much on that."

"Explain once more how she reacted when her mother — that would be your grandmother, right?" Ronny nodded and Brady continued, "Okay, when your grandmother um… died, I want to know what Morgana said to your mother. I want to compare that against what I found in her diary."

"I have told you most of it." Ronny sighed. "Do not forget, I was not there. I only know what Mother and Aunt Morgana have told me." She rubbed her eyes before speaking again, and I noticed she looked far more tired than when we got there.

Her eyes changed, became distant. "Aunt Morgana never liked the Mundane. For years going back into your antiquity, she played tricks, some with dire results, against your kind. I have told you that many of your stories are based on Aunt Morgana. She has been called Maleficent, Medusa, Morgan le Fey, Hecate, even the Snow Queen. Aunt Brigana, her eldest sister, and Aunt Morgana together played Sirens, Harpies and Banshees. And for a time Aunt Titiana, their youngest sister, joined them. The three of them were known as Furies."

She slumped back in her seat. "After my grandmother was forced to sacrifice herself to save her children, Aunt Morgana's dislike of the Mundane turned to hatred. She and Aunt Brigana swore vengeance, and Mother said the two of them tried to outdo each other in terrifying and persecuting the Mundane. Many died."

She shifted in her chair as if she was uncomfortable, but I didn't think it was anything physical. From the look on her face, this discussion bothered her. "Aunt Brigana was found dead in Kansas. Mother said the Mundane there began accusing Aunt Brigana of witchcraft. Instead of leaving that place, she stayed and flaunted what she was, sure she could not be caught. Aunt Morgana was convinced the Mundane killed her. She was incensed when L. Frank Baum used rumors of her death in his story. You might have heard of it — *The Wizard of Oz*. He wrote of her death like it was a good thing."

She looked at us pleadingly. "You must understand how close they were. Aunt Brigana was her surrogate mother after my grandmother was killed. When Aunt Brigana died, Aunt Morgana swore she would wipe the Mundane from the face of the earth. Mother was terrified she would lose her entire family, and created the idea of Chimera to keep them safe."

Ronny uttered a short laugh that lacked any trace of humor. "Of course, that infuriated Aunt Morgana. It grew even worse after my mother married my Mundane father." She gave a strained smile. "Which is rather ironic, since it was Aunt Morgana who brought Father to Chimera in the first place."

She twisted her hands in her lap and added, "Even though Aunt Morgana was angry, I still cannot believe she would have caused real harm to any of her sisters."

I thought she sounded more like she was pleading for us to agree than actually convinced her words were true. Then she said flatly, "I am certain Aunt Morgana would not do something that could destroy Chimera. That is where the source of our magick lives."

Brady asked, "What *did* she do to your Mother?"

Ronny sucked in her breath. "She tried to make Mother lose her place on the Council."

She uttered another short laugh. "Creating Chimera did Mother little good. She still lost most of her family. First her mother, then Aunt Brigana in Kansas. Next Aunt Titiana died just outside the doorway in the cemetery, soon after Chimera was created. There were few Mundane here back then. Many questioned how it could be a Mundane who killed her. Some suggested it might be someone from Chimera, and even suggested Aunt Morgana. Mother refused to believe that."

Ronny shifted in her seat and looked at me. "I was an only child, so I do not know what it feels like to have a sibling, but I have been told no one wishes to believe a sister or a brother could do such a thing."

I nodded. "I understand why she didn't want to believe it. I wouldn't believe it if someone told me Chris had done something like that."

She gave me a half smile. "Of course, my Christopher would never do such a thing. And I have to believe that Aunt Morgana would not either." She shook herself and said, "Where was I?"

Brady told her, "That's all I need to know right now." He had a strange look on his face but sounded normal enough when he added, "As soon as I can look at everything, I'll share what I find with you."

"I am not sure I want to know everything you find," Ronny told him, then shrugged. "But of course you must tell me. I can't be like an ostrich and hide my head in my hand. I cannot tell you I will look forward to hearing it. But as always, I appreciate everything you are doing."

We said our goodbyes quickly and left. I was curious what Brady was thinking, but I was sure he had no intention of telling us until he had a chance to figure out more. Darn it!

Chapter 30/August/Santa Ramona

How Do You Become a Know-It-All? Ask Questions. Lots of Questions

It was weird to think we'd be out of high school in less than two years, but that day couldn't get here soon enough. It was harder than ever to avoid the Rejects now. It didn't help that they were angrier with us than usual. Of course, we *had* left them in a house that was throwing things in the hallway, where the floor heaved and sank under your feet. I couldn't help wondering how long they'd tried to get through those last rooms with all the doors. Had they been able to get through and use the window? Or had they given up and gone back through that horrible hallway and out the front door? The idea of going through that twice made me shudder.

However many times it had been, they hadn't enjoyed it, and as usual were blaming us for it. Ray actually screamed at us right before class, when the hall was filled with people at their lockers. "How did you throw all that sh—"

Andrew elbowed him and said something I couldn't hear. Probably reminding Ray that he could get expelled for cursing in here.

Ray scowled and suddenly plowed through the hallway, nearly knocking over a small group of new kids who hadn't seen him coming. For a moment there were shouts of "Hey!" and "Watch it." and "Who do you think you are?"

All five of us were together that morning, so I was determined to hold my ground. After all, everyone was staring. Ray couldn't really try anything *too* bad. But I cringed back half a step when he stalked right up and shoved his face only inches away from Doug. Unfortunately, Doug was standing right next to me, which meant Ray was way too close for comfort.

He was flushed red with anger, and ground out, "No one gets away with throwing sh—"

Olivia threw her hands over her ears and started humming loudly so I missed the next few words. Then Ray raised his voice, not loud enough for the others in the hall to hear, but loud enough that I couldn't miss it. He turned on Olivia first. "Grow up. A few bad words aren't going to hurt you." Then he let his eyes rove over the rest of us. "If you ever hit me with anything, *any*thing, you're all dead. Every single one of you."

My knees trembled. Ray and Andrew had threatened us before. But in the past they'd mostly sounded like they were just threats. This time, Ray sounded like he was making a vow. I really didn't want to believe that *anyone* I knew, even Ray, could really plan to commit murder. But the churning in my stomach told me my body believed it, even if my mind didn't want to.

We'd always been careful to avoid the Rejects and travel in groups, but from now on, I planned to be much more careful.

-xXx-

We met after school to go back to Chris and Ronny's. Brady had managed a few more translations and had more questions. As usual, he refused to discuss anything until we got there, saying he didn't want to keep repeating himself.

The wait nearly drove me crazy.

I didn't enjoy making a bunch of wild speculations; that pretty much seemed like a waste of time. But Olivia didn't feel the same. She was always trying to guess which stars were dating each other, who would be cast in movies she wanted to see, what grade she'd get on her last test. Really, she just liked to speculate.

So it was no surprise when she started bugging Brady on the way to Ronny's. "You found out how to stop the Rejects?"

Brady sighed. "Of course not. I wouldn't make you wait to hear something like that."

"Okay, okay. Sooooo, it's…I got it. You now know exactly where to find the next object we need. That's why you're so excited."

This time Brady came to a complete stop and stared at her. "Really? Look at my face. Do I look like I know exactly what we need to do next?"

I snorted with laughter. I couldn't help it. His face had never looked so far from excited.

"Fine," she said, her lower lip jutting in a pout. "You found out—"

"Stop with the guessing already," Faith said.

Olivia's eyes tightened and I was sure the two of them were going to start arguing, but we were turning onto Chris and Ronny's street and would be at the house in moments.

I cleared my throat and said brightly, "Oh, look. We're almost there. Can't wait to hear what Brady's gonna say." I walked a bit faster and was relieved when the others followed me. Silently.

It was Ronny who opened the door for us. We entered and got seated before anyone could say anything else.

"You have more information?" Ronny looked almost normal; better than she had in months, and I felt something inside me relax.

I was suddenly sure that everything was going to work out.

"I found something that I think is important." Brady said. "It was just lying on a work bench in the middle of several scattered papers. I have no idea how it came to be there. Perhaps *you* can give us your thoughts on that."

Ronny looked as confused as I felt. "I will certainly try to help you in any way that I can."

Brady nodded. "I found a page written by Ghalynn. It was in plain language, not his normal cryptic poetry, so I'm sure it wasn't meant for us. It sounded like he was writing to a friend." Brady didn't bother pulling the note out of his backpack. No doubt he remembered every word.

He told her, "I won't read the entire note. I'll sum it up. Ghalynn wrote that something was going wrong with the magic in Chimera. He repeated the Annihilation Prophecy. Then he wrote about the group in the South, how they were experimenting and joining up spells that shouldn't be joined. He referred to Sleeping Beauty and spell amplification and wild magic. He wrote that their efforts might be causing changes in Chimera. How it wasn't safe to go anywhere near the center any longer."

Brady pulled out the map and looked at it carefully, then said, "It isn't just the center. It all continues to change." He passed the map to Ronny who looked stricken by what she saw. She passed it back quickly, like she didn't even want to touch it.

"He wrote that the group in the South insisted on hiding an object somewhere in town." Brady pushed up his glasses, his eyes distracted.

Ronny moved restlessly and Brady refocused. "Ghalynn described several dreams that he called prophetic. Strong as any he'd had when he was younger."

"Do you think this South group used that huge place hidden by the hedges?" Doug asked. "The one we couldn't get into."

"As it is the largest building we've seen, that seems like a reasonable hypothesis." Brady folded the map and put it back in his pocket. "Ghalynn mentioned one other thing. He said 'put not too much trust in Elementals'."

"What are Elementals again?" Olivia asked.

"Don't you remember the Gnome, the Undine and the Sylph?" Faith sounded…disappointed. "You know, the ones who gave us clues from Ghalynn?"

"Those things?" Olivia grinned at her. "Okay, they were cool. And you said we'll see some sort of fire lizard next?"

Brady cleared his throat, probably worried we were going to get totally off topic. "Yes, we were told to look for a Salamander." He leaned forward and spoke directly to Ronny. "He mentioned once again that he didn't trust Morgana; that she might be part of what was wrong with Chimera. He was disappointed in Glenna because she would not listen."

Ronny frowned and spoke more forcefully than I'd ever heard. "That is not fair. Mother was always close to Ghalynn. I cannot believe she would ignore him unless she was sure he was incorrect. And no one believed Ghalynn's dreams anymore. They ended up wrong as often as they were right." She set her jaw. "I am quite sure Mother knew Aunt Morgana far better than Ghalynn. So if she did not believe

Aunt Morgana was trying to destroy Chimera, then I do not either." She sat back and crossed her arms over her chest, eyes tight with anger.

I could tell she was done talking and I guess Brady did too. He asked her abruptly, "What is the significance of items being grouped in threes or sevens?"

"What?" Ronny's eyes lost their tension, going wide with surprise.

"I have noticed that most houses in Chimera have items arranged in threes or sevens," he said. "I've seen it so often it can't be a coincidence."

Olivia spoke up, sounding smug. "Everyone knows it is a basic of design; odd numbered groupings, usually three or five items, are the most aesthetically pleasing."

Brady stared at her as if she had announced that she was from another planet. But Ronny laughed and said, "While it may indeed be more pleasing to the eye, the numbers three and seven are considered powerful numbers in magick. You will have heard stories of the seventh son of a seventh son, yes?" When we all nodded, she continued, "And that things always seem to happen in threes."

"My parents say that," I said. "That things always happen in threes."

Ronny nodded, "Three is a powerful number. As Brady has noticed, many in Chimera place groups of three and seven objects around their homes. It can help to intensify any spells they leave running, even when they are not there."

Doug sat forward. "Could those spells be growing in strength, for example, making their defenses stronger because the magic is growing more unpredictable?"

After a brief pause, Ronny said, "I do not know. If that is the case, I would have to ask you to stop going into any of those houses. It would be far too dangerous." I could see sorrow beginning to darken her eyes. I hurriedly assured her that nothing too dangerous had happened. I kept my crossed fingers hidden at my side.

Doug added quickly, "I was just curious."

"We'd stop going if it got too dangerous," Faith assured her.

That seemed to reassure Ronny.

"See, there's nothing to worry about," I told her and grinned.

A magic storm erupted just as I said that. The sky grew black with clouds. The wind rose until it roared around the house, and the lights went out, plunging the room into darkness.

Faith covered her eyes and pushed back into the couch as if she was trying to disappear into it.

I, on the other hand, couldn't pull my eyes away from the destruction I could see out the window. Branches and dirt were tossed around the yard. Parts of lawn chairs and fences and roof tiles struck the house with violent thuds and bangs.

I was surprised I could even hear those. The claps of thunder were brutally loud, shaking the house. And they were followed by enormous bolts of blue lightning. Those speared from the sky, so bright I could barely see.

Brady was yelling something I couldn't hear over the rising wind.

I didn't think it could get much worse, then it began to rain. The drops were striking so hard they popped and snapped like water falling into a hot greased frying pan.

Maybe Faith was right. I wrapped my arms around my head and bent over, praying the house would hold together, fighting the urge to whimper like a little kid.

Then, as suddenly as it had begun, it was gone.

I expected Ronny to say this storm proved Chimera was becoming too dangerous. Instead she smiled weakly and said, "Such small storms are actually a good thing, though it might not seem like it. It is rather like the small earthquakes you have here. When small bits of magick are released such as this, they will reduce some of the magickal pressure in Chimera. When they are small, there is not so much reason to worry."

"Small?" Faith's voice came out as a squeak. "That was *small?*"

At Ronny's nod, I huddled back against my chair. If that was small, I never wanted to see a *large* one.

"Maybe we should all put lightning rods on our houses," Brady said. "I've been studying them."

Ronny looked puzzled. "What is a lightning rod?"

"It's a metal post attached to the top of the house." Brady sat forward and pushed his glasses up his nose. Obviously this topic interested him. "It attracts lightning and funnels it safely into the ground. It— "

Doug interrupted, "Would lightning rods work on magic lightning?"

Ronny shook her head with a small smile. "It would not matter if you had them. Metal posts could not do any good against a magick storm. Metal does not attract magick."

Brady's enthusiasm deflated and he sat back. I got to my feet and said I should probably get home. The others didn't argue; they jumped up and said quick goodbyes.

-xXx-

That night started normal enough.

I brushed my teeth. I got into the t-shirt I liked to wear to bed. I pulled down the bedspread. I folded back the sheet and bent one knee, placing it onto the mattress.

And before I could pick up the other foot, something grabbed my ankle. A low harsh growling erupted from under my bed.

My heart squeezed into a small hard lump, like it was trying to hide inside my chest.

I'd forgotten how incredibly long, thin, and *strong* those fingers were. How cold and hard they felt around my ankle.

For a moment I was tempted to scream for help. But that hadn't worked so well last time. Dad hadn't believed a word I'd said about monsters. And I didn't believe he'd change his mind tonight. So it was up to me.

Yanking against its grip did nothing. In fact, my foot ended up closer to the bed than it had started as that thing tugged back. My little hard lump of a heart fluttered in panic. I tried to think of all of my favorite fighting moves from movies, but they required two available legs. Therefore, whatever *it* was, I had to make it let go. It took three strong, painful heaves, but I managed to jerk my captured foot back several inches from the edge of the bed. Giving me, I hoped, just enough space.

I took a deep breath and thought about what I was going to do. And what could go wrong if I messed it up.

Then those fingers tightened with crushing force on my ankle, and I knew it was about to make another try to drag me under the bed.

I was out of time.

I jerked my knee off the bed, and turned my foot sideways so my heel was in front of my trapped foot. I gave a quick fervent hope that I was about to stomp on the arm of that thing and not on my own toes, then brought my foot down with all of my might, putting all of my weight into it. Grinding my heel down violently.

There was an unearthly screech that left me nearly deafened, but those fingers let go and disappeared under my bed. This time, I was standing there calmly when my father rushed in, looking frantic. I think he kept asking what had made that sound, but I couldn't really hear him. I finally just shook my head and pointed at my bed. "It came from under there," I told him.

I think my voice must have been too loud, because he gave me a strange look, then dropped down to peer underneath it. He stared at what I was sure was an empty space for a long time, then stood up and shook his head. Fortunately I heard him say, "There's nothing there."

I smiled and said, "It must have come from outside then."

"I can't imagine what could make that sound," he said, "but you must be right. There's nothing in here. You just go back to sleep now, okay?"

I nodded and as he began to turn away, making shooing motions at my mother hesitating out in the hall, I leapt onto the bed, threw the covers over my head and prayed for sleep to come.

Just sleep.

No dreams.

-xXx-

I got my wish. There were no dreams for me that night. But I woke up sure of one very annoying fact. Everyone would be going on and on about TSYE at school.

I could have won a million dollars, if I'd been able to bet anyone with that kind of money. The halls were filled with talk about THE-STRANGEST-YEAR-EVER. People were claiming to have seen ravens flying backwards and dozens of toads swarming around some parts of town.

By lunchtime the latest rumor had made the rounds — how a curse had been laid against Santa Ramona by the witch buried in the cemetery. How there'd be a year of strange and terrible things every sixteen years until the curse was broken. How her spell book, buried in the cemetery with her, was the only way to break the curse.

This appeared to thrill everyone at school; the excited talk was everywhere, along with plans about trying to find it.

If I ever wanted a chance to get my hands on that book, I'd better start searching. Perhaps next Sunday while Faith was practicing soccer and Olivia was watching her younger brothers and sisters. No one would miss me.

But first I had to make it through the rest of the day. And I had to tell the others about what had happened in my room before lunch was over. I thought I described it to them pretty calmly, but their reaction was worse than I'd feared.

"Dammit, Kat, that's the second time," Doug said, his voice rising so that others in the lunch room turned to look at us.

Olivia opened her mouth, probably to ask Doug not to curse around her, but he pointed a finger at her and said, "I don't want to hear it."

He turned back to me and said, a bit accusingly I thought, "You've got to check under your bed after magic storms in the future." His tone of voice made it clear I was stupid for not thinking of it. And that I was obviously too dim to think about it for myself next time.

Right. Like I should have known it would happen again. And like I wouldn't be checking under my bed on a regular basis from now on.

What I didn't know was why it wasn't happening to anyone else. I nodded at him and said, sarcastically, "Yeah, thanks for the tip. Maybe you should do that too."

He didn't look like he thought this conversation was over, but the bell rang and we had to go to class.

TSYE talk was growing increasingly wild. Finally I started humming under my breath as we moved through the hall between classes, trying to block it out. By the end of the day, I was more than ready to get out of school.

Thank goodness I didn't have to put up with TYSE talk from my friends. Instead we talked about how unfair it was for Mr. Harper to give us three chapters of US History for homework. On top of the English paper due at the end of the week from Mr. Kline, and the biology test Ms. Gates told to us study for. It was like teachers didn't bother to talk to each other. Didn't they know their class wasn't the only thing going on?

The others were still complaining when I waved goodbye. I'd nearly reached my house when I heard a loud cawing from the tree beside me. I looked up, expecting to see a crow, but the bird perched there was far too big to be a crow. It turned its head and glared at me out of a shiny black eye, then croaked, "Nevermore, Kitty-Kat."

I honestly didn't remember screaming, but Doug insisted that I sounded louder than the whistle on a tea kettle. What I did know, was that it took almost no time for him to reach me. One moment I was staring at that horrid black thing, the next Doug was there, one arm wrapped around my shaking shoulders, demanding to know what was wrong. I waved my hand feebly at the tree and the huge bird lifted off and flew away. Backwards.

"What the hell was that?" Doug demanded.

"It spoke to me," I said and gulped, fighting to get myself back under control. "I think it threatened me."

"What are you talking about?" He sounded skeptical, and I couldn't really blame him.

"It said, 'Nevermore, Kitty-Kat'." I shuddered one last time, then felt calm enough to step away from him. I added, "It made this horrible cawing noise as I walked under the tree, then it spoke to me when I looked at it."

"I…I…" I couldn't really blame him for not knowing what to say, either.

"Doug, it knew my name. My nickname!" I clasped my hands together tightly as they started to shake. "How could it know that?"

He glanced where it had disappeared and shook his head. "I don't know." He looked back at me and said, "I don't like it."

I smiled wanly. "Me neither." I waved goodbye and headed into my house. I had to forget about the stupid bird. It was going to take forever to get all my homework done, and I couldn't afford to fail biology.

-xXx-

At school the next day, during morning break, I came around the corner and saw Olivia and George. They looked tense and unsmiling, so I put my head down and started to hurry past. I almost changed my mind when George had the nerve to say, "Olivia, you're a pretty face. It's not like I'm dating you for your brain. Which is a good thing." He sounded so kind and reasonable it took me a moment to realize just how bad that was. He'd just called Olivia stupid.

It was only the thought of how humiliated Olivia would be if I popped up and read him the riot act right there in the hall that kept me moving. But I couldn't resist turning to look back, to make sure she was okay. She was giving him her I'm-the-Queen-and-you're-just-a-minion look. I couldn't hear what she said to him, but she brushed past and walked over to where I waited, linked her arm through mine and hustled me down the hall and into the bathroom.

It wasn't until we were safely inside that she said, "I can't believe he talked to me like that. I thought he liked me." That's when the first tears began leaking from the corners of her eyes, dripping one at a time down her cheeks. Leaving long thick smears of mascara in their wake.

"Obviously he doesn't really know you." I dampened a paper towel, knowing the first thing she'd want to do was fix her make-up. "After dating you for months, he obviously doesn't *want* to know you. That's on him, not you."

She smiled wanly, snatched the damp towel from my hand and began blotting at her face. "Thanks, Kat."

"Seriously, the guy's got a problem. You're well rid of someone like that."

"Darn right," she said, voice not as angry as I'd have liked. But at least she no longer sounded…flattened? Defeated? Wounded.

-xXx-

I was pleased when Olivia looked okay at lunchtime, so I was really surprised when she suddenly blurted, "How can I make people see me for who I am? I do well in school. I do lots more things than sit in front of a mirror all day. How could anyone think I'm just a pretty face?"

I wasn't sure what to say. Then Brady spoke up. "Of course you're more than that. Everyone could see that if they paid attention."

Olivia sniffed and asked, "Oh yeah? Like what."

Brady told her with a calm surety, "You are a good friend. You would like to stand up to Ray and the others, but you don't because Faith doesn't want you to. You keep your promises, even when it makes your life more difficult. You are good at talking to strangers, comfortable in large groups of people, and not afraid to speak up in class. You stand up for others, like that new girl."

At her surprised look, he said, "Kat told me about it. He smiled and continued, "Also, you're really good with Pyg. You think fast, like when you mixed the neutralizers into a paste. And I know you're donating most of your allowance, and whatever other money you earn, to the no-kill animal shelter."

I looked at Olivia in amazement. She was giving her money to the animal shelter? He couldn't be right; she'd have told me. Besides, if he was right, how did he know about it when I didn't?

Olivia didn't shake her head or try to deny it. Instead she blushed, fiercely. Her eyes seemed to focus on him, in a way I hadn't seen before. Surprised. Intense. Speculative. Intrigued.

Then Brady said, "It helps to mitigate your propensity to be ten minutes late for everything."

At that, her eyes heated and her blush receded. "Late, schmate! And just how do you know all that? No one knows all that stuff."

Brady shrugged and gave a lop-sided smile. "I guess I notice everything about you." He stood up quickly, tossed the remainder of his lunch in the trash and walked out of the room without a backward glance.

Olivia stared after his retreating back, opening and shutting her mouth, looking a bit like a fish. She'd have hated that if she'd known. Plus she was blushing again, a deep crimson. She touched her cheeks then looked down at the remainder of her lunch and let her hair fall around her face, screening it from view.

For several minutes there was no sound at our table.

I was wondering how Brady managed to know things about my best friend that even *I* didn't know.

My thoughts felt like a ping-pong ball, getting smacked back and forth across a table.

Why didn't she tell me?

Was I a bad friend because I didn't know?

Why hadn't she ever told me?

Why did I have to find out from Brady?

Back and forth.

I looked at Olivia and decided now was not the time to ask about it. But that time would come.

Chapter 31/September/Santa Ramona

A Sorrow Nothing Heals– Though a *Real* Family Might Help

Brady's call that Saturday surprised me. It was a week before Chimera opened — why was he calling me now?

He sounded so choked up I could barely understand him, but once I did, I agreed to meet him and the others at Doug's in an hour. When I got there, last even though I lived the closest, Brady had his head buried in his hands, his shoulders hunched as if to deflect a blow.

I opened my mouth to ask what was going on, but Doug shook his head and motioned for me to sit down. I looked at the others, puzzled, and they just shrugged. We sat there, waiting for Brady to tell us why we were there.

Brady finally broke the long silence. His voice was thick and hard to understand, and I had to lean forward to make out what he was saying. He stopped and cleared his throat and started again. This time it came out in a rush of words, like a dam had broken.

"Grandpa Chuck is dead. Myocardial infarction."

He ignored our quick murmurs of sympathy and surprise. "I miss him so much already. It's like I have no one now. He watched out for me after Dad married again, you know? *She* acts like I should be over it already. After all, *she* said, he was old and old people die every day. Can you believe it?"

His voice iced with bitterness. "She actually said this will give me more time to be with my real family. As if she and Judy could *ever* be my real family. That will never occur."

He straightened, his face growing as cold as his voice. I was relieved to see that his eyes were dry, though his nose was very red. "It's like she suddenly imagines I'm no longer going to be an embarrassment to her. Which is pretty terrifying, really. What does she expect of me? Did I tell you Judy persists in informing me she's thankful she's not in high school? Because being related to me would have ruined her *popularity*."

He snorted in disgust, then slumped back, eyes tightening. "Dad refuses to talk about it. He keeps instructing me to be mature and deal with it. Of course, that's quite simple for him. I think he hated his father."

I started to protest thinking Brady was letting anger cloud his thinking, but he frowned at me and I subsided. He took a couple deep breaths and looked at each of us. "I'll always be grateful to have you as my friends. I didn't have many before I met you." He shot a quick glance at Olivia and gave her a thin smile. "That's why I never got upset when, ah, one of you teased me."

I spoke without thinking. "I thought maybe you just didn't get sarcasm."

"I live with the most sarcastic person I think the world has ever known." Brady gave me a forgiving glance. "After Judy, there's probably very little sarcasm I wouldn't recognize. You treated me like a friend. A bit of sarcasm was a small price to pay."

I glanced quickly at Olivia then averted my eyes. Her face was flaming. Even the part in her hair was a deep red.

He blew out a breath then stood up. "Thanks for being there. I just wanted to be sure you'd all be at the funeral. I think I'll need the moral support." All of us assured him we would be there, and he swallowed hard before saying, "I'll let you know the date as soon as possible."

He said a quick good-bye and left a deafening silence behind him.

-xXx-

At school the next day, he told us the funeral would be the following Saturday. Maybe it should have been obvious, but none of us expected the funeral to be held on the day we were supposed to go to Chimera.

We made sure Brady didn't know, but there were several arguments how some of us, meaning Doug, should still go to Chimera. Because some of us, meaning Doug, didn't have the right clothes for a funeral and wouldn't feel comfortable there anyway. And how it would be a shame if we, meaning the rest of us, allowed Brady's schedule for checking houses to get behind by a whole month. And wouldn't it be a better way to show support if some of us, meaning Doug, followed Brady's plan?

After Faith, Olivia and I wasted at least fifteen minutes arguing with him, I finally put my foot down. "You promised the very first time we took you into Chimera that you would do what we said in there. And you promised us you would never go there without us."

"Yes, but—"

"There are no buts, Douglas Oliver Geller. You made a promise and you are going to stick to it. Now suck it up. It doesn't matter if you want to be there. What matters is that Brady wants you there."

And that, thank goodness, was that.

The day of the funeral was foggy and cold. As we made our way through the now extremely familiar cemetery, I realized I hadn't yet made good on my idea to search for the witch's book. I had to make a plan.

The place where Brady's grandfather was being buried was on the far side of the cemetery, not near the back where we usually went. As we passed the area that led back to our tree, I craned my neck trying to see it. At first I wasn't sure I was looking in the right place, because if I was, another faceless angel statue had moved.

I shuddered and turned quickly away.

-xXx-

I'd never been to a funeral before. Mom told me to be respectful, don't hang all over Brady, and don't do anything to upset the other adults. I did what she said, but it was hard. At the graveside, Brady huddled miserably between his Dad and his step-mother, with Judy on the other side of his step-mother, looking bored. No one in his family was paying any attention to him, and I wanted to run over and hug him.

As the service progressed, I was forced to remember that Brady thought his father hated his grandfather. Brady's dad looked nearly as bored as Judy, stony-faced, glancing at his watch several times, tapping his foot impatiently. The few times he glanced at the casket, he looked angry, rather than sad, as if he was blaming his own father, Brady's grandfather, for making him be there.

-xXx-

In the days that followed, I began to wish I *had* gone over to hug him. Brady had been excused from school until Thursday and he didn't respond to any of our texts. I asked Mom what I should do because I was worried about him, but she told me to give him some space. That he'd answer us when he was ready.

On Thursday, Brady shoved his way into class, brushing by the rest of us before we could say a word. He threw himself in his chair, pulled out a textbook and buried his nose in it. I barely recognized him. His hair was cut all stylish, he was wearing completely different clothes than I'd ever seen on him, and he wasn't wearing his glasses. In fact, he looked as if he'd just stepped out of a Teen Vogue ad or off a teen fashion spot on the internet. I was all too familiar with those because Olivia liked to shove them under my nose on a regular basis. He looked as unlike Brady as possible. Even the bright copper penny red of his hair had changed; it didn't look as bright as in the past.

We didn't have a chance to talk to him until lunch, and even then he didn't say anything, but merely led the way outside. As we gathered around him, he tried to hike up his slim black pants with low-slung front pockets. He'd never worn anything that tight in his life. Though his plain white shirt was looser than the pants, the sleeves were rolled above his elbows, and he had a tight black t-shirt beneath it.

A light weight black jacket, decorated with fancy metal studs, was clutched tightly in his right fist. His knuckles showed white around it.

He raised one hand as if to push up his non-existent glasses, then dropped it to his side with a grimace. The movement dislodged his hair which had been cut longer on top and one side, and so short it nearly looked shaved on the other. The longer hair fell over his forehead and hung to the top of his eyes. That was wrong. Just wrong. Brady liked to shove his hair straight back from his face.

Judging by his expression, he hated everything about his new look. Because I was his friend I'd deny it to my dying breath, but I thought he looked pretty hot.

"What happened to you?" Doug asked incredulously.

Brady made a guttural sound in his throat, threw his jacket in the dirt and stomped on it repeatedly. With each stomp we got a bit of explanation.

"Since Grandpa Chuck is dead," stomp, "she said I didn't have to keep dressing like a reject from the fashion police." That earned a double stomp. "While I was downstairs going through a few of his things, SHE…" This one ended up more of a kick than a stomp. "SHE took everything out of my closet." Stomp. "I have no idea what she did with them; she won't say." This earned a combination of a stomp and a grinding foot motion. "Then she dragged me out to the car, bought me these stupid clothes, and forced me to the barber for a haircut of HER choice." There were so many stomps during this part, I lost count. "That was followed by a trip to an optometrist for contact lenses." He shoved his foot under the discarded, nearly demolished jacket and tossed it toward the trash can.

Then he tried, and failed, to shove his hands in his narrow, low slung front pockets. That caused a frustrated growl.

Olivia, who was not always as tactful as I was, said, "You look fantastic, Brady. Who knew you could look like this. It's awesome…" At the last minute she must have noticed me shaking my head at her, because that final word just trailed away. There was a moment of silence during which I thought Brady might explode.

Then he walked over to a nearby bench and slumped down on it. "I'm not me in these clothes. I don't want to look like the guy in a magazine ad. I don't want people to stare at me." He motioned to a group of giggling girls who were throwing him interested looks. Olivia moved in front of him so their view was cut off.

Their discontented grumbles floated back to us.

"I feel miserable in my own skin, can you understand that?" He looked at us with longing, so I nodded. I could at least imagine feeling that way.

Olivia stepped closer to him. "I know I'd feel miserable if someone made me dress like Faith." She quickly turned to Faith and said, "You look great as an athletic type. It suits you. I'd look like a Pekinese pretending to be a Greyhound."

Faith grinned at her and said, "And vice-versa, baby."

Olivia laughed and turned back to Brady. "I know how to fix this."

He shook his head morosely, so she turned and sat next to him in one fluid motion. "I know how to fix this," she stated calmly. She batted her lashes and pouted her lips. "Do you think I look this good naturally?"

That brought Brady's head up. He scrutinized her as she gave him a can't-you-see-how-gorgeous-I-am look. He gave her a small half smile. "You always look beautiful."

She shook her head but he continued, "You're beautiful even when you're climbing all fresh-faced and half-drowned out of a lake."

Olivia's eyes widened momentarily and settled on his face. She sounded nearly breathless when she spoke. "Yes, well, I spend a lot of time and attention on looking good. Mom hates make-up so I carry it with me and use it on the way to school each morning."

She said that like we should all get her meaning. When we didn't start applauding and telling her how smart she was, she rolled her eyes. "After school, you and I are going to the second hand shop on Main Street."

"Wait, we're what?" She certainly had Brady's attention now.

"We're going to find you clothes you feel comfortable in. Well, you may be stuck with the pants, there's only so much room in your backpack, after all. But I'll show you how to roll the clothes you like up so they won't wrinkle and will fit in your pack. While I'm making myself awesome, you can be switching out the new threads with some you like. Switch back at the end of the day and SHE won't know any different."

Now Olivia did earn a small smattering of applause. She bowed at the waist and said, "Thank you, thank you."

That won a real smile from Brady.

-xXx-

It was just before dinner time when Olivia called that night.

"There's so much more to him than the science stuff," she said.

"More to who?" I asked.

"Brady of course," she said impatiently. "Keep up." Then her voice softened. "He always made me feel twitchy. I thought it was all his geek-speak. But, I think, it's more than that. He's really considerate, you know? He sees people for who they are. He certainly sees me. And he hardly ever complains or gets angry."

There was a brief pause while I considered what to say, then Olivia spoke again, sounding thoughtful. "I'm not sure how he does that, actually. I never saw all these sides of him before. I'm intrigued."

"All those sides were always there," I told her.

"Maybe. But I didn't see it before, did I?"

I managed not to say what I was thinking. That if she'd ever stopped sniping at him, she might have been able to see him a long time ago.

She said, "I'll have to pay better attention from now on."

I opened my mouth to agree then shut it, slowly. After all, I'd missed several things about Olivia.

"Oh, I almost forgot! Can you believe it?" Olivia sounded like she was practically bouncing off the walls. "When we got to the second-hand shop, there were all of Brady's clothes. All of them! We got as many as we could. He said he's going to keep some in Chimera so there's no chance SHE can find all of them. You know. Just in case."

"How was he? Was it hard for you?" I tried to keep the hesitation out of my voice, but kept remembering her strange reaction when he told her she was always beautiful. I'd seen her turn that kind of comment from others into a joking acceptance on several occasions. Never had I seen her stare at someone like she had at Brady.

"Oh, he's totally fine now. Though he swears SHE had better leave him the hell alone."

"Olivia!" She was in her house and she'd cursed over the phone. "Where's your Mom?"

"What? Oh, I slipped didn't I? Darn. I haven't needed to put anything into the curse jar in over a year. Oh well. It was worth it. And that *is* what he said, after all."

I was still puzzling over the correct response to that when she said, "Tah tah. Got to go start dinner for the babes. See you mañana." And she hung up the phone before I had a chance to say anything else.

At school the next day, Brady looked a lot more like his normal self. His hair was slicked back and he was wearing jeans and his normal blue button down shirt. The only thing different was his glasses. His lack of glasses. That was going to take some getting used to.

"Did she throw away your glasses?" Doug asked, grinning.

Brady pushed self-consciously at the bridge of his nose, then shook his head. "No, I still have them. But I find my visual acuity to be far superior with these new lenses. She paid a lot of money to find lenses that could correct my severe astigmatism." He grinned. "What would Ronny say? There's no point throwing away the baby along with all the stuff in the bathwater."

"Well," I said, "I don't think she would put it quite like that, but I get your meaning,"

"Plus you look great in contacts," Olivia told him, grinning. "Want to grab a Coke after school?"

Brady glared at her and said, "Oh, so now I look good enough to spend time with at Johnny's Burger Shack? Forget it."

Before he could turn away, she grabbed his shoulder. "Are you forgetting what we spent yesterday afternoon doing? If I was that shallow, I'd never have helped you get your clothes back." She sniffed loudly and turned away from him, nose definitely aimed higher than normal.

Faith and I followed Olivia down the hall, and ended up being the first ones in the classroom. Olivia took advantage by turning to us. "I teased him too many times, didn't I? Now he'll never believe I want to be there for him." She clenched her hands into fists and rested them on the desk before her.

Faith gaped at her in astonishment and choked out, "Uh, what?"

But I remembered our phone call and wasn't surprised.

"Well, you heard the way Brady talked to me after George and I broke up. Brady pays attention to the things I do. He appreciates *me,* not just my face. I really like that."

Faith spoke slowly, choosing her words with care. "Don't you think you'll get tired of being with someone who only likes to think about geeky science stuff all the time?"

Olivia raised her left eyebrow, letting it climb up her forehead and under her bangs before shaking her head. "I don't expect guys to like my fashion magazines. He can do science stuff and I'll watch E!. I'd just like to do it together."

"What have you done with my friend Olivia?" I demanded, only half joking. You didn't wake up with some creepy pod next to your bed this morning, did you?"

She threw back her head and laughed. "No, I just finally gave myself permission to believe someone smart could like me, just as I am. Brady actually appreciates a lot of things about me. I need to come up with a way to convince him— "

She cut off as the rest of the class began wandering in, leaving me wondering. *Convince him of what?*

-xXx-

Olivia was extremely agreeable at lunch. Uncharacteristically so. I actually found myself missing her usual sarcasm. It became clear after a while that whenever there was any type of disagreement among the five of us, she took Brady's side. I wasn't sure if anyone else noticed, but I was going to watch this development.

The rest of the week seemed fairly normal. New normal. We avoided the Rejects. Olivia agreed with Brady. Brady changed his shirt in the morning while Olivia decorated her face. I'd just started to get comfortable with it when Brady cornered me in the only class I didn't have with Olivia and Faith. He walked over as I gathered up my books and asked, "What's up?"

"Nothing," I said, startled, looking around in case I'd missed something.

"Not here. Olivia. What's up with Olivia?" He sounded hunted.

"What about Olivia?" I asked carefully. So I might not have been the only one to notice her new of-course-Brady-is-right attitude.

He slung his backpack on the table and threw himself into the chair next to mine. "I was always the one she argued with. Now she's agreeing with me all the time."

"Really?" I asked, but I could tell my voice sounded weak.

"Kat, I'm socially inept, not stupid. And I remember every word she's ever said to me."

Was Olivia really sure about being with Brady? I couldn't imagine having a boyfriend who remembered every word — every single word — I ever said. "Well, maybe she started paying attention and realized that you're frequently correct." I cringed after I said that; it sounded so dorky.

"You don't believe that," he said. "Today you and I disagreed at lunch. No way should she agree with me over you."

Darn it, he was right. "Well, in this particular instance, she must've agreed with you." It took a bit of courage to say that; he was starting to look angry. Obviously he wasn't buying the bull I was trying to sell him. Not that I could blame him. "Anyway, you told me you liked her," I accused him. "Isn't this a good thing?"

"I just can't trust it. She never wanted to have anything to do with me before." He turned a face that looked as upset as Olivia's earlier that week. The two of them could pose for Greek tragedy masks.

"I can't help it. It hurts to think Olivia only likes me now that SHE made me look like a fashion magazine."

I couldn't break the code of silence with a Blood Sister, so I couldn't tell him what Olivia had said about Brady. But I might be able to help. "Maybe since you started telling her nice things she wants to be nicer to you."

Okay, so my first attempt pretty much sucked. He shot me a disbelieving look and stood up. "I gotta go."

Between classes, I tried to tell Olivia as much about that conversation as possible, without betraying Brady. Really, trying to keep secrets that they liked each other was becoming ridiculous! "I think Brady might believe you suddenly like him because you saw how good he can look." There, that was truthful yet vague. And Brady *had* looked pretty hot.

Olivia sniffed. "I already told him that had nothing to do with it, or I wouldn't have helped him get his ugly old clothes back."

"Well, see, if he heard you say that he'd be sure it had something to do with how he looks." Actually, I was sure that Olivia didn't feel like that, but she needed to stop and think before blurting out stuff like that.

"Don't you think he'd freak if I started bragging about his kindness? About his ability to see me for who I am? About his intelligence and insight?" She smiled, a soft dreamy sort of smile, and added, "About his beautiful eyes?" She shook her head as if coming back from somewhere else and focused on me. "I've been checking him out. Did you know he's been donating to the same animal shelter I do? For almost a year now."

I shook my head and she sighed. "Like I said, he's kind. You can always count on him, no matter what." She paced a few steps away from me then back again. "I've started paying attention, and I think I'm getting to know him pretty well. I *know* he'd freak if I said any of those things to him! Which leaves, what?"

In a quick change of mood, she struck a pose — chin raised, eyelashes fluttering, hands clasped near her heart — and pitched her voice up, sounding enthralled. "Oh, Brady, your perfect understanding of the scientific principal drives me wild." She looked at me and gave a half-hearted smirk. "That just sounds stupid."

"Yeah, you're right. Don't ever say that again." I laughed, I couldn't help it. But Olivia looked more dejected than she had before and I suddenly couldn't stand it. "Look, why don't you just tell him it's nice to have our old Brady back. He'd probably like that."

She rolled her eyes. "That sounds stupid too," she insisted, but there was a momentary flash of interest across her face.

-xXx-

It was just two days later when I got to see the conclusion of all that angst. They'd obviously been able to work things out between them.

I didn't mean to listen to them. Or to look!

I'd dropped some papers at the end of class and stooped down to gather them up. Everyone else left, so I was alone in there. Crouched down beside my desk, on the far side of the room, no one could have seen me. It would have seemed deserted to anyone looking for a private spot.

The door, which was normally quiet, thumped shut like it had been pushed with some force. By the time I looked up, it was too late; I didn't want to be seen.

Brady and Olivia were standing just inside, where they couldn't be seen through the small window in the door. Their arms were wrapped around each other so tightly I couldn't tell where one began and the other ended. And their mouths were locked together like they'd been starving for each other.

I crouched down even further and prayed they wouldn't decide to come any deeper into the room. My abused muscles were quivering in outrage by the time they broke apart.

Olivia gasped and said, "It's just that…lately you were kinda mean to me."

"Well," Brady said, his voice husky and unsure, "you were always going out with someone else. I couldn't stand it."

A loud clang of a metal locker being slammed right outside startled them. They looked into each other's eyes for a moment, then grinned. Brady pulled Olivia next to him and the two of them left the classroom together. I might have been able to shove one of the papers I'd just picked up between them. But not more than one.

I wasn't sure how I felt about this development. I *was* glad the two of them wouldn't act like they were trying out for the part of saddest sophomore in school anymore. But they looked pretty serious. Especially Brady. What if they hurt each other, got angry with each other, broke up with each other? What would that do to our group? To our exploration of Chimera?

I'd have to trust them. They liked each other, right? They'd be careful, right?

-xXx-

The next day, our history teacher, Mr. Harper went on enthusiastically for nearly half the class about how wonderful the Mayor and Council were. How they kept trying to protect the town's reputation from all the horrible reporters who were only out for the next big story. How any talk of paranormal events was dangerous, and none of his students should be spreading gossip that would make the town sound…odd. How there must be some type of natural formation causing compasses and GPS not to work properly at times. That we should all be grateful for our leaders' diligence on our behalf.

That evening, the City Council requested that there be no posts on social media about anything happening in our town. To protect the town's reputation, of course. They were asking that the citizens refrain from all mentions of strange or paranormal phenomena. And to avoid taking any pictures that could be *misinterpreted* by outsiders.

So later that week, when Ray and Andrew started screaming at me in the hallway that my brother Chris was part of the town's *paranormal problem* and should be run out of town, I wasn't even surprised. What did surprise me was how tempted I was to say he didn't know the half of it. That Chris was married to a woman from another world. The very place causing all the strangeness. I almost laughed out loud; it sounded like the perfect romance novel — The Paranormal Investigator and the Half-Magic Sorceress.

I managed to restrain myself, though. Well, other than flipping the two of them off before turning away.

-xXx-

I wondered when Olivia and Brady would tell the rest of us that they were seeing each other, but I had a long wait. I was able to see it since I was looking for it: they stood a bit too close; their eyes lingered on each other; their fingers brushed a bit too often. They might not want to talk about it, but if they kept that up, everyone would know soon enough.

We went to Ronny's on Saturday. Brady brought it up, and all of us agreed that we missed going to Chimera that month. Going to Ronny's to talk about it wasn't the same, but it was better than watching Brady and Doug play their newest shoot-at-everything-that-moves video game.

"We've been going into Mystic for months now," Faith said as we took our usual seats. "I've been wondering what it was like growing up there."

"Mystic," Ronny assured her, "was a marvelous place to grow up." She smiled reminiscently, then a frown passed quickly across her face. "I did sometimes wish for friends my own age. And of course, there were those who didn't like that I was half-Mundane." She shrugged and pulled her smile back. "But those were minor problems. My mother did her best to make sure I was happy. And we grew especially close after we lost my father."

"How old were you when that happened?" I couldn't imagine losing my father. Even when he sometimes drove me crazy.

"I had been alive for only thirty-two years," she said. At that, most of us gasped, though not Brady. He would have remembered that she'd lived in Chimera for nearly seventy-five years before being banished. I sometimes forgot that her magic had kept her much younger than if she'd lived here. Her next words echoed that. "Don't forget, in Chimera thirty-two years is no time at all. But at least I did have him that long."

"And he told you he was happy there?" When Ronny nodded, he said, "I'd like to believe that could happen. After all, my great-grandfather disappeared. I'd like to think something good might have happened for him. My Grandfather used to say he would never have chosen to leave him. Dad got tired of hearing about it and told Grandpa Chuck he was crazy. It was one of the few things they ever really argued about. That and me, I guess."

There was a moment of silence then Olivia stirred next to me. I saw her surreptitiously pat Brady's leg before asking, "What was it like to live in a magical place?" Ronny frowned as if she wasn't sure how to answer her. So Olivia added, "I mean, how's it different than living here?"

"Ah." Ronny's expression cleared. "That is an interesting question, but one I am not sure I can really explain. In Chimera, there is so much more color." All of us nodded. We'd seen that for ourselves.

Ronny smiled and said, "It is much more than that, of course. There is a low hum of conversation and magick all the time. As if the air itself is filled with energy from all the spells being cast. The best I can describe it is like a newly poured soda, where the bubbles push against your face. Like the air itself fizzes with magick. There is an abundance of interesting sounds and smells around every corner as spells are cast and used. The trees are filled with flowers of every shape and size, many of which make music in the breeze."

She'd worn a dreamy expression during all that, but now her face split into a huge grin. "And there are the Jabbertock birds that nest in the trees near my home. They could talk to me."

Brady looked startled. "Did you say they could talk?"

"Yes! They would call out and offer praise and insults regarding everyone's wardrobe choices, their hairstyles, whether you were leaving your home later than usual or bringing someone home with you. They would share their opinions of everyone who lived in our neighborhood with everyone else. No one went unnoticed. Not even the town's sole child trying not to be caught for getting into mischief," she said and laughed. "They loved tattling on me." She was smiling like this was a pleasant memory, but the thought made me shudder. I couldn't image birds repeating every single thing about me to everyone I knew. It gave a whole new meaning to the term *stool pigeon*.

Note to self – When we get to Ronny's neighborhood, don't do anything *in front of those birds!*

Doug cleared his throat. "There's something I've been thinking about. It seems clear that our familiars reflect our personalities in some ways. I was wondering if that means something."

There were a few moments of confusion as everyone spoke over the top of the others. It was Ronny's amused laugh that finally got us to stop.

"Of course it means something," she said. "The magick in Chimera created them to help you. They were created specifically to match who and what you are."

"Like what?" Faith asked. She crossed her arms defensively over her chest, as if afraid of what Ronny might say.

"From everything you have told me, Doug and Rusty are sometimes a bit impetuous," she said. "Even when it might not be in their best interest."

There were several nods, though now it was Doug who crossed his arms over his chest, and frowned.

"Faith and her fox are a bit…timid," Ronny continued with a quick smile at Faith. "Brady and his bat like to hang back and assess things." Brady wasn't the only one who nodded at this.

Ronny turned to Olivia and said, "Olivia and her owl are always ready to try to do something to stop those bullies that have been such a problem for you, isn't that right?" That earned another set of nods.

Doug stood up and said he had to go. The rest of us scrambled to our feet. As we headed for the door, I turned back. "What about me?" I asked, not entirely sure I wanted to know what she thought, but very sure I didn't want to be the only one left out.

She looked surprised by my question. "You and Shadow are there to help the others. To try to keep the peace. To keep everyone looking for answers. You are the glue, Kat."

Glue. How...blah. As we headed for home, I kept trying to make that sound more adventurous. More dramatic. More satisfying. But glue was just so...blah.

-xXx-

That night a bit of putrid fog was reported in the cemetery. The town council was split over the possibility of a chemical spill off shore or someone that hadn't been buried properly in the cemetery. When no further traces could be found the next day, the whole issue mysteriously disappeared from conversation. Almost like no one remembered. When I mentioned it to Doug, he said they probably didn't want to remember.

I wished I could forget that easily, because I was pretty sure I knew where it came from. It had been some of the stinking yellow fog that we'd encountered before in Chimera.

The day after that, huge flocks of birds appeared. Lots of birds. All mixed together. Seven of them perched on every single lamppost throughout town. Now instead of TSYE talk, people were talking about Hitchcock's *The Birds*.

I really didn't like that any better.

Chapter 32/October/Chimera

Death by Floor

I was early and dragging my feet, worried about getting to our corner too soon. I didn't want to be standing there by myself if the Rejects came by. My view was blocked by a large hedge, and I slowed as I turned the corner. I came to an abrupt halt and simply stared. Brady and Olivia were already there.

How had Olivia beat me? She never got there first, especially when I was early.

The two of them didn't see me. They were plastered against each other, lips locked. Then Olivia pulled back about an inch and said, "When you kiss me, I don't feel twitchy anymore."

Brady laughed low in his throat. "I guess I need to run some experiments on that. Maybe lots of experiments."

"You can perform as much scientific analysis as you want," Olivia told him, and reached for him again.

I took a quick step back, putting myself on the other side of the hedge. I started whistling before I came back around the corner. The two of them were standing a couple feet apart, looking innocent.

Too innocent.

If I hadn't already seen them, I'd have been wondering what the heck they'd been doing after taking one look at those innocent faces.

Brady was in his fashion magazine clothes and he stayed in them all the way through the cemetery and into Chimera. The moment we were through, he shrugged out of his pack, yanked off the shirt his step-mother had made him wear, and leaned back, letting the sunlight wash over his face. With his eyes still closed, he hooked his sunglasses in the neck of his sleeveless t-shirt and heaved a relieved sigh. I'd known he hated wearing his step-mother's choice of clothes, but seeing his relief in getting that shirt off made it real.

I glanced over at Olivia then quickly away. Her eyes were wide with something that resembled hunger and it made me uncomfortable. Like bursting in on her when she just stepped out of the shower or something. As I glanced away, I realized Brady had opened his eyes and had seen the look on Olivia's face. He must have felt uncomfortable too; he turned away, a flush climbing his cheeks.

"Well," Doug said heartily. "We should get going."

No one spoke as we started down the path, except to quickly greet our animals as they came running up. I scooped up Shadow and buried my face in her fur, then set her back down.

We'd all agreed to make it a short day if possible, and hurried down the road and into the town. I thought we might have set a record.

Brady pulled out the map and frowned in concentration. He pointed to the houses we could see off to our right, just past those we'd explored during our second month in Mystic. There were four of them, and they were large, at least the size of the mini-mansions we'd checked a few months before. The only difference I could see was these were made from different materials.

Olivia put her hand on my arm and whispered, "Don't you just love that little wrinkle he gets between his eyes when he concentrates on something?"

"Um…no. I never noticed any such thing," I whispered back, then grinned to myself before asking, "Since when do *you* notice such things?"

"How long have you known?" she asked.

I opened my eyes wide and asked, "Known what?"

She shot me a sideways glance and said, "Katherine Alice Taylor, I've known you since you were just a few years old. I know when you've seen something that embarrassed you. That's when you start whistling *Pop Goes the Weasel*.

Darn! How embarrassing to find out I did something so obvious. "Well, I…you…"

"You're my very best friend. And who else could I talk to about Brady?" She laughed at the blush that swept up my cheeks, and bumped against my shoulder. "Okay, I'll change the subject."

I smiled at her, but was grateful that we were nearing the houses. They looked even larger now. One was made entirely with bales of straw. The second was covered by wood siding. The third was made of bright red brick. The fourth was made of heavy gray stone. All had ornately framed windows enclosing stained glass. The doorways had highly decorated wooden frames and the doors themselves were intricately carved.

I noticed several statues positioned around a large flower bed at the center of the houses. It was filled with small trees and flowers that looked like someone had combined Dr. Seuss with Disney's *Alice in Wonderland.* I might have been tempted to look closer, but seeing all those statues made me uncomfortable. What if they *were* some kind of memorial for those that had disappeared? That was…disturbing.

When we reached the first house, the straw house, we told our animals to wait outside. This door didn't have any booby-traps. It simply opened and let us enter.

Then everything went to hell.

I was getting really tired of everything going to hell.

One at a time, sliding over the door and windows, bars, metal shields and thick wooden barriers moved across every opening. Some came up from the floor, some down from the ceiling, others from one side or the other. I lost count of how many there were. Each made loud clunking, clanging, thumping or crashing sounds. When they finally stopped, the silence seemed even thicker and heavier than before.

"What's up with things sliding over the doors and windows?" Doug asked, disgustedly. "Can't they be more original?"

"Um…" I couldn't believe he would say something so idiotic. "I'd rather deal with things we know."

"But this time we're on the inside," Olivia pointed out.

"How are we going to get out of here?" Faith asked. She wrapped her arms tightly around her waist and I realized I hadn't seen her do that for a while.

"We'll need to huff and puff and blow the house in," I said and started laughing. It was half-hysterical, but at least I was able to laugh about it.

"There must be some trigger to get it open again," Brady said, sounding calm and reasonable. "We just need to figure it out."

He was right, I realized. Between the five of us, we were bound to figure something out. And I might as well go first. "You mean like saying Abracadabra?"

He turned to me, clearly about to say no, but Faith said, "How about hocus pocus?" I was glad to see she'd relaxed her arms.

"No, it's probably Alakazam," Olivia said with gusto.

Brady crossed his arms over his chest, shaking his head but looking indulgent now.

"Maybe Presto-Chango," I added.

"Supercalifragilisticexpialidocious," Faith said, then giggled.

"Bibbidi-bobbidi-boo!" Olivia yelled.

"Open Sesame," I said, then stopped. There'd been a momentary quiver in the air. Like I'd come close.

"Open up," Faith said. She must have noticed it also.

"Open the doors," Olivia said.

Each time, there was that same quiver that died away in the middle of the second word. It seemed 'open' was right; we just had to find the next word.

"Open the heck up," Doug growled, rubbing absently at his bad leg. I wasn't surprised when his command didn't do any more good than mine, but he frowned and muttered something under his breath.

"Open sesame seeds," Faith said.

This time the quiver seemed stronger.

"Open turmeric," Olivia said.

"Open what?" I asked, puzzled.

"It's a type of spice. Like sesame seeds," she said.

I shrugged; it was as good try as any. "Open rosemary," I said.

This time, the quiver was definite.

"Open sage," Faith tried. There was another heavy quivering, but still no open doors.

"Oh for heaven's sake," Olivia said, disgustedly. "There's dozens, probably hundreds, of possible herbs and seasonings. How are we supposed to know which it is?"

"Open parsley, sage, rosemary and thyme," Faith said dispiritedly.

And lo and behold, there was a grinding, screeching sound, and one at a time the coverings over the doors and windows re-opened.

Faith threw her arms around me. "We're saved!"

Once all the coverings were out of the way, we could hear our animals making sounds of distress. I stuck my head out the door and said, "We're fine, guys. Don't worry. We'll check this place and be out soon."

A contented silence settled behind us as we started checking through each of the rooms inside the house. We explored several, but most seemed unused. The dressers and closets were all empty, so it didn't take long to get through.

As we made our way back to the front door, I asked, "Why do you think so much of the house was empty? Doesn't that seem weird?"

"Not really," Olivia said. "A lot of the large manors in other countries have an entire floor or even a whole wing that's not in use. It happens. Why keep a bunch of stuff in rooms you won't be using?"

"Okay, I guess I buy that," I told her. "But this is a magic place. You'd think they could just make rooms they no longer want disappear."

"You might have to reconfigure the entire space if you take one or two rooms out of an existing space," Brady chimed in, unexpectedly. "Unless you wanted to leave strange empty spaces in your floor plan."

He opened his mouth like he was going to keep talking about spatial planning and other things I really didn't care about, so I said, "I'll take your word for it."

When we emerged from the house our animals surrounded us and seemed especially affectionate. "We're fine," I assured Shadow, stooping to stroke my hand down her fur. I could still hear her purring when I stood up.

The next house was a repeat of the first, only made from wood and missing the crazy door and window coverings. There was nothing exciting or scary in there. And thankfully, no wolf outside.

We started toward the next house, the one of brick, when the sudden sound of squawking came from the trees over our heads.

"You are the first we have seen in so long," a strange voice said. It reminded me of internet videos of parrots trying to talk. I looked around until I saw several brightly-feathered birds perched in a tree not more than five feet away from us.

Apparently Faith hadn't seen them. "Who said that?" she asked and twisted around.

I laughed and pointed, right as one of the birds said, "It was I, stupid mortal."

Faith sucked in a shocked breath and bit her lip.

"What are you?" Doug asked. I thought Brady might say something, but he was merely staring in fascination.

One bird hopped closer and turned its beady eye on us "We are Jabbertock. Birds of gossip. Rumor-mongers. Fowl tellers of tales."

Ronny had told us about these birds. I'd hoped we wouldn't run into them. "Well," I said brightly. "Gotta go. See ya."

If I'd really hoped we'd leave them behind, I would've been sadly disappointed. They kept swooping from tree to tree, landing only a few feet ahead. Each time, they spoke to us.

"Why are mortals in Chimera?" asked one. It had long blue and red feathers that trailed far behind it.

"Just visiting," Olivia said, and we made it several feet before they landed in front of us again.

"Where are you going? We can help." This bird was yellow and green with iridescent markings on the tip of each wing.

"No, we're fine," I said in a cheerful voice. "See ya."

"Wait," Brady said. "What do you know about why Mystic is empty?"

One of the birds hopped closer and turned its head until it was leaning over parallel to the ground. "Empty? No. We are here."

"Empty of most who lived here," Brady clarified.

"Here then gone," one said. "Here then gone."

Another hopped over next to the first. "Long time now."

Then they were all speaking. "Yes, long. Very long." "Empty." "Abandoned." "Alone."

I spoke loudly to make myself heard, "Yes, but why?"

The birds just sat there without a sound, twisting their heads back and forth, blinking their large black eyes.

Okay, that was pretty clear. They didn't know any more than we did.

This time, we made it to the door of the brick house before they flew after us. I fervently hoped they'd be gone by the time we were done in there. At least there were only four houses to check today, and we'd already finished two.

But this house had something new to throw at us. Once we were inside with the door shut, Doug's wristband shot out a blue-green glow. At the same time, the ground began to quake underfoot. It was as if the wooden planks had turned into thick, unyielding quicksand.

Olivia shrieked and Brady grabbed her "I've got you," he said, holding onto her as she scrambled up on the coffee table.

Faith held onto the arm of a chair and tried to pull her feet free. One foot slowly inched out with a disgusting sucking noise. I expected to see it covered in mud or a thick, sticky liquid but it looked perfectly dry. And all the while, her other foot continued to slowly sink.

Just like both of mine.

The others had all been able to climb onto, or at least desperately cling to, various bits of the furnishings. Except me. The closest piece of furniture was the couch, and it was several feet away.

Death by floor sounded amusing, but the reality was far from funny.

I pulled as hard as I could but my feet were trapped in something that moved like gummy molasses sinking slowly down into a deep hole. And it was taking me with it. I grunted with effort, the sound raising in pitch and volume as panic set in. My feet weren't coming back out.

Not an inch.

Not a centimeter.

Not. At. All.

Somehow Doug began forcing his way toward me. The floor began sucking him down as I watched. He kept pushing through, first ankle deep, then calf deep. Coming slowly closer, eyes determined, muscles in his neck tight with effort.

And all that time, I was slowly sinking deeper into the floor.

Whatever was under the surface was not level; my right leg was sinking faster than the left. As Doug battled with the floor to get to me, I was waging my own battle. I had to constantly shift my weight, struggling to keep my balance.

And just like that, I lost. I could feel my body begin to tip over backwards, and the idea of my entire body touching that floor and getting sucked into it made me scream.

I pin-wheeled my arms wildly, fighting to stay upright.

Doug's eyes were intent on me and his face was red and sweating with effort. Several excruciatingly slow moments passed as I fought for balance, and I nearly sobbed with relief as he reached me. He grabbed my shoulders tightly and got me stable. I could feel his hands shaking where they gripped me. But when he spoke, his voice sounded calm, nearly casual. "Having some trouble, Taylor?"

"You creep," I said, then laughed, giddy with relief. "Get me out of here." I struggled again, up to my knees now.

Doug laughed, too. He grabbed me around the waist and slowly began pulling me from the floor. It felt alive, as if it had its arms wrapped around my legs, refusing to let go. The grip tightened painfully, then it gave with a slurping sound, like I was being sucked up out of a straw.

As soon as my feet were loose, Doug scooped me up and waded with me toward the couch. "For once, I'd prefer it if you were a light-weight," he said, panting with the effort of carrying me and moving us both through the thick floor, continuing to sink deeper with each step. I wasn't sure how he was doing it; the floor was only an inch of so below his knees now. He boosted me onto the couch with a theatrical grunt, then dragged one of his legs free and also got it up on the couch. Then with a grimace he used that leg, his injured leg, to vault up next to me.

"Um, some help here!" I'd forgotten about Faith — too worried about myself. She hadn't been able to pull her other leg from the floor and was now stretched to an uncomfortable angle; one leg perched on the seat of the chair, the other now trapped nearly to her thigh.

Balancing carefully, Doug and Brady made their way around the room to her, moving from one piece of furniture to another. As they drew near, I saw the panicked tension leave her face. It took both of them, with as much assistance as Faith could give, to get that leg out.

"Thanks," Faith said, then leaned over and placed her hands against her knees as she dragged in several deep breaths. Then she straightened and pressed her lips to first Doug's cheek, then Brady's, in a quick kiss of thanks.

I almost laughed out loud at the nearly identical looks of horrified embarrassment on their faces. They mumbled something, then Olivia interrupted. "Why is the furniture okay? I mean, it isn't sinking like we were."

"Excellent question," Brady told her and smiled. "I was just wondering the same thing."

"Duh," I said crossly, feeling tired and *so* done with magic at the moment. "We set off some kind of anti-intruder spell. The people living here wouldn't want their furniture sinking into the floor if someone broke in. Obviously."

"They could just make more," Doug said, clearly not seeing this as a big thing. Of course, it was really ugly furniture, mustard yellow flowers on a pea soup green background. Who'd care if it did disappear?

"No," Faith said impatiently. "You can't create matter out of magic, remember?"

"Then how did it snow on us a couple years ago?" Olivia asked.

"That would be the moisture in the air being cooled by the spell. The water turned to snow, we didn't create it," Brady said slowly. "Good point, Faith."

She turned away, but I saw her grin with pleasure.

Brady cleared his throat, "We need to successfully navigate our way over to the door." He pointed at the far end of the room. At the doorway, several feet away from any piece of furniture. I looked down at the soft, squishy couch, and let my eyes sweep across the overstuffed chairs. I rocked my weight and felt the cushions give alarmingly under my feet. Getting from here to the door would be easier said than done.

We began clambering over the soft cushions toward the other side of the room. It probably would have looked hysterical if someone was watching us. Five sixteen year olds, lurching, totally undignified, over the furniture. Leaping from couch to chair to ottoman to coffee table. It took a while, and there were a few times one or another of us almost fell, but we did reach the other end without putting our feet on the floor. Thankfully.

I was panting a bit with exertion, but asked "Is anyone else totally sick and tired of these damn houses attacking us?"

"Kat. Language!" Olivia huffed.

"Sorry." I rolled my eyes but didn't push it. I was sure the others had to be as tired of it as I was.

We finally all made it over to the last piece of furniture in the room, a long, low table. My stomach twisted as I realized it was more than six feet from what we'd thought was a doorway. But there wasn't a hallway inside that opening, there was a staircase. Somehow we were going to have to get from the table onto a narrow step, which was farther away than the length of my entire body.

"I'm going for it," Doug said, and launched himself off the table and onto the stairs.

Fortunately they held firm underneath him.

Chapter 33/October/Chimera

Arthur

With Doug helping to catch us, we made that leap one at a time until we were all standing on the stairs. Some of us, more vertically challenged, wind-milling our arms and fighting for every inch of that space. As soon as Brady made the final jump, the floor rippled and firmed back up.

Of course.

"I wonder if we'll have to get out the same way we got in," I said, looking back. It had been bad enough launching ourselves from that table to the stairs. How hard would it be to do it in reverse?

We searched through the house quickly, and even though Brady asked the map and Doug waved his wristband around, we ended up with nothing to show for it. Brady stuffed the map back in his pocket with more force than usual. I could tell by the look on his face that even patient Brady was getting frustrated by our lack of progress.

There were no other exits in the house and we hesitated as we reached the bottom of the staircase, staring out at the living room. Doug stepped tentatively on the floor, Brady holding his arm in case it didn't hold. I sucked in my breath as Doug staggered. Then he laughed like that had been a funny joke, and stepped out boldly, the floor firm beneath him.

I thought crossly it would serve him right if he took a few more steps then hit a soft spot and dropped in up to his neck.

Brady and Olivia stepped down at the same time, just as hesitant at first as Doug had been. Faith followed, then it was my turn. My movements were awkward at first, until I was sure *I* wouldn't be the one up to my neck.

At least the floor stayed solid as we left, walking faster and faster, ready to be safely out of the disappointingly empty house.

When we walked outside, there was no sign of those obnoxious birds. I grabbed Shadow and swung her around in an exuberant circle. She laid her ears flat against her head, not pleased with me, but didn't try to get down. At least if we didn't find anything, we didn't have to put up with any more surprises out here.

The fourth and final house for today stood ahead of us. It was the largest and most beautiful. Masses of brightly colored flowers grew around the edges of the building, which was painted a nearly blinding white with lemon yellow trim and a shiny candy apple red door.

Lemon trim? Candy apple door? Clearly I was getting hungry. I fished a granola bar out of my backpack as Doug carefully pulled open the door. We crowded into the house behind him, ready to help if necessary, but there didn't seem to be any booby traps.

Not here, anyway.

We made short work of the rooms downstairs, then made our way up to the next floor. This floor was also broken into a number of nearly empty rooms.

In the third room, Doug's wristband seemed to glow for a second, and we spent the next ten minutes knocking on walls and floorboards. My hands were trembling from the adrenaline rush. I kept thinking this could be it. We might finally find the fourth object!

We searched everything and finally had to give up when Brady insisted the map showed nothing and nothing Doug did was able to coax another flash from the wristband.

Nothing happened in the rest of the rooms, and it didn't take long to explore them. This house was different than the others. It had a third story. We trudged up, some of us walking more slowly than others. I didn't know about anyone else, but this day was beginning to feel very long.

Especially when Doug's wristband couldn't be trusted. I hadn't realized how much I'd been hoping we were finally going to find *something*.

The top floor was taken up by mostly one bedroom. It had a large walk-in closet filled with clothes. I had to drag Olivia out of it; she'd probably have spent the rest of the afternoon in there. There was also a surprisingly modern bathroom.

The walls of the bedroom were a soft blue, trimmed in that same bright white as the outside. One was covered with pictures of people. Lots of pictures; some looked like photographs, while others were paintings. I wandered over to get a closer look and saw a handsome young man in a sepia toned photo, standing in a Mundane street, wearing a dark suit and a hat. Next I found a picture of Ronny sitting with a slightly older woman who had her arm wrapped around her. In another, four young women stood in a row with their arms around each other's waists. They looked so similar in coloring and features I was sure they must be sisters. There was also a very old painting; dark and cracked with age. It was of a woman in a long gown. She looked similar to those sisters, though her face looked drawn and weary, and her eyes were dull.

I was suddenly sure who was in these pictures. "This house belonged to Ronny's mother," I said.

"What makes you hypothesize that?" Brady asked interestedly.

I pointed to the picture of the four sisters first, explaining why I thought they were related. Brady agreed that was a reasonable deduction. Then, I pointed to the older picture of the woman who looked similar, and said, "I think that's Glenna's mom. The one who was burned at the stake."

Brady frowned as if he was going to argue, and I pointed again. "Look at the paint. It's old, at least several hundred years old. I learned about paint darkening like that in Art History."

"Okay, I'll agree that it might be old and there is a likeness," Brady allowed. Like I needed his agreement.

"And last," I pointed at the picture of the woman, definitely one of the four sisters standing next to a younger Ronny. "I believe that is Ronny and her mother."

Everyone stood there, silently. Wondering if we were really looking at a picture of Ronny's mother Glenna. Standing there in her house. And once again, the feeling that we were violating people's privacy swept over me, nearly making me suggest we leave.

Faith wiped her hands on her pants and said, "Well, let's get this over with. We'll have to get back and tell Ronny everything we can remember about this place. I'm sure she'll want to hear." She turned and looked at Brady. "You have that magic memory of yours working?"

He grumbled something about a scientific anomaly and not a product of magic, but everyone ignored him and got to work.

After looking through most of the large dresser against the far wall, Faith got frustrated and slammed one of the drawers. Unfortunately, she didn't get her finger out of the way in time. She gave a loud shout before sucking on her pinched finger, grimacing around it in pain.

Her shout startled Olivia. She backed into the shelves lining the wall, causing one to rock then tipped alarmingly. Though she managed to catch a glass paperweight before it hit the ground, a small box fell to the floor with a loud thump. For a long moment that thump seemed to echo through the room. Then the top of the box, surprisingly similar to others we'd found, burst open with a flash of blue light and a sound like a small explosion.

At the same moment, Doug's wristband flashed blue-green.

When the sound died away, there were a few pieces of jewelry, a letter written on thick creamy paper, and a bulky watch on the floor.

Olivia's breath came out in a shocked gasp and she stooped down. "Look at this."

I knelt next to her and she pointed at one of the necklaces. It looked just like the one Ronny had been wearing every day, right up until it broke. It had been sitting next to her chair for months now and there was no mistaking it. I wondered if Ronny's mom had bought one to match the one she'd given to her daughter.

"That's weird." I reached out and poked it gingerly, and when nothing bad happened, I scooped it up and examined it closely. "It looks identical." I looked at the small pile of jewels and trinkets on the floor and said, "I think we should take all of this to Ronny. She'd want her mother's things."

I was scooping them off the floor when Brady uttered a bitten-off curse. "I was right! Damn it to hell and back."

I looked at him curiously, but he reached past me for the watch. His fingers shook as he picked it up. Then he sank to his knees and cradled it in his hands, muttering, "No. No, no, no."

He flipped the watch over and stared at the back, his face frozen in anguish or horror. He knelt there, unmoving and unresponsive as we tried to talk to him. Finally Olivia reached over and touched his shoulder. A faint tremor began in his hands and worked its way back to his shoulders.

Then he tipped his head back, and let that strange emotion out in a roar that must have scraped his throat raw.

I took a startled step back, and Faith stuck next to me. I had no idea Brady could sound like that. What was wrong?

Brady clutched the watch tightly in his fist and rocked back and forth. Olivia threw her arms around him, muttering, "It's okay, whatever it is, it'll be okay. Talk to us, Brady."

Instead he shook her away, ripped his backpack off and dug around inside. I was startled to see one of the books we'd found on our last trip. The one from the bench in the inventor's room. He yanked out the map he'd stuffed inside and stared at it. "Of course it's familiar," he said. "How could I miss something so obvious with my supposedly infallible memory?"

"What is going on?" Olivia demanded. "Talk to us."

"I should have recognized these." His finger stabbed at several spots on the map. "Or perhaps I did and just didn't want to admit what they meant."

"I can't make heads or tails of what you're saying," Olivia insisted, "Explain. Please."

I think it was the please that finally got through to him. He pulled himself together with an effort, then said quietly, "I inherited all of Grandpa Chuck's belongings. That included a box of papers and other items from his father. My great-grandfather Arthur." He paused for a moment as if that should have some significance for us.

When none of us reacted, he ran his hand through his hair and made a gesture like he was pushing his non-existent glasses back up his nose. He closed his eyes briefly, then stared back at the map. "Great-grandfather Arthur loved to draw maps. He used several symbols of his own devising to mark special points of interest."

Brady pointed again to several of the places he'd pointed before. "Do you see this triangle inside a circle, this circle inside a square, and this cross inside a diamond?" When we nodded, he said, "Those were the codes he used. They stood for things that interested him; unusual plants, interesting buildings, geologically interesting features.

"So what are you saying?" I asked slowly, staring at the marks on the map. Once he'd pointed them out, I could see a number of them.

Brady held up the watch he'd been cradling in his hands. On the back were three initials: ATJ. They were written like a monogram, with the initial in the middle much larger than those on either side. "Those are his initials," Brady said tonelessly. "Arthur James Truman."

"You are *not* saying what I think you're saying!" Faith said, like she was arguing with him.

"I'm saying that Ronny's father Arthur, and my great-grandfather Arthur are one and the same." He bit off each word as if they hurt him.

All of us looked from the watch to the map and back.

Faith said, "I'm sorry Brady, but you're jumping to conclusions. Just because there are a few marks on a map you found here that are similar to those on a map your great grandfather had, doesn't make them from the same person."

"You're forgetting about the initials," he said. At least his voice didn't sound as furious as it had before.

I felt an uneasy flutter in my stomach, which I tried to ignore. This couldn't be right.

"For all you know, those are supposed to be ATJ, just like they're written," Faith argued. "Maybe the middle initial is larger because that was the name he normally used. Or maybe it's just larger because that's the largest part of the watch and it looked better bigger."

Brady leapt to his feet in one quick motion. "You're clutching at straws." His voice grew bitter as he said, "At least now I know what happened to him. He didn't just take off and leave my grandfather. Not by choice."

"You can't know that," I protested, alarmed by his expression. The flutter was growing into something that rumbled like a freight train. He looked terrible; even worse than when his step-mother got rid of his clothes. "It's just a theory, right? An hypothesis."

Brady glared at me, angrier than I'd ever seen him. "You just hate the idea that your precious sister-in-law's aunt kidnapped my Great-grandfather."

That made me shut up. I hadn't even thought about what it meant. But he was right, no *way* did I want to think that.

Everyone else began talking, growing louder and louder as they tried to be heard over the commotion. Through it all, Brady stood, his arms hunched protectively in front of him, the map clutched in one hand, the watch in the other.

I looked around and wondered what I could do to fix this. Everyone was getting angry. We wouldn't even be able to leave until we got this under control or we'd attract the Mimps for sure. Plus all this fighting was making my stomach hurt worse than ever. Like something was jumping around in there, trying to claw its way out.

I climbed slowly to my feet, turned my back on the others and started opening drawers and rifling through them. We had to finish checking everything and we had to do it quickly so we could get to Ronny's.

She'd better have an explanation. A good one.

-xXx-

It took a while, but the others slowly ceased their shouting and helped me. All but Brady. He was still in that defensive, frozen posture, staring at the watch. I was nearly done with the dresser when he whispered, "It's self-winding. Just like the one on my wrist. It began working as soon as I started moving. This is the watch he created. The one that disappeared with him."

He looked up, his eyes red-rimmed and dark, like he was ill. "Are you done? Can we go now?"

I finished the drawer I was looking through and shut it quietly, not wanting to make any sudden sounds. The air practically vibrated with tension and I was sure the least little thing could set everyone off again.

Which is when Doug slammed the drawer in the small table by the bed and yelled, "Look at this!"

Faith dropped the bottle of water she'd just pulled from her pack. I watched for a moment as water spread, then began to disappear into a crack in the floorboards.

I glanced back at Doug. He was holding a beautiful leather journal. The pages inside were covered with handwriting I'd seen before and I realized it must be Glenna's journal. Brady quickly moved the watch into the same hand as the map and strode over to grab the journal from Doug.

He slipped out of his pack, carefully placed the watch, letter, and map in a side pocket, then flipped through the journal. There were several pages throughout the book with no writing. Why did she skip pages in her journal?

"It's Glenna's diary," Brady said flatly. "I recognize her writing. I'm going to read this before we give it to Ronny." His voice dared us to argue, but none of us said a word.

He gave a short stiff nod, then tucked the book in his pack as well.

"Um, guys?" Faith's voice sounded startled and we all looked at her. She pointed to the crack where the water had been disappearing. From it, a thin line of brilliant green smoke drifted up.

"Leave it—" Before Brady could finish, Doug stooped down, pried the edge of the floorboard loose and pulled it up. Under it, lying nestled in a bed of green silk, were several other journals. Doug scooped them up and told Brady, "I'll carry these. Your pack is full."

There was a moment of tense silence during which I was suddenly sure Brady was going to insist on carrying them himself.

Then he shrugged and turned away. "Thanks. As long as you remember to give them to me before we talk to Ronny."

"Absolutely," Doug assured him, then stuffed them in *my* backpack.

Brady glanced at the watch on his wrist. "Actually, it's getting so late I suggest we make plans to meet with her Monday. By then I should have some idea what's in all of them." He lifted his pack and slipped it on, and turned to the door.

-xXx-

I couldn't really blame Brady. He'd had a terrible shock. We all had. But he chose the worst possible time to get distracted. To forget to check the map. I was only a step behind him when we exited from the house, and I could swear I felt their eyes on me.

"There they are." That was Andrew's voice.

"Get them!" That was definitely Ray.

"We've got you now."That cold, sure voice made me shudder. I could have sworn the temperature dropped.

The Jabbertock birds instantly repeated their triumphant calls. The knowledge that there was no place we could hide stopped me. No matter where we went, those stupid birds would give us away.

The Rejects were still down the road, but heading toward us at a dead run. I froze, my mind blank as I tried to think what to do. Next to me, Faith made a gagging sound. When I looked over, her face was rigid with dread. That's exactly how I felt, like every one of my muscles were frozen with fear.

Fortunately Doug was made of sterner stuff. "Brady, find us the quickest way back to that transporter house. The one that took us back to those houses near the bridge."

Our familiars turned and ran into the trees. I crossed my fingers that they'd understood Doug and were heading there to wait for us. Brady jerked the map from his pocket as we all turned and ran the other direction; away from the Rejects. Brady took the lead and we followed him down one path and onto the next. Even though we were running full out, I could swear Ray and the others were growing closer with each passing minute.

I refused to look back, but it felt like they were breathing down our necks. We weren't going to get away this time.

Faith was letting out small moans every few steps. I wasn't sure if it was because the Rejects were so close or because we were heading back to that house. The one that made her sick the last time we'd been in it.

Then, as if chasing us through Chimera wasn't enough, Ray started shouting abuse after us. Insulting us. Telling us how he was going to take us apart, piece by piece. Arnold chimed in occasionally, using language so foul I wouldn't have been surprised if his tongue turned black and fell out of his head.

I grimly wished the teachers at school could hear what was pouring out of their mouths. Golden Boy's I'm-so-perfect image would never be the same. Olivia was running with her hands clamped over her ears, probably almost as afraid of her mother's wrath if she said one of those words as she was of getting caught by Ray.

I should have realized there would be another down-side to being shouted at like that. I could see what Doug called the transporter house now —though still some distance away — when I heard maniacal chortles heading our way.

That's all we needed, to be attacked by Mimps!

But I'd forgotten one important fact. Mimps attack whoever is doing the yelling. And that wasn't us; we were too busy running. As we crested a low rise only a few hundred yards from the house, I saw Mimps ranged along the path on both sides. We were too close to stop before we reached them.

Fortunately, it wasn't necessary. *We* were ignored completely. But as soon as the Rejects crested the rise, now just a short distance behind us, the Mimps started hurling everything they could put their hands on; leaves, twigs, small branches, even rocks. At the Rejects.

I heard howls of anger and pain from behind us even over those freakish giggles. I was too busy watching where I was putting my feet to look back, but the sounds from the Rejects grew slightly muted like they were falling behind. I'd spent the last few months hating the idea of those stupid Mimps, but right now they seemed like the best thing we'd ever encountered in here.

We reached the transporter house ahead of the Rejects. Actually far enough ahead, they couldn't see us right now. We'd left enough foot prints the last time we'd been here; they'd have no idea which house we entered now. If it took them a while to search for us, we might actually get clean away.

I felt the same strange resistance I had last time as I crossed the threshold. The door slammed behind us and the world and everything in it spun crazily, nearly knocking me off my feet. I heard the sounds of violent retching, and shut my eyes, wrapped my arms around my chest, and waited for the stomach-churning movement to be over.

Like the last time, just as suddenly as it had started, everything went still. We'd made it. We were standing on the rough wooden floor, with thin gauzy curtains that changed colors over the windows. And through those thin curtains, I could see thatch hanging from the roof's edge.

Faith was standing farthest from the door, head hanging near her knees. She slowly straightened and wiped her mouth with the back of her hand. She had to clear her throat twice before any sound emerged. "Are they coming? Did we get away?"

Brady checked the map. "They're still back where we last saw them. Probably chasing the Mimps now."

"Um…you don't think they'd hurt those Mimps, do you?" Faith bit her lip, looking pale and sweaty.

"Of course they would," I told her. "The Rejects like hurting things."

Now Olivia looked as worried as Faith. "Ronny said hurting Mimps is dangerous."

Doug flung the front door open. "Let's get out of here. None of us want to find out just how dangerous that could be."

I was relieved to see all of our animals waiting for us outside. Doug gave Rusty a quick pat and said, "We're in a hurry, boy, let's go."

Rusty trotted at Doug's heels and the rest of our animals ranged out around us as we half-ran, half-walked down the road, leaving the town behind us. Doug set a pace that was fast and had me out of breath, but I managed to keep up. I was *determined* to keep up.

Doug was rubbing at his leg. I wasn't surprised; mine felt like they had lead weights tied to them. My shoulders didn't feel much better where the straps of my backpack dug in. When the tree came into view, it looked so far away I was suddenly afraid I wouldn't make it. That I would fall down and not being able to get back up.

"We're going to…make it," Olivia wheezed out.

"I don't know if I am," I said.

"Yes you can, Katherine…Alice…Taylor. Don't you…give up on…me."

Olivia's hair was plastered to her head and her make-up had smeared where she'd tried to wipe sweat from her eyes. She looked even worse than I felt. If she could make it, so could I. Somehow.

We'd taken only a few more steps when I heard Ray whoop, voice echoing oddly. Brady scanned the map and looked confused. Then with that same strange echo, Ray yelled, "You *got* one Arnold! Is it dead?"

A loud buzzing, like thousands of angry wasps erupted all around us. When Ronny had said it was dangerous to hurt a Mimp, I hadn't understood *how* dangerous. Of course, nothing could possibly have prepared me for this.

It felt like the world was coming apart around us.

The air shimmered and everything seemed to…fade for a moment. I'd been looking at Shadow who was loping along next to us. She seemed to shimmer and fade as well. I bit back a muffled scream and reached for her. The ground heaved up underneath us, then fell with a harsh smacking sound, knocking us off our feet.

I rolled onto my knees and looked at my friends. They were sprawled around me looking as dazed as I felt. The ground heaved again, and I changed my mind about getting back up.

One of the rock sculptures in the field to our left snapped off near the base and crashed to the ground, and a large cloud of dust erupted around it. Howls erupted in the woods flanking the road, but these sounded like a warped CD; the sound grew louder, faded, then roared back to full volume, over and over again.

I closed my eyes when I realized the woods were fading in and out of view in sync with those howls. As if Chimera might fade away altogether.

With us inside it.

Terror twisted up inside me and wrapped itself around my throat, nearly choking me. At least that kept me from opening my mouth and howling too.

I peered out of half-closed eyes and stared hard at my hands. The tightness in my throat began to loosen. My hands didn't fade. Even when Chimera seemed to recede, my hands remained solid and unchanging. Whatever was happening here wasn't affecting us.

Not yet, anyway.

"We need to get out," Doug said. Another of the rock sculptures crumbled into broken bits in the field. "This place is coming apart."

"I agree," Brady said, stuffing the map in his pocket. "We don't know how the doorway is being affected by this phenomena."

The ground seemed momentarily still and we got to our feet to stagger the remaining distance to the tree. Somehow, even though at times insubstantial, our animals followed us. I scooped up Shadow, held her tightly and buried my face in her fur. "Are you okay?"

Of course she couldn't talk to me. But her loud purr managed to convey that she hadn't been hurt.

"I hate to leave you like this," I told her, and her purr seemed to grow even louder.

"It's beginning to stabilize," Brady said in satisfaction. "I was concerned about the potential effects if the fading occurred while we were inside the tree, but I don't think we'll need to be concerned with that now."

"What could it do to us?" Olivia's voice was small and quiet. She sounded like she wasn't sure she wanted to hear Brady's answer.

"It's possible, if the magic wasn't strong enough while we were in transit, that it wouldn't be able to return us to our world." Brady didn't look as horrified by this idea as the rest of us. He mostly looked interested, like he was trying to perform complex equations in his head.

I wanted to scream in fear and frustration. That wasn't interesting to me! I knew exactly how getting stuck would feel. I didn't ever want to experience it again.

Then Brady said, "That would be a possible result, but I believe it has settled enough that it shouldn't be an issue now."

He was right; I hadn't seen anything fade in the last minute or two. I patted Shadow one last time and set her down. "We'll see you next month," I told her. She held her tail in the air, waving it gently back and forth, then turned and began walking down the road with the other animals following after her.

Fortunately for the state of my mental health, the trip back through the tree was one of the quickest and easiest I could remember.

-xXx-

Olivia called me that night. She started droning on and on about how wonderful Brady was. So smart. So practical. So understanding. So caring. So practically perfect in every way.

I said "Um," and "Oh," and "Really." A lot.

She didn't seem to need me to say anything else. Finally she said, "Thanks for listening, Kat," and hung up.

Thank goodness.

I mean, I like him, but fifteen minutes of The-Wonderful-World-of-Brady was a bit much.

-xXx-

For several days, Brady refused to let me make plans to meet with Ronny. He kept insisting he had to understand what happened to his great-grandfather before talking to her. The way he said it made me think he meant arguing with her, rather than talking. I started dreading that meeting. I felt torn between loyalty to Brady, and loyalty to Ronny, and through Ronny to my brother. The thought of having to choose one over the other kept giving me a headache.

The five of us made our way through the halls at school like a small pack of zebras, afraid of the lions roaming around our territory. Because even though the Rejects were the ones that nearly caused the destruction of Chimera, they were even angrier with us than usual. Ray had made that clear the one time we got a bit too close. He blamed us for all the chaos.

"Arnold grabbed one of those little monsters and threw it against a tree," he said and sneered at Faith when she let out a strangled noise. "I had to do something to convince those creepy little things to leave us the fu— alone." Olivia's panicked hiss had covered Ray's expletive. I think that would have amused him, but he was too angry. "You should have warned us those things were dangerous. Do you see Andrew at school today? No. He sprained his wrist. Do you see Arnold? No. He broke his glasses and needs to get another pair before he comes back.

His face split in an evil grin. "You should hear what Arnold has in store for you." Whatever Arnold planned, Ray was thrilled. A sick excitement shone briefly in his eyes. "It involves pain and possibly breakage. Both Arnold and Andrew will be here tomorrow, and the three of us are going to make you pay."

He ignored Polly when she grabbed his arm and said, "Four of us."

He glared at Doug and said, "It's not like he did serious damage to that thing, anyway. He just bruised it a bit. The others didn't have to go crazy and try to pull one of those buildings down on us."

"Next time maybe you'll pick on something your own size," Doug said. I wanted to kick him. Was he trying to pick a fight with Ray right here? *He* was nearly Ray's size.

Sound swelled in the hallway as other students crowded around us. They looked enthralled at the thought there might be bloodshed at any minute. Here and there, I thought I heard muttered cheers. At least a few seemed to like the idea of someone standing up to Ray. I just hoped Ray couldn't hear them. It would only make him angrier.

He glared around, realizing we had an audience. He turned back to Doug and hissed, "Tomorrow, Geller." Then he pushed Polly ahead of him toward their next class.

We managed to stay out of their way the rest of that week. I'd just begun to relax when Brady called and asked me to arrange a meeting with Ronny after school the next day. He refused to talk about what he'd found or what he intended to say. He would only say we'd find out soon enough.

Soon enough for what?

Chapter 34/October/Santa Ramona

Annihilation

Brady had looked grim all day, growing even more so as each hour passed. By the time we got to Ronny's once school was over, my nerves were shot. Ronny opened the door and Brady shoved by her without a word. My stomach tightened as I watched confusion sweep over Ronny's face.

My nerves drew even tighter when we got seated and Brady leaned forward, his movements abrupt and his expression antagonistic.

"There are several things we need to discuss," he said. "I believe I've determined the type of object we need to discover, though you will not like how I reached that conclusion. We also need to discuss the Mimps, or at least the possible results of harming them, because the Rejects hurt one of them and it caused a disturbance in the force. I mean, the magic."

Brady paused briefly as Ronny made an inarticulate sound of distress. Then he continued implacably without any change in expression. "But first, we are going to talk about Arthur."

"Father?" Ronny blinked twice, and her look of confusion deepened. "What more do you want to know about him?"

"Everything!" Brady spat, his voice so low it was nearly a growl.

Ronny pushed back into her chair, confusion turning to alarm. "I don't understand."

"Your father was my great-grandfather Arthur. No, don't shake your head at me. I had started to wonder if it was possible, and now I have proof. Your people stole him from his world and kept him prisoner in yours. You stole him from his family — *my* family — and nearly destroyed it."

Brady glared at her through eyes dark with emotion. "Grandpa Chuck was ten when he lost his father. He always believed Arthur had been kidnapped or injured; that he would have come back if he could. *My* father, on the other hand, was certain Arthur simply got tired of having a family and left on purpose. It caused terrible arguments between the two of them. Dad called Grandpa Chuck a sentimental fool. It kept growing worse until they hardly spoke at all."

He ran a hand over his eyes and added, "The worst part was I hardly ever got to see my grandfather the last few years because of it. And then he died."

He looked at Ronny again and gave a cynical laugh. "Arthur was Grandpa Chuck's father. That makes him your half-brother."

I watched the blood drain from Ronny's face, leaving her pale and shaken. She gave an inarticulate cry and Chris rushed to her side, demanding to know if she was all right. She shook her head and grabbed his hand tightly in her own. After taking a deep breath, she gave him a shaky smile and said, "I will be all right, love. It is only that Brady has made a mistake." She turned and looked at Brady. Her voice was pleading as she said, "It has to be a mistake."

"There's no mistake," he said coldly. "My great-grandfather is your dad. That makes you my great half-aunt." He gave her a twisted, ugly smile. "How you doing, Auntie?"

Chris stood up, towering over Brady. "I understand that you're upset," he said coldly, "but you need to keep a respectful tone when you talk to Ronny in this house." Brady's lips tightened and Chris told him, "If you can't, you can leave."

The two of them stared at each other for a long moment and it was Brady who looked away first. He dropped his gaze and gave one short nod.

Ronny leaned forward. "You said you have proof." She tugged Chris down on the arm of her chair, never taking her eyes off Brady. "What proof?"

Brady kept his lips pressed tight as he placed his backpack on the floor between his feet. First he pulled out the watch he wore into Chimera each month. "My grandfather bought this watch in memory of his father, my great-grandfather, Arthur. He was an inventor."

A low sound issued from Ronny at that. Brady ignored it, but his voice changed. It was still angry, but underneath I could hear pain. "Arthur was working on a special watch that he thought would revolutionize the watch industry back in the day." He pulled the watch we'd found at Glenna's house from his pack and laid it next to the first, though this one he laid on its face so the monogram on the back showed clearly.

"My great-grandfather's name was Arthur James Truman. Those are his initials. Carved into the back of the watch I found in *your* mother's house." He shot a look I couldn't interpret at Ronny, who had her hands clasped tightly in her lap.

She looked so sad. How would I feel if someone said my dad had been stolen from his original family? I'd feel glad that I'd had him. And I'd feel guilty. Very guilty.

Brady dug into his backpack and pulled out several papers and the map we'd found in the inventor's house. He waved them at Ronny before slapping them down on the table. "Some of these papers are in my great-grandfather's handwriting. I have other examples of it if you need me to prove that to you."

Ronny shook her head, staring at those pages, horrified. She looked at him and said, "He was my father and we were happy together. I'm sorry. I suppose I should have, but I never even wondered whether he had another family. I never considered what it must be like for them. I'm so very sorry."

Brady hesitated a moment, considering her words, then nodded. "We found these right here, in someone's workshop." He stabbed his finger at one of the houses on our map of Chimera. "According to these documents, whoever lived there worked with Arthur to create something that would be able to generate electricity in Chimera. They kept trying to continue the work, even after Arthur," he paused and swallowed audibly, "died."

He placed most of the papers on the table, then held out the map we'd found in that house. "This is also a map of Chimera. But it has a number of symbols added." He pointed to a few, then laid the map on the table next to our Chimera map. Ronny opened her mouth, but he held up his hand and said, "Wait."

He pulled a third map from his pack and placed it on the table as well. "This is a map of Long Beach, California. That's where my great-grandfather lived when he...disappeared." Ronny gasped and grabbed Chris so tightly I saw him wince. "This is one of the maps he used there. You can see where he made the same sort of symbols that are on the map of Chimera."

He was right. They did look the same. But without pausing for any of us to comment, he dug back into this pack again. This time he pulled out the journals we'd found in Glenna's house. Ronny gasped at the sight of them and reached out her hands. "Can I have those, please?"

He handed them to her without a word. Ronny stroked the leather with her fingers, a wondering look on her face. "I never thought I'd see these again. They were my mother's. She wrote in them every day, as far back as I can remember."

"Yes, they did belong to your mother," Brady said. "And all but the last journal are just notes of things that happened each day."

He hunched his shoulders and took a deep breath, then admitted grudgingly, "It's clear that she and my great-grandfather cared for each other. I'm glad that he found some happiness, at least."

"He did, Brady. I promise you. I had him for thirty-two years and I am so grateful for every minute." She looked at the books in her lap and stroked her finger again over each of the covers. "I am so sorry my happiness was built upon your loss. It is so hard to lose someone you care about."

Brady took several deep breaths then shook his shoulders as if shaking off his anger. When he began speaking again, his voice was nearly toneless.

"After you were banished, your mother paid some attention Ghalynn, though she believed most of his pronouncements were foolishness. However, she finally believed enough that she snuck into Morgana's house and stole her diary." Ronny gasped, which Brady ignored. He pointed to the last journal. "She wrote in here that she hid the stolen diary and made sure Morgana didn't know she had it. Many pages in this journal are blank, but what she does write shows she'd started to distrust Morgana at the end."

"Blank pages?" Ronny sounded agitated and let go of Chris. "Show me please." She held out the stack of journals to him, and Brady pulled out a small journal covered in plain brown leather. He flipped through it and I could see blank pages scattered throughout. Ronny grabbed the book from him and looked through it until she came to the first blank page. She turned to Chris and begged, "Get me salt, water and the bottle of earth I keep by my bed."

He squeezed her shoulder and left the room. He was back shortly with those things and Ronny said, "I'm sorry, love, I also need a small bowl."

He gave a long-suffering sigh, which was cancelled out by the wink he gave her. It only took a moment before he was back with a small glass Pyrex bowl. Ronny mixed a few pinches of salt and earth in the bowl with her fingers, then slowly added water, chanting under her breath. When the water, salt and earth mixture was thinned to the consistency of tea, there was a small blue flash from the bowl. Ronny grinned, dipped her fingers into the watery mixture, and stroked it over the blank page. For a moment, nothing happened and I sat back in disappointment. Then, slowly, words formed on the page.

"Disappearing ink," Ronny said.

Brady was on his feet and around the table, staring at the words as they appeared. He began reading them out loud.

I wish I'd never taken Morgana's diary, for now I know the full extent of her hatred. It is a malice that has festered for years, like an abscess rooted deep in her soul. She hated me even before Chimera, back to the time our mother died. She blames me for mother's death, for dragging her into Chimera against her will, for blocking her revenge upon the Mundane. She even blames me for Titiana's death.

All these years. How could I not have known?

Ronny turned to the next blank page and treated it with the muddy liquid. Brady continued to read what was revealed out loud.

She forced more of the Mundane into our world than any other. Now I must live with the knowledge that she tormented them while they were here. I should have known. I should have stopped it.

My greatest happiness and my greatest suffering came from her.

It took my beloved Arthur years to forgive what she did. After that, the years we had together were the happiest in my life, and he said he felt the same. We were overjoyed when our union produced one of the few children Chimera has seen. With my magick to slow his aging, we should have had hundreds of years of happiness together.

All of us were sitting forward now, impatient to hear what was on the next blank page.

Now I must live with the knowledge that Morgana destroyed this. Her twisted hatred of me and of the Mundane, created the most terrible revenge.

Morgana described each detail in her diary. She gloated over it. She conjured the rock fall on the path that Arthur used. She was disappointed that I wasn't with him.

She murdered my Arthur and used my devastation to turn members of the Council against me. So many suggested I step down until my grieving was done.

I nearly did as they suggested.

Ronny flipped through until the next empty page and rubbed the mixture over it. Soon more words began to form.

That was not enough for Morgana. She then turned her sights on my beloved daughter.

I have read of her plan to convince Rowena to spend her time in the Mundane world. Though it would not be as fast as crushing her under a mountainside, my sister knew Rowena would age quickly outside Chimera's protective magick.

Morgana described with great pleasure how she convinced the Council to banish my lovely Rowena, knowing she will age and lose her magick and die there like any Mundane.

And Morgana gloated at how this new grief would incapacitate me.

Ronny made a low sound of distress and stared blankly at those words. Then she shook herself and reached out as if to turn the page. Her hand was shaking so hard she fumbled twice.

She motioned to Brady to find the next blank page and coat it with the mixture. Then he cleared his throat and read the rest.

I owe Ghalynn an apology. His warnings about Morgana were correct. And so, perhaps, may the other things he has tried to tell me. I admit I paid no attention, though he insisted he knew something of great import to Chimera.

That last time he tried to warn me, a pale red glow formed about his neck. He struggled to breathe, then abruptly left. I paid no attention, then.

But Ghalynn was right about Morgana. What if he was right about the rest? It is too bad he cannot be found.

I must now consider it was a geas placed upon him by another. I do not know who might be responsible, for all geas are prohibited in Chimera.

This at least cannot be laid at Morgana's door, She never once mentioned Ghalynn in her diary.

Brady quickly turned to the next page, covered it with the mixture and began reading.

There is an enemy, or perhaps more than one. I fear for myself, for Ghalynn, for Chimera. How can I protect any of these?

I do not know if I will survive what is to come. I will hide this information in my journal, and hope it will be found, if the worst happens.

There was a long moment of near silence, broken only by Ronny's ragged breathing. Chris moved behind her chair and put his hands reassuringly on her shoulders. She blurted, "Morgana was trying to keep me from Chimera." She rubbed her hand quickly over eyes sheened with tears. "I did not give her enough credit it seems. For I never once believed she actually wanted me…dead."

Her eyes grew remote, staring at something the rest of us couldn't see. Then they snapped back into focus. Her voice flattened when she said her aunt's name. "Morgana always told me the Greeks thought of us, the Magickal, as gods. It is true that many of the Greek gods were patterned after members of the Magickal community. Morgana could never accept that things had changed."

Olivia said drily, "The way I heard it, Egyptians used to call cats gods and they've never forgotten either."

I snickered, then thought of Shadow. She never seemed remote and superior; she was my companion.

I glanced at Ronny's face and felt sorry. First Brady had yelled at her about her father. Not that I blamed him, really. But then he rubbed her nose in the fact that she and her mother had been far too trusting about Morgana. When, from everything Ronny had told us, Morgana had been a really terrible person.

Brady said, "There are a number of blank pages at the back of the journal. They probably were never used, but we should test them to be sure."

"I'll have to mix more Revelatorium to do that many," Ronny said. She began making the mixture the same way as before, but something went wrong. About half way through, it began to bubble and hiss, and an acrid smoke rose in a thin black plume from the bowl.

Ronny hissed between her teeth and turned to Chris. "I'm sorry, love, you must dispose of this bowl. Wrap it in several layers of aluminum foil before placing it in the trash. We must never use it again. I'll try again, but it would be best if you got me one of the cheap glass bowls."

"What happened?" I asked, staring at the smoke that had flattened out above us leaving a greasy black smudge on the ceiling.

Chris made a sound of disgust, and Ronny followed my gaze. "Oh no, I'll need to clean that up later. Oh well." She looked back at me and her shoulders slumped. "There is too much negative magick leaking from Chimera. It affects how magick acts here. Unfortunately, there seems to be more each month."

"Negative magic?" My voice squeaked a bit and I coughed like I had something stuck in my throat. "What do you mean, *negative* magic?"

"At first it only happened after the magick storms. The ones that carry the blue lightning. But for the past few months, I feel it leaking out the entire time the doorway is open. There's a stream of magick flowing from Chimera now. And it has been twisted somehow. I fear this must be the last magick I try. It is becoming far too dangerous."

Ronny's eyes were dark and sad, but more determined than I'd ever seen. She carefully performed the magic again, and this time there was the blue flash I'd come to expect.

She wiped the mixture over each of the remaining pages in the journal, but nothing further showed. Her shoulders slumped when the last page remained stubbornly blank.

"Um…" I broke the silence timidly, but I had to get an answer to this question. "Should we be worried going through the tree each month? Could we be absorbing too much magic in the doorway?"

Ronny looked at me blankly, then began to concentrate. I could practically see the wheels turning behind her eyes. Finally she shook her head and spoke in a sure voice. "You will absorb some of the magick. But you are Mundane, and what little you are exposed to should not be enough to cause concern."

I relaxed gratefully back into the couch.

"Why does it happen around the full moon?" Faith asked.

Ronny laughed. "Have you not heard how there are strange calls to telephone operators and emergency personnel at the full moon?" Brady, Faith and I nodded. The others shook their heads. Ronny said, "Even the Mundane are affected by the pull of the moon. Magick is affected even more so. We do not know why, just as your scientists have not been able to identify what causes this to affect your people."

There was a moment of silence, so I said, "We met up with your Jabbertock birds. They wanted us to stop and talk to them. I was surprised; they seemed awfully smart for birds."

Ronny laughed again, looking more relaxed. "They are not smart. They cannot truly think for themselves. They cannot carry on real conversations, with themselves or with others. Oh they can answer very simple questions. But mostly they repeat things they see or hear."

"They almost caused us a lot of trouble," Doug muttered. "Guess I was right when I called them stupid—"

"I have a question." Faith's abrupt announcement interrupted whatever else Doug might have said. "It's been bothering me for months." She sat on the edge of the couch and leaned forward. "What's up with the house that keeps moving around? It's been all over."

I sat forward also, interested in hearing the answer to that.

"That was Brigana's house," Ronny told Faith. "After she died, without her to anchor it, the house seemed to lose its connection. It has been moving randomly around Chimera ever since that day. No one has been able to enter it, not since she…well, you know."

"That house has moved ever since that day…" Brady leapt to his feet and went over to the curio cabinet in the corner of the room. He let out a growl of frustration and thumped his hand against the glass next to one of the boxes we'd brought from Chimera. He whirled around and said, "I should have known what that combination meant. Days have special meaning."

We all stared at him, shocked by the intensity of this outburst. Chris straightened up and looked ready to defend Ronny if necessary.

It wasn't.

"What good is my memory when I don't put pieces of data together?" His eyes looked nearly wild. "I should've known last year when you told us about your father's chest," he told Ronny. "The combination is 03-28-24?" He paced away, then back. "That's a date."

Ronny shrugged, then nodded, not sure where he was going with this. I wasn't sure either.

"That was the date my grandfather —Arthur's son — was born." He stared at Ronny then said, "I've been furious about what happened to my great-grandfather. But I must accept that he and the rest of my family have been as much a victim of Morgana as you and your mother."

"The rest of your family?" Ronny asked, confused. Though I could see a barely formed worry pinch at her mouth and eyes.

"Arthur's wife, Jenniffer, died two years before he disappeared. Arthur tried but couldn't raise Grandpa Chuck alone. So he sent him to Santa Ramona to live with Arthur's sister, Linda. It was supposed to be temporary, but my great-grandfather disappeared only a few months later."

Brady came back over and let himself drop back onto the couch. "That was the start of it. Four generations, angry and divided, because of that disappearance."

Ronny sucked in her breath, but Brady wasn't looking at her. He was staring where his hands rested on his knees. "Linda always believed he abandoned my grandfather, leaving her to care for a child she really didn't want. She told Grandpa Chuck terrible things about Arthur. My grandfather left her house when he was sixteen, refusing to believe the things she said. He never graduated high school, let alone went to college. My father always held that against him. In the end, he didn't want me to mention his name in our house."

He looked up then. "Grandpa Chuck used to meet me at the park to talk about Arthur. He wanted someone to believe that his father was a good person."

Tears glinted in Ronny's eyes. She leaned forward and wrapped her hands around Brady's. "He was a very good man. I wish you could have known him."

Brady pulled his hands away from her; but carefully, not as if he were angry. He sat back and said, "So tell us what could happen if a Mimp is seriously injured."

Ronny blinked and looked like she wanted to say something else, then she also sat back. "You must make sure that never happens. I told you they are tied into the magick."

"Yes, you did," Brady said. "But the Rejects don't know that, and I'm sure they hurt one."

"What makes you think so?" Ronny's brow tightened and she looked at Brady sharply.

For a few moments pandemonium reigned as everyone spoke over each other, describing how everything faded in and out, including our animals, the woods around us, the sound of buzzing, the howls. The way the ground heaved under our feet. The sculptures that crumbled into bits of rock in the fields near the tree.

Finally Chris bellowed for silence and instantly all conversation ceased.

Ronny looked as shocked as I'd ever seen her. Then it morphed into anger. "Yes, I agree with you, Brady, I am sure one of our beloved Mimps was harmed. You have been right all along; those children are bullies. Dangerous bullies. You must do your best to make sure they do not do it ever again."

"I'll be more vigilant about checking the map," Brady assured her. "If the Rejects don't see us, they will have no reason to start screaming, drawing the Mimps to them. Besides, we have only one more area to check in Mystic."

At Ronny's surprised exclamation, Brady pointed to map, showing all the areas he'd crossed off. Then he indicated the few remaining houses we hadn't been able to check yet. "Those three," he said, pointing, "look like they'd been abandoned before whatever went wrong. They've been partially destroyed."

Ronny turned away for a moment, swallowing convulsively. Chris patted her hand and she smiled wanly. She stroked her finger over one of the houses on the map and said, "This one was mine. The others were the houses of close friends. They most likely decided to move when I was banished. It would not do for them to be associated with me any longer."

Brady moved his finger to the area where we'd found the large building. "We saw something here a few months ago," he told her. "We went all the way around it, but there were no doors or windows. We need to know how to get inside."

Ronny stared where his finger pointed. "It's in the South end of Mystic. The South," she said quietly. "I wonder if this is the location of the South group that worried Ghalynn and Mother so much. A number of witches lived there, but they were known as The Coven. Many in Chimera laughed at them behind their backs; they really were not strong witches. They had to cast spells together to make them work at all."

She looked up at Brady. "You said there were no doors or windows?" At his nod, she said, "You should wish for them to appear. That should trigger any available spells."

"We tried that the last time," Doug told her. Although he spoke politely, there was a definite edge of duh-we-are-not-stupid in his voice.

Ronny looked at us for a long moment, biting her lip. Her voice was hesitant when she said, "You should not be able to use regular spells, not the ones which must be created new each time. But there is so much magick leaking from Chimera… Perhaps one could work for you, one of the general unlocking spells. You should try Activatotum Alomura. Or you could try a general reveal charm, such as Activatotum Apeersium."

"Those sound a lot like charms from *Harry Potter*," Olivia said, raising one eyebrow, clearly disbelieving.

"Well, much of the magickal community has used the same charms and spells," Ronny told her. "I believe there are still a few witches and wizards living in the Mundane world. There is no reason for them to have changed the spells, even if it has been several hundred years."

Olivia stared at her a moment, then rolled her eyes. "You don't understand. *Harry Potter* isn't real."

"Are you sure of that?" Ronny asked. At Olivia's emphatic nod, Ronny said, "Perhaps the writer knew someone magickal, or overheard a witch or wizard."

I sat back, stunned. Parts of *Harry Potter* might be *real*? That was incredible. Freaking awesome! Now I totally had to read those books again.

Brady didn't look like he was buying that idea, but he didn't argue. He held up his hand when Olivia looked like she wanted to, and shook his head at her. "I believe I've figured out the next object we need to locate." He ignored our questions. Instead he grimaced and added. "You aren't going to like it."

That got everyone to stop talking. I sat forward but Brady didn't say anything else. Finally Doug punched him lightly on the arm. "Just spill it."

Brady rolled his shoulders and cleared his throat nervously. "For those of you who don't have an eidetic memory, I need to quote something."

Time shall come when silence rules
Echoes of what was remain
East and South dark MALICE pools
Set loose as protections wane.

Two worlds WITH one dire test
With the entrance breached by man
Mundane MAGICK marks the quest
Fate awaits the final plan

Only clear to those with Sight
Direction is necessity
Paths revealed within the Light
Resolution is the Key

Greed with evil SPELLS entwine
Without courage faith will quail
Magick and Mundane COMBINE
For one without the other fail

ANNIHILATION

"Why are you quoting that?" I asked, a chill skittering down my back. "We've all heard it before. And what could it possibly have to do with the fourth object?"

"Let's talk about what it says for a minute," Brady shot me a quick, enigmatic glance. "We know a time did come when Chimera became silent. We experience it every time we go there. It's why Ronny asked us to start our search."

I nodded, reluctantly. The others did too.

"On a few occasions, Ronny has described creatures in Chimera that do not possess much intelligence. She has called them echoes." When Faith and Doug looked confused, Brady touched the side of his head. "Eidetic memory, remember? Just go with me on this."

Again, there were reluctant nods around the room. Chris shifted closer to Ronny and tightened his grip on Ronny's hand. He didn't take his eyes from Brady's face.

"Let's skip the next two lines for now and concentrate on the next stanza. I believe we can agree that the term *two worlds* most likely refers to this world and Chimera." He stated this without a shred of doubt. "I believe we can also agree that 'entrance breached by man' refers to us." Then he added, "Well, us and the Rejects."

Olivia huffed that she was no man and he merely grinned at her. "I'm sure that is meant to be the generic term for someone from the Mundane world, as opposed to someone from the magical world." I saw Ronny give a short nod then Brady continued, "We have been using Mundane magic inside Chimera, every time we set off an existing spell."

He abruptly grabbed a piece of paper from his pack and wrote the words key, lantern, compass, followed by a question mark.

Next to key, he wrote Resolution is the Key.

Next to lantern, he wrote Paths revealed within the Light.

Next to compass, he wrote Direction is necessity.

Next to the question mark, he wrote Only clear to those with Sight.

"We've found three objects. I think they fit extremely well inside this poem. Too much so to be coincidental. The only thing we're missing is something to help with sight. It could be binoculars, or a telescope, or glasses, that type of thing. No matter what shape it takes, it will have something to do with the ability to see."

We all stared at the paper in silence.

I gulped, feeling like my stomach was learning how to tap dance. Then I blurted, "Are you trying to tell me, Brady Albert Truman, that you think the Annihilation Prophecy is happening now? That it was written about us?"

He hesitated a moment. "I suppose we could be just a small part of the prophecy," he said slowly. "But clearly, we are a part. Even Ghalynn thought so."

An incoherent babble broke out as everyone spoke at once; only quieting when Brady took out a letter written on thick creamy paper from his backpack. I recognized it from Glenna's house. He laid it on the table and quoted it.

Three have I known and sent you clues
The fourth's location they refuse.

Inside the mansion the last hides;
They did not let it from their sides.

Hard to find and perhaps constrained,
And yet the fourth MUST be obtained.

No second choice; you must not fall,
Or Annihilation ends it all.

There was another long moment. "Well, that's not much help. We knew most of that." Doug said finally. "Although you may be right about Ghalynn thinking the Annihilation Prophecy is connected. So what do you make of the last bit in the prophecy? About *Magick and Mundane combine, for one without the other fail*?"

"I'm not sure," Brady admitted. "It may mean that we'll need to use more of the uh, magic, in there before we're done."

"Do you think there's anything significant about the words that were written deeper in the wall?" I asked this hesitantly. It was quite possible that I didn't want to know the answer.

Brady shut his eyes, then quoted, "MALICE WITH MAGICK SPELLS COMBINE. ANNHILATION."

His eyes popped open when Ronny let out a shocked gasp. "Mother used that word. Something about a malice that has long festered in Morgana."

Brady quoted off the top of his head, staring at Ronny, "It is a malice that has festered for years, like an abscess rooted deep in her soul."

"Yes, I remember now," Ronny said. "And Ghalynn spoke of magick spells being cast from a group in the South." She pulled her hand gently from Chris and closed her eyes. She wasn't just sitting there; under her eyelids, I could see her eyes twitching back and forth. Then they popped open.

She stared at Brady. "You have already figured this out, have you not? The prophecy refers to malice from Morgana and that group."

I almost asked her why she'd stopped calling her *Aunt* Morgana, but her next words distracted me. "If two powerful spells were let off close together... If they contradicted each other..." Ronny's face lost color as she continued to lock eyes with Brady who was nodding slowly.

My heart bean to pound. This didn't sound good; both Brady and Ronny looked uneasy. She said, "This could be quite bad. Such spells could combine and interact with each other, creating something completely different, something that would react unpredictably." She ran her hand over her face, then whispered, "That could destroy all of the magickal creatures and people in Chimera."

Brady nodded more decisively. "Yes, that is what I suspected. It is the scientific principle of synergy, wherein the whole is greater than the sum of its parts."

She turned to look at me, eyes brimming with sorrow. "I have had you looking for the impossible. Holding onto a false hope that they might be somewhere. But if this thing has happened, my mother and all I know have been wiped from existence." She dropped her head into her hands and sobbed. We just sat there, unable to do anything.

Chris gathered her into his arms and lifted her, slid onto the chair and held her in his lap. He lifted her face to his and kissed her, murmuring low words of comfort as he stroked her back. Finally she sat up and looked straight at me.

The others were talking in low voices but I couldn't hear what they were saying any more. I was caught by Ronny's gaze. It was filled with pain, begging me for understanding. For forgiveness. I hoped my gaze was telling her what I felt. That I was sorry her hopes were ended like this. That there was nothing for me to forgive.

Brady cleared his throat. "I hate to bring this up, but you are forgetting the most important issue." That broke the silent communication between Ronny and me.

He looked at us slowly, meeting each of our eyes in turn. I'd never seen him look more serious. "The prophecy says that both worlds will face a dire test and that we may fail."

Everyone was speaking over the others. It was useless trying to make out anything important. Finally Doug whistled sharply, stopping the cacophony in an instant. He said, "Have we accepted that the prophecy refers to us?"

Slowly, reluctantly, we took turns nodding. I was last and looked quickly at Ronny's white face before adding my nod to the others. My head felt too light and I suspected if I tried to stand I'd end up passed out on the floor.

Brady said, "Okay, we're agreed. Next, we must consider what type of dire test may be coming, and what happens if we fail."

Ronny sat bolt upright, fingernails digging into the arms of her chair. "It has already begun," she choked out. "The magick storms. They are caused by wild magick that is out of control. It has been leaking faster and faster into this world, growing in strength over time. I kept waiting for it to die back like it did sixteen years ago. Now I know why it has continued to grow rather than disperse."

You could have heard a pin drop in that room. She twisted to look back at Chris, love and terror etched on her face. "There can be no doubt of how much damage such storms can cause in this world, for we have already seen that, with only a small part of the power that is surely to come."

She reached out and grabbed Chris's hand again, holding on tight. "There is nothing in Chimera to stop these storms. They will continue to pour forth, destroying more and more of Santa Ramona. Then they will spread from here until this entire world is consumed."

Doug stood up and squared his shoulders. "Then I guess it's up to us to find the remaining object." He glanced quickly at Brady. "The object that will help us see."

"Yes." Brady stood also. "That much is clear from the prophecy."

Doug turned back to Ronny and gave her a lopsided smile. "We'll find it. And then we'll do whatever has to be done next."

Chapter 35/November/Chimera

Clues!

Fortunately for all of us, Brady seemed to calm down over the next week. We spent too much time staying away from the Rejects for him to brood much. Arnold had reinforced the need for us to be careful.

Early that week, Arnold had trapped us against a locked door when Olivia Faith and I stopped briefly to review Ms. Mahoney's homework assignment. He'd loomed up from the hall, blocking our escape. I was grateful I couldn't see the expression behind his dark glasses. The implacable contempt on his mouth was bad enough.

He took a long, slow step toward us and pulled a metal ruler out of his backpack. He struck it against his palm twice and I realized with a sick dread that he'd done something to it; it was no longer a flimsy metal ruler. He'd made it heavier and inflexible in the middle. One long edge caught the light, gleaming as if it was razor sharp. He avoided touching that side.

I felt like a rabbit caught in the light, unable to move as I watched that thin flashing edge. As he stepped closer, to us. As an anticipatory grin twisted his lips into something horrible. If he'd started sprouting fangs and claws, I wouldn't have felt a bit surprised.

His outsides might not show it, but there was a monster lurking in there somewhere. On the whole, I'd have preferred giants spiders or a troll.

I don't know what might have happened if Mrs. Lott hadn't come by. Even though there were three of us and only one of him. Him and a knife sharp, foot long weapon. We got lucky that time. When Brady and Doug came pounding up to us, it caught Mrs. Lott's attention. She came over and reminded us that there was to be no running in the halls. Brady and Doug apologized and the five of us left when she did, leaving Arnold standing there by himself.

He was so angry at getting interrupted, I could feel the fury vibrating off him as we walked away.

-xXx-

Even though Brady seemed calmer, I was nervous when he knocked on my door that next Saturday. Had he come to yell about Ronny again?

A sigh escaped me as I ushered him into the living room.

He sat in my Dad's favorite chair but didn't look comfortable. He was perched on the edge and kept shifting around in a very un-Brady-like manner. Normally I'd have asked him to spill whatever had him so jumpy, but I wasn't sure I wanted to know.

Then he stilled abruptly and asked, "Does Olivia like flowers?"

I was so surprised by the question, I stuttered a bit. "Flowers? Olivia? I…I guess. Yes, um…orchids."

"How about candy?" he asked quickly.

"Candy?" I realized I sounded like a parrot. "Um…not really." Olivia was always working on keeping her figure. "She's actually more of a jewelry kind of person."

His eyes lit up. "Jewelry. Thanks, Kat."

He jumped to his feet and was gone.

WTH?

-xXx-

Olivia called me that evening, wanting to talk about wonderful, marvelous, fantastic Brady. Again.

I finally interrupted and asked, "Where did this all come from?"

"What do you mean?" Olivia sounded genuinely puzzled.

"For years you've been annoyed by him. Then suddenly, he's all you talk about and you're kissing him every time I turn around. That's what I mean!"

"Well, he sees me — really sees me, Kat. The good parts and the bad parts. He doesn't expect me to try to be things I'm not. He just loves me for who I am. Ad I feel the same about him."

I was silent, stunned actually. Completely caught off guard by the 'L' word. Olivia had never used it before. Not about a guy.

She didn't seem to notice my silence. She laughed, delightedly. "Even though he still annoys me on a regular basis!"

"Yeah, but he's doing more than annoying you now," I said. I sounded a bit like I'd just sucked on a lemon. "I still don't get it."

"I'm just as surprised as you." Olivia laughed, then her voice dropped. "I guess I didn't know he thought about anything but his science books before."

"Really? I did," I muttered, glad I hadn't missed *every*thing about my friends.

-xXx-

A few days before our next trip into Chimera, Brady asked all of us to meet him in a small area in school that was typically empty during lunch. We all kept a lookout, because the teachers wouldn't like us back here.

Brady pulled one of Glenna's journals from his pack.

"Glenna wrote some things in a handmade code. It took me until last night to break it." He flipped the journal open to a page covered with small Chimeran letters. Folded into the journal was a piece of paper. "First, I need to read this part of her journal." He didn't bother actually read the words on the page. Of course.

Ghalynn dropped a cryptic message while he walked in front of me. When I called to him, he ran and I could not find him. The message is brief but has me worried."

Brady paused while he pulled the piece of paper from the journal. "This is definitely from Ghalynn; you'll recognize that right away."

Beware the dark magick,
For it pools and grows.
Now it is far too late;
None here can oppose.

Take these my final words;
Geas-bound I expire.
The Salamander guards the
Fourth within his fire.

Thus fate must rest upon
Those who were foretold.
I've helped them all I can;
Now it must unfold.

The Prophecy does tell,
Much that they should know.
Yet this must be discerned -
Be it friend or foe?

Faith bit her lip and frowned. "What do you think that means?"

"And what's with all the bad poetry?" Olivia asked in frustration. "Why can't he ever just *say* things?"

I turned to Brady. "What do you think he meant by 'geas-bound I expire'?"

Brady kicked at a straggly clump of grass, then looked at me. "He wrote about accepting a geas not to talk, remember?"

"Yes, so?"

"Ghalynn wanted this information found but couldn't talk about it. He tried to get around that by writing the information and leaving it where Glenna would find it, but that was walking a very fine line if he was under some magical compulsion." He looked away as he said, "I believe he thought that by violating the geas he would die." When he looked back at me, his jaw was set. "He must have thought it was very important for Glenna to get this information if he was willing to risk his life, don't you think?"

"Ghalynn left that message for us," I said, suddenly very sure. I had no proof, of course, other than the fact that it was written in his typical bad poetry, but I knew I was right. Brady started to shake his head and I forestalled whatever he planned to say. "It tells us about the next elemental *and* refers to a fourth object. He had to mean for us to have it."

Doug snorted. Brady opened his mouth then closed it slowly, his eyes becoming abstracted. One of his I'm-really-giving-this-serious-scientific-analysis looks spread over his face, then he gave me a lopsided smile. "Okay, let's utilize your hypothesis for now. We haven't seen any fires in the dwellings we've searched so far. Therefore it is a possibility that we will not finish with the town this month. We may need to search the more distant corners of the town, not just the houses, after we get through the mansion."

"If we can get into it," Doug said. When I turned and glared at him, tired of him being so negative, he said, "You heard Ronny. She doesn't really believe we'll be able to use those spells she gave us. And if we can't, there's no way to get inside."

Brady grinned, and his smile widened as he looked at Olivia. "I'm not counting on spells. I'm bringing my climbing equipment." Olivia gave a delighted laugh as he finished, "We might find a way in from the roof."

"Oh!" Faith sounded first alarmed, then amused. "That's actually pretty great. You and Olivia will go up and get into the mansion. Then you'll find a way in for the rest of us that doesn't include scaling the side of a building." She grinned at him. "I like it."

I remembered when we'd climbed up to an opening high inside a cave the first year we'd been in Chimera. Faith had hated it, and very nearly slipped and fell. I still remembered the terror I'd felt, knowing she could've fallen and died.

On top of that, her mom had been really pissed at her; she'd ruined her new pants.

Hopefully Brady and Olivia could find some way in that didn't involve Faith climbing up a rope.

-xXx-

The next day when we got to school, Olivia dragged Faith and me into the girl's bathroom.

"Look!" She touched a pretty piece of jewelry hanging on a thin chain around her neck. "Do you know what this is?"

"No," Faith said, although I thought it looked familiar. Olivia's face clouded so Faith added, "It's really pretty."

I looked closer, then realized I recognized it. "I know that. It's Arwen's necklace. The one she gave to Aragorn in *Lord of the Rings*. You always said you liked it."

"Nice!" Faith told her. She would have said more, but the bell rang. It was noisy in the hallway and I took advantage by whispering to Olivia, "Brady gave you that."

She blushed and nodded as we entered the classroom. We didn't have a chance to talk about it further. But later that day, I saw Olivia fingering the necklace and Brady smiling to himself, I leaned over and murmured, "Good job," in his ear. He turned away, a flush climbing his cheeks, but his smile grew even wider.

-xXx-

The next morning didn't start well. For once, I wasn't the only one freaked out by the angel statues. Slowly but surely, moving during each magic storm, they were closing in around the tree.

"Do you think they'll go through the tree into Chimera?" Doug asked Brady.

Before Brady could answer, I said, "Maybe their intent isn't to leave. Maybe they just want to block the entrance so we can't get in." They were already close enough that I felt a shudder work its way down my spine when we walked by them to get to the tree.

"Do you think this will be one of the fast trips," Faith asked, eyeing the tree, "or one of the long ones?"

"Quick and easy gets my vote." I thought my voice sounded light and cheerful. I worked really hard to make it so. There was no need to let everyone know how frightened I was, still, about going through that tree. I must not have been as successful as I thought; Olivia looked at me with sympathy clear on her face.

"Here's to an expectation of a positive outcome," Brady said briskly, leaning against the tree. Brady would be going through first from now on, so he could check the map as soon as he got there.

I just wanted to get the tree over with, so I took a couple deep breaths and leaned against it. Instantly the cold, clammy darkness closed in around me, smothering me. I began my slow count, thinking *quick and easy, quick and easy,* over and over. Like a mantra.

It wasn't exactly quick and easy, but I only got to 103 before being ejected into the warmth and intense silence of Chimera.

Time shall come when silence rules… The thought echoed uncomfortably in my head. I shook myself, trying not to think about annihilation.

Brady folded the map, and shoved it into his pocket. "No sign of the Rejects. As soon as the others are here we should get going."

It only took a couple minutes for everyone to emerge from the tree. Our animals rushed to meet us as we headed toward Mystic.

At first Brady kept pulling the map from his pocket and checking it compulsively every few minutes. After a while that must have gotten old. Pretty soon he just kept it out in his hand. I'm not sure I'd have noticed if I hadn't been watching him carry the map, but the watch around his wrist wasn't his usual watch. He was wearing the one his Great-grandfather had designed. The other watch had always looked too big on Brady's wrist. But this one looked as if it had been designed specifically for him.

I had a sudden memory of the first time Ronny met Brady. She'd seemed uncomfortable. I'd put that down to springing him on her with no warning. Now I had to wonder; how much did he look like Arthur? Could she have been startled by some vague resemblance to her father?

Brady glanced again at the map and smiled. Clearly the Rejects still hadn't entered Chimera. We might actually have time to finish looking through the last couple houses and get into the mansion before they showed up.

That was, If we could get into the mansion.

We walked past the tall hedge that hid the mansion from the road. Beyond it were three smaller houses. These looked different than others we'd seen in Chimera. They were derelicts; boarded up, falling apart, paint peeling, dead leaves covering the porches, weeds growing tall and wild in the yards.

One was more than derelict. It appeared to have been vandalized. The windows were broken, and strange letters and symbols had been painted on the walls.

These were the first houses since we'd found Ghalynn's cabin, the first year we'd come to Chimera, that looked like they'd been abandoned long before everyone disappeared. Most looked as if their owners had simply stepped away a few minutes ago.

Why were these different?

Then the memory of Ronny, pointing to this area on the map and telling us she'd lived there, came back to me. One of those houses had been hers.

The idea of searching her house made my skin itch. How would I be able to tell her we'd gone through her things?

At least these were small, thatched cottages. They shouldn't take long to search.

We didn't spend much time inside the first abandoned building. The one nearest the edge of town, where the forest crowded close, was completely empty. Our feet rang hollowly on the floor. Other than a slow creepy drip from the faucet in the kitchen, there was absolutely no sound. If anyone said they could hear dust settling on the floor, I'd believe them.

The next house was partially destroyed. Everything that had been left inside had collapsed into a mess of shattered wood and broken glass. Doug stirred the litter carefully. "It doesn't look like there was anything much in here," he announced. "I think the next house was Ronny's. We should check it next."

It felt strange to walk into my sister-in-law's abandoned house. At least we knew there were no booby traps on this one. Even better, when Brady made his usual "I wish to see anything we should find or anything left for us by Ghalynn," there was a flash of blue from one end of the room, from inside a small drawer in the table next to a comfortable chair. At the same time, the stone on Doug's wristband flashed a bright blue-green, and a blue 'X' appeared on the map.

"I'd say we found something," Doug said. We crowded around, staring at his wristband. We finally might have found something important! Maybe the object itself! It was possible, even if there was no Salamander hanging around…

Olivia was frowning. She clearly didn't share my excitement. "Well, it's something," she said, dubiously.

"What do you think it is?" Faith asked, rocking forward on the balls of her feet. At least she was showing enthusiasm.

Brady tried to open the drawer, but it was stuck. He jerked and yanked on it before stepping back and staring at it with narrowed eyes. "Someone, probably Ghalynn, added some sort of lock to this. If I was Ghalynn and wanted to be sure no one else could get in here, what would I do?"

Brady stood there, tapping his chin with his fist, staring wordlessly at the table. It felt weird just standing there watching him doing nothing, so I wandered to the back of the room.

Just like her creepy aunt, Ronny's house had several items from fairy tales on display. But none of these represented the nasty stories Morgana enjoyed. Instead, on one shelf a glass slipper was displayed on a red velvet cushion. On another there was a large golden lamp, like the one in the Aladdin stories. A tall umbrella stand sat on the floor, holding several staffs, looking like they belonged in *Lord of the Rings*. There was an entire glass case filled with wands; it reminded me of Olivanders in *Harry Potter*. But the most interesting was the carpet. It looped slowly around this end of the room, about a foot below the ceiling. Though I looked carefully, I couldn't see any wires or anything holding it up.

A thought started to form as I stared at the flying carpet, but before it came clear Brady called out in triumph.

"Got it!" I turned back in time to see him press what looked like a knot hole. The drawer gave a series of clicks, then Brady threw the drawer open and searched through it. If Doug hadn't been standing there, we might have missed it, but there was a blue-green flash from his wristband when Brady touched a ragged piece of paper. There must be magic attached to it, somehow.

Brady held it up. "It's in English," he said, stunned. Then read it out loud, voice faltering over the uneven meter.

I left this first, it is not yet last,
Find the next in my friend's box locked fast.
It is the only one locked by date.
Use it well to help you find your fate.

- Ghalynn

As soon as Brady finished, the paper flamed up and disappeared in a small puff of purple smoke. Brady was left staring at empty purple-coated fingers.

Olivia raced over and cradled his hand in hers. "Did it burn you?" she demanded, twisting his hand to see it better.

"No." Brady sounded dazed. "The flames were the same temperature as this room. They just startled me."

"I guess we should get started on the mansion," Doug said.

"Not yet." Brady looked up toward the top of the house. A ladder attached to the wall led up to a small trap door about two feet square. We had one like that in our house; it accessed the attic. I didn't have long to wonder why Brady was so interested. He said, "Don't you remember, we need to get my great-grandfather's chest."

"What chest?" Olivia asked.

"I don't suppose you would remember," Brady said, fortunately without bitterness. "Ronny said her father's chest was at the top of her house, in a small space in the eaves. The one with the combination lock with the date Grandpa Chuck was born." Impatience crept into his voice. "Ghalynn's note?" made air quotes with his fingers and repeated, "Locked by date?"

"Oh!" I said, feeling slow. At least I hadn't been the only one.

He turned away. "Just wait here, it will only take a minute." He shrugged out of his backpack and sprang up the ladder. When he pushed against the trap door, it swung up and he disappeared up over our heads.

I felt a moment's giddy relief that he hadn't said 'I'll be right back'. That had been the death knell of teenagers in dozens of horror movies.

I'd just begun to worry when he finally appeared at the top of the ladder, carrying a small wooden chest. When he got down, he asked Faith if she could carry a few things from his backpack so he'd have room for the chest.

Why couldn't Doug ask me like that?

When that got sorted out, Faith said, "You realize this means we have only one place left to look? What happens if we don't find anything at the mansion?"

"Ghalynn stated the fourth object was hidden in the mansion," Brady told her.

"But what if he's wrong? He couldn't find it," Faith insisted, and shoved her hands into her pockets. "I'm not climbing up a wall to get into a building unless I know we're going to find something in there. I hate heights."

Brady said dismissively, "I'll figure it out."

Olivia narrowed her eyes. "Don't you mean, we?"

Brady grinned, showing a lot of teeth. If it had been anyone other than Brady, I'd have said he looked wolf-ish. "Sure," he told her, "*we'll* figure it out." He ruined it by rolling his eyes.

"Don't you dare make it sound like the rest of us are incapable of thinking up stuff," Olivia snapped.

"You think of lots of stuff," he said readily. Then added, "But let's face it, I have a logical mind that's well suited for reviewing the available facts, formulating possible alternatives and calculating which will work best. That's what I'm good at."

Olivia flushed and her eyes glittered. She slapped her hands on her hips and leaned forward. "Now you listen here, Brady Albert Truman. You are good at lots of things." She paused to suck in a breath and I decided it was past time to get the conversation back on track.

I turned to Faith. "It'll be okay," I told her. The expression on her face made it clear how unimpressed she was by this reassurance. I tried again, "We'll get in and we'll find it. You'll see."

"Sure," she said. "And we'll solve the mystery of Chimera while we're at it."

"That's the spirit," Doug said heartily and gave her shoulder a bump with his fist. He turned to Brady. "Are we done here?"

Brady pulled out the map and wished to be shown anything else we should know about, but nothing showed up. He turned toward the door and said, "We'd better get going."

"Wait," I interrupted. "There are two things we need to do first."

"Like what?" Doug asked skeptically.

"Like, first I want to check Ronny's bedroom to see if she left anything here. She might like to have it back."

Doug tipped his head back and forth like he wasn't sold on the idea but was willing to go along with it.

"Second," I said triumphantly, "we need to grab that flying carpet in the living room. In case we can't find a way to open anything on the ground floor of the mansion." I grinned at their puzzled looks. Brady wasn't the only one who could think up stuff! "We can use it to fly up on the roof."

Chapter 36/November/Chimera

Find the Fire

The flying carpet did fit into my backpack, but wrestling it down and getting it rolled up took three of us. Trying to shove it in my already stuffed backpack was even worse.

I grumbled at Doug, "Why do you keep putting all this stuff in my backpack!"

His voice was low when he answered. "I trust you with my things. I know you'll take care of them." That nearly shut me up. It was really sweet.

And still really irritating.

"Maybe you shouldn't trust me quite *this* much in the future," I panted out as we wrestled the carpet into my pack.

I managed to get the overfull backpack settled on my shoulders, but even then, the carpet wasn't still. I could feel it twisting and writhing in there, strong enough to throw me off balance. A couple times I thought I'd end up doing a face-plant in the dirt.

I held Olivia back a moment. "Are you and Brady okay?"

"Sure," she said, brows drawing together in puzzlement. "Why wouldn't we be?"

"Well," I said carefully. "You were arguing. You've done that a few times lately."

Olivia threw back her head and laughed. Ahead of us, Brady looked back over his shoulder and smiled, eyes fixed on her face. Olivia linked her arm through mine and sped up. "We're fine. We *like* to argue. I think we've been doing it so long, we miss it when we try to stop."

I shook my head and laughed back. But I was hoping they wouldn't argue all the time, like they used to.

We pushed our way through the hedge, and it was just as bad as last time. The sharp pointy ends of the hundreds of small twigs poked at me through my clothes, scratched my hands and twisted into my hair. It felt like I'd pulled half the hair off my head by the time we got through.

The mansion was just as forbidding and blank as the first time. The house was huge; at least three stories high. Which would make it around thirty feet tall. Suddenly my idea of using a flying carpet didn't sound so clever. Who wanted to ride a carpet thirty feet into the air? We didn't even know how to control it.

The hedges reached so tall and thick around the house that the first ten feet were covered in dark shadows. It would have been hard to see anything — if there'd been anything to see. Unfortunately, no doors or windows had miraculously appeared since the last time we were here. I hadn't realized I'd been hoping they would be there, until they weren't.

Olivia was still plucking twigs and leaves out of her hair. One in the back was giving her trouble. I stepped over, planning to help, but she didn't see me. Instead she turned and said, "Brady, can you get this out for me?"

"Of course." He stepped up and with surprisingly gentle hands began to untangle it from her hair. It wasn't going to be easy; the half-foot long twig was really stuck in there. I'd have given up and suggested we cut it out by now, but Brady kept working at it patiently.

"Um, maybe there's no way for you to get it untangled," I finally suggested.

"Of course I can untangle it," Brady said without looking away from his hands. "It's like any other logic puzzle." He made a few more gentle tugs and suddenly the twig was lying across the palm of his hand. I didn't even see any of her hair wrapped around it.

"Thanks," Olivia told him, and gave him such a brilliant smile I turned away.

I cleared my throat and said, "Well, we know wishing for doors or a way in didn't work. What next?"

Brady shrugged out of his pack and opened it, saying, "We climb." He pulled out some ropes and metal bolts.

I glanced at Faith who looked positively gray. At the same time I felt my pack twitch as the carpet tried to get loose again. I took a deep breath and said, "Maybe we should try those spells Ronny gave us first."

"Why bother?" Brady asked shortly, eyes on the rope he was twisting and knotting. "When we use a wish, we are activating existing spells. I can accept that. But it's not logical to believe that we can control a magic spell that does not already exist in this area. We are not magic; therefore it won't work for us."

"Well, then, it certainly won't hurt to try, will it?" I asked, frustration starting to leak into my voice.

Brady looked up then, but before he could say anything I exclaimed in a loud, firm voice, "Activatotum Alomura."

"That was foolish," Brady said angrily. "It could have triggered something other than what you expected."

I got my hopes up when there was a loud clicking sound, almost like a key being turned in a lock, but nothing else happened. There was still no way in.

Brady relaxed and I crossed my arms over my chest and said, even more firmly, "Activatotum Apeersium."

To be honest, I hadn't really expected anything to happen. Because Brady was right, we weren't magical. I couldn't cast spells. So I was as surprised as he was when several feet away from us the shadowy outline of a door appeared.

It was insubstantial, as if created from the shadows cast by the hedge. But it was definitely there.

Everyone froze for a moment, then Doug rushed over and ran his fingers over the insubstantial shape. It remained a shadow door and wouldn't budge when he tried to turn the door handle. I felt my shoulders slump in disappointment.

Brady was muttering something under his breath that sounded suspiciously like cursing. He went over and began running his hands over the barely discernable edges, but it wouldn't open for him either. At first I thought it had all been for nothing, then I remembered something Ronny had said months earlier. Something about only the person who cast a spell can operate it.

I walked over to the door and carefully closed my fingers around the indistinct shape of a doorknob. I gasped as I felt my fingers close around something that definitely had substance. I twisted it slowly and the door groaned as it pivoted open on shadowy hinges.

Everyone crowded around me, speaking in excited whispers. But I couldn't make out what any of them were saying. I was too busy quietly freaking out.

I'd just cast a spell.

I wasn't magical, but I'd still done it. So just how much magic had we been absorbing from this place?

Just how much had we changed?

Then Doug gave me a silly half-bow, pulling me back to the present. "You opened the portal," he said grandly. "You should enter first, milady."

I snorted. His chivalrous knight routine could use some work. But I pushed the door fully open and stepped inside.

It was really dark in there. No light entered from other doors or windows, and the little bit of light that reached in from this doorway didn't penetrate more than a foot into the room. I turned around and asked, "Who brought candles?"

"Wait!" Faith stepped in next to me, took a deep breath and said, "I wish there was light."

I gaped at her. Faith never wanted us to try wishes in here. But it worked. The room brightened dramatically.

"What?" Faith asked, seeing the incredulous expression on my face.

"You never wish," I said. Only it came out more like an accusation.

"Well, I hate using candles in a house. What if someone trips and catches the rug on fire?" She grimaced. "This just seemed safer, somehow."

"Yeah, okay," I said weakly. Magic spells that could go horribly wrong were safer than an innocent candle? "I guess I can see that."

Olivia snickered. "Yeah, you can see that because Faith turned on the lights."

I groaned but couldn't keep a grin off my face.

Faith had been busy looking around the room. "Just how many people do you think lived here?"

I glanced around and understood what she meant. It looked more like a common room at Hogwarts than the living room of a house. It was filled with tables, couches, chairs, large soft floor pillows and benches. The walls were filled with shelves of mugs, bowls, plates, and boxes of cookies and crackers.

There were no books or papers anywhere in the room, and no dressers, side boards or anything else with cupboards or drawers.

"Well," I said. "At least there's nothing we need to check out in here."

We made our way to the right, through a doorway at the far end of the room. Inside was a large, rather dirty kitchen. It wasn't only the pots and pans stacked into the sink, with food so old it was just a powdery residue in the bottom where it had flacked away into dust. It wasn't even the mugs and dishes stacked all over the counters. It was the gritty, sticky floor and the grime on the walls. Clearly, whoever lived here wasn't overly concerned with housekeeping.

After a few glances around, I swore I was going to take better care of my room. No way did I want someone coming in and feeling so disgusted about me.

The cupboards and drawers in this place contained only utensils and boxes of what had been food. At the far end, a door led to another room.

This turned out to be a long, narrow dining room. A huge dark table took up most of the space. It was set with at least fifteen chairs on each side. Other than a few ugly tapestries on the wall, depicting witches hovering over steaming cauldrons, there was nothing else in this room.

But at the far end, a staircase led out and up.

We trudged up the long flight of stairs; I was afraid to touch the grimy banisters of heavy carved wood. The newel post was large, carved into a dragon several feet high. It stood on its hind legs with its clawed arms extended. Its mouth gaped open, displaying rows of long, sharp wooden teeth.

Why would anyone want something that looked like it was about to take a bite out of you in their house?

Beyond the dragon, the stairs ended on a narrow landing. We were at the corner of two corridors, one branching off to our left, the other heading straight ahead. A series of doors lined one side of the hallway.

"Stick together, or split up and meet back here?" I asked.

Doug said, "You three girls go that way," he said, pointing to the left. "Brady and I will go this way." He motioned down the hallway directly ahead of us.

Olivia lifted her eyebrow and her lip curled disdainfully. "Girls?"

Doug snorted. "Girls, females, non-male persons. Whatever you want to call yourself. Just go that way."

Olivia gave him a saucy grin. "Us *women* will go that way. And we'll beat you *boys* back here."

We turned and hustled away, laughing and nudging Olivia. Faith said, "That was awesome."

We made short work checking out each of the rooms on this hallway. They were small, austere bedrooms; most had very little in them.

When we reached the end of the hallway, it made a sharp 90 degree turn and headed parallel to the hallway Brady and Doug were taking. I realized rooms filled the middle of the building, with corridors around the outside.

There was an air of expectation this time. We knew we were looking for something to do with seeing. And it was likely, though not definite, that whatever it was would be in this building.

I tried really hard to hold onto my enthusiasm as we looked through the rooms. They were little more than cells. Grey walls, no windows, no decorations, hard flat mattresses, very basic dressers with small drawers. At first I thought about calling Doug to wave his wristband around to make sure we weren't missing anything. But after looking through the skimpy belongings, I realized that would be a waste. There was absolutely nothing of interest in any of the rooms.

We'd just finished checking the last one on the second hallway and had turned down the third when Doug and Brady came out of a room a few feet away.

"Anything?" Brady asked. Clearly they hadn't found anything, or Brady would have said so. It felt like my whole body slumped in disappointment.

"No. You?" Olivia asked, walking up to him and standing just a little too close.

He grinned at her. "No. But I'm very interested in what lies on the other side of those rooms." He motioned to the room they had just left.

"What do you mean?" I asked. "Don't they just back up to the rooms on the other side?"

"It's clear from the interior dimensions that the center has been blocked off. A space at least 3 meters by 3 meters square exists in the middle of those rooms."

"And what is that in feet?" Olivia asked, hands on hips.

Brady's grin widened. "About 9 feet, 10.1 inches."

Olivia grinned back. "*About* 10.1 inches?"

"Well 10.109375 inches if you want to be more precise," Brady told her. And the two of them stood there, looking at each other with foolish grins on their faces. I turned away so they wouldn't see, then rolled my eyes.

Note to self — Do not ever stare at a guy like that! Not where people can see you.

Faith said, "I don't think there's anything else on this level. Should we try the next?" She brushed past Olivia and Brady and headed back toward the stairs. I followed her with Doug on my heels.

Before Faith had a chance to step onto the stairs, Brady called out, "Wait!" He held up his hand in a just-a-moment gesture. He pulled the map from his pocket and wished to see if there was anything else we should see here or anything from Ghalynn.

Brady stiffened and a sharp breath hissed out between his teeth. I looked at the map, and there in bright blue was a small 'X'. Fortunately, it was in a nearby room. Brady hurried over to it, opened the door, and we all crowded into the small space.

There were several books piled on the floor next to the unmade bed. With a grimace, Brady began moving them one at a time, riffling through the pages. Faith and I jumped over and began to help.

I immediately understood why he didn't like touching these books. Not only were they dirty, they felt greasy and...wrong. Like a low level current was running through them. Just strong enough to make your fingers tingle, unpleasantly.

Faith found it. She picked up one of the books, grasped both covers and gave it a vigorous shake. A small piece of parchment fell out and Brady snatched it up before it hit the sticky, grimy floor. He opened it and read out loud.

- **Ghalynn Thurinor Haeredon, Seer, Prognosticator, House of "Quidrittch", Survivor of the Noldorin Elves**

"What kind of note is that?" I asked, disappointed.

"I'm not sure, but I'm going to keep it. Maybe there's hidden writing on it or something." Brady shoved the note in his pack. "Okay, let's go."

Olivia moved past me and went to stand by Brady. He quickly motioned for the rest of us to go first. As I left the room, I glanced back surreptitiously to see if Brady and Olivia were following. They were, but they were walking slowly, so close their shoulders kept brushing, whispering to each other.

When we got to the stairs, Faith lifted her foot to place it on the first step but Brady shouted again. "Wait!"

Faith turned, confused, and placed her foot back on the floor.

"That sign," Brady said, pointing to a small metal plaque with a jumble of Chimeran letters. "It says 'Do not enter here without first speaking the password'."

"What's the password?" Faith asked, confused.

"Abracadabra," I said, facetiously.

"We don't have a password, so we need to try climbing up anyway," Doug said. He set his foot on the stairs, then grabbed the railing, his eyes going wide. The stairs had jerked into motion beneath him, rising like a circular escalator. The rest of us piled on before he could get too far ahead. But every time someone else stepped on, the stairs circled faster. And though it was definitely climbing, it was soon apparent the steps were somehow going nowhere. I groaned and clutched my head; the constant revolving was getting to me.

Brady let out an exclamation and slung his pack off his shoulder, letting it dangle from his arm. He dug out the message from Ghalynn. "I thought so," he said in satisfaction. "I noticed these small quote marks around one word. I thought it was just a mistake, but now I believe this is the clue Ghalynn left for us."

"Don't just talk about it," Olivia yelled. "Do something!"

Brady took a deep breath and said, "Quilldritch."

Instantly, the stairs began to slow, then delivered Doug onto the third floor landing.

This was definitely the top floor of the house. The ceiling directly over the stairs was criss-crossed with huge beams of dark wood holding up large slate tiles. On this level, there were no other rooms. The entire floor was open. And around the center of that open space, a railing enclosed an area about ten feet square. I started to go over to look, but Brady said, "We need to do this logically. Let's start here, work our way around the outer part of the room, then see what lies at the center."

I turned away reluctantly and followed Brady over to the long, low tables that were pushed up around the walls.

"It's like a laboratory," I said, looking at the cauldrons perched over charred spaces on the tables. The ceiling overhead was covered in burn marks, like something hot had shot up and splattered. There were jars of strange ingredients, some with colors that assaulted my eyes, others were dark and murky and nasty looking. A few others, I could swear, were moving.

Yes. One was pulsating in a slow, uneven rhythm.

Everywhere I looked, spills covered the tables. Crusty bits had settled in the bottom of cauldrons. Dirty glass tubes and beakers sealed with wax and metal, incised with strange symbols, were scattered around the room. Worn leather books were stacked in haphazard piles, while others lay opened to incomprehensible pages covered with strange diagrams in spidery faded brown ink. Candles stood everywhere, in dozens of different colors of wax.

"Not a laboratory," Brady said, disgust lacing his voice. "A laboratory should be bright and clean and modern. This is a room for potions and spells."

We made a complete circuit of the room. Brady said most of the books were the same as those we'd found in the book shop, although one had notations in the margins. Brady held it gingerly by the corner and dropped it into his backpack with a grimace.

"Okay," I said. "Can we go look over the railing now?"

Brady nodded and shifted his pack higher on his shoulders, shrugging as if the weight of that one book was making him uncomfortable.

I hurried over. How cool was having a hidden space inside a house? My fingers closed tightly around the railing and I looked down. My gasp was clearly audible in the silence. Everyone ran over.

"What's wrong," Faith asked and touched my shoulder. I pointed at the flames leaping far below.

Doug gave a sharp whistle between his teeth and his eyes gleamed with excitement. So did the stone on his wristband, blazing with blue-green light.

I turned to look back down and still couldn't believe what I was seeing. We'd done it! I nearly broke out in a happy dance.

Below us, swimming through leaping flames, was a large orange and yellow lizard-like shape.

Brady looked around, then pointed to the small staircase that spiraled around the edges of that space, heading down into the building. The top of the stairs began across the room. I was the first one to reach them, somehow beating Doug for once. Then I hesitated to take the first step down. The narrow stairs appeared to be floating. At least, I couldn't see what was holding them up. And there were no handrails, just steps less than one foot long and half a foot wide.

If they'd gone straight down like normal stairs it might not have bothered me. Or at least, not so much. But these curved around first one way, then another like a staircase maze. And they went all the way down to the ground floor without a landing or a place to get off. Once you started down, it would be nearly impossible to turn around before going all the way to the bottom.

Doug touched my shoulder. "I'll go," he told me and gently pulled me back out of the way. He started down carefully, testing each step before placing all his weight on it. He called back, "They seem solid enough. They aren't wobbling or moving under my feet."

One by one the rest of us began following him down. Then Doug yelled, "Whoa!" and the stair he was on dipped to one side, nearly throwing him off. He widened his stance, making sure he was balanced before looking back over his shoulder. "This one feels loose on one end. Be careful."

We continued down, moving a bit more cautiously than before. I couldn't remember which stair had given him the problem. But even though I'd been careful where I placed my feet, I felt it move the moment I stepped on it.

The step shifted under me, then jolted to the side, nearly dumping me off. My eyes were drawn against my will to the ground, still nearly twenty feet below. I took a quick step down then waited until my heart stopped pounding and my knees lost their momentary weakness. I stood perfectly still, just enjoying the feeling of the unmoving stair under my feet. Then I continued down, even more cautious than before, and heaved a sigh of relief as my feet touched the wide, solid ground.

Doug grinned at me, but I thought he looked pale and the corners of his eyes were bright. "You almost took a header, Taylor." His voice was light, nearly taunting.

I glared at him, but relented; I knew him too well to let some teasing get to me. But you'd think he could have been a little concerned.

Once we all got off the staircase, Brady cautiously approached the huge fire blazing in the center of the stone floor. I was creeped out to see at least a dozen statues ranged around that fire. What was up with all these statues? Why would you stick them down here?

I glanced up and realized the roof was open directly above the fire. I hadn't noticed that before; I had been too intent on looking down. The ceiling had been designed specifically to hide that fact unless you were down here. This place just kept getting weirder —why would someone leave a hole in the roof?

Faith stepped up next to Brady, pointed at the lizard shape and whispered, "That's a Salamander. The Elemental of fire."

The creature opened its eyes and regarded her. "Precissssely," it hissed. Its voice reminded me of the sound fire made when a new piece of wood caught in a campfire. The hissing sound as the water in the wood flash-dried.

"Ghalynn said you might have a message for us," she said.

"Ghalynn. Yessss. I have a messssage. If you are the right onessss." It rolled over in a long, convulsive movement, then continued, "It hassss been growing harder, to hold myself together." Another convulsive roll made it hiss as though in pain. "There issss too much uncontrolled magic. I felt itssss creation. Two different spellssss.

They collided. They mingled. As they fused they grew wild and unrestrained. It is no longer either spell, but something elsssse instead. And it issss pulling all the magic from thissss world, draining it. Including me. I do not know if I can lasssst much longer."

I leaned against the side of one of the statues, thinking this might take a while. Brady kept trying to question the Salamander, but its replies seemed evasive, almost rude. I wondered if it spoke to everyone like that, or if the draining magic was making it grouchy. Or, maybe it had something personal against us… But why? It didn't even know us, right?

Now the Salamander was trying to convince Brady it had nothing to tell us. Nothing to give us.

And I was suddenly very sure it was lying. I straightened up to warn Brady, but something else caught my attention. Something was different about the statue I'd been leaning against. When I'd first rested on it, it was hard and cold to the touch, even though it was just a few feet away from the blazing fire. But now it felt softer somehow, and I could swear I saw a hint of color under that smooth stone exterior.

Without thinking, I blurted, "It's like when I froze you guys."

That got everyone's attention. Even the Salamander stopped its oh-so-reasonable speech-i-fying.

I pointed to the statue I'd been leaning against. "Look. There. Touch it. Is it different than the rest?"

The others came over and did as I asked. They seemed pretty skeptical, but agreed there might be a *slight* difference.

Brady turned back to the Salamander and asked, very casually, "So what is going on with all the statues?"

The Salamander rolled over, and swam through the fire. If a lizard could look confused, this one did. It said, "Of what do you speak? There are no statuessss here."

Brady pointed to the one next to me. "What is that then?"

"That issss Helga," the Salamander said. "Or at least, it wassss Helga. I cannot in all actuality tell you if it issss still Helga after all thissss time."

I took a quick step away and brushed frantically at the side of my shirt where it had touched 'Helga'. I was fighting down the urge to vomit. I'd been leaning against a frozen woman? A frozen magic woman? Ugh! Brady pulled out the map and asked to see all of the statues of people in Chimera.

Instantly, small brown dots appeared on the map. There were dozens. The forest and the field where we'd seen them last year. Those around the fountain where we'd first seen them in town. All the others we'd seen around fountains and other places the last few months. And there were many more that we hadn't seen.

And then there were all of them in here.

"They are all situated in outdoor locations," Brady said, in full techno-science-geek mode. He scanned the map again. "Every statue is outside or has contact with the sky. Not one is in a house."

"This isn't outside," Olivia protested.

Brady pointed up where we could see blue sky over the interior of the house.

"Oh, right," she said, a flush brightening her cheeks.

"The spellssss," the Salamander hissed. "I could feel them both assss they were cast. One had a far greater effect on thosssse under a roof. I do not know if the onessss touched by that spell continue to exisssst at all. But thosssse who were not covered were caught between them both. I could not recognize either spell, but it rendered everyone I knew assss you see thesssse."

"You are saying these are actually people?" I felt my stomach roll uncomfortably, and swallowed hard.

"They were," the Salamander said. "I cannot tell if they sssstill are."

While I stood there, shuddering, Brady took a step back and cleared his throat. "We must locate an object related to sight. Will you help us?"

The Salamander said nothing.

Brady gave a quick, fierce grin. "If *you* do not possess such an object, can you inform us of its location?"

A crafty look lit its strange orange eyes. "I have no object. I do not know what it issss you sssseek."

I would have left it there, but fortunately Brady was made of sterner stuff. He said, "I wish to see the object Ghalynn wants us to have."

The Salamander hissed angrily and a small case flew up into the flames. The Salamander grabbed it in stubby front legs, while a vicious growl erupted from its throat.

"Ghalynn said the Elementals would help us," Brady said. "The others have. So why aren't you?"

There was no answer from the Salamander.

"You have to help us," Doug said. "We can break the spell. Ghalynn said so."

The Salamander snarled furiously and spat, "The days of the Mundane and Magickal are at an end. It issss time for my kind now."

I took an involuntary step back. That thing had grown larger as it spoke, as if its anger fed it.

Brady glared at the forbidding creature for a moment, then grinned. He took a deep breath and said clearly, "I wish to see anything else I need to know about, or anything that could help us."

In a far corner of that space, a small fountain shuddered to life. It was shaped like a lotus blossom extending above a deep bowl filled with water. The petals slowly opened and it began to sing.

Literally.

Its voice was high pitched and garbled, but I could make out what it said with a bit of effort.

THE SALAMANDER BROODS IN EVIL AND STONE.
IT HAS BEEN LEFT TOO LONG ALONE.
WITH TIME ITS HEART HAS TURNED TO BONE.
THE NATURAL ORDER IT SEEKS TO DETHRONE.

"You are curssssed to evaporate in my heat." The Salamander's voice was low and rough with anger. "If you wissssh to live, go back to ssssleep." I realized it wasn't just anger I was hearing, it was a threat.

For a moment the fountain reached up, sending water spilling over the top of the bowl, clearly aimed at the Salamander. A few drops got through the flames and struck it, making it hiss in pain. The flames surrounding it reached out toward the fountain and its water began to dissipate in a large cloud of steam.

The voice from the fountain sounded thinner and drier as it sang once more.

NOW ITS PROMISES IT CHOOSES TO DISOWN.
SUCH CHOICES NONE CAN YET CONDONE.
TRUST NOT ONE WORD THAT IT MAY DRONE.
NONE NOW CANNNN… Cannnn…

The fountain's song faded away as the bowl ran dry.

While the Salamander was still busy aiming flames at the silent fountain, Doug grabbed something out of my pack and rushed forward. The box was floating near the top of the flames, at least ten feet over his head. He flicked the flying carpet open, jumped on it and grabbed some of the fringe in both hands. He steered toward the box, aiming the carpet by pulling up on one corner. The carpet soared up into the air. I balled my hands into fists, terrified he would fall.

Doug started to overshoot and hauled frantically at both corners to come to a stop next to the box. He'd just touched it when the Salamander whipped its body back around. Its flames shot toward us, enveloping Doug.

I screamed in terror.

Doug yanked the carpet back from the fire, box in one hand. It plummeted back toward the floor carrying Doug just ahead of the flames. He hit the ground hard, rolling himself and the carpet over and over, crushing out a few lingering flames. When he stopped, he sat up and pumped his fist. He was still holding the box and looked fierce.

He was sooty and singed, and began to climb to his feet.

I stepped over to him and shoved him back down. "Are you all right?"

"I'm fine," he said. He gently pushed me aside and got to his feet, then stumbled and clutched his leg.

"No, you're not," I said, annoyed that he felt the need to lie to me.

"I'll be okay. Seriously,"

I sighed, not bothering to argue, and grabbed his arms. I checked them over carefully while he stood there, rolling his eyes. He was right. His skin was red, like he had a bad sunburn, but it wasn't blistered.

"You know," I said, being oh-so-patient-and-calm, "You don't always have to be the hero. There are four other people here."

He gave me a jaunty grin. "Where would be the fun in that?"

I threw up my hands and turned away from him. But other than a lingering irritation with Doug, I was feeling pretty good. Ecstatic, in fact. And I could tell by the pleased chatter between Olivia and Brady, and Faith when she could get a word in, that they all felt the same.

We'd done it!

We'd found the Salamander and we'd found the object we'd just spent months looking for! I was sure of it.

It must be very important; the Salamander had tried to keep it for itself. Now we just had to get it ba—.

A sudden inferno of flame and hot ash shot toward us. It missed us, barely, but scorched the air around us. I felt sweat break out on every inch of skin, only to dry away instantly leaving it feeling hot and tight. A swelling rumble of sound rose toward us, climbing from a low snarl into an ear shattering roar.

"You shall not win," it bellowed. The entire room shuddered and one of the statues…people…fell over with a crash.

Doug stumbled back against the carpet and nearly fell onto his knees. He steadied himself with a quick push against it, then we were all scrambling toward the narrow curving stairs.

I actually thought we'd make it away safely until Faith screamed.

Chapter 37/November/Chimera

Escape the Fire

Bits of fire, some as large as basketballs, swarmed up the stairs after us. From below, the Salamander bellowed, "Be swift, my spritessss. Stop the intruderssss. Take back what is ourssss. Do not return until it issss done."

I ran up the thirty feet of stairs faster than I'd ever run before. So fast, the tipping step barely moved under my feet. The sprites were fast, but they were clumsy, knocking into things as they followed. Everywhere they crashed into the walls behind us, they left a trail of fire. At this rate, everything inside this building was going to burn.

Including us.

Below, the Salamander kept roaring, growing angrier as we increased the distance between it and us. With each bellow, the flames grew higher. My throat felt parched by the intense heat and my eyes were so dry I could barely see.

The thought of being burned in those flames, like Ronny's grandmother Gloriana, made my head pound as I tried to fight down terror.

"It's not fair," Faith said, puffing only a little, dang it. I could barely get enough breath to keep moving.

"What's…not fair?" I panted.

"We already almost died from fire," she said. "We shouldn't have to escape from it again. Damn it all."

I hoped Olivia hadn't heard her. Although, if there was ever a time to start cursing, this seemed like a good one. Fortunately, she and Brady were a couple steps below us, having an intense discussion. A snippet of their conversation drifted up to me.

"I'm not leaving you," Olivia insisted.

"I may be able to slow them down. I'm not going to risk you," Brady insisted.

"Save your breath. It's the two of us from now on." Olivia's voice was rock solid. I knew that voice. Nothing Brady could say or do was going to change her mind.

I don't know what Brady would have tried, but we emerged onto the top floor and raced across over to the rotating staircase that had carried us up. When we reached it, my breath was expelled in a horrified gasp. The stairs were still heading up!

Brady didn't pause. He shouted "Quilldritch," and gave me a light shove to keep me moving. With a creaking, grinding sound, the stairs reversed direction and began to rotate down.

We hit it at a run.

My feet were flying so fast, I almost tripped and tumbled down the stairs. Doug grabbed my elbow and kept me upright. I looked back and saw one of the sprites dart forward and shoot a narrow flame toward Olivia. I yelled and suddenly the carpet darted between Olivia and the sprite. The fire touched it —it made a muffled screech and the smell of scorched fabric reached my nostrils. Fortunately, the carpet showed no sign of catching on fire.

We made it to the landing on the second story and raced around the fancy dragon newel post, plunging down the next flight of stairs leading to the first floor. I knew it wouldn't change things, but I kept looking over my shoulder to see how close the sprites were. It was horrifying to see flames clawing up the walls behind us. The only thing that had saved us so far was the carpet. It continued to dart across the space behind us, trying to stop the fire spurts from reaching us.

There was one heart-stopping moment when I heard Olivia scream. I slowed, ever so slightly, looking back over my shoulder, trusting my feet to land in the right places. The carpet was busy guarding Faith, and Olivia was unprotected. I nearly turned back, but Brady threw himself between Olivia and a sprite that was aiming at her head. He'd pulled a bottle of water out of his pack and took careful aim. When Brady splashed water onto it, the sprite shrank in size for a moment. I felt a spurt of pleasure, followed by a thread of hope. Then the fire flared back to life, even larger.

Doug yanked on my arm to get me moving faster and I had to turn away before I saw what happened. I tried to tell myself that Faith and Olivia's silence meant they were okay.

Please let them be okay.

We were nearing the bottom of the stairs to the first floor when one of the sprites made it past the vigilant carpet. It had been mostly successful in defending us up to now. This sprite managed to get close enough to singe the hair off my arm before Brady poured a whole bottle of water over it. The sprite steamed and shuddered and hissed, growing smaller and smaller.

"I'm melting, melting. What a world," I said, a bit shocked at my intense pleasure in seeing it disappear.

Faith let out a shriek and beat at the hair on the top of her head, and put on a burst of speed. We seemed to be holding up pretty well, but the carpet was definitely beginning to look the worse for wear. It was singed in a number of places and had a few small holes showing through the thickly woven wool. I felt a proprietary interest in it, since I was the one that had dragged it here.

It swooped again, protecting Brady this time. The sprite turned away and Brady yelled to the carpet, "Not me. Protect Olivia."

She probably would have snapped at him for risking himself, but she was out of breath. I could hear it sobbing out of her as she ran. Of course, I wasn't much better. I was getting a stitch in my side and was pretty sure I couldn't keep this up much longer.

The smell of burning was growing stronger by the minute. I couldn't bear the thought of smelling my own burning flesh.

The carpet swept past me, darting between Faith and one of the sprites. Again I could smell burning cloth. Hopefully that was the carpet, not Faith's clothes.

Hopefully the carpet would be okay.

If it made it out of here, I'd offer to take it to Ronny. Although, it was so obviously magical it might not be interested in going to a non-magic world.

The sprites nearly caught us as we ran through the dining room. There was more and more disgusting smells behind us. Smells of charring wood, burning wool, singed hair and overheated skin. We made it through the kitchen to the living room. Fire was spreading through the wooden floors and furnishings, shooting up the wood-paneled walls, roaring overhead. Sparks were raining down on us as we neared the front door.

Only, it wasn't there.

I desperately choked out "Activatotum Alomura" followed by "Activatotum Apeersium". Through the smoke and embers I could see the door appear in front of us. We nearly stuck in the doorway, all of us trying to push through at once. Doug stepped back and grabbed my elbow long enough for Faith, Olivia and Brady to make their way out. Then he shoved me through so hard and fast I sprawled on my hands and knees in the dirt.

I was coughing so hard I couldn't even yell at him for being so rough. All of us were breathing hard, coughing and choking.

We'd made it out alive, but I didn't have enough air to celebrate. I decided staying on the ground was actually a good idea. I wasn't sure I wanted to take the energy necessary to stand up.

There was only one thing wrong. All of us were busy pulling cool clear air into starved lungs. None of us thought about shutting the door. If someone had asked, I'd have said the sprites couldn't follow us outside the building.

My mistake.

The carpet plastered itself across the doorway, then made a loud whooshing sound as all the sprites hit it full speed. There were a few seconds resistance, then it went up like a torch with a high pitched whine like a dentist's drill.

Brady grabbed the edge of the door and slammed it shut. That cut off the last of that horrible whine. It made my teeth hurt almost as much as it hurt my heart. I'd just thought of it as a carpet, something we could use. I'd stuffed it in my backpack without thinking. It had hated that based on all its squirming. Then Doug used it without even asking it for help. And in spite of all that, it had saved us from the fire sprites over and over again. Then it allowed itself to be burnt to nothing but ash. To save us.

Olivia threw her arms around Brady and kissed him. She finally pulled away enough to tell him, "You were wonderful!"

Faith opened her mouth to say something, then gasped and pointed.

One of the sprites had made it through the doorway.

It was darting back and forth, as if trying to decide which of us to hurt first.

Then it threw itself at me. Shadow darted toward me, hissing and growling. I scooped her into my arms and huddled over, trying to keep her safe from the flames.

The heat was intense. I heard Shadow give a high pitched shriek that sounded all too similar to the carpet, and I screamed.

One side of my back felt like it was on fire. I could feel blisters rising and bit back another scream. Behind me I could hear someone cursing.

With a sudden crack of thunder, clouds gathered overhead and I was instantly drenched with cold water. The sprite yowled as if the water hurt it.

I looked up and saw Olivia looking at Brady defiantly.

"What happened?" I asked, dazed.

"I made the wish you did the first year we came here," she said. "I remembered how it rained on us, but nowhere else. I thought it would help." She glared around rebelliously, though no one was arguing with her.

The dirt quickly absorbed the water, turning into mud beneath my feet. The sprite hissed and sputtered, growing smaller and smaller until it disappeared in a large puff of steam.

I sat there in the muck and began frantically checking Shadow. I ignored Doug and the others asking if I was okay. Shadow looked completely bedraggled, her long fur flattened against her skin, dripping with water. Olivia tugged impatiently at my backpack until she had it off, then jerked the back of my shirt up and checked me thoroughly.

I was vaguely aware of her saying my skin was mostly just red, but I had an area on my side a few inches long that was badly blistered. I knew Shadow had been hurt more than me. I still had that sound stuck in my head. I finally found a spot about three inches long where the fur had been burned off her tail. It was red and heavily blistered with a few white spots where the skin had burnt nearly to the bone. I burst into tears, hugging her tight.

I finally realized Olivia was talking to me, asking if I knew how I'd received such a bad burn when my shirt hadn't been burned at all. As she described it to me, the pain grew, sinking its teeth into my side. This was going to be really bad. I cast my thoughts back over what had happened with the sprites, but I couldn't remember a single moment when this injury could've happened.

Then a sick feeling washed through me as the spot became increasingly, painfully hot. It began to throb, deep into my skin, like I was being stabbed by a white hot poker. I asked Olivia to describe it to me again, then had her look at Shadow's tail. She gasped and stepped back so fast that she stepped on Faith's feet and the two of them nearly fell.

"It's the same, isn't it?" I asked dully.

"It, it…it's identical," she said, horrified.

Brady hurried over and compared the mark on my side and Shadow's tail, careful not to touch either. "She's right. They *are,* as far as I can determine without exact measurement, indistinguishable." He sounding puzzled. "That's not empirically possible. Shadow's tail and your side were never in the same place."

"I kept turning away from that sprite," I said, "trying to protect Shadow. There was no way for it to hit me there. The only reason it got Shadow was because she was whipping her tail back and forth. It got in the way of its fire spray."

"So if it never touched you, how did you get marked the same as Shadow?"

"Yep," I said, shrugging uncomfortably as the pain in my side sank deeper. "That would definitely be the question."

Shadow stirred in my arms, swept her injured tail up and began to carefully wash it with her tongue. I knew cats washed injuries like that, and I'd read it could be helpful. I just wasn't sure if that applied to serious burns. Then Shadow began to purr and as I watched, the burn began to grow smaller.

"What's going on with your side?" Olivia asked. I looked up quickly at the sound in her voice. Her brows were drawn together and her eyes were narrowed. She actually took a step back, clearly weirded out.

"Is the burn getting smaller?" I asked, feeling the throbbing pain begin to dissipate.

"How did you know that?" Brady asked sharply.

"Look at Shadow's tail," I said quietly. It was growing better by the minute. At the same rate as I was feeling better.

"How is that possible?" Faith asked blankly. "And why did Kat have the same injury as Shadow?"

Brady's forehead was creased with worry. "We know our familiars are magic. Ronny told us Kat's wish brought them into existence. I'll have to think about this, but I would hypothesize that we are more closely linked to them than I previously thought."

I looked down at the purring cat in my arms. She was nearly healed now, her skin merely red where she'd been washing it. My side felt nearly healed, too. Brady might be right.

"Really, that's all you can say?" Doug's voice was harsh as he whirled around to confront Brady. "You'll have to think about our animals? What about Kat? What about what happened to her?"

Brady stared at him, not speaking. I was glad Doug cared about what happened to me, but his reaction seemed weirdly extreme. Why was he being so intense? After all; my side was nearly healed now.

Doug collapsed on the ground and flopped over onto his back, setting the box down next to him. Rusty came running over and Doug ran a gentle hand over the little dog's back. "Guess we'll have to be a bit more careful with you guys, huh?"

Rusty barked, then gave Doug a doggy grin before licking his face enthusiastically.

Brady gave a startled exclamation and pulled the map from his pocket. His eyes tracked back and forth rapidly until he gave a pleased grin. "The Rejects are near that herb shop we checked a few months ago. Hopefully they won't destroy it." He grabbed the box where it sat next to Doug and said, "There's enough time for us to go see Ronny tonight. Let's get out of here."

Who knew I'd ever think the Rejects just weren't that important. But they weren't. Not at the moment.

Chapter 38/November/Santa Ramona

Home Again, Home Again, Jiggity Jog

I was still holding Shadow, not ready to let her go. Doug insisted on carrying my backpack so it wouldn't hurt my side. I tried to tell him I was nearly fine, but he didn't want to hear it. And okay, I didn't argue too much. After all, it sounded like a pretty good idea since he kept piling stuff in there without my permission.

But I couldn't ignore how badly he was limping before we were even halfway back to the tree. We were still quite a distance away when he stumbled the first time.

He righted himself quickly enough, but I asked to have my backpack. After all, I was feeling nearly better now. He merely glared at me and walked faster. He kept it up for a while, but stumbled again, then again. The last time he nearly fell. Without saying anything, Brady pulled a collapsible walking stick out of his backpack and handed it to Doug.

The look of distaste on Doug's face nearly made me laugh. But the fact that he accepted it and began to lean on it, heavily, nearly broke my heart. Doug liked to act like a tough guy. He must hate for us to see him like this.

I decided I would never, ever hassle him about using my backpack. But I was absolutely going to ask him to pack lighter!

Brady was carrying himself indefinably different. I was able to find a moment with him, while Faith and Olivia giggled together about something.

"You look different somehow," I told him. "What's up?"

"Oh, I am," he said, with deep satisfaction. "I defeated a monster. I got the girl." He shot a quick emotion filled glance at Olivia. I was glad she didn't see it, or this conversation would have been over. No way could Olivia resist a heated, love filled look like that!

He looked back at me, "Even better, I did those things and could still be me. *Science-Techno-Geek Brady.*" His voice had changed and I realized he was imitating me. Ooops!

His voice dropped back to normal and he threw back his head and laughed. "That's pretty cool, don't you think?"

"Yeah, Brady," I said. "I think it's plenty cool."

Olivia came over and slid her arm through Brady's. "I can't believe we found it! And everyone is all right. Mostly. Everything's great."

He squeezed her arm, but said, "I'll feel a lot better when we know what's in that chest."

I carried Shadow the entire way back to the tree. I couldn't bear to let go of her. By the time we got there, my side felt fine and other than a patch where the hair was missing on her tail, I couldn't tell that Shadow had been injured.

I stroked the fur on her back and told her how brave and wonderful she was. Her low rumbling purr was reassuring, and when we finally got back to the tree I set her down, promising to come again as soon as I could. I still wasn't sure how much she really understood, but I reminded her we wouldn't be coming next month. Some of us would be gone visiting family in other areas and we wouldn't be back until January.

Her purring didn't diminish, but she stroked against my legs three times before turning to head back up the road, tail held high.

The others had said goodbye to their animals and we took turns going through the tree.

This passage was bad.

I felt like I was being buffeted back and forth by an invisible wind, and the damp cold seemed to sink straight down into my bones. My soot filled lungs burned even worse than usual. They felt like they were about to burst by the time I fell into the cemetery. I nearly rolled into the angel statue that was now uncomfortably close to the tree.

A shudder shook me, and I scrambled away on my hands and feet, desperate to put some distance between it and me.

I jumped up and got out of the way as the others followed me through. Brady came last and said, "The Rejects started back to the tree. We should have no trouble getting to Ronny's before they get out."

"You're going to be nice to her, right?" I was afraid of causing a fight, but wanted to make sure it didn't happen while we were there.

"I called her last week and we worked things out," Brady said. "Don't worry about it."

I pulled my phone out of my pocket, glad to see it working again. I called Ronny and she said she'd be waiting for us.

When I told the others, Brady said, "I hope she has cookies. Lots of cookies. This may be a very long discussion."

"Why?" Faith asked curiously.

"First there's my great-grandfather's case. Second, there's the case Doug got away from the Salamander. Third, there are the messages Ghalynn gave us. Fourth, there's what the Salamander and the fountain told us. Along with a few others."

"Yeah," I said, "like getting her flying carpet destroyed. She needs to know how brave it was and how it saved our life. There's also the whole that's-not-a-statue-that's-Helga thing. I don't know how Ronny's going to take that."

"We don't know how much we can believe the Salamander," Olivia reminded me. She could hear how worried I was. "After all, it tried to kill us."

Chris opened the door when I knocked. "I thought you were still gone on your latest ghost hunt," I said.

He grinned at me and reached out like he was going to ruffle my hair. I quickly stepped out of the way. What was up with that? I was sixteen years old, for heaven's sake.

"I got back a couple hours ago," he said. "Unfortunately the trip was a bust. Loose pipes in the walls and badly hung doors. There was an explanation for everything they'd been experiencing."

Brady perked up. "So you try to debunk paranormal claims?"

"Of course," Chris told him and smiled. "No one will believe your evidence if you're a sloppy investigator."

"And you use scientific principles and logic?" Brady sounded even more intrigued. Hadn't I ever told him this?

"Those are essential. I also use several types of equipment. You've probably used many of them, like electronic temperature monitors, electro-magnetic meters, sound monitors, voice operated audio recorders, thermal imaging and multi-spectrum cameras. I also use other equipment created just for the type of work I do."

Brady looked like he wanted to keep discussing ghost hunting equipment, but we had more important things to deal with right now. I cleared my throat, loudly, and said, "That's all very interesting, Chris. But you and Brady can talk about it some other time. We have things we have to discuss with Ronny."

Chris followed us into the living room and perched on the arm of Ronny's chair. Brady uttered an embarrassingly loud cry of pleasure and all but dived on the plate of cookies sitting on the coffee table.

Ronny sat back in her chair with a large smile. It was good to see her looking so happy. Which made me feel bad, because I was pretty sure some of what we were about to tell her would wipe that happiness away.

Brady sat forward. "I'm not sure where we should start."

Ronny grinned and said, "Is it not always best to begin at the beginning? That is what your poor Lewis Carroll wrote, after he escaped from Chimera."

Brady laid the locking box on the table in front of Ronny. She clasped her hands together and asked, "Have you opened it?"

"I thought you'd want to be there when I did that," he told her.

She smiled at him. "Thank you."

He turned the dials on the combination lock to 03-28-24, then slowly lifted the lid. I stood up and looked over his shoulder. The first item was a letter. "It's from Ghalynn," he said.

He read it out loud, voice faltering as he repeated Ghalynn's words.

I must break my geas, time is short,
And thus with Death I must consort.

So I shall share all I now know,
There will be two to cause such woe.

This much is clear from dreams and legends
Two worlds at risk from two obsessions.

Of the first, my knowledge is slight,
Yet spells they cast inflame the blight.

Of the second, I know much more,
The Council's rules they do abhor.

Complex spells both cast for power,
When these meet they shall devour.

The second spell you may yet end
Four objects, in concert, will suspend.

~ One to see when all is grey.
~ One to show you your direction.
~ One to light you on your way.
~ One to resolve disconnection.

These can't work until you enter
Where they pierce the magick's center.

This will require all your care,
For monsters roam and traps ensnare.

When one spell breaks, potency is lost,
Though this may have a dreadful cost.

Otherwise — Annihilation

- **Ghalynn Thurinor Haeredon, Seer, Prognosticator, House of Quilldritch, Survivor of the Noldorin Elves**

Post script:
I must believe you will succeed
And save our worlds both from their greed

Perhaps I will rest easy kno

"That's all there is," Brady said. "It just stops."

Ronny was staring at the letter in confusion. "Why would Ghalynn leave that letter in my father's chest?"

"I would hypothesize that he felt it would be safe from others in there," Brady told her.

"Maybe we should check out the rest of it," I said, curiosity eating at me.

The inside of the box was divided into two sections. On one side, there were old black and white photographs, faded with age, of a very young child held by a beautiful woman. She was smiling out of one of the photos, a look of joy on her face.

Brady sucked in his breath and reached out a tentative finger, tracing the face of first the woman and then the child. "That's my grandfather," he said, voice husky. "And that's my great-grandmother, Jenniffer. It's hard to believe she was dead a few months after this picture was taken."

In the other side of the box, there was a handkerchief with a smudge of rusty brown. Beneath it, there were several pressed flowers taped to a note in painstaking English. Below that was a small box with one small baby tooth.

Ronny laughed. It didn't sound quite steady, but it was a genuine laugh. "That is my baby tooth," she said, and laughed again. Then she lifted the note and read it slowly to herself. When she set it down, she sighed. "My mother wrote this for my father. It was how she let him know she loved him. It's the only time I've ever seen her write something in English."

I cleared my throat nervously then said what I was thinking. "It's a memory box. He kept all the things that meant the most to him in there. And he had parts from his life in this world, and his life in Chimera. I think it means he loved both sides."

Ronny and Brady stared at me for a moment. Then Ronny smiled and said, "I always thought he was happy. Thank you, Kat."

Brady nodded slowly and looked away. I wasn't sure how he felt about what I said, then it seemed like tension lifted off his shoulders and evaporated.

"So…" Ronny hesitated then said, "Now will you, please, begin at the beginning?"

That surprised a laugh out of Brady. "Okay, from the beginning then." He described the two derelict houses that looked as though they'd been abandoned.

She interrupted, "They belonged to friends. They would not have wanted to stay by my home after I left."

"We went in your house, as you know," he told her.

"Wait," I said and moved so fast I almost fell off the couch. I grabbed my backpack off the floor and pulled out the jewelry and drawings I'd found in her house. When I held them out, her face lit up. She thanked me profusely, totally losing track of what Brady had been saying.

The more she thanked me, the worse I felt. "Um, don't thank me yet," I told her. "I, uh, borrowed your flying carpet."

"Icarus! I so enjoyed riding him." Ronny leaned back, lost in memories. Pleasant memories, that I was about to destroy

I cleared my throat, "Your Icarus was very brave. He saved us."

That snapped her eyes back into focus. "What do you mean?"

"Well, it…uh… We…" I gulped, not sure what to say.

Brady took a deep breath and said, "First, there is something important we need to discuss." He picked up his backpack, and pulled out the chest Doug had taken. "We found the Salamander." He tapped the box and said, "And we believe the last object is in here. We'll need you to open this; it's locked by magic." He set it on the table near Ronny.

She picked it up and hesitated, turning it over in her hands. "I swore I would do no more magick. It is dangerous."

Chris touched her shoulder and she gave him a wan smile. "I know, I must risk it. But still I am afraid." She sucked in her breath, then waved her hands over it and muttered something that sounded familiar. There was a flash of blue light and the lock released.

I wasn't the only one who breathed out a sigh of relief.

The lid popped open about half an inch. She flipped it open quickly and looked inside. I was watching her face, trying to guess what she was seeing. Whatever it was, she looked puzzled. She reached in and pulled out a strange pair of glasses. There were three layers of glass that opened independently. One layer was a rich blue. One layer a deep red. The last layer, dark green.

Ronny handed them to Brady. "I have never seen anything like these."

Brady tried them on, then made an odd sound.

"What's up?" I asked.

"They're opaque. I can't see a thing." He waved his hand in front of his face, then pulled them off and stared at them in confusion. "How are we supposed to use these? Do you understand how they function?"

Ronny shook her head. "I do not know. I can only hope it becomes obvious to you when the time does come." She held out her hand and took the glasses from Brady. She stood and with a bit of ceremony, placed them in the cabinet in the corner that held all of the things we'd found so far in Chimera.

When she got back to her seat, Brady said, "Unfortunately, the Salamander decided it didn't want any other magical people or creatures in Chimera. It thought it was the time for the Elementals to take control."

Ronny was sitting stock still, staring at him, waiting. Brady's rigid posture made it clear there was more. He said, "It tried to burn us with things it called Sprites."

"It did what?" Ronny sounded horrified.

Brady described our encounter with the Salamander. How it had ordered the Sprites after us. "We would all have been seriously burned if it wasn't for your carpet. Icarus. It kept them off of us."

"It was wonderful," I told her. "Icarus covered the doorway so most of the sprites couldn't get out, even though the Sprites were burning it. Him. In the end, we got the door shut, but not before Icarus went up in flames. I'm so sorry. I wanted to bring him out for you, but there was nothing left." I felt the tears welling into my eyes and dashed them away with the back of my hand.

I held my breath, afraid Ronny would be angry or hurt by this loss, on top of all the others she'd had. I wondered if she ever regretted choosing to be here.

"Oh, I am so proud," she said, and gave a shaky smile. "Father," she shot a glance at Brady and then said, "Arthur gave me that carpet for my tenth birthday. He said I was always getting myself in some sort of danger, so he had a protection spell woven into the threads. I am so happy that protection transferred to you."

I decided I'd better get it all over with at once. "There's more," I told her. I pretended not to hear the small sound of protest she made. "When we were talking to the Salamander, down in the open space in the middle of the mansion, there were several more statues. And one of them, well…" I hesitated then said in a rush, "One seemed to warm slightly when I leaned against it. It even seemed to get a slight bit of color."

Ronny made a sound like she felt sick. I ignored it, wanting to finsih. "I asked the Salamander why a statue would change like that. It told me there were no statues in there. When I pointed to the one I'd been touching, it said it wasn't a statue, it was Helga. Or at least, it had been Helga."

"It was lying," Ronny said, slowly shaking her head from side to side. "It must have been. I have been thinking about these statues you have been seeing. No witch or wizard, or any magickal being for that matter, would allow its likeness to be used on a statue. It could be used by an enemy in sympathetic magick. These statues can't be based on real people."

"Did you know anyone named Helga?" Doug asked curiously.

"Only one," Ronny said shortly.

"Did she have long hair in braids that hung to the small of her back?" Olivia asked Ronny. "About Faith's height, but with a, um, sturdier build? And long narrow features with her nose tipped up slightly at the tip and a wide mouth?"

Ronny's face registered surprise. "You saw her picture? How did you know it was Helga?"

I reached across the table and grasped Ronny's arm tightly. "She's describing the statue. The one the Salamander called Helga."

"No." Ronny pulled her arm away, then moaned and clasped her head in her hands. Her voice was hoarse as she asked, "How many of those statues have you seen?"

"I haven't counted them," I said quietly.

"I've counted thirty-four," Brady said. "All of them were people, not any mythic creatures, and all of them were outside. The salamander gave us a theory. I have to think about it to see if I agree that it is a viable hypothesis."

Ronny licked her lips and sank back in her chair. "Thirty-four. There were ten times that number living in Chimera. If those are truly my friends and family, where are the rest?"

"Well, those are just the ones I saw," Brady said patiently. "According to the map, there are more."

"Nearly three hundred and fifty more?" Ronny demanded.

"Improbable," Brady told her, "but not impossible."

I wanted to say something more comforting, but Ronny seemed content with his statement. She nodded. "I would very much appreciate you trying to describe all the statues…the, ah… the people that you have seen there. I would like to know if I recognize any." She reached out her hand toward the necklace lying on the table next to her, then winced and jerked her arm back.

"What's wrong?" I asked, knowing how much she'd always liked touching that necklace. It was the necklace her mother had given to her. I stilled, caught by that thought. Why did that make me feel like I'd forgotten something important?

"I have not been able to touch it since that last magick storm," she said peevishly. "Touching it makes me feel so weak and tired."

The necklace from her mother. Why did that keep twisting through my head? Why did I suddenly feel like remembering was urgent? Something that Ronny needed to know?

Then I had a light bulb moment. I'd forgotten to tell Ronny about the necklace we'd found at her mother's house. I'd stuffed it in my pack along with a couple other pieces of jewelry, but had forgotten about them with everything else that happened. What with Brady finding out about his great-grandfather living in Chimera and being murdered.

I grabbed my pack again and dug in the pocket. Olivia was asking me what I thought I was doing, but I ignored her. Then my fingers closed around the small pieces of metal and I pulled them up and held them in front of Ronny.

"I found these in your mother's house," I told her. "At first I thought you'd like to have a few of her things. Then I found this." I held up the necklace identical to the one Ronny was unable to touch any longer.

She stared at it, perplexed at first, then a grim coldness spread across her face, freezing her features, sharpening them. "Let me see that," she said in a voice I didn't recognize.

Chapter 39/November/Santa Ramona

Lightning and Fog and Storms, Oh My!

I handed her the necklace, and she held it carefully in her hand. Then her hand tightened into a fist and she let out a sound of pain. It seemed to vibrate from her toes up through her entire body, and lasted far too long. It took a moment for her to even recognize that Chris was holding her shoulders, asking what was wrong.

Finally she came back to herself. Her eyes cleared and she reached out a hand to Chris. "I'm sorry."

"Don't be sorry," he told her. "Just tell me what's wrong."

"I have held the necklace that I thought was from Mother all this time. It never felt right, but I thought it was because it was in the Mundane world, not Chimera. I clung to it as the last thing Mother had given to me. But that," she flicked her hand toward the necklace on the table, "is not from Mother. I can tell the difference now."

She caressed the necklace I'd given her and said, "I can feel Mother in this. The fact that it is in the Mundane world does not affect it. I feel no ill effects from it. In fact, I believe it was designed to feed me magick from Chimera."

She turned to look again at the necklace on the table. "I have to know," she whispered, then held her hand above it and muttered something I couldn't catch. It only lasted a moment, but there was a sudden vague impression of smoke that formed briefly into a face, then dissipated.

Ronny's voice was hard and bitter. "That was Morgana. That necklace was from her, not Mother."

She waved her hands and said something else I couldn't catch. There was a scent of wet ashes and burnt hair, then a streak of red flashed out of the necklace and nearly hit Ronny. She must have been expecting it. She jerked to the side and it shot past her. It hit the wall and sizzled a moment, the paint bubbling. The wood beneath it began charring before it finally disappeared with a loud pop.

"What was that?" I couldn't stop the words; they just burst out. But from the grim set of Ronny's mouth, I didn't want to know.

"It was the reverse of the spell Mother used on her necklace. *That* contained a draining spell. It was stealing my magick. It was supposed to feed it to the creator of the spell inside Chimera. It should have been feeding Morgana."

"But she's missing, like the others," Faith said.

"If the energy could not go to the creator of the spell, where would it go?" Brady asked, somewhere between fascinated and concerned.

Ronny nodded at him. "You are right to worry. Ordinarily, this spell should have died if the creator was dead. But it did not. If it isn't going to Morgana, I believe each of the magick storms has been able to release whatever was stored inside. It would be sucked out into the storm's wild magick. That would increase the damage in this world."

"You need to destroy it," I said. "Those storms are bad enough without adding more magic!"

"I would love to destroy it, but that would most likely cause something similar to an explosive decompression on one of your airplanes. I do not know what the effect on this world would be. I will have to give it some thought, but in the meantime, I will put it inside the same box that held the glasses. It is shielded, and I can lock it in there."

Ronny stood and did it quickly, touching Morgana's necklace with distaste. As soon as she locked the box, she placed it in the curio cabinet. For years that cabinet had looked fairly empty. Now, it was beginning to look pretty full.

Ronny sat back down, but looked so upset we made our excuses and left, promising to come back and talk to her again soon. After all, we hadn't really talked about the worst part — the information that Ghalynn had left for us.

-xXx-

Olivia called me that night.

"It's so great to be with someone who respects me for who I am," she said. She was practically cooing. "Brady makes me feel wonderful."

"If things are so *wonderful,* why do you guys keep acting so…so…" I wasn't sure what word I wanted to use.

"Snarky?" Olivia supplied helpfully.

"Yeah, snarky," I agreed. That was a good word for it. "Why are you so snarky to each other?"

"We like it," Olivia said.

"But it's not the way it's supposed to work when you love someone," I almost wailed.

"Says who?" Olivia asked and laughed. "It works for us. It makes us think in different ways than we're used to." She ignored my over-loud snort. "It's kind of…our thing."

"But I always thought of you as a hearts and flowers and poetry type," I told her.

"I always did too," she said, then her voice grew dreamy. "But this is much more interesting. And he is romantic, in his own way!"

She refused to explain that statement, and I guessed I'd have to be satisfied.

-xXx-

Brady came to my house on Sunday. My parents were home so we sat in the backyard, even though it was cold and damp.

He had on his thoughtful how-is-the-best-way-to-say-this face. Finally, I grew tired of waiting and said, "Spill it, Brady."

He squirmed in his seat, then blurted, "She really liked the necklace. Thanks for the suggestion."

"I only told you she liked jewelry," I said. "The necklace was your idea."

"Yeah," he said, and grinned. It was a satisfied ear-to-ear type of grin. "But I still want to thank you. I would probably never have taken the chance. With Olivia I mean. But you didn't laugh at the idea like I expected. You encouraged me. So thanks."

"It seems to be working okay then?" I still wasn't sure how Brady felt about being snarky.

His grin changed. It grew wider and deeper. It sank into his eyes where joy and contentment stirred and spread until everything about him radiated satisfaction. "I used to think Judy might be right. That I was an embarrassment and a freak."

How could he think that after being friends with us for years now? "But—"

"It helped when we became friends," he said, as if he could read my mind. "But I still felt different than most people. I have a high IQ, and I'm a *science geek,* which made things hard enough." He moved restlessly, then twitched his shoulders. "I've also got my eidetic memory. So, I'm different. But that's okay. I've got friends who like those things about me. In fact, I have been extremely useful at times. And even better, Olivia accepts me just the way I am."

The color rose in his face, but he kept his eyes steady on mine. "Last night I offered to start wearing the clothes SHE bought me if Olivia would prefer them."

He was still wearing his regular button-down Brady clothes, so I wasn't sure where this was going.

My confusion must have showed because he laughed and looked smug. "She yelled at me for more than five minutes."

"Um…that's a good thing?" I asked. I knew Olivia; I'd hate it if she yelled at me for five minutes!

"Very good," he said. "She was furious that I would suggest being something I'm not. She doesn't want me to change, not even the clothes I like to wear." His eyes lost focus as if he was remembering their conversation. He voice was almost dreamy as he said, "She likes me for who I am."

He stood up and headed for the door, then turned and said decisively, "And so do I!"

He was out the door so fast I didn't have a chance to answer.

And maybe I didn't really need to say anything.

-xXx-

That had been a good, if strange, day. The very next night, I thought the world was going to end.

Or, at least my part of it.

This storm was the worst ever. The flashes of blue lightning were almost continuous. The power went out and stayed out for hours. The noise from the thunder was deafening; there was no way any of us could sleep through it. Mom and Dad got out a small battery operated radio and after several moments, were able to pick up an all-news-all-the-time station in Los Angeles.

It was even worse than I'd feared.

This storm was being experienced from Oxnard to San Luis Obispo. Although many news crews had been dispatched to cover the strange storm, none of them were able to report in. Their equipment kept failing. Meteorologists were scrambling to come up with any reasonable explanation.

I knew what was causing it.

That nasty yellow fog, the one that was icy cold and burned where it touched was back in Santa Ramona. It crept around our house, reeking like something had died in it. Nothing electronic worked, even after the power came back on. Lights blinked red or green on the cable box, TV, DVR, DVD and my computer. Like they should be working, but nothing happened when I tried to use them.

Finally the storm began to dissipate and the yellow fog retreated back toward the cemetery. It was like something out of a movie about *The Fog*. I'd thought that movie was pretty stupid when I watched it. Unfortunately, it didn't feel so stupid when it was actually happening to me.

As soon as the fog and lightning retreated, my phone and everything else started working normally again. I called Ronny and asked if we could see her the next day. But Chris asked that we wait until at least Thursday before coming. Ronny had been seriously affected by this storm and was in no shape for visitors. I told him I was really sorry, and I'd check with the others to be sure Thursday would work.

That night, the news reports would seem unbelievable to anyone who hadn't lived through it. The local newscasters certainly seemed to find it all very amusing. Birds talking. No GPS. Compasses spinning. Garage doors opening and closing every few minutes. Plants dying and then coming back to life. Living things, from amphibians to fish to reptiles, falling from the sky, a few at a time or by the dozen.

My parents were offended that people kept reporting such foolish tales when there must be real destruction from the storm. I didn't bother arguing; how could I explain why I believed every single one of those strange stories?

I was so worried about Ronny and what the storm's fury could mean for us that I barely noticed all the buzzing in the hallways about THE-STRANGEST-YEAR-EVER. I didn't even care when three of our teachers mentioned it in class.

I did notice how Olivia's entire face lit up when she saw Brady walking toward us on our way to the cafeteria for lunch. I'd read about that expression, but had never really thought someone's face could do that. But it was as if Olivia had stepped out of shadows into the bright summer sun when she saw him.

I hoped fervently, not for the first time, that this new relationship of theirs wouldn't end badly and require everyone to pick sides. I really liked Brady, but Olivia and I were Blood Sisters.

At lunch the five of us huddled together. Brady was clearly worried. "I found handwritten notes in the margins of the books we found at Morgana's. I haven't had a chance to finish translating them, but I'll finish before we go to Ronny's on Thursday. I think she needs to hear them."

Although Olivia teased him unmercifully, he refused to explain further. Merely saying everything might change once he finished. And he didn't want to upset us unnecessarily.

That didn't sound good. What had he found that he thought might upset us?

-xXx-

As soon as we got to Chris and Ronny's on Thursday, Chris explained that he had some work he had to get done in his home office and excused himself.

Before we had a chance to sit down, Brady announced, "It's not just here."

I glanced around and felt relieved that no one else seemed to understand that cryptic sentence either. Then he pulled the map from his pocket and spread it on the coffee table in front of Ronny. "You said the wild magic was causing damage here. But it isn't just here." He pointed to the blank center of the map. "Chimera is being destroyed from within."

There was no denying the fog at the center had been growing; we'd known that for years now. What was new was how much faster it had grown recently. Nearly a third of Chimera was covered by the blank spot that represented the putrid fog.

He pulled a book from his pack and opened it on the table next to the map. He pointed to writing in the margins. "I believe this is from your Aunt Morgana," he told Ronny.

She nodded slowly, looking at her aunt's handwriting on the page, horror dawning on her face.

Brady asked her, "Do you want me to read it to the others?"

Ronny looked around, then shook her head. She picked up the book and began to read in a shaky voice, pausing occasionally to take a gulp of air.

"My foolish sister informed me that several people have tattled to her about me. She actually apologized. She said she doesn't believe the rumors that I have been trying to destroy everyone on the Council.

Then she started in with ridiculous tales about the Coven. Like those foolish amateurs could cause damage to Chimera.

At the very least, those tales are keeping her busy.

If they were truly the problem, she would be right. But she is never right. She is blind.

She has never truly seen me for who I am.

She has no idea what I am capable of.

That is all about to change."

I had my eyes pinned on Ronny's face. She looked up, stricken. Brady flipped a few pages and pointed to more writing. She dutifully read.

"Sister dear told me how happy she is that we still have each other. I nearly spit in her face.

I would give a thousand of her to have Brigana back."

I managed to stifle a gasp, not wanting to distract Ronny, but I *seriously* disliked her Aunt Morgana.

"At least I do not have to tolerate Titiana anymore. Foolish Glenna keeps telling me how the anniversary of Titiana's death makes her sad. She is completely unaware that I am the one who betrayed Titiana to the Mundane."

This time Faith and I gasped in unison. Olivia reached over and grasped Brady's hand as Ronny continued.

"It was supposed to trap them both, but that cursed Glenna was called away on Council business. And I allowed myself to be so distracted by the ruination of my careful plans that I did not get Titiana's spellbook.

The stupid Mundane buried her with her book somewhere in their cemetery. And because she was an accused witch they did not mark her grave. I am no longer sure I will ever find it.

When Titiana died, I did not miss the looks some sent me. I will need to bide my time before trying something else against Glenna."

Ronny was holding the book so tightly that her knuckles were white. She made a choking sound then blurted, "I do not believe this. It cannot be true. Mother said Morgana was devastated when Titiana died. Nearly inconsolable. And now I am to believe that was all an act?"

"You said Titiana died in our cemetery?" Faith asked.

"Aunt Titiana was found dead in your cemetery, shortly after Chimera was created," she said. "She had been trapped and beaten. There should have been enough magick for her to defend herself, but even the strongest witch can be helpless when alone and ambushed by well-armed men."

"Our cemetery?" Faith asked. "I've heard a witch was killed, but no one said she was beaten to death."

"The Mundane are very good at ignoring things that make them uncomfortable." This time Ronny's voice held a trace of bitterness. "I won't say magickal beings were always nice to the Mundane. Some, like my aunts, have even done great evil. But it was the Mundane who decided to exterminate us. Why are your people so cruel to others just because they are not the same?"

"How can you be so sure it was the Mundane who killed her?" Doug asked.

"A paper was left on her body, warning that all who practiced the black arts would meet the same fate." Tears overflowed Ronny's eyes and tracked down her cheeks. "Aunt Titiana was only ten feet from the doorway. She nearly made it home."

Olivia wrinkled her nose. "Why aren't there stories about it? You know, stories that warn about staying away from Santa Ramona if you're a witch."

"There *are* stories," I said flatly. "Everyone knows about the witch buried in the cemetery with her spell book."

Olivia turned to Ronny, "So, is Titiana's spellbook really missing? Could it actually be in the cemetery?"

"For three hundred years," Ronny told her, "Morgana has searched the cemetery for Aunt Titiana's spellbook. We know only that she had it with her when she died."

"So maybe whoever killed her destroyed it," I suggested, and felt a brief flash of disappointment. I'd always wanted to find that book.

"No, that is not possible. Our spellbooks are protected by powerful magick. They cannot be destroyed by fire, water, earth or air. They cannot be torn, changed, or written upon. You cannot cover the writing with ink or any other substance. And spellbooks cannot be understood or used by the Mundane. That is what makes us believe it is still hidden in the cemetery." Ronny's tone was completely devoid of emotion as she added, "It is believed that Aunt Titiana hid it with magick when she felt her life slipping away."

Brady turned several more pages and pointed again to the margin. Ronny had to blink a few times before she could read it, but her voice stayed steady.

"The Greeks thought we were gods. When my sisters and I were young, we were magnificent. All except Glenna the Good. The rest of us enjoyed destroying the Mundane after Mother's murder. Glenna was sure we were turning the Mundane even further against us. How stupid. And what would it matter if it was true?"

After they killed Brigana, Glenna wanted to save me. She thought I would be grateful. Grateful! To be locked in this prison.

Ronny started to sit back, but Brady shook his head and turned several more pages. "I don't know that I can read any more," Ronny said, her voice rough with strain.

Brady nodded, closed his eyes, and quoted from memory.

"Glenna doesn't see it, but I hate her far more than all of the Mundane. The fool does not deserve to head the Council. It should be me."

He paused a moment and I saw his eyes moving behind his eyelids as if he was reading. Then he began again.

"She has contaminated everything in my life. I will destroy her, but first I will make sure she sees the death of all she loves. Just as I have."

He hesitated, opened his eyes and looked at Ronny. "This next part gets pretty bad."

Ronny called out hoarsely, "Chris, I need you."

Chris came at a dead run. He took a quick look at her face, then came over and sat on the arm of her chair. He reached down and picked up her hand in his, holding it gently. "What do you need?"

"Just be here," she told him and gave him a wavering smile. Then she nodded to Brady and said, "Continue, please."

He nodded then grimaced and closed his eyes. I knew he didn't really need his eyes closed. He probably didn't want to look at Ronny's face as he began quoting again.

"Getting rid of that disgusting parasite Arthur was easy. Next will be her mongrel daughter. She refused to stay in Santa Ramona, where watching her age would have been so satisfying. But it was easy to convince the Council to overrule sister dear and banish Rowena when she threw her life away on a Mundane."

Brady shot a quick look at Chris, then shut his eyes again and continued.

"Glenna was nearly crushed by her loss. She has allowed herself to become pitiful and weak. So now the time has come to destroy her. I will take control of the Council and Chimera, then declare war against the Mundane. I will destroy them and take back the world which should have been mine all along."

Brady kept his head down as he turned a few pages, getting near the end of the book. He cleared his throat and said, "There are only a few more lines."

Olivia muttered, "Good!" I elbowed her in the ribs, careful not to let Ronny or Brady see.

"The spell is set. All will be frozen in place until I make my final arrangements. I will awaken the Council first. They will be panicked by Glenna's gruesome death and the time they have lost. They will turn to me for help. If they do not, I will eliminate them as well."

Brady laid the book back down on the table and turned to Ronny. "Could Morgana have frozen everyone into statues first, then something happened that disrupted the rest of her plans?"

Ronny shook her head. "Her description sounds like an ordinary freezing spell, but most who live in Chimera would have protections against something so commonplace. She must have done something more. But if something happened to her, the spell would have broken. I just cannot make sense of it."

"It's as if everyone was like Sleeping Beauty," Faith said. "You know, cursed to sleep for a hundred years."

"Morgana would never use a Sleeping Beauty spell," Ronny told her. "She always said she should have destroyed those fairies in the tale you call Sleeping Beauty. She hated that they believed they were so clever, changing her spell. When I was a child, Morgana would sometimes mutter, 'Not in death but in sleep. Those fools!' I promise you, she would never use a spell like that."

I hated bringing her more pain, but I thought we needed to talk about what Ghalynn had said. "Brady, can you remember those…uh…poems that Ghalynn left for us?"

Brady glared at me then snorted. "Of course I remember. Why wouldn't I?" He turned to Ronny and said, "I could quote all of his terrible poetry, but I will keep it to the critical pieces of information."

"I must break my geas, time is short,

Two worlds at risk from two obsessions.

When they meet they shall devour.

The second spell you may yet end
Four objects, in concert, will suspend.

~ One to see when all is grey.
~ One to show you your direction.
~ One to light you on your way.
~ One to resolve disconnection.

These can't work until you enter
Where they pierce the magick's center.

When one spell breaks, potency is lost."

Brady leaned forward, sudden excitement in his eyes "What would happen if your Aunt Morgana set off a freezing spell at the same time another group, like Ghalynn's group from the South, cast a Sleeping Beauty curse?"

Ronny sat there, staring at him. He continued with more animation. "It's what the Salamander said. I discounted it, after it tried to kill us. But what if the group in the South and Morgana's spells combined. It isn't just the Salamander that said it. It's what the prophecy says. Two spells together? They could be causing the edge of Chimera to destabilize.

He held up his right hand and said, "South group. Sleeping Beauty spell."

Then he held up his left hand. "Morgana. Freezing spell. With, as you suggested, something added to make it more potent."

He brought his hands together and laced his fingers together. "What would happen if those spells were let loose and they combined?"

Ronny's face went white. "I don't know. I... I..." She clasped her hands to her head, and moaned. "Oh Great Spirit. Could this all be due to Morgana's curse?"

Pandemonium broke out as we all asked what that meant. Shouldn't she have told us there might be a curse involved?

Chris gave a sharp whistle that brought a moment of silence. He said gently, "Explain what you mean by a curse, love."

Ronny gave him a tremulous smile and said, "Morgana refused to believe it could do anything. She said no Mundane had enough power to harm her. But Mother worried about the Gypsy girl's curse."

"What kind of curse?" Faith asked.

"It happened in the early 1900's, though I do not know the exact date. Mother never told me what Morgana did, but it caused the death of an entire Romani family in Southern California. Only one survived for a short time; the teenaged daughter. She was devastated by the loss of her parents and brothers. As she lay dying Morgana mocked her pain. With her dying breath, the girl called a curse down upon her.

Brady said. "I don't believe in curses."

I snorted. That seemed like a ridiculous statement considering we were discussing the possible destruction of our world by two conflicting magic spells.

Ronny looked at him and shook her head. "For the Romani, a curse is a form of magic. It is not magick as my people know it, but there is power there. Mother said she could feel the force of it still clinging to Morgana when she came home."

"So what was this curse?" Olivia asked.

"Though it takes one hundred years, your evil will rebound upon you ten-fold," Ronny said. "Morgana laughed it off when Mother expressed concern. She always said, 'You cannot believe that Mundane spawn could do anything to me."

There was a moment of silence and I said the first thing that came to mind to fill it. "That's weird. It has been a hundred years since the early 1900's." Then as I listened to my words, a shiver worked its way down my spine. I wished that I could be like Brady and not believe, because I didn't like the idea of out of control spells were mixing with curses. And all of them working against us.

"Oh no." Ronny shook her head emphatically. "I do not care how strong that Gypsy girl was, she could not possibly affect everyone in Chimera."

"What if it didn't have to be everyone?" I said slowly and clenched my hands into fists to make sure they didn't shake. "What if it only affected Morgana as she cast her spell?"

Ronny flopped back limply in her chair, staring at me with horror-stricken eyes. She said dully, "You believe this curse affected Morgana's spell."

"I don't know what to believe," I told her. "But the idea is making me sick."

"If that is what happened, it was more like a perfect storm of spells," Brady said. His eyes were narrowed in concentration. "Ghalynn was afraid the spell cast by the group in the South was too big and strong for them to control; that the smallest misstep could cause it to burst apart. So what we're really talking about is a curse interfering with a spell cast by a powerful magic user that collided with a dark and complex spell let loose by a group whose competence was in question. I believe Ghalynn said he would not trust even the most skilled and sure wielder of magic to perform such a spell, and the group in the South were far from skilled."

Ronny was staring down at her hands where they were clasped tightly in her lap. She didn't look up as Brady quoted the first part of the Annihilation Prophecy.

Time shall come when silence rules
Echoes of what was remain
East and South dark MALICE pools
Set loose as protections wane.

Brady stared intently at the top of Ronny's head. "Chimera has gone silent. Only those things you have referred to as echoes, those with no real intelligence, still exist in Chimera. Your Aunt's house was the one furthest to the East. She was planning a spell to take over Chimera. Ghalynn wrote that a group in the South prepared a spell far too complex, in order to take over Chimera. I'll ask again. What if they were both set loose at nearly the same time? One hundred years after Morgana was cursed. While your mother was here for your wedding. At the time they knew there would be less protection in Chimera."

Ronny gave a small nod of her head but kept her eyes on her hands. I sat up straighter and asked Brady, "What was the next part?"

Two worlds WITH one dire test
With the entrance breached by man
Mundane MAGICK marks the quest
Fate awaits the final plan

Doug said, "The two worlds refers to our world and Chimera." Brady nodded even though Doug had been making a statement, not asked a question. He added, "We've already agreed that we're the first Mundane to go into Chimera without being, um, *escorted* in." Brady scowled and flicked a glance at Ronny, then nodded to Doug.

He continued, "We've already discussed whether we've been using Mundane magic. I think we can agree that we've used some form of magic." This time everyone nodded. "So what's the next part?"

Brady said, "The prophecy and what Ghalynn said are very similar. This is the prophecy."

Only clear to those with Sight
Direction is necessity
Paths revealed within the Light
Resolution is the Key

"And this," he said, "Ghalynn wrote."

One to see when all is grey.
One to show you your direction.
One to light you on your way.
One to resolve disconnection.

"They obviously have considerable similarity," Brady said. "And I believe we can all agree they correspond well with the objects we've found."

I glanced over at the cabinet in the corner that held those four objects. The strange opaque glasses we'd just found. The small metal circle we'd found last year, with a compass inside. One that looked disappointingly similar to any other compass. The foot-high lantern we'd found the second year we'd been in Chimera at the bottom of the lake. It was trimmed in tarnished metal carved with the shapes of ferns and flowers, surrounding a glass chimney that was warped and pitted and slightly milky. The fourth item was the one we'd found the first year we'd come here. It was an old-fashioned brass key, more than three inches long with a shaft as big around as a pencil. It was topped by a fancy Celtic design.

Brady was right. They all fit the prophecy and Ghalynn's letter far too well.

Brady squared his shoulders. "It's the next section that made me wonder about the potential effects if the spells combined. Both spells are about a desire for power. About taking control of Chimera. I think that could be considered as greed, which is how the next part begins."

Greed with evil SPELLS entwine
Without courage faith will quail
Magick and Mundane COMBINE
For one without the other fail

He sat back. "I think it's warning us that the wild magic will continue to grow unless we are able to, somehow, use magic along with those objects," he pointed toward the cabinet, "to stop it."

"You think we need to fight two competing magic spells, one that is dark and complex?" Faith sounded incredulous. "I think you'd better think again."

Ronny was huddled in her chair. She finally looked up and slowly pulled her hands apart, only to cross her arms and cup her elbows in her palms instead. "What frightens me is that these spells seem to be destroying the magick that created Chimera in the first place. I do not believe Chimera can continue to exist so very much longer."

I interrupted, suddenly worried about her. What would the death of Chimera do to her? Chris had said Ronny was being serious affected by the magic storms. "What about you?" I demanded abruptly.

"I do not know what the effect will be on me. I feel increasingly weak with each storm, but that is not my biggest concern at the moment." She ignored Chris and me when we tried to argue. She simply raised her voice and kept talking. "Have you thought about what will happen if the magick continues to pour out of Chimera in an ever-increasing flood? Already parts of this world have been affected. The Mundane world was not designed to stand against such an onslaught. It may well be destroyed as well if too much magick pushes through."

"You're saying that Chimera is falling apart and it might take our world with it?" Olivia didn't sound frightened. She sounded…amused. Like that couldn't possibly happen. That anyone who suggested such a thing was being silly. She usually reacted to end-of-the-world-as-we-know-it movies that way.

Too bad this wasn't a movie.

I was distracted by a sudden but distinct feeling that someone was staring at me. I turned my head quickly and caught Doug's eyes pinned on me. As soon as I met his gaze, he jerked his head away and stared down at his hands. He'd looked…concerned, like he was worried about something.

What was up with that?

Brady said, "I've been the last one to accept the possibility of magic."

All of us nodded and made fervent sounds of agreement.

He gave a brief smile then looked at Ronny. "I don't think we can ignore this. It is only logical, based on all the facts, to treat the Annihilation Prophecy as real. There are simply too many parallels to be a coincidence."

He pulled a page out of his backpack. It was covered with his precise writing. "This is a copy of one of the letters we found. It was the last thing I had to translate." He sighed. "It was also from Ghalynn." He didn't bother actually reading from the paper. *Of course.* But I was sure his words were exactly the same as Ghalynn's.

No one will listen.

No one believes any longer in my visions, but I am sure the time of the Prophecy is upon us.

I have studied the old texts. The Mundane must penetrate the center of Chimera, the source of our magick, to break the spells and set it right.

That will be a perilous journey, fraught with untold dangers.

I can understand why the others choose not to believe me. Mundane using magick? Going into the center, where none have ever returned? No one wants to believe this.

But I am certain. It is the very limited magick the Mundane possess that will save them in the center.

And if my visions are correct, they must succeed.

Or our world, and theirs, will pay the price.

Brady set the paper on the table. "I guess we need to talk about what we intend to do."

Doug glanced at me out of the corner of his eye. "I'm not about to risk our world being destroyed, so of course *I* intend to go. But maybe the girls should sit this one out."

That had the three of us *girls* on our feet, arguing. Although when I paid attention, we weren't arguing exactly the same way.

Faith was just angry about the whole *girls* thing, like he thought we weren't capable of continuing.

Olivia was arguing that there was no way Brady was going to go in there without her.

I was arguing that we'd promised to stick together on this quest, and that's what we were going to do. My heart was pounding so hard my whole body was vibrating with it. There was no way high-and-mighty bossy Doug got to decide who stayed and who went. I made sure my voice was the loudest and repeated, "We made a promise to stick together on this quest."

After one baleful look at me, Doug said, "Great. So we're all going on this *quest*?"

Okay, that might be a ridiculous word for it. But there was no way I was staying behind. My hand was up like a shot, but Olivia beat me to it. And between one heart beat and the next everyone's hand was raised.

Chris cleared his throat. "I'd go with you if I could. I've tried several times to get into Chimera, but nothing I can do gets me inside. I'd like to say that Kat should stay here."

I started to bristle and he held up a hand. "I don't know which of you, or perhaps all of you together, might be needed to fix what's wrong. It would be foolish of me to stop you from going only to have our world destroyed because of it."

He gripped my shoulders in a hard grasp and said, "I think it's possible that all of you might be needed in order to succeed. Each of you brings something the others may require."

"All for one?" I asked and held out my hand. The rest of them reached out and stacked their hands on mine, before dipping them and raising them toward the ceiling. Olivia was looking at Brady, but spoke for the rest of us when she said, "One for all."

Chapter 40/December/Santa Ramona

The Strangest Year Ever, Once Again

Another magic storm hit Friday afternoon and lasted, off and on, until the next day. It made it hard to sleep and I was in no mood to wake up early on Saturday morning.

Unfortunately, Doug began pounding insistently on the front door before the sun was fully up. I let him in, rubbing sleep from my eyes and croaked, "You're lucky Mom and Dad aren't home. They'd have killed you for making that kind of racket on the weekend. At," I held my phone in front of my face and squinted at it, "seven a.m."

Doug shoved past me and slapped some folded pages on the coffee table. I felt my mouth draw down into a frown as I realized it was the town's excuse for a newspaper. The one published by Andrew's father. I never read it. I didn't want to do anything that would support Andrew's father and, therefore, Andrew.

"Why'd you bring that in here?" I knew I sounded like a grouch, but he knew how I felt about what was little more than a cheap tabloid about how great the rich people in town were.

He jabbed his finger at the front page. "Read this."

I rolled my eyes and plopped onto the couch, not even trying to hide my irritation. I picked it up and Doug once again thrust his finger at an article that took up the whole left side.

> **Santa Ramona Tribune** **December 20th**
>
> **Local Student Found Dead in Cemetery**
>
> Officials are still trying to determine the cause of death for Tricia Allen, who was found dead in the Santa Ramona Cemetery on Friday morning.
>
> The senior from Santa Ramona High School was found near the back of the cemetery, in the oldest section. It appears she, and most likely other students, had been moving some of the statues back there. The police have no explanation as to why they were doing this.

I stared at Doug in horror. "I know Tricia Allen."

"I know. She was only one year ahead of us," he said. "I thought they'd canceled the cemetery trip when that storm came through."

I crushed the paper between my hands. "Oh no, if they were there during the storm…"

"It means she didn't move that statue; it moved on its own while she was in there."

"And it killed her," I whispered.

"We don't know what killed her," he said. "Finish reading."

I spread the paper back out so I could finish the article.

Santa Ramona Tribune **December 20th**

It is a long established practice for seniors to look for the gravesite of a reputed witch buried in the cemetery hundreds of years ago. Such a practice has occurred for at least the past fifty years.

Some speculate that Ms. Allen suffered heart failure because she tried to move too much weight, even though she recently passed a physical exam. Others believe that she was hit during the strange lightning storm Friday evening. Still others have raised the possibility of a prank gone wrong. She reputedly looked like she'd literally been scared to death.

The Santa Ramona City Council held an emergency meeting Friday night. They approved an Ordinance requiring those under 18 years of age to be restricted from access to the cemetery unless accompanied by a parent or guardian.

My hands were shaking as I placed the paper back on the table. I looked at Doug and met his worried eyes. "We aren't allowed in the cemetery?"

He merely shrugged.

I jumped to my feet and grabbed his arm. "We just found out that our world could be destroyed by what's happening in Chimera. We promised we'd go back and find a way to stop it." I shook his arm as I shouted, "Now they aren't going to let us in?"

He placed his hand over mine, tightening his arm until it felt like I was trying to shake concrete, and looked grim. "I think that sums it up pretty well."

I tightened my grip further and felt my fingernails dig into his arm. "Doug, what are we going to do?"

The conclusion of the Chimera Chronicles will be available December 2016.

Brady's Map

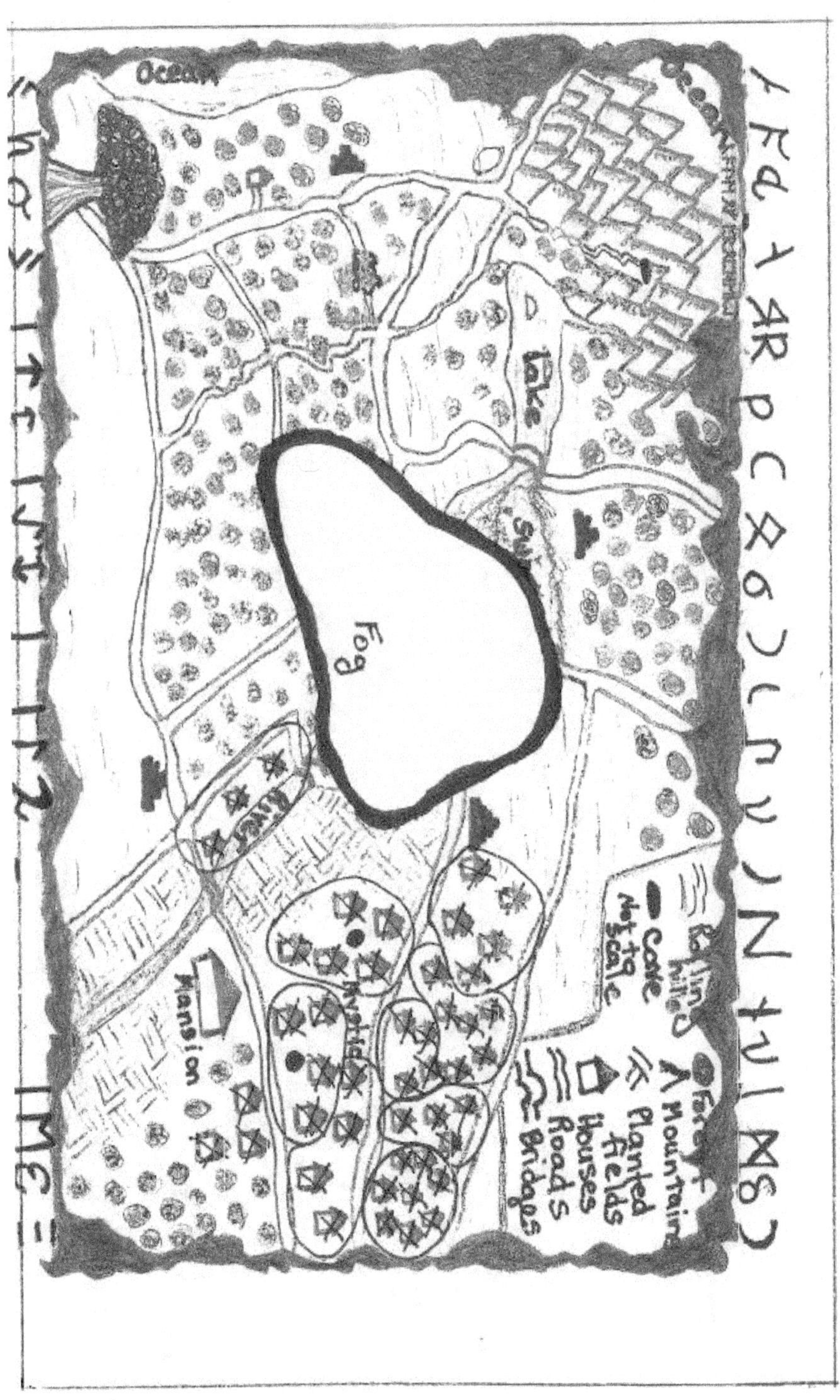
Ocean
Ocean
Lake
Fog
River
Mansion
Mountains
Planted fields
Houses
Roads
Bridges
Cave
Not to scale

www.ingramcontent.com/pod-product-compliance
Lightning Source LLC
Chambersburg PA
CBHW071147250626
47159CB00001B/11

* 9 7 8 1 6 8 0 1 2 2 7 6 3 *